THE CORPSE FACTORY

And Other Stories

The DANCING TUATARA PRESS
Books from RAMBLE HOUSE

THE CORPSE FACTORY

And Other Stories

The Weird Tales of
Arthur Leo Zagat
VOLUME #2

Arthur Leo Zagat

Introduction by

John Pelan

RAMBLE HOUSE

Introduction © 2013 by John Pelan
Cover Art © 2013 Gavin O'Keefe

The Corpse Factory, *Dime Mystery Magazine*, Mary 1934
A Lodging in Hell, *Horror Stories*, February/March 1936
Death Lands a Cargo, *Dime Mystery Magazine*, October 1935
Death's Mistress, *Dime Mystery Magazine*, September 1934
Madman's Bride, *Dime Mystery Magazine*, January 1935
Satan's Bedchamber, *Dime Mystery Magazine*, August 1936
Soft Blows the Breeze from Hell, *Dime Mystery Magazine*, December 1937
The Little Walking Corpses, *Dime Mystery Magazine*, November 1934

ISBN 13: 978-1-60543-720-0

Cover Art: Gavin L. O'Keefe
Preparation: Kathy Pelan and Fender Tucker

Dancing Tuatara Press #29

THE CORPSE FACTORY

And Other Stories

TABLE OF CONTENTS

ARTHUR LEO ZAGAT— MAGISTER TRISMEGISTUS OF THE MACABRE

Born in 1896, Arthur Leo Zagat had the writing bug from an early age, trying his hand at verse (as with his contemporary, John H. Knox, the poet's eye for language is readily apparent in his prose). Of course, the number of poets that can make a living from their work can usually be counted on the fingers of one hand, and this was certainly true in the early 1900s. Zagat also wrote a humor column while attending New York's City College; but neither avocation gave much of a hint as to the work he would be remembered for.

Zagat served in the First World War in the Signal Corps and upon returning to civilian life got married and returned to school obtaining a law degree from Fordham University in 1929. Unfortunately, during the Great Depression there wasn't a huge demand for young lawyers and Zagat found himself working a variety of low level jobs until, like much of America's workforce, he found himself unemployed with just a few dollars to his name. Borrowing a typewriter, Zagat set out to make his mark as a writer of fiction. With the poet's natural gift for language, Zagat was an instant success, selling his first story immediately and finding editors clamoring for more of his work. What was to prove a brilliant career was launched.

Zagat's forte was the novella, or as the hyperbolic editors called them, "the feature-length novel". These "novels" generally ranged from 12,000 to 25,000 words in length, thus, in any definition save that of the pulp magazines, these were novelettes. Writing works of this length not only guaranteed top billing on the covers, but usually qualified the author for a slightly higher word-rate, often an additional half cent a word. Zagat's output was prodigious, rivaling that of Arthur J. Burks. He turned out mysteries, science fiction, and many other types of fiction. In addition to lead "novels", he was also a dependable writer of shorter fiction, including the popular Doc Turner stories in *The Spider* and the *Red Finger* series that ran in the pages of *Operator #5.*

Finally, in 1934 Popular Publications took a bold step, changing the format of *Dime Mystery Magazine*, a publication known for its publishing of staid novels that were a cure for insomnia if nothing else. In October, 1933 the change was made with the appearance of *Dance of the Skeletons* by Norvell Page. The weird menace genre was born, and by January, 1934 Arthur Leo Zagat was on board with a short story in *Dime Mystery Magazine* and when Popular expanded the line in September 1934 with the publication of *Terror Tales* editor Rogers Terrill turned to Zagat to write the lead "novel". Zagat responded with *House of Living Death.*

Zagat took to the weird menace genre like a fish to water; Terrill needed dependable wordsmiths, and particularly authors that could be counted on to turn out "feature novels" on a regular basis and Zagat filled the bill with gusto with some three dozen such pieces for Popular Publications as well as another dozen or so for their competitors.

Zagat's work was rife with the tropes of the early Gothics: decaying mansions, dark family secrets, bizarre cults, and scheming madmen. What sets Zagat's work apart from many of his contemporaries is the poet's sure touch with language putting him in the company of the great John H. Knox. In fact, fellow author Roger Howard Norton dubbed him "magister trismegistus of the macabre"; were this monicker applied to anyone other than Zagat or Knox it would be ludicrous; bestowed on Zagat, even with tongue slightly in cheek, it's perfectly appropriate.

In addition to colorful descriptive phrases such as "lambent gloom" and "choking fetor" Zagat's tales featured a good deal of introspection from his characters, leading the reader to feel a growing sense of dread. When Zagat pulls it off, he's able to sustain a growing feeling of unease over a twenty-thousand word story—a very difficult feat. When he falls short, it's often when he's using the female point of view. These cases aren't complete failures. Zagat has the words, but he hasn't got the tune; it feels like watching Charlie Daniels playing Mozart; all the technique is present, he's hitting all the notes, but something doesn't ring true.

The truly remarkable thing about Zagat is not only the generally high quality of his work, but the amazing quantity of work that he produced. From his debut until the war years he was writing at least one "feature length novel" and four or five short stories every month. In 1935 at the height of the weird menace years Zagat suffered a near fatal attack of pneumonia and one of his editors felt it necessary to alert fans as to the impending lack of Zagat stories. Amusingly enough, there were already so many Zagat stories in inventory that readers were unlikely to have noticed any difference at all, and likely thought the editors must have been drinking on the job.

When the weird menace genre faded away at the end of the decade Zagat continued his prodigious output, though his time was now split between mystery stories and science fiction yarns. Tragically, Arthur Leo Zagat died of a heart attack in 1949 at the age of fifty-three. At the time he was one of the most sought after and highly paid authors in the pulps. One can only imagine what he might have gone on to accomplish had he lived another ten or twenty years. As it is, Arthur Leo Zagat did leave a magnificent body of work for such a short career. In fact, the body of work he produced in the weird menace genre surpasses the combined output of Hugh B. Cave and Arthur J. Burks combined! Readers can be assured that there will definitely be more volumes of weird fiction by Arthur Leo Zagat from Dancing Tuatara Press.

John Pelan
Midnight House
2013

THE CORPSE FACTORY

Chapter 1

THE KNIFE FROM NOWHERE

The road was wide and well-surfaced, as it would have to be for the trucks I had seen back there in Roton, the huge green tank trucks that brought their loads of Neosite fifty miles to the nearest railroad. But on either side the light of my headlamps sprayed out into a blank nothingness, and when the way curved their beam swept over flat swampland, vacant and desolate. The humid air, too, was heavy with a rank miasma, an odor of putrescence. I felt seeping away from me the elation with which I had started toward the biggest job of my career, the superintendency, no less, of the plant whose cheap and super-efficient product was driving other motor fuels from the market. I tried to shrug off my growing depression, but it weighed on me more and more heavily as the car that had been waiting for me at the shipping point bored on into the night.

The highway lifted in a gradual rise whose crest was sharply defined against the pale glimmer of an overcast sky. A chemical engineer should have no imagination, but I had to fight off an eerie feeling that there, just ahead, was the end of the world; that beyond was sheer emptiness. My skin prickled as I saw a formless black excrescence on that ominous skyline, a black and brooding blob of too solid shadow ... Then I neared and the anomalous bulk took on human contour. Almost involuntarily my foot lifted from the gas pedal, shifted to the brake and slowed the car to a stop. I leaned out.

The fellow my headlight revealed was seated on the ground at the roadside, his long thin arms clasped around gangling, up-bent knees. I judged him to be young, about eighteen, but there was ageless vapidity in his leathery, hollow-cheeked face, dull incuriousness that was not youthful in the lackluster eyes with which he met my own. I could read not even the intelligence of an animal in his countenance; somehow it was flat and featureless as the very swamp from which he appeared to have sprung.

"How far to Newville, buddy?" I called to explain my halt.

He looked at me, unblinking. He didn't reply, but the narrow rim of his forehead wrinkled under his stringy, unkempt black hair. I repeated my question in a louder voice, as if mere noise could penetrate his stupidity.

"Five er ten mile." His husky voice was quite inflectionless and his lips scarcely moved.

"Thanks." I couldn't keep the sarcasm out of my tone. "That tells me a lot." I might as well have spared the effort; he seemed already to have forgotten my presence, was staring unseeingly through my car. I trod on the starter button . . .

Then, from somewhere beyond, a moaning wail sounded— low, muffled, but vibrant with an agony that was somehow uncomprehending. Like the plaint of a hurt cat it welled in a crescendo of suffering.

"Good Lord!" I gritted. "What's that?"

"Mom."

The youth showed not the slightest flicker of interest.

I tried to peer into the blank wall of darkness past my headlights. "What's the matter with her?" I asked.

"Nothin. It's 'Lije. He's dyin'."

" 'Lije?"

"M' brother." There was a slight tinge of expression in his tone this time, of exasperation at my continued questioning.

I switched the car lights off. The wail came again— unutterably sorrowful. The blackness faded. I saw a bulk of darker shadow, ahead and to the left of the road, and a pale rectangle of flickering yellow luminance that might be a window. "Maybe she needs help," I said sharply. "A doctor."

"Ain't no doctor kin stop the Peelin's. Ain't no doctor nigher'n Roton anyways." He sat like a clod, motionless, uncaring.

I slid to the ground and made for what was now defined as a crazily leaning hut. Maybe I wouldn't do any good, but I couldn't go on without finding out. I'm not built that way.

My feet sank into soft, sucking mire, found a narrow path of muddy but firmer ground. There was no lock on the drab door of unpainted rough boards and I pulled it open. A stench of decayed food, human filth, was febrilely warm around me. There was another scent, pungent and foul, that I could not identify. I stepped into a cluttered, grimy room where one feeble candle flickered on a debris strewn table. The beastlike wailing twisted me to a corner.

The woman was on her knees, crouched over what was at my first glance a flat pile of dirt-colored rags. The garment she wore was pulled tight over the abject curve of her back and I could trace the humped line of her spine showing through. Her hair was scraggly, streaked black and gray; and broken, black-rimmed fingertips curved claw-like over the thin lines of her shoulders.

Apparently she had not heard my entrance. I moved toward her, my lips parting to speak. And froze as I glimpsed that over which she moaned.

It wasn't a face on that pallet of rags, not such a face as even the foulest of nightmares could present. Nor was it a skull. That at least is bone-clean and dead. This was stripped clear of flesh, except where some blackened shreds still clung, but the bared muscles were there, and white threadings of nerves, and there was a quivering of agonized life over the blurred surface. The eyelids were gone. From the dark pits they should have covered, sightless balls stared a chalky, translucent white. Seared lip edges were eaten raggedly away from a yellow, rotted grin. And the head had

neither nose nor ears. The rest, mercifully, was hidden from
sight by a dirt-crusted, tattered blanket.

I must have made some sound, though I was not aware of
it, for the woman turned. Had it not been for the other, her
countenance might have inspired horror in me, so lined with
suffering, so emaciated it was. Strands of bedraggled, grimy
hair fell across her brow, and from behind them her eyes glittered, rat-like. Something like a rat, too, there was in the furtive startlement of her expression, in the snarling lift of her
thin lips.

"What d'yer want?" she squeaked.

"Your son told me you were in trouble," I managed to
speak—steadily, I hoped. "Is there anything I can do?"

"Who're you?"

"Thorndal's new superintendent. I was—" The blaze of
hate in her face cut me off. She leaped to her feet and
shrieked:

"Thorndal! Git out! Thet's whut yer kin do. Git out o' here.
He's done ernough ter me, he an' his devils!" She snatched
up a carving knife from the table. "Git out 'fore I fergit I'm a
God-fearin' woman an' use this on yer."

I dodged to the door. "But—but—"

"But nothin'. Ye'll git th' other too—Zeke'll be thar to-
morrer! But he ain't yers yit. Not ternight." She lunged at
me, the knife sweeping in a long arc, and I dived out, slam-
ming the ramshackle panel behind me. I missed the path, and
as I floundered through the patch of swamp between hovel
and road the door flung open behind me. "I hope yer mother
has to look at yer," the virago shrilled after me, "a month
from terday." Cackling, obscene laughter rattled in the dark.

I lurched into my car, kicked blindly at the starter. The
roadside watcher, Zeke, had not moved, had not even turned
his head to the clamor. But he spoke now, above the roar of
my motor, and I throttled down to listen to him.

"Thar wuz a nut loose on yer license plate," he said. "I
fixed it."

Gears rasped and I hurtled away from there as if ten thousand devils from Hell pursued me.

Chapter 2

EYES OF PITY

The road along which I fled curved in a long line, dipped, and rose again. The land to the left rose with it, and here and there a tree showed, gaunt and somehow solitary against the brooding quarter-light of the horizon. I realized that the ground must be firmer here, firm enough to support the stills and gigantic retorts shown on the blueprints Andrew Thorndal had displayed to me.

He hadn't told me much about the process in the interview at which I had been engaged, at a salary startling in these days of slow recovery. There were non-patentable steps, he had explained, in the manufacture of Neosite that his competitors would pay hugely to purloin. "I'll go over the whole thing thoroughly when you get out to Newville," he had rumbled. "Where I can make sure the secrets won't be blabbered."

There had been a challenge, and a threat, in his steely eyes when he had said that across our luncheon table at the Chemist's Club in New York. I had met the challenge frankly. "My first principle is loyalty to my employers, Mr. Thorndal," I had responded. "Through self-interest if nothing else. A man in my profession who does not adhere to that policy finds his career ended very quickly."

The full lips had hardened grimly under his close-clipped gray mustache. "Stick to that, Sutton," he said, "and we'll get along. Otherwise—we're pretty well cut off from the world at Newville and I have my own methods of dealing with—traitors."

Cut off was right! I had asked him why there was no railroad spur to the plant. Even then it seemed to me his reply was evasive. Newville was surrounded by a thirty-five mile stretch of bottomless swamp land; there were no other factories or towns in the region. But the tremendous production of his own industry would have rendered a one-track branch line profitable, and the well-built highway along which I was now journeying could not have presented any lesser engineering difficulties than the building of a railroad. I wondered now whether his isolation was not deliberate.

And my thoughts returned to the scene I had just left. The flesh-stripped face of the dying man had not vanished from my inward vision; it will, I am afraid, never entirely disappear. What disease could have produced that condition? I am somewhat of an amateur physician—one has to be in the outlands to which my work takes me—but I could think of none. It wasn't leprosy—that turns the sloughing tissue an unholy white. Cold rippled along my backbone. *Was it a disease at all?*

A cluster of lights came into view ahead. This must be Newville, the small town Thorndal had built for his truckdrivers and skilled mechanics. My headlight picked up a barrier across the road, striped black and white for visibility, a tall, green-uniformed figure standing in front of it. I skidded to a stop, and the guard came alongside my running-board. There was a revolver in the hand he lifted to the sill of the open window to my left, and his heavy-jowled visage glowered forbiddingly.

"Who are yuh, and what do yuh want?" he demanded.

I flushed at his overbearing manner, but one doesn't argue with a man whose gun snouts at one's diaphragm. "Stanley Sutton, officer," I answered. "I'm the new superintendent at the works."

"Where's yuhr pass?"

I remembered a card Thorndal had handed me at our parting and which I had inattentively stuffed into my wallet. I got it out. The man scrutinized it, handed it back. "That looks okay," he muttered. "Yuh're to park yuhr car in the. garage an' wait there for orders."

"I thought I was to put up in the town. Why—?"

"I don't know nothin'." A secretive veil appeared to drop across his face. "That's what I was told to tell yuh, an' that's all I know about it." He didn't seem to be much impressed by my new dignity. "The garage is straight on, 'bout a quarter mile. All right, Joe."

He stepped back and a dim-seen figure to one side bent and seemed to be operating a lever of some kind. The barrier lifted jerkily, and I let my clutch in. Surely the guarding of a secret process did not require an armed road patrol a mile or more from the plant where it was being carried on. What was I getting into? I fought down a sudden impulse to turn the car around and make for Roton and civilization.

Would God I had obeyed that impulse! I had no difficulty finding the garage to which I had been directed. It was the first building I reached, stretching about five hundred feet beside the highway and correspondingly deep. As I rolled up to it I glimpsed rank upon rank of vehicles within—tanks like those I had seen at Roton, enclosed vans, platform trucks, six- and eight-wheeled trailers, all painted a distinctive, vivid green. A number of green-uniformed guards lounged in front of the structure; hard-faced individuals whose big hands were never far from their holstered guns. There was an electric feeling of tensity about the place, a brooding expectancy. But it left untouched the overalled attendant who slouched up to meet me.

He seemed of a different race. He was painfully thin, lax-jawed and dull-eyed, cut from the same pattern as the lout whose sodden indifference to his brother's terrible fate had appalled me more than his mother's agony. They were typical of the natives of this region, I found—an inbred, moronic species hardly fit for the most unexacting of common labor, dregs of humanity. The man regarded me bovinely.

"I'm Stanley Sutton," I said. "I was told to bring this car here."

"Yeh. Yer ter wait."

"For whom? How long?"

"Dunno." The infinitesimal motion of his knife-blade shoulders might have been a shrug. "Mister Mowrer 'phoned ter tell yer ter wait."

"Who's Mowrer?"

"Unh?"

"Who is this Mowrer?" I repeated, slowly and distinctly.

"Boss's secatary."

There was evidently nothing to be gotten out of the creature. I slid out of the car to stretch my legs. The guards had clotted in a knot, were pretending elaborate unconcern, but I knew, as one does know those things, that I was the subject of their low talk, their furtive inspection. This was natural enough; I was destined to assume a rather important place in the community. Yet there was something other than appraisement in the one or two glances I managed to intercept, something very like compassion, it seemed to me. Nonsense! Why should anyone pity me when I had just been given a position men of twice my age might well envy?

A distant thrumming came to my ears, rose swiftly to a booming roar. From a side road a long-hooded, black Lancia thundered up, halted in a cloud of dust. Its door flung open and Thorndal popped out.

"Sutton!" he bellowed. "Glad you're here!" His big hand engulfed mine. "Waiting long?"

"Just arrived." I am no mean height, yet his massive, iron-gray head loomed above me. There was physical power in the spread of his shoulders, the hugeness of his frame; and his face, sculptured in broad, powerful strokes, was eloquent of a mental strength that explained in some part his swift conquest of an industry that was the stamping-ground of financial giants. Just now his countenance was lined with weariness, the hard glitter of his brown eyes was somewhat dulled, but the dominant virility of the man still showed through like the luminance of an inward blaze. Somehow, other men faded in Andrew Thorndal's presence like a candle in the glare of a thousand-watt airport lamp.

"Get your bag and get in!" The moment of greeting past, he was brusque, commanding. "Snap into it."

His big car was filmed with the dust and mud of a long journey. Thorndal slid under the wheel. I evinced no surprise at this; one didn't expect this man to be driven by a chauffeur. The Lancia leaped into motion.

"Pleasant trip?" asked Thorndal.

"Good enough." We were purring along Newville's Main Street; as we passed there was a perceptible tightening in the bearing of the few men on the narrow sidewalk, even of the shambling, vacant-faced natives. I could see no women.

"Can't say the same. Roads were rotten from Akron. Had to straighten something out there and the damn fools kept me longer that I expected. But this car's good for a hundred or more when she's pushed, so I was able to meet you as I planned."

"I rather imagined I was to put up in town," I said.

"No. You'll stay at the house."

Newville's trim houses dropped behind and the road was bordered by trees that arched overhead and made out path a tunnel of blackness.

"I want you where I can watch you," he added. "You might get notions."

He smiled without humor, and once again I felt as if the coils of a web were tightening around me. All these elaborate precautions must be intended to conceal something more than a mere secret process . . .

And then an uneasy question obtruded itself. Jimmy Haynes, my classmate at Tech and my predecessor here, was of course acquainted with all I was about to learn, all that Thorndal was going to such elaborate lengths to prevent me from communicating to the outside world. How had the manufacturer made certain of Haynes' silence? I realized now that no one had heard from the little man since he had gone, as I was going, to assume charge of the plant at Newville. *Where was he now?*

Something nicked the outer edge of the Lancia's beam, was revealed as a man in the center of the road, waving in a signal to stop. Thorndal grunted, but did not slow. The car hurtled at the figure . . .

"Look out!" I yelled. "You'll hit—" But at the last instant of catastrophe the man leaped aside; we flicked by. Some-

thing thudded against the tonneau side and glass crashed. "Good God," I jerked out. "You almost killed him!"

My employer's mouth was a straight, cruel slash. "His fault," he said. "No business getting in my way."

"But you can't—" I caught myself.

Thorndal's voice was a low growl. "Can't what?"

"You can't kill a man for getting in your path."

"I can't, eh? I wouldn't advise you to try it." His eyes were smoldering. "You might as well learn right now, young man, that getting in Andrew Thorndal's way is dangerous. Especially in Newville."

I didn't answer that. What could I say? I didn't want to talk anyway. Something beside the callous ruthlessness of my chief was making the pit of my stomach squirm.

For the second time in an hour I had seen a man from whose face the blackened flesh was sloughing in rotten decay, baring the quivering, raw muscles beneath. And there had been no covering at all on his waving hand, only gray sinews lacing skeleton fingers!

A red light showed ahead; the Lancia skidded, stopped. I saw two guards advancing, and behind them a high fence of copper wire in parallel strands. It came out from the right, crossed the road and disappeared to the left. But it was the square white sign hanging from it, man-high, that caught my eye. The letters on it were a staring red:

DANGER
This fence is
ELECTRICALLY CHARGED
It is
DEATH
TO TOUCH IT

"Evening, Mr. Thorndal," one of the uniformed men was saying. "I'll have the current off in a minute. Had any trouble on the way up?"

The magnate's voice was sharp. "Why? Expect any?"

The fellow shuffled his feet uneasily. "No, sir. Only there's been someone hangin' around in the woods off there, and a couple stones were thrown at Miss Thorndal's car when she came in last night."

"What? What's that? Nan here?" There was no doubt about it, consternation was vibrant in his tones. "How did she pass the outer lines?"

"I—I dunno. Guess they didn't dare stop her."

"Look here," snapped Thorndal, "the orders are that no one gets in without a pass. No one, do you understand, my daughter or the devil himself. Tell Captain Daley that. No! Tell him to call me at once. I'll flay the hide off him."

The man saluted, awkwardly. "Yes sir. I'll pass the word." The tiny red light at the top of the fence blinked out. "Power's off, sir." I thought there was resentment in the guard's eyes, but his swarthy face was masklike. A panel opened in the fence, gate-like, and gears clashed.

"The brat," Thorndal muttered to himself. "I told her to stay away from here! Well, she'll go back in the morning or I'll know the reason why."

Chapter 3

GOD OF VENGEANCE

Gravel crunched under our wheels. I was aware of a house ahead, of windows warmly lighted. We rolled to a stop, a door opened at the head of a short flight of stone steps, and a man came out. Despite his livery he shambled down the stairs, his long arms lax at his side, and there was something queerly robot-like in his movements.

"Take Mr. Sutton's bag to the room Haynes had," Thorndal snapped. Then he turned to me. "Come on in, Sutton, and I'll introduce you to your new quarters." I thought the weariness in his face had deepened in the last few minutes. Certainly there was a hint of worry in his eyes.

There was a priceless Ispahan on the floor of the entrance hall, something baronial in the lift of the curving staircase toward the rear. I thought of the hovel back on the road, where a faceless man lay dying. A door to one side opened and someone came out, peering through thick spectacles.

"Hah, Mowrer!" Thorndal rumbled. "Got those papers ready?"

The secretary was a gray little man, bent and shriveled. "Yes, Mr. Thorndal," he answered. "They are on your desk. Glad to see you back safely. Were you . . . Did they . . ."

"No. I couldn't do anything with those imbeciles. They insist there has been absolutely no change in the composition they're using on the suits. By the way, this is Stanley Sutton, our new superintendent. My secretary, Carl Mowrer."

Mowrer mumbled some sort of acknowledgment of the introduction, turned back to his superior. "Johnson reports ten additional laborers incapacitated, sir," he said. "And there's three died today."

Thorndal's face hardened. "The devil! That means more slowing up of production while they break in new hands."

"It is annoying, sir." Was I mistaken, or was there a faint hint of irony in the little man's bland voice? "Hampden is waiting in the study to see you. I told him you would be too tired for business tonight, but he insisted. Said he had something you would want to hear about immediately. Shall I tell him to come back in the morning?"

"No. I'll talk to him now. Take care of Sutton for a minute." The manufacturer wheeled eagerly to the door from which Mowrer had come, slammed it shut behind him.

The secretary sighed, and turned to me. His jaw jerked sidewise. "So you've come to take Jim Haynes' place, eh . . . You're not afraid?"

"Afraid?" I echoed wonderingly. "Of what?"

"Of him and his devil's brew. Hasn't he told you how Neosite is made?"

"No. He's told me nothing."

The fellow's gnarled fingers twined nervously with one another. He moved closer to me and peered up into my face. "You're young," he muttered. "Too young. Go away. Go away before he tells you. He'll let you go now. He won't after you know. You'll want to run to the end of the world. But it will be too late then. Too late!" Suddenly he was laughing, soundlessly but horrible. "Too late!"

I grabbed his thin arm, dug my fingers into it. "For the love of Peter," I gritted. "What's this all about? What's going on here?"

"Mowrer!" It was Thorndal's voice from the study door, but brittle, menacing as I had never hear it. "Come here." He had an opened letter in his hand and his face was livid with repressed rage.

"Yes sir." The old man's eyes were fixed on the letter Thorndal held. Suddenly his cheeks were the color of death. "What is it, sir?"

"Did you write this?" He thrust it at Mowrer. "Did you?"

"Where—how—"

"How did I get it? What do you think I pay Hampden for? Did you think he wouldn't know that you gave it to a truck-driver to mail in Roton?"

"Yes—yes, sir."

"Well, you have another think coming. So it was you, not Haynes, that Tri-State Oil was dickering with!"

The man made a little helpless gesture.

"You were going to sell me out for a hundred thousand, and they were willing. But they balked at sending a plane in to get you out." Thorndal's voice rumbled lower and lower, till it was like nothing so much as a volcano about to erupt. Mowrer was almost groveling before him. "Speak up! I want you to admit it with your own lips."

"It—it was the only way I could escape from here. And I had to *get* away—" his voice rose shrilly—"before I went completely mad. I had to get away from this hell . . ."

Did Thorndal flinch, infinitesimally? You couldn't tell it from the deep, deadly murmur of his tone, as he said: "You'll taste real hell, Mowrer, now. They need men in the nitration room. Go to Johnson and tell him I said you were to work there."

I felt let down. All this to-do, and then a mere demotion! What . . .

Then Mowrer shrieked, "Not that! Oh God! Not that! Jail me! Kill me! But don't send me there!" His lips were absolutely colorless, his eyes stared horror. He dropped to the floor and squirmed to Thorndal's feet. "Don't make me work in there!"

The tycoon shoved him away with a heavy shoe. "You should have thought of that before you tried to double-cross me." His face was granite, his eyes contemptuous. "You'll go into that room tonight, and if you make any more fuss you'll go without a suit."

"Without a suit . . ." Suddenly, so quickly I did not see how he managed it, Mowrer surged to his feet, was swarming, an infuriated midget, over Thorndal's huge frame, his clawed hands scoring scarlet furrows across the magnate's cheek. The big man staggered under the unexpectedness of the onslaught, tore blindly at the whirlpool of mad fury the other had become. I heard a maniacal, snarling whimper, saw Mowrer's nails go for the big man's eyes. I saw a knife flash in his other hand. And sprang.

I grabbed, caught the knife wrist, jerked it back till the little man screamed in agony, got an arm around his neck and clamped it tight. Mowrer's feet lashed out, struck Thorndal square in the belly—and then I had ripped the maddened man away from his astounded victim. I tripped, stumbled backward, crashed to the floor with the mewling, screaming fellow atop me.

A whistle shrilled, and I was threshing about the floor, scarcely able to hold the armful of explosive energy terror had made of the meek, near-sighted clerk, fighting to keep the gleaming knife out of my flesh, the clashing teeth from my skin. The tramp of heavy feet was all about me. I saw green uniforms, felt Mowrer ripped from my hold, and I lay gasping, exhausted.

Thorndal was dabbing a white handkerchief at his scratched face. Little lights crawled in his dark eyes, but there was no expression on his countenance save two white spots that came and went on either side of his nostrils. The secretary was limp in the grasp of two burly guards.

"Take him to the nitration room," Thorndal said grimly. "And tell Johnson he is to work without a suit."

Mowrer lifted his head. He had lost his glasses in the struggle, his pupils were tiny, the whites of his eyes blood-shot. But there was no fear in those blurred orbs. Hate peered from them, hate and an awful threat. Words dripped from his twisted mouth . . .

"There is a God, Thorndal, a God of Vengeance," he said. "He knows what you do, and prepares His punishment. Even the least of His creatures may be His instrument to that end. Even I." Then his look dropped to me.

"And you, poor fool," he said. "You have made your choice. I shall not forget you when the time comes. Pray, if you can, for you are doubly doomed."

"Take him away," Thorndal gestured imperatively. Mowrer went steadily toward the door, proudly erect be-tween his captors. Torn, bleeding, disheveled, he dwarfed us all in that moment. The hatchet-faced manservant let them out.

I got to my feet, painfully. Thorndal stared at me, for a moment, as if he were seeing me for the first time. Then he spoke:

"I'm glad you saw that, Sutton. You'll know better than to try to fool me now."

Footsteps sounded overhead.

"Dad. Daddy! What's happened?" I twisted to the flute-like voice from the stair head. "What was all that noise?" The girl came running down the stairs, filmy draperies streaming out behind her, white face anxious. I saw full-curved, red lips, great lustrous eyes, a coif of ebony hair. "Ohhh, you're bleeding!"

"Nan!" There was a throaty tenderness in his ejaculation. He held his arms out to her and she nestled within them.

"But Dad—that's an awful scratch—"

"Never mind that." He pushed her away from him but still held a tight grip on both her arms, just above the elbow. It seemed to me his glance drank her in thirstily. Then suddenly his face was granite once more, his eyes hard. "Why did you come here, Nan? You know I forbade you to."

It was the gruffness of his tone, rather than the words, I thought, that brought the hurt look to her face. "I know. But I was lonesome for you, and Bill Lannon was motoring up this way. So I came along. He's upstairs. You'll like him."

The white spots of rage were visible again, at the outcurve of his nostrils. "You brought someone here." He said it slowly, icily.

She was petulant now, in the way girls have when trying to avoid the consequences of a transgression. "But Daddy, he's swell," she said. She half-turned, and called, "Billy . . . oh, Billy. Come down and meet my father."

"Coming."

He was a typical playboy, the fellow who rattled down the staircase, meticulously dressed, his little blond mustache waxed, his hair slicked back. His round face was insipid, his blue eyes insolent. He reached the lower floor, halted.

"This is Bill Lannon, Dad," said the girl. "Isn't he nice?"

Thorndal grunted. Lannon bowed. "I have been very anxious to make your acquaintance, sir," he said. "Nan's father, I was sure, must be exceptional."

That to the man who had swept like a meteor across industry's sky! Could the chap possibly be so arrant an ass? He looked at the girl fatuously, and I knew I disliked him heartily. But I didn't realize, then, why I did.

"Thanks." Dryly. "I hope you find the sight worth a long trip for a short stay. A very short stay . . . Nan is leaving here at once, and you also."

The chap looked bewildered. But Nan flashed around to her father with something of his own spirit. "Dad," she said. "You can't do that! You can't chase us out the minute we've gotten here."

Thorndal's mouth was grim, but I fancied there was anxiety mixed with the smouldering wrath in his eyes, as he answered. "I can't have you stay here, Nan, not even one night. There's something—I am too busy. And you know I don't allow visitors in Newville."

"I know. I shouldn't have come. But you're not going to send me right away. Without even a chance for one little chat with you, Daddy . . ."

He weakened. "All right. You may stay overnight, with the understanding that neither of you is to set foot outside this house."

The girl's lips firmed, but she knew when not to press an advantage. "All right, Dad. I won't go outside tonight and I won't let Bill." I noticed she said nothing about the morning. "We'll just sit around the fire in my sitting-room and talk. Come on up."

"Not now," he said. "I must go over matters with Mr. Sutton, my new superintendent." She looked at me for the first time, coolly. My heart skipped a beat. "We have lots to do before I can rest."

"I'm Nan Thorndal, Mr. Sutton," she said then. "I was wondering how soon Dad would see fit to introduce us."

I muttered something, I'll be hanged if I know what. She rattled on. "You must join us after you're through. Mr. Haynes and I were great pals till dad exiled me to Florida a month ago."

"We were classmates at Tech," I told her. "But he kept away from the rest of us. Sensitive about his appearance, I imagine."

"He did look rather like a queer old gnome, with his tremendous head and shriveled-up little body. But how could he have been your classmate? He must have been forty-five at least."

"No. He was no older than thirty."

"Come on, Sutton," Thorndal interrupted. "Let's get to work. You two run along."

He watched them scurry up the stairs, and his mouth twisted. I don't think he realized that he spoke aloud. "I'd give ten years of my life if she weren't here."

From somewhere outside there was a shriek, muffled shouts, the dull thud of a shot. Thorndal hurtled to the outer door, slammed it open and lunged out into the night. I followed.

A hundred yards away, across a sloping lawn, a line of red lights marked the fence, and I could see slumped forms in a dark knot just beneath one of them. As I dashed after my employer's running form an excited murmur came from the group, a shocked oath.

There was something hanging from the wire, a quivering shape outlined by a faint blue haze of electricity. My scalp tightened and my throat was dry. The shredded face seemed to be grinning at me through black lips, and the hand that was clamped to an upper wire was nothing but muscles and bones. It was the man Thorndal had tried to run down. Fire smoldered in the tattered jacket that covered the twisted torso of the tortured corpse. I sickened, then looked again. The man had an enormous head, and his body was shriveled, tiny.

I moved further away from the lethal barrier as the ground seemed to heave under my feet. Could there be anyone else with precisely the deformity that Jim Hayne's had? Anyone else with that gnome-like shape?

My employer's voice was devoid of emotion. "What happened here, Lansio?"

One of the men in green uniforms who stood on the other side of the fence answered him: "I see him come out from the woods. He got knife in hand. I holler. He no answer. Holler 'gain. He start running. I shoot, get him in leg. He fall 'gainst wire. That all."

The red lights were gone, suddenly, and the body slumped to the ground, horribly. Someone pulled it away and the lights came on again. Thorndal turned on his heel. "We'll never get through at this rate," he grumbled. It seemed to me he was watching my face, speculatively.

What was it the woman had shrieked after me, back on the road to Newville? "I hope yer mother has to look at yer a month from terday."

I tried to say something, but the words stuck in my throat. I wanted to tell him I was going away from there. He could have his job. But that would mean I should never see Nan Thorndal again.

I followed Andrew Thorndal into the house, into his study, sat down in the chair he indicated and watched while he got paper from a drawer, adjusted an automatic pencil. And all the time I was thinking of Mowrer's warning: *"After he tells you it will be too late."*

Chapter 4

"I AM THE LAW!"

I listened to Thorndal's voice, flowing on and on, and watched his busy pencil jot down chemical equation after equation. There seemed nothing particularly intricate about the synthesis of Neosite so far, nothing that any ordinarily skilled chemist might not deduce from an analysis of the product itself. What was the dread secret?

"From here," he rumbled, "the liquid is piped to the nitration room. This is where my new technique comes in. As the nitric acid is poured in I also add one-tenth of a per cent of—" He named a certain organic compound. "The resultant reaction is this, rather unexpectedly." Letters and symbols formed a new line on the scribbled sheet.

I emitted a low whistle and pointed to a cabalistic inscription. "I've never run across this gas." It was a by-product. "But from its formula I should judge it to be extremely caustic."

"It is. The fumes that fill the nitration room dissolve flesh like water does salt."

"You take no chances, of course. The nitration is performed in an autoclave."

He looked at me rather queerly, I thought. "No," he answered.

My skin crawled. "Then how do you guard your laborers?"

"By suits and masks made from a special rubber compound I have devised. They are fairly efficient."

"Fairly!" I was trying to match the unemotional steadiness of his tone. "Not perfectly!"

"No. We have had occasional failures. In the past two weeks they have grown in number, inexplicably. That's why I went to Akron. I thought the trouble lay in the manufacture of the suits. But it isn't there." There was just the slightest trace of cloudiness in his eyes. "We've lost twenty men from the nitration room in the past fortnight. Breaking in new ones is hampering production."

"Twenty men!" I couldn't keep the horror out of my voice any longer. "Good God—they must die horribly!"

"They do." He said it with an utter lack of expression, but his eyes were smouldering coals. "I'm afraid that stupid as are the people around here they will soon refuse to work for us, even with increased pay."

I pushed against the tabletop with my hands, pushed myself to my feet. "Look here, Mr. Thorndal," I gritted through cold lips, "I may need the money and the job you've offered me. But I can't be mixed up in this. I'm resigning."

His mouth twisted. "Not any more, young fellow. You know too much. You're going to stay here and work for me—as superintendent or in the nitration room alongside Mowrer."

There was sodden, brooding silence in the somber room. His head lifted slightly, so that his agate eyes held mine, and his mouth was a hard, straight line. I thought of the armed guards outside, the death-dealing wires.

"All right," I said. "I'll continue as superintendent." After a while his vigilance might relax, I might see a chance to get away. "But I shall try to find a way to protect the workers."

The corners of his lips lifted in a satiric smile. "Try. But make damn sure you don't make it cost more than the expense of the labor turnover if you want me to adopt it. I won't raise the price of Neosite, and I won't cut my profit."

I shrugged. "After all, there isn't a bridge or a skyscraper built without a couple of deaths. There are fatal accidents in every factory." I must make him believe I had capitulated without reservations. "It is the price of progress."

"Now you're talking," Thorndal exclaimed, and there was satisfaction in his tone. "Sit down and we'll go on with our work."

I was searching for a weak point in the defenses, a loophole through which I might escape. And I found it!

The basic material of Neosite was crude oil, brought into the plant by pipeline from Pennsylvania fields. The huge underground tube was indicated clearly on the maps. But there was another similar but fainter tracing, angling off to the south.

"Another pipeline," he explained. "For emergencies. It connects up with the Texas tube. It's empty, never been used."

I talked about something else, disinterestedly. But my pulses throbbed. There was the road to freedom! I noted carefully that its entrance was just below a window of the nitration room.

At last we were finished. Thorndal looked at his watch. "Three a.m., by George!" he said. "I'll show you your room." Upstairs, he added: "If you get any ideas during the night, remember Mowrer." He opened a door at the other end of the hall and disappeared.

Enough illumination came in from outside for me to undress, and I didn't switch on the light in the room. My pajamas were folded across the pillow; I got into them mechanically and stretched out. I was dog-tired, physically and mentally, but I could not sleep.

I closed my eyes, and Nan Thorndal drifted across my imagining, her white grace in poignant contrast to all the horrors I had seen, gayety and fervor for living dancing in her eyes.

The loathsome triangle of a snake's head rose behind her, peered over her shoulder. I saw its forked tongue darting, saw that it was poised to strike. It hissed warningly. Its eyes were like Thorndal's, glittering hard . . . The hissing grew louder—I tried to yell a warning to the girl—and woke trembling.

But the hissing continued, low, insistent. It was somewhere in the room. There was a faint odor too, rank, pungent, like the unfamiliar stench in the hut where 'Lije lay dying. It had grown darker; the ceiling was only a faint, pale glimmer. I forced my head around, against the paralysis of inexplicable fear that held me—forced it around to the seeming source of the sibilant noise. And saw a green-glowing mist billowing along the floor!

It came from the gloom of the further corner, a thin veil of iridescence rolling ominously; its advancing edge sharply defined. It was coming swiftly toward my bed. Before I could gather my sleep-bemused faculties and guess its meaning, the ominous tide was lapping at the legs of my couch, was reaching tenuous, hungry filaments up toward me.

A sound at my door—someone breathing heavily—snapped the spell that gripped me. I gathered myself—launched myself in a flying leap that sent me almost to the exit. In the instant it took for me to grasp the doorknob and get the portal open, my bare feet were immersed ankle-deep in the green vapor. Then I was through, had crashed the door behind me and leaned, gasping, against the wall. Agony seared my feet where they had dipped into the gas, the excruciating torture of a burn from boiling acid.

Something scattered to my right. I twisted, saw someone flick down the curving stairs. I had only a glimpse of him in the wan light of the single burning lamp. I shouted something unintelligible, started after him—and whirled to the boom of Thorndal's voice. "Sutton!"

He was gigantic in the dimness, and he was much too near to have come all the way from his room since I had slammed the door! Red rage exploded in my skull.

"You devil," I squeezed out through a tightened throat. "What are you trying to do—kill me in my sleep?" I took a step toward him, my hands fisting, and stopped as pain shot up my legs from my scorched feet. The pain was growing worse.

His face was a frozen mask, but there was a red glow in his eyes. "What do you mean?" he rumbled, speaking low. "What's going on here?"

Doors were opening along the hall. "You know damn well what I mean," I snapped. "The gas in my room—if I hadn't wakened in time I'd be dead!"

Behind him Nan came out into the hall, a pastel-shaded negligee tightly clasped around her exquisite form. She was sleepy-eyed, pale.

"Gas in your room." There was no surprise in his calm voice.

"Yes. The green hell-gas. Look!" I lifted one foot. Already the skin was black. It was like a skin-tight shoe.

"Get in there and wash it off!" He jerked a thumb at a bathroom door, just across from my bedchamber. "Use plenty of soap. If you've had only a touch that will stop it. Hurry!" The impact of his authoritative command, my terror that in moments the flesh would peel from my extremities, drove anger from me. I dove into the room he indicated, snapped on the light and twisted bathtub spigots in frantic haste. But I left the door open, listened and watched as I flinched from the sting of the soap I had snatched up.

"Dad." Nan asked. "What . . .?"

"Nothing, dear. Just an accident. Sutton was fooling with something Haynes left in there and burned himself. Go back."

"But—but I'm frightened, Dad. I want to stay with you."

"Please go to your room." His voice was commanding, but his eyes devoured her. The outer skin was peeling from my feet and ankles as I rubbed the lather in, and the soap burned like fire. "You will be in the way here," he said. "I'll come to you later. Go, please."

She sighed, vanished. Lannon came into sight, in orchid pajamas. Not a hair was out of place on his head or in that tiny, pointed mustache of his. But his insipid face was colorless, and he clutched a pearl-handled pistol in one white hand. "Is anything wrong?"

The big man ignored him. He was looking at the floor, at
the threshold of the room I had quitted in such haste. I swung
my legs out of the tub, reached for a jar of cold-cream. The
burning was gone from my feet and ankles, but they were
raw, tender. The salve relieved the pain somewhat, and I
stood up gingerly, peered to see what it was Thorndal
watched.

Along the lower edge of the door green smoke was seeping
out.

Thorndal's head lifted. "That's got to be shut off or it will
fill the home. Here you—" He turned to address someone
beyond my vision, "Go in and see what you can do."

I hobbled out of the bathroom and looked to see whom he
was ordering into that death-filled room, that chamber of
horror. It was the robot-like servant, uniform trousers hastily
pulled on over a drab, grimy union-suit in which he evidently
slept. The man shambled forward as I came out, his vacuous
eyes fixed on his master's. Was it ignorance or mechanical
obedience that was sending him unprotesting to terrible
death?

"My God!" I ripped out. "You can't let him go in there.
The room must be filled with the stuff by now. Why, it's
murder!"

Lannon's jaw was dropped, his mouth gaped stupidly.
Thorndal looked at me and his gaze was basilisk. "Keep out
of this, Sutton," he said icily.

The man's hand was on the door-knob, but my cry seemed
to have penetrated his dull intellect. He said, fumblingly: "Is
it the Peelin' gas, boss? I don't know as I want ter go in."
There was something pathetic in his irresolution. Evidently
defiance of Thorndal's orders was quite beyond his concep-
tion.

"Go in and turn it off," the latter snarled, and jerked the
door open. The ominous hissing flashed out, and the room
was fogged with the green haze of death. "See it?" Thorndal
shouted. "A drum in the corner." His big hand struck Jever's
back, thrust him in. The door slammed behind the man, and a
muffled scream sounded from within—a scream of anguish.

I thought I heard stumbling footsteps going across the floor. Then there was the thud of a falling body.

Thorndal's ear was against the panel. "The hissing's stopped," he said. "He shut it off before he dropped."

"Good Lord," I yammered. "It's murder. Murder!"

The other's eyes were bleak. "Not murder, Sutton. Justice. Someone had to cut the gas off or we'd all be killed. Jevers could be spared the best. And besides he had it coming to him. He helped Mowrer get his double-crossing messages out."

My pulses hammered. "You have no right to take the law into your hands!" If it meant that I would meet the same fate I had to say it. "You—"

"I *am* the law in Newville. Get that fixed in your mind, young man. *I am the law.*"

With an effort I shrugged and turned away. If I ever got out of here alive I would show him there was another law, stronger than his.

Thorndal's voice broke in upon my thoughts. "Where's that nincompoop Lannon?" he asked.

"He was here a minute ago," I answered heavily. "Right here."

"I want to tell him—"

A room door had opened; the playboy bustled out. He had gotten into clothes, and he had a heavy bag in his fist. His cheeks were the color of putty.

"Hey, you! Where do you think you're going?" growled Thorndal.

"Away. I'm going away from here."

Thorndal moved toward him ominously. "Oh, no, you're not," he said grimly. "You're staying right here. You've seen too much."

Hysteria leaped into Lannon's voice; I swear there were tears in his eyes. "Don't touch me," he quavered. "Keep your hands off me!"

"I wouldn't touch you with a ten-foot pole. But if you're looking for trouble just put a foot outside this house. You'll get it."

"Good Heavens!" The bag dropped from his nerveless fingers. "I should never have come here."

"That's the first sensible thing you've said," Thorndal commented dryly. "Now, get back in your room and stay there."

Chapter 5

THE LIVING DEAD

Throbbing pain rendered sleep impossible, and I sat in the new room I had been given, my feet on a pillow and my chin cupped in a hand whose elbow rested on the windowsill. The sky bad cleared, and below my vantage point the lawn sloped, moonlit, to the circling line of red pin-points marking the electrically-charged fence that had already taken a life that night.

Somewhere a clock struck four. Two hours to daylight yet. Three hours till I should have to go into that factory where horror stalked—till I should have to face Andrew Thorndal again.

For I knew now that it was a battle to the death between us. I must smash him, smash his fiendish mill—or die. As long as his power remained I was a prisoner, a slave, sending other helpless slaves to incredible tortures.

What kind of man was he? Incredibly hard, ruthless, murderous. And yet he was sane. In all his long exposition of the intricate manufacture of Neosite, in the hours that I had studied him, there had been no hint of anything to the contrary. He was no madman, but merely one utterly without human feeling, driving straight to his objective of the production of his motor fuel cheaply and in quantity, without regard to what sacrifice that objective entailed.

And when he discovered a spy, a traitor, he sent him to death as spies and traitors are sent to death in war—utterly without compunction.

My brow knitted. All this seemed logical—devilishly logical. But why had he tried to kill me with gas hidden in my

room? That was not like him. If he trusted me, there was no
reason for such an attempt. If he did not, he would not hesitate to shoot me down like a dog—or send me to the nitration
room. I was utterly in his power. There was no need for de-
ception, for the planting of an opened drum where it would
take me in my sleep.

He had not bothered to deny my accusation. But somehow
I could not believe him guilty of that abomination. *Someone
else had tried to kill me!* Who, and why? *Would he try
again?*

My scalp tightened. The struggle against Thorndal that had
been forced on me was alone a titanic task. What could I do
against another enemy, unknown, striking at me invisibly
from the night?

At this unpleasant point in the whirligig of my tired mind I
became conscious of a furtive murmur, voices too low to be
intelligible. This was curious!

I looked along the house-side, and saw that someone was
squatted on the slanting verandah roof, two windows away.

Could it be that the secret enemy was lurking in that chamber, unknown even to Thorndal? It would have been easy
enough to steal along the slanting boards and slip a tank of
gas into the room where I had been sleeping. Holy Moses!
Maybe it had not been intended for me at all; perhaps it had
been meant for Thorndal himself. No—he slept at the end of
the hall; no possibility of a mistake. For Nan, then! My blood
curdled. Perhaps the plotters were planning even now to rec-
tify their error!

The man on the roof moved, just then, and slid over its
edge. He was a shadow flitting across the lawn. A patch of
moonlight caught him, momentarily, and I saw that he was
tall, painfully thin, his hatless head a high, hairless dome. He
went into shadow again, and vanished.

And then I saw something that drove the puzzle from my
mind. The long arc of red lights blinked out! Dim forms appeared suddenly from the black cluster of the bordering
woods, all along the fence, and suddenly there were silent,
shadowy struggles everywhere. Not one of the surprised

guards had time to shout or shoot. Even at this distance I sensed the venomous quality of those struggles.

Almost before I realized they had begun they were over, and a swarm of dark, distorted forms were climbing the wire barrier that was no longer impregnable. They were running across the lawn, queer distorted shapes, more fearful for the silence of their coming. The foremost reached the swath of moonlight and I saw that he was Mowrer, had Mowrer's slight figure at least, though the face I glimpsed was as black as coal, black as my feet had been after an instant's contact with the green gas.

Thorndal's victims had risen at last, were coming to take their vengeance. Let them come! Swift elation rose in me, then vanished. Nan! What would they do to her if they won into the house? Nan!

I plunged for the door, slammed it open, and yelled, "Thorndal! Thorndal! They're coming!"

He must have slept lightly or not at all, for he was out of his room almost before I could turn towards it. "What is it?" he snapped. "Who's coming?"

"Mowrer and a gang from the plant! They've killed the guards and—"

He had popped back through his door, was out again instantly with guns in his hands. Nan appeared, and Lannon, his blue eyes popping from his head. There was a crash from below and through the upper windows came a shrill tumult of cries, the arid yells of a bloodthirsty mob.

"Here, Sutton, take this," Thorndal shouted, and tossed a gun to me. "Watch the stair head."

He twisted to Lannon, handed a revolver to him. "Get back in your room and guard the porch roof."

"Give me one, Dad. You know how well I can shoot." Nan was pale but calm. There was something of her father in the set of her little jaw. He looked at her, and obeyed.

"God bless you, girl! You watch the porch, too; I don't trust that milksop."

She smiled bravely, jerked open the door of her bedroom and disappeared within. The bedlam from below was terrific now; something was thudding against the entrance door in great crashes that shook the building, and there was the smash of breaking glass.

Behind me there was the sound of moving furniture. "Here, help me with this," came Thorndal's voice. He was hauling a huge chifferobe out of a room close by. I sprang to his aid and got it across the stair head. It filled the space, would shield us well enough, while at either flank there was just sufficient space for us to see past and shoot I crouched at one side, Thorndal at the other. And the entrance portal crashed in!

They poured through and filled the lower hall, a howling, shrieking mob. It was dark down there and I could see them only dimly, but the foul stench of their putrescence swept up to me, and the pungent aroma of the green gas. A black shadow leaped for the stairs and my gun spat. He fell—crashed down, and sprawled in the dimness.

"Too dark," I grunted. "Too dark down there," Gun-flash answered my shot and bullets thudded into our barricade. "I can't see to shoot."

"There's a switch here," my companion growled. "Wait."

A click, and light flooded the milling crowd. It was greeted by a volley of shots and shrill, weird yelpings that made a madhouse chorus. Thorndal's weapon thudded, but for a hor-rified instant I could not fire.

Down there, in that luxuriously furnished lobby, some gro-tesque nightmare had spilled its creatures in an affrighting, obscene throng. Not one of them was human-looking. Not one. They ranged from some who were merely blackened by the first touch of the gas, through gibbering, mad-eyed be-ings whose cheekbones protruded and whose lips were frayed, to the incarnate horror of the dead-alive from whom all flesh had vanished. Cheekless, noseless, earless corpses, they still jerked about in a simulation of life, with a shim-mering play of exposed muscles and flickering nerves whose agony was horribly visible.

If it had not been for the thought of Nan, in that moment, I should have thrust the barricade aside and thrown down to them the man who had made them what they were, thrown him down to them and plunged after. But she was there, somewhere behind, and I could not abandon her to their vengeance. I dared not think what her fate would be.

The chifferobe was jerking under the impact of their shots. They surged on.

My finger squeezed trigger and I felt the gun jump in my hand. Flayed figures fell, twitching, on the steps. Thorndal's weapon thundered beside me, took its deadly toll. But still they came on; mouthing, grimacing figures from Hell! They came slowly because they had to clamber over the contorted bodies of the fallen. Slowly, because my lead and Thorndal's was hurtling into them, driving them back. I saw one gaunt skeleton topple, his open mouth gurgling a scream, his tongue only a blackened stump in the dark cavity of his throat.

Where was Mowrer? He had led the charge across the lawn, but I could see him nowhere now. The question flicked across my horror-numbed brain, and then the hammer of my gun clicked on an empty shell. A raw, featureless face stared through my firing slit, its eyes twin pits of damnation. The chest rocked under the impact of the attackers, toppled. I sprang backward . . .

And from somewhere behind a shriek ripped high above the triumphant clamor of the mob. A woman's shriek. *Nan!*

I whirled, and hurtled down the long corridor, Thorndal's berserk roar ringing in my ears. I was conscious of Lannon's white face, his open mouth shouting something I did not hear, and then I was hurling myself into the room where I had seen the girl go.

The window framed struggling figures. I glimpsed Nan's flailing arms, the ex-secretary's face, black save where mad eyes rolled whitely under lashless lids. I leaped to them. Someone loomed at my side. I dodged—felt the breeze of a club that just missed my head—flung a fist at the dim-seen form. It thudded sickeningly against moist flesh. I heard weakened bone crunch, and twisted again to the window. It was open, empty. I lunged to it, thrust head and shoulders out.

"Help," Nan screamed from the roof-edge. "Dad! Bill! Help!" She was still fighting at the roof-edge, against Mowrer and another dark, tall form. I shouted something unintelligible, lifted a leg to the sill. A shot barked—to my right. Something crashed against my skull—crashed me into oblivion.

Chapter 6

FREE?

I think the first thing of which I was conscious was the pain in my feet. It seemed as if they had been rasped with sharp files and salt rubbed into the wounds. Then the racking pain at the back of my skull obtruded itself, and the weight that lay across my chest. I opened my eyes. My sensations were still purely physical—I recall that. Thought was not yet functioning at all. There was a roar in my ears and a lurid red light was all around me. I felt warm, although I was clothed only in pajamas, and I hurt all over.

Something was digging into my back and I tried to turn over. I could not move! The blow that had knocked me out had paralyzed me. I realized that I was still on the porch roof, that something lay across me, pinning me down, that I could not stir. And that the roaring I heard, the dancing red light, and the unnatural warmth could mean only one thing. Fire! The house was on fire and I could not move!

Flames licked along the upper window-sash, just within my vision, tiny jets of yellow, and red, and lucent green. Acrid sting of smoke was in my nostrils, and heat beat at me. Glass crashed somewhere and the voice of the blaze was deafening. I smelled hair burning. My own? I turned my head toward the window and saw a red face on the sill, black flesh peeling away from it, its scant hair frizzling in the heat.

Soon my hair would frizzle like that, and the fire lick across my body. What a way to die!

I had turned my head! Did that mean the paralysis was gone? I heaved up, throwing off the body that lay over me. Something clattered on the roof, a cudgel. There was a bullet wound in the back of the corpse's neck and blood still seeped from it. I was on my feet, the hot tin roofing doubling my agony. A flame licked out from the window, almost caught me. I leaped from the porch-roof, doubling my feet under me, ducking my head between my shoulders, taking the fall on my back and rolling as I had been taught in gym-class at Tech. But the impact knocked the breath from me.

I struggled erect. Every move I made was painful, the grassy stubble was a torment, my head was a gigantic, whirling globe on my shoulders. I limped toward the fence where the danger lights no longer glowed, trying to gather my incoherent thoughts. Someone had shot the fellow who had stunned me just as the cudgel fell. I had been left for dead, I was free to escape from this infernal place, from this Hell on Earth. *I was free to escape!*

I reached the fence, crawled between copper strands. A mound in the road attracted my attention and I bent to it. Shredded bits of green cloth told me what lay there had been a uniformed guard two hours ago, filled with life. I looked away quickly to save my sanity.

I stood there, swaying. I was free to escape, I told myself; but something inside me denied it. I couldn't go away from here. There was something I must do. What was it? I put out a hand to the wire to steady myself—and remembered.

Nan! Nan Thorndal! Mowrer had her, he whose eyes had glared with such hate at her father, at me. He who had led the ravening throng of the green gas's victims to their long overdue uprising, he who had proclaimed himself God's instrument for vengeance! Would his crazed mind extend that vengeance to her? Had he not left the direct attack to the others while he stole behind our defenses and snatched her from her room?

I groaned, and shuddered with cold, despite the heat-blast that rolled across the lawn from the blazing house. What was he doing to her, what unimaginable torture was he inflicting on that lissome, slender, dreamy-eyed girl? What had he done to her, where had he taken her? I looked around wildly, and saw the looming bulk of the plant, saw that most of the windows were darkened, but that four were alight, near the ground. And against their staring oblongs, dark figures moved.

I cudgeled my brain for the plans Thorndal had shown me. And cursed as I got a glimmer of what Mowrer's scheme must be. That was the nitration room, the place where the gas was born that stripped men's flesh from them and killed them too slowly. Good Lord! Had he taken her there?

I dove across the road, was swallowed up in the shadow, and started toward those yellow windows, calming myself to coherent thought as I forced my way through underbrush that tore at my scantily covered body and slashed my already lacerated feet. I must have traced a trail of blood through those woods, but I did not feel it then. I was racked by a greater torture, hag-ridden by the vision of Nan Thorndal in Mowrer's power, in the power of his fiendish horde. Nan Thorndal—whom I knew at last that I loved, had loved from the moment I had seen her.

What could I hope to accomplish, weaponless, almost naked, weakened by all that I had passed through? I did not know, knew only that I must get to her, get to Nan, help her or share her fate.

Dread hammered at me for speed, but I could not go fast. I was too weak, the brush too thick. So I moved slowly, and had time to think.

Mowrer might be insane, but his attack had been well worked out. The stealthy gathering of his forces in the woods, their sudden silent onslaught the instant the power was off in the wires . . .

Hold on! How had that come about? The master switch was on the lower floor of the blazing building. That I knew from the blueprints. *Someone in the house had cut the current!* Jevers was the only servant who slept in—Thorndal had told me that—and Jevers, I realized grimly, could not have been the one. There was left, as far as I knew, myself, Thorndal and Nan, and Lannon.

Was there someone else, someone unknown even to the manufacturer? The same one, perhaps, who had planted the gas in my room? The one who had engaged in that midnight conversation with the prowler of the high-domed, bald head? Where had the latter gone, anyway—of which party was he? What had that furtive talk been about, and with whom?

A vast roaring twisted me toward the burning home, a tremendous crash. The roof had fallen in, the walls were toppling, crashed even as I looked, and the triumphant flames soared heavenward in a furious outburst, a geysering of lurid, blazing gases, of great beams exploding upward, of cascading sparks and fluttering, whirling embers. Through the split open building-side, I saw the curving staircase shatter and drop into the roaring lake of avid light, saw a body wrapped in flame swirl in that inferno, a human torch. I shuddered to think that if my coma had lasted a bare ten minutes longer my corpse too, or my still-living body, would have been enveloped in a fiery shroud.

There was an open space between the edge of the woods and the long low building that was my goal, a space shielded from the fading glow of the ashes so that sightless dark lay there.

A grotesque, twisted shadow flitted across one luminous aperture; thin shoulders, and a profile that showed no irregularity marking nose or chin. I crouched, shivering a little in the before-dawn chill.

One advantage alone I had—Mowrer's ignorance of my continued existence, his belief that I was dead.

An oath, deep-voiced, came faintly to me from within, and the intonations of a protesting feminine voice. The pall of dread lifted from me ever so slightly as I realized that Nan was still alive. But the sounds stirred me into action. I started across the clearing, moving gingerly to spare my feet and avoid untoward noise. The footing here was soft earth, a blessed relief after the torture of grassy stubble and twig-covered forest ground. My burning soles felt cool iron, and I bent to it.

Groping blindly, I felt that a metal disk was embedded in the ground, some three feet in diameter. By sheer luck I had blundered across the manhole cover to the unused pipeline, the steel-lined tunnel I had forgotten—but that now, I realized, must make an essential part of my plan.

Weakened as I was, blinded by darkness and hampered by the necessity for avoiding noise, it was a gigantic task to move the iron plate. But at last I managed it. Then I turned once more to the nitration room windows, just beyond.

They were frosted, as I have mentioned, blocking vision. But I could hear sounds, the padding of many feet, someone speaking in a high shrill voice, the noise of pouring liquid. A hairline of brighter light along the sill showed that the window was not quite tightly shut. I bent to see if I could peer through.

And someone leaped on me from behind! An arm slid around my neck, clamped tight. A knee dug into the small of my back. "Got you!" the garrotter grunted, and I could not breathe. I twisted desperately, flailing fists backward at empty air. But his grip was iron, the dig of his knee into my kidneys excruciating. "Mowrer!" he shouted. "Mowrer!"

My eyes were popping from their sockets, my lungs bursting. Dimly I knew that dark figures were crowding about me; the secretary's blackened face danced dizzily before me in the window-glow. The choking arm relaxed, but hands gripped my arms, my legs. I was lifted from the ground.

"Two birds at one throw," I heard Mowrer's gloating voice. "Grab Johnson, too, and bring him in."

"But I'm on your side." It was my captor's voice, thin-edged with hysteria, "I'm on your side, Mowrer. I caught the fellow for you."

Johnson! Where had I heard that name? Oh, yes. The one in charge of the nitration room, of Thorndal's hellhole!

"On my side!" said Mowrer. "Only because you can't help yourself . . . You can't get past my watchers where the road bottle-necks into the swamp and you think you can escape punishment this way. Nothing doing, friend Johnson. You have a long roll of misdeeds for which to answer."

There was no way out then—except through the pipeline! Good thing I had opened that manhole! Much good it would do me now. I was done for.

"I couldn't help myself," Johnson protested. "I only obeyed orders."

"You'll obey my orders now. Mine, and His whose instrument I am." There was the exaltation of the religious fanatic in Mowrer's voice, and the cold cruelty of the triumphant oppressed! No hope for mercy there, or justice. "Take him, men."

I couldn't see what was happening in the dark, but there was the sound of a scuffle, and the wordless wail of one in mortal fear. A nightmare sound! "Gag him!" Mowrer ordered implacably. Then those holding me started to move, and I saw the dark wall of the building drifting by.

Up steps, through a huge door, a vast space, shadowy, eerie with towering tanks and weird machines, half-seen. I closed my eyes to shut out the sight of my bearers, to shut out the unholy vision of those horrible faces; more horrible now for the flare of triumph, the little crawling lights of sadistic anticipation in their lidless eyes. A door opened. They lifted me over a threshold, and I heard the door shut again. Heard Nan scream, "Mr. Sutton. Oh God! They've caught you, too!" I forced myself to look, then.

I was in a long room, ablaze with the uncanny blue of spluttering mercury lamps. A line of iron pillars marched down the center of the loft, and there were three forms bound to the columns: Nan, her fear-distorted face staring white in the luxuriant frame of her Stygian hair; Lannon, his mustache still ludicrously pointed and immaculate against the fish-belly gray of his cheeks; and Thorndal! Lashed immovably to an iron post, helpless, his clothing was half-ripped from his great frame, there were angry red weals on his hairy torso, and blood dripped from a cut over one ear. But he was poised, defiant, his massive head was proudly erect and his rough-sculptured features were overlaid by a brooding thunder-cloud of wrath. Lightning flickered in his eyes as he saw me.

"Tie them up!" Mowrer's command crackled in the sudden silence that followed Nan's outburst.

Skinless, dreadful hands fumbled ropes around me, pulled them ungently tight, and I sagged, unable any longer to stand, supported against the metal stake by those ropes alone. A knot of gargoylesque figures about the next column to mine disintegrated, and I had my first view of the man who had taken me and had in his turn been nabbed. Johnson, foreman of the nitration room, was the tall, high-domed individual who had crouched on the porch roof and whispered secretively to someone within the house!

Chapter 7

JURY OF THE DAMNED!

There were perhaps a score of them in the long room, chattering among themselves like so many apes.

Now and then one would laugh, a cackling, lascivious laugh that sent new tremors of detestation through me. Mowrer was bent over a huge rectangular vat that spread along the farther wall of the loft, watching a great pipe gurgitate into it a flood of viscous black liquid. He was talking to someone whom I could not make out. Above him there hung from the beamed ceiling a smaller glass tank, and it was filled with an iridescent fluid that I knew to be Thorndal's secret reagent. From it a pipe dipped down and ended just over the larger tank, and the corrugated wheel of a valve was within easy hand reach.

My eyes clung to that wheel and my blood curdled, for I knew that when it was turned the contents of the tank above would pour into the black fluid—and the green gas of death would boil up to dissolve the flesh, the muscles and very bones of any who might be in that room and unprotected! In an hour anyone immersed would be tracelessly dissolved!

My eyes sought Nan's, a wordless message passed between us. My pulse leaped, the blood hammered in my veins, and emotion surged within me—wonder that the miracle I read in her veiled glance could have occurred. Then a grinning, lipless skull passed between us and our peril was recalled to me full force. My brain raced. Was there any way in which I could kill her, swiftly, before the gas seared that young beauty?

"Enough," Mowrer spoke crisply. Someone grimaced with bared facial muscles and pulled a lever over. The stream of oil cut off with a sucking sound. I could just see the surface of the black pool, two feet below the level of the floor. It heaved like some foul prehistoric monster, and noisome colors rippled over it. Mowrer turned slowly, and the man with him. My throat contorted in a soundless shriek.

His body was shriveled, tiny; the skull, all that remained of his head, gigantic. God Almighty! I had seen him dead, hours before, clamped rigid to wires vibrant with lethal lightning, seen that deformed body alight with a blue aurora that was blasting every cell within it! And now Jimmy Haynes walked across the floor, his skeleton hand on Mowrer's arm, his sightless eyes deep pits wherein white marbles rolled!

Was the little old man, whom Thorndal had condemned, indeed the instrument of God's vengeance? Had he been infused with power to raise the dead? Was this concourse of inhuman figures a gathering of the damned, raised from the grave to visit retribution upon their slayer? The solid walls rocked around me and the floor, heaved beneath my feet . . .

There was a desk on the dais near the entrance to this corner of Hades, and two chairs had been placed behind it. Those two went directly there, Mowrer guiding the other with infinite tenderness. They sat down. There was something appalling in their slow progress, an awful threat in their grim, still faces. To my tortured vision Haynes was Beelzebub himself, the ebony-skinned Mowrer his chief disciple.

In response to a motion of the secretary's hand the others ranged themselves to one side, intent, listening. Utter silence clotted in the room. The foul odor of rotting bodies was stench in my nostrils, and the mercury lamps added the last touch of horror with their ghastly light and the huge shadows they cast across the floor. It seemed to me that vast black wings beat overhead . . .

"Andrew Thorndal!" Mowrer's tones had lost their shrillness, the thinness that had spoken of age and pain. They had a husky quality, were hushed, though clear and penetrating, as if he were himself appalled by that which he was about to do. "Andrew Thorndal! That you may not hereafter complain you were unjustly condemned, a jury of those you have wronged will hear you. Have you anything to say?"

An instant Thorndal's nostrils flared, then he was speaking, calmly, steadily: "With what am I charged?"

"With exploiting for your private profit the people of a countryside. With condemning to torture and death men too dulled and stupid to withstand you."

"They were starving when I came, were clothed in rags. I gave them work, money with which to buy food and clothing."

The voice of the accuser was implacable. "You lured them into your power," he said. "You gave them suits that at first protected them, but when you had set up your fences of death and your cordons of armed guards so they could not escape, the suits failed. You cheapened them, to save a few paltry cents in the cost of the only defense they had against the hell-gas you devised."

"No!" The syllable blasted into the room. "No! The suits failed, but that was not my fault. They were the same. I swear to you they were the same. I do not know why they failed." I felt that he was not answering Mowrer then. He was answering something within himself, some question that had robbed him of sleep, that had clouded his eyes even when I brought the subject up in our first talk an eternity before.

Mowrer returned to the attack. "If that were so," he demanded, "why did you not shut the plant till you had determined the reason and remedied it?"

Thorndal looked at him unbelievingly. "Shut down! Why I could not do that. We could not meet the demand as it was. Tri-State Oil had their backs against the wall. Another month and they would have folded up. Neosite would have been in every car and airplane tank in America. Close and give them a chance to say the supply of Neosite was unreliable, could not be depended upon! That's what they wanted; that's why I had armed guards on the road, so they could not send their agents in to shut me down. They tried it, persistently. I had to go ahead. Had to!"

Good Lord! This general of industry, this master of men, was himself a slave, a Frankenstein to the monster of his own creation! In a flash I saw it. He had given himself to the service of Neosite, and Neosite had become a Juggernaut riding down and crushing out every atom of humanity in him! He would sacrifice himself to Neosite as he had sacrificed the poor, maddened creatures around us, without the least hesitation. Somewhere deep within me was born a tiny spark of pity for the man.

But not so with Mowrer and the others. The prosecutor broke the silence with, "That is your only excuse?"

"That is all." Thorndal's brown eyes had retreated again into lethargy. Something like contempt hovered about his lip corners. "I have nothing more to say."

Mowrer half-turned to the hulk in whom I had recognized Haynes. "Andrew Thorndal has condemned himself from his own mouth. Need I say more?"

The gigantic head moved slowly in negation. Then a whisper came from its mouth, an awful sibilance of sound that was like nothing save one's imagining of a voice from beyond the grave, a voice from the fleshless lips of a skeleton dead so long that even the worms had lost interest in it. Yet the words were clear: "You have heard charge and defense. What is your will?"

And that jury of the dying, those who still could talk among that jury of the damned, roared their answer: *"Guilty!"* Like the yapping of wild dogs it was, like a fiends' chorus from Hell.

Haynes nodded. "Andrew Thorndal," he whispered. "You will die as they died. It is my regret that you will die more quickly."

Mowrer stopped, spoke again: "Nancy Thorndal! You have danced while men died that you might clothe yourself in silks, have given yourself to pleasure while mothers' hearts were wrung with despair that you might drink fine wines . . ."

I shouted something, and Thorndal's voice thundered: "She knew nothing about it. Let her go, you devils!"

" 'The sins of the fathers shall be visited upon the children . . .' "

"Jury," said Haynes. "What is your will?"

"Guilty!"

God! Even they could have spared her. I ripped curses at them, but I might have been crying in a desert for all the attention anyone paid to me.

And the inexorable voice of the judge came back from the dead, husked the sentence, "You shall die in the gas."

"Stanley Sutton!" The farcical trial went on. "You were warned and persisted. You aided Andrew Thorndal and defended him from me and from his other victims. You shot down the messengers of vengeance."

"Go to hell," I snarled. "What's the use of my saying anything?"

"—Die in the gas."

I didn't care. If Nan were to go that way I was satisfied to go with her . . .

"Randall Johnson! You were foreman of the nitration room and sent men to their death without compunction. You sat at this desk in the only suit that functioned and watched them labor in the shadow of their doom."

The tall man turned to his accuser. "I helped you in your plot," he said. "When nobody could get through the fence I told the guard something was wrong in here and I must see Thorndal at once. They passed me through and I shut off the current that would have held you back."

So it was he who had done that! But that did not tell why he had been engaged in a covert confab with someone else on the bedroom floor. Nor could it have been he who planted the tank of gas in my room. I wished now that I had not awakened then. At least I should not have had to watch Nan die.

Mowrer was pondering Johnson's plea. He raised his head now. "No!" he said. "We used you, but that did not win for you absolution from your sins." There was a murmur of approbation from the macabre group of listeners. "You were in our power and you thought to bribe us with your offer of aid. Your guilt is too black to be washed white by one act of repentance, if repentance there was."

Thorndal was looking at the bald man with burning eyes. If he were free, I thought, he would tear him to pieces with his bare hands.

Again the ritual of reference to the jury, the chorused "Guilty," and Haynes' eerie voice pronouncing sentence: "You will die in the gas."

Johnson sagged against his lashings, and his eyes were the orbs of death. "No," he whimpered. "I can't face it." He surged up as far as his lashings would permit and screamed, "Oh, God! Don't let them do it!"

A lank creature whose face was a red blob yelled, "Shut up, yuh rat. Yuh held a gun on me when I wanted ter git out o' here."

Mowrer, ignoring Johnson's screams, peered nearsightedly past the four of us who had been condemned. "You, there," he said. "What is your name?"

"Wuh—William Lannon." The popinjay's jaw shook visibly as he answered.

The little man who had brought about this holocaust turned to Haynes. "I know nothing against this man," he said. "His presence here is pure accident, and he did not fire at us when we attacked the house. But he must die that God's work that we do may go unpunished by man's blundering law. We dare leave no witness."

"Gentlemen!" Lannon's voice rang out. "I won't say anything. I swear it by everything that is holy to me. I won't say anything if you let me go."

There was a momentary pause. Then Haynes projected toneless words into the room: "You swear silence as to all that has passed?"

"I swear by my dead mother's name, by my only hope of salvation." He was cringing, pleading. "No one knows that I came to Newville. No one will ever know if you will only let me out of here." He slavered at the mouth in his eagerness.

Someone called, "Let the poor fool go! He ain't done nothin'."

Haynes considered a moment, then nodded. Mowrer pointed to one who was less burnt than the rest. "Release him," he ordered.

"No!" It was a squeal so shrill that for an instant I could not locate its source. "Stop! I'll be damned if he'll go free and leave me to suffer." Johnson was yammering those words, straining at his ropes, his bound hands clawing at his sides. "Listen to me! Listen."

"What is it?" Mowrer clipped.

"Johnson! Don't tell them!" Lannon screamed, wild-eyed. "For God's sake, don't."

"Silence!" Haynes husked. "Silence. We shall hear him."

That voice from the dead struck Lannon dumb. But his mouth remained open in a soundless scream, and the terror in his eyes was an awful thing to witness. Yes, even in that chamber of horrors there could be a greater horror: his naked soul revealed in those staring orbs. My scalp tightened as I guessed what Johnson had to tell.

That one was speaking, malevolence vibrant in his now steady tones: "His name ain't Lannon. It's Rand, Morton Rand, and he's a vice-president of Tri-State Oil."

An inarticulate roar from Thorndal blasted the man's next words, a thunder-sound of fury.

"Silence," came the command of the judge who had been dead and was now alive. "Silence!"

"He got me, no matter how," Johnson went on. "A hundred grand they paid me—to put Neosite on the fritz. A hundred grand. For that I smeared oil on the rubber safety suits, so that they'd be porous an' let the gas through. I didn't put it on my own . . ."

"You lie, damn you. You lie!"

Lannon's shriek set off a cataclysmic tumult of noise. Thorndal's boom, "You dogs! You cowardly dogs!" Johnson: "It's the truth. I can prove it." Mowrer mouthing: "God's vengeance. God's wrath upon him." And the agonizing screams of the victims of the gas: "Kill! *Kill!* KILL!!!"

Only I was silent, horror-stricken at the lengths to which greed could go—I, and Nan. I saw that she had fainted, her head lolling, her silk-clad body erect only by virtue of the lashings that held it to the steel column next to mine.

They surged down the long room toward Lannon, those men whose tortures of the damned had been his procuring—a wave of maddened fiends. I saw one, faster moving than the rest, clutch a fleshless hand in the man's blond hair, and closed my eyes lest I see him ripped limb from limb. Someone scattered by me, and I heard Mowrer's voice: "Stop! Stop men! That death's too good for him! I claim him for the vengeance appointed by God!"

There was a scream, the spat of blows, and the sounds died away. When I looked again they were going back to theftplaces, and Lannon—or Rand—was still bound to his post, still alive. Alive, but his face was a raw, bleeding mass, one side of his mustache had been literally torn out by its roots, his torso was bare and scored with deep, gory furrows.

The blind Haynes had not moved from his seat. He waited till they were quiet again, and then rasped out: "Go on!"

Johnson's features were twisted now with bitterness. He looked odd with that towering, hairless head of his, his long neck with the Adam's apple moving up and down as he talked. "I thought the first touch of the gas would scare the men out, or make the boss quit," he was saying. "But things went right on, an' I had to obey orders and keep on making Neosite. Last night I caught sight o' Rand drivin' up to the house, an' knew he'd come to see what was what. Afterwards he told me he'd gone to the beach where Miss Nan was and kidded her into bringing him to Newville."

"Afterwards! Then you talked to him?"

"Sure. Three times. The first was through the fence, right after the boss got home. Rand told me Thorndal had brung a new super that looked smart, wanted me to fetch him a tank o' gas so's he could scare Sutton off . . ."

Scare me off? Murder me! Rage was cold within me as I realized the viciousness of the man . . .

" . . . I brung it to him the second time, when the current was cut off so's they could take Jim Haynes' corpse off the wire, an' the third was when you made me go. I wanted to tip Rand off, to tell him not to fight you an' he'd be all right." Johnson had been pouring out his amazing confession in a rush of hurried words, but suddenly his voice broke into a high, venomous shrillness. "I risked my neck for the devil, but I'll be damned if I'll let him get scot-free while I die for what I've done. He's the cause of it all. He—"

"Enough! We've heard enough." Mowrer's voice was surcharged with pent fury; it was the voice of doom. "He shall not escape. 'Vengeance is mine! saith the Lord.' "

And in a dread antiphony Haynes husked the sentence, "He shall die in the gas."

If ever a man deserved death Morton Rand did. But we others . . . Nan . . .

"Men!" I twisted to the sudden bellow from Thorndal. "Men! Listen to me!" His eyes were blazing, his face alight with inspiration. "Listen!"

There was a rustle. Someone shrilled, "No! We've heard enough from you!" But Thorndal went on, roaring down all opposition: "Listen! The suits are good! You know it now—I knew it all the time. The suits are good and we can make

Neosite safely. We can make Neosite and sweep Tri-State off the map. I'll raise your wages, I'll treble production. I'll give you pensions—build schools—Newville will be the wonder, industrial city of the world!"

A hissing started, venomous. High-pitched cries from blackened lips: "No!—Stop talking.—We've had enough!—Murderer!—Torturer!—The gas—*Turn on the gas!*"

Thorndal roared on, unhearing, uncomprehending. He was mad with renewed hope, not for his safety, not for his daughter's, but for his Neosite . . .

"Hell! I don't want to make any money out of this. I'll give all the profits to the workers, run the thing for nothing! Just let me go on making it. You can't kill it! You can't kill Neosite, the best damn fuel that was ever invented, the fuel of the future. It will revolutionize transportation if you give it a chance. Listen to me . . ."

"Silence, Thorndal." The impact of Haynes' awful voice got through him. "Silence!"

Thorndal stopped, and for the first time there was consternation in his face, realization of defeat. Not make Neosite! He just couldn't understand it.

The whisper of doom from the dead man's lips came again. "No, Andrew Thorndal," he said. "Though it was not your fault that the suits failed, yet when they did fail you drove on despite that failure, despite the black death it brought on those over whom you cracked the whip of your will, the dumb, helpless creatures your enslaved. For this you merit the death you gave them, you and yours, you and all your works. The sentence of the court stands."

And Mowrer's harsh accents put a period to hope: " 'Vengeance is mine, saith the Lord Jehovah. Vengeance is mine!' "

Chapter 8

THE DEATH WHEEL TURNS

I was watching Nan with anxious eyes, praying that she would not revive till the gas had done its foul work. The room was clear now of that awful company. We five were alone, bound to the steel columns that were to be our stakes of martyrdom, alone save for one ghastly figure. Haynes stood with his skeleton hand on the fateful valve-wheel, Haynes who was dead already and so was not afraid to die again. He stood there, the muscles that criss-crossed his skinned head taut with some inner tension, his grotesque skull canted as though he were listening through the tiny orifices where ears had once been. What sound was he listening for, what awful sound heralding our doom?

Somehow I could not believe that this was the end. There was no hope, and yet my brain still struggled for some way out. And . . . inspiration flashed on me! Perhaps—now that he was alone . . .

"Haynes!" I cried. "I'm Sutton, Stan Sutton, from Tech. Your classmate. You can't kill me, Jim Haynes!"

The figure there at the wheel started, turned toward me his black sockets wherein sightless white orbs rolled. "Who calls Jim Haynes?" he asked.

"Stanley Sutton! We've studied together. Remember Prof. Carlon and the campus songs? Remember the night we licked Yale? Remember commencement and the two *cum laudes,* you and I?" Was I getting it across? Tech has a strong hold on her grads; was it strong enough to stop him? "You wouldn't blast Stan Sutton with the green gas, Jim."

His rotted teeth moved in signal that he was about to speak, and I stopped, held my breath. His voice came, that hushed, spectral voice of his that had pronounced sentence of death in the court of the damned.

"Jim Haynes is dead," it said . . . Then the awful thing was true . . . "Thorndal killed my brother Jim and I watched him die." I rocked back against the pillar. Once, once only, I had heard Haynes speak of a twin brother, Sam. "Now Thorndal dies, and his child, and his minions who have done his will."

Haynes—Sam Haynes—turned, and twisted the valve-wheel! The iridescent fluid gushed from the pipe-mouth in a six-inch stream, struck the black pool and spattered. Some of it reached me, wet my clothing and the rope that was wound around me. A drop hit my hand, stung. It was an organic acid, I recalled, caustic almost as the green gas it produced.

"I'm coming," Haynes squalled. "I'm coming, Jim," and plunged into the black pool, disappeared beneath its surface! He shrieked as the acid burned him, and his struggles mixed the reagent with the processed oil it would change to Neo-site. As by magic the fluid cleared, turned pink, then a milky-white. I stared at the faint green mist that formed on its surface, that spread rapidly, that boiled up in manifold tiny bubbles from the depths below. The green gas was rising in a lifting tide of death.

God! It rose so slowly, so deathly slow. It would be hours, hours before it reached the level of our heads. I had shuddered at the thought of swift, searing extinction by that burning mist, but I had not envisioned the dragged out torture that was in store for us. Now the awfulness of our fate burst upon me full force. Tied, helpless to move, the green gas would creep up on our tormented frames, inch by slow inch, corroding our flesh, searing deep to bone as it rose, while still we lived, while still we were conscious of every agony, every torture of that slow advance!

The tendrils spread, coalesced, formed a thin pool on the stone floor, a pool that rolled nearer, gradually nearer with its terrible threat. I pulled my eyes away from it, sought Nan again. She was awake! She was staring at the green gas and her eyes were pits of terror.

"Nan," I called. "Nan!" And, forgetting they were bound, I tried to raise my arms to her.

Tried to! Almighty God! They came up! The rope snapped, and my arms lifted!

I gazed at my hands unbelievingly, saw white marks of acid burns on them. The reagent that had splashed on me— the iridescent acid . . . I glanced at the frayed rope-ends, moist and blackened . . . The acid that had spattered on them had eaten through the thongs binding me—had freed me!

"Nan," I gibbered, laughing hysterically. "Nan, it's all right. I'm loose! Heads up, Nan!" I worked frantically at my lashings and got them off, leaped to her and liberated her. There was a long shelf under the windows, a shelf on which bottles were arrayed. I lifted her to that. "Stay there till I get the others untied," I said. She should be safe there, safe for thirty minutes at least, so slowly was the gas coming.

Thorndal was exultant as I plucked at his ropes. "Good work, Sutton," he said. "Good work! We'll get out of here and start all over again. We'll build another Neosite factory somewhere else and you shall be my partner. You'll run the plant and I'll attend to distribution."

My hands dropped away from the knots. "Nothing doing, Thorndal. Swear to me there will be no more Neosite or I'll leave you here."

"No more Neosite! Man! You're crazy!"

"I will be crazy if I let you start making that hell's brew again."

"Hurry, Stan. Oh, hurry!" Nan called to me from her perch. "Look, the gas is near you. It will burn you and dad!"

I twisted. There it was, inches away from my feet, the burned feet whose pain I had forgotten in the blazing excitement of all that had happened. It was spreading all through the long room, but there was time yet. I turned back to Thorndal. "Well, what do you say?"

"No! I'll never promise that. If I did there would be no reason for me to continue living." He was honest, at least. He could have given me the promise I demanded, and broken it later.

"Then you'll stay here."

I turned away. And Nan screamed, "Stanley! Stanley Sutton! What are you doing? You're not going to leave my fa-

ther. You're not!" She started to scramble down from her
refuge.

"Get back there! Get back, I say!"

"Not unless you untie dad. If you don't, I shall."

I stared at her determined little face, so like Thorndal's
now, and weakened. "All right, Nan," I answered. "Get
back." I don't know whether I would have gone through with
my bluff, but I had been determined to extort the promise
from him. The first touch of the gas would have—But she
had settled that. It took me seconds to complete the job.

"Fine," Thorndal grunted, stretching. "Get Nan away. I'll
take care of the others."

"All right," I snapped. I was beginning to fear someone
would come back to see why Haynes had not emerged, for
surely they could not have known of his contemplated suicide. "We're going out the window . . ." I leaped for the
shelving, thrust up the window. It screeched in its disused
grooves.

It was broad daylight now. I saw the round black hole from
which I had removed the cover . . . My eyes lifted, and far
beyond the woods I saw figures turning to the sound of the
window's opening. They started to run back, but one remained behind. I saw a rifle lift to his shoulder, saw the flash
of its firing. "Come on, Nan," I gasped. "Quick."

She clung to me, frightened. "We can't get away, Stan,"
she said. "They'll catch us."

"Come on!" I got an arm around her, thrilling even in that
instant to the warm softness of her body, and jumped. It was
only a step to the opening to the oil pipe, but a bullet whistled uncomfortably close to my head as I took it, half-
dragging Nan with me. Then I was kneeling, peering down
into the pit. It looked dry, clean. "Down here, Nan," I said.
"It's our only chance."

She hung back. "Dad. He isn't . . ."

"He's freeing the others. He'll be right along. Hurry!" Another bullet spat dust a foot from us. "Slide in and I'll lift
you down. Quick!"

She was sitting on the well-curb, her feet within. I took her hands, swung her down. Her face lifted to me, a pale oval in the dimness of the shaft. "I can't reach bottom with my feet," she told me.

"I'll drop you. It's only a foot or two." I let go, and heard her thud to the bottom. "Are you all right?"

"Yes. It's a tunnel, Stan. I can stand almost straight in it."

"I know." I looked up. The running men were nearer, and the one with the rifle was aiming more carefully.

"Is dad coming?"

I glanced back. Thorndal was heaving through the window and something metallic gleamed in his hand. I slid into the bore, hung from its rim by my hands. "Look out, Nan!" I cried, and let go.

The hole was deeper than I thought, ten feet at least, its sides smooth. The shock of my landing sent pain shooting up my legs. The light-disc above darkened and I ducked back into the conduit. Distant shouts came to me, and Thorndal dropped down the well.

"I have a gun, Sutton," he said. "It was in the lab and I knew we'd need it. Cartridges, too, this time. We can stand them off indefinitely here."

"Johnson! Lannon! Are they coming?"

"Coming?" he snarled. "Hell! That double-crosser and the hound who bought him? They won't bother us any more. They're stewing in the tank."

My mouth opened, closed. I couldn't say anything. They deserved it, but only Thorndal could have done that. My mind flashed back to the scene in the lobby when Mowrer had been dragged off to the nitration room at his command. He hadn't changed. All he had endured was powerless to change him!

Sunlight streamed down the shaft, and dust motes danced in it. Then a shadow fell blackly down.

"Keep back," Thorndal shouted. "Keep back or I'll shoot!" He backed away from the bottom of the well, crouching, the bulldog revolver snouting . . .

There was a muffled clamor above, the shrill voices of the gas-blasted men whose doom we had escaped. The shadow flickered away, returned. And suddenly a twisted shape thudded down!

The thunder of Thorndal's gun deafened me. Nan screamed, and her father's full-chested bellow echoed in the pipe behind: "One down! Any more coming?" There was a note of triumph in his tones, the exultant lift of a fighting man at the smell of battle. I moved back to where Nan knelt, got an arm around her. The man Thorndal had shot was a crumpled heap in the light. He rolled his flayed face toward us, the ligaments quivering. His eyes glazed, and he didn't move again. We waited, but nothing happened.

"They're licked, Sutton," Thorndal growled. "They don't dare come down. We've got them licked!"

I could distinguish Mowrer's high-pitched voice, crisp with command, and doubted Thorndal's statement. They couldn't come down to pursue us, but he would find a way to get at us. He was indomitable, implacable. He would not allow us to escape his revenge so easily. Thus my thoughts, but to Nan I whispered, "We've won, darling. We've won! They can't touch us now." The term of endearment came naturally; I had not forgotten the message of her eyes . . .

"That horrible face!" She shuddered. "I can't stand it. Stan, it's driving me mad."

"Here. Hide your eyes against my shoulder."

Chapter 9

NIGHTMARE FLIGHT

Minutes dragged. The huge pipe in which we had found refuge stretched back behind us into blackness, its steel walls rusty. I knew that it stretched so for miles, till it met the pipe-line from the Texas oilfields.

"Sutton," Thorndal called, without turning his head. "About two miles back this pipe comes to the surface and lies along the top of the swamps. There's another manhole there, for cleaning purposes. You and Nan make for it, and get help from Roton. I'll hold the fort here."

"That will take hours. You can't keep vigilant forever. They'll catch you napping and grab you again; come after us. I'll stay here with you, and Nan will go for help."

She stirred in my arms, pulled away. "No!" she said. "No! I couldn't go through all that long dark alone. And besides, I won't leave dad and—and you, Stan."

"Good God, girl!" I burst out. "You must. It's the only way, the only way we'll ever get out of here."

"You go, dear." Ineffably sweet, that word on her lips. "You go. I'll watch here with dad. I can shoot."

"Ridiculous! I—"

There were ominous clinkings at the surface. "Sutton!" Thorndal exclaimed. "They're sticking a big pipe down the manhole, one of the conveyor tubes from the processing room. What do you think they're up to?"

My scalp prickled. "It's some devilment . . . Mowrer isn't beaten yet!"

"By God! He'll be beaten before I'm through with him! Beaten to a pulp!" Thorndal banged his free hand against the steel side of the pipe in an ecstasy of defiance. "Beaten to a pulp."

"Shhh!" Nan hushed him. "What's that sound?" We fell silent, listening intently. I heard a dull throb, throb; thought it was the sound of blood in my ears. Then I was certain it was not.

"Sounds like a pump," I whispered. "But it can't be! What would they be doing with a pump?"

"I'm frightened," the girl breathed in my ear. "Stan, I'm—"

"Great Jupiter! . . . Look!"

There was a green glow, suddenly, in the aperture. We watched Thorndal's bulking frame silhouetted against it. He leaped back, cursing. I smelled an unmistakable odor. A trickle of the emerald vapor crept lazily into the thin cylinder of sunlight that still came down from the world above.

"Run!" I shouted, choking. "Run!" And even as we turned to flee the first great gush of the death-gas billowed forth to follow us! Mowrer had found a way indeed! Bullets were of no avail against the weapon he had devised to confound us!

We ran into the pitch blackness of that long tube, and the green glow of horror rolled after us, aided by the down-pitch of the tube, spurred by the throb, throb of the pump, the echoing thud of which followed us mercilessly.

I can't remember much of that nightmare flight, except that the steel was sharply curved, and its roof so close down that I was half-stooped over as I ran, that the soles of my feet were torn once more by rust and my scalp bruised again and again by some inequality overhead. Nan was somewhere in front, I next, then Thorndal—cursing, cursing in a rumbling monotone as he ran. His voice thundered as it echoed through that long tube, the pump throbbed, the green gas followed us with its deadly luminance. We stumbled onward through an infinity of lightless constricted space, an eternity of time.

How long, I thought, how long can we last? We may go on and on, but finally we must drop, and the gas will roll over us, over Nan, and Thorndal and me, and blacken our bodies as had been intended from the first.

It seemed to me I could hear Mowrer intoning his awful refrain: " 'Vengeance is mine, saith the Lord.' "

Under my tortured feet the pipe curved, slanted upward. The ascent slowed us, but it slowed the gas still more. We drew ahead of the threatening glow, and I began to hope that perhaps we should beat it. If only we were far enough ahead when we reached the manhole of which Thorndal had spoken, that we might have time to get it open before the misty death caught us!

"Faster," I gasped. "Faster, Nan!" I could barely make out the pale glimmer of her, ahead.

And suddenly she was gone! Her shrill scream echoed back to me, but I could not see her. "Stop, Stan," she cried. "Oh, stop!"

I skidded to a halt. "Nan! What's happened? Where are you?"

"Here!" Her voice came from my feet, from below me! "Here. There's a deep hole here; I slid into it. The other side's vertical. I can't get out."

"A sump hole." Thorndal was right behind me. I could feel his hot breath on my neck. "A depression to clear the oil of sediment."

I threw a fearful look over my shoulder. The gas was distant, but it rolled toward us implacably. "Watch out, Nan," I said. "I'm coming down for you."

"No, Stan. It's not far across. You and dad can jump over. Don't come down here."

I took a cautious step, another. The conduit floor flattened out, slanted steeply downward. I pushed my feet over the edge, skidded, bumped into Nan's soft body. I must have fallen ten feet, at least.

"Oh, Stan! You did come! Now you can't get out, either. Feel here . . ." She seized my hands, placed them against the opposite wall of the sump-hole. It was straight up and down, slick.

"All right," I grunted. "I'll lift you out."

"And you?"

"Don't worry about me. I can climb like a fly. I'll follow you."

Of course, I lied. I could get her up, but I would have to stay behind. The gas would reach here in moments, would pour over the lip of the depression and swallow me.

"I'll be all right," I assured her. "Hurry! Up on my shoulders, then grab the top and pull yourself up. Quick!" I must not give her time to think, to argue! "Up with you!" I got hands around her waist, swung her to my shoulders. She scrambled erect, I felt her heels digging into me. Then they were gone.

"I'm up, Stan. Come on."

"Go ahead, Nan; I'll be with you in a minute. Go ahead, Thorndal, jump across. It's only three feet."

"Stan! You can't get out. Oh, my dear!"

"Run, Nan, run. If you love me, run."

She was safe . . . And Thorndal could save himself. It was an easy leap.

"Watch it, Sutton," Thorndal said. Good Lord! What was he doing? Why didn't he jump? The question had scarcely framed itself in my mind when he was at my side. "Up with you, boy."

"Mr. Thorndal, you—"

"Shut up. She's my daughter and you saved her life. It should have been I . . . It will be. Up with you—quick!"

No time for futile argument. Perhaps it was just that he should be the one to go. Rand and Johnson had paid the penalty of their crimes; why should Thorndal escape? Protesting nevertheless, I let him hoist me to his shoulders, lifted myself erect and pulled myself out of the death-trap!

I glanced back. The awful glare of the gas was close— terribly close. In seconds now it would pour down into the hole where Thorndal was.

"Nan's away," I told him. "She's safe! Maybe I can find something to help you out, maybe I can save you yet!"

"Good-bye, boy. Take good care of her. Good-bye!"

I twisted to start off.

"Stan!" It was Nan, only yards ahead. "Stan! There's something queer here. Hurry!"

I was at her side. The roof of the pipe lifted here; I could stand up straight. I felt overhead—felt a flat plate. My pulse hammered.

"It's the manhole, Nan!" I cried. "The manhole in the swamp. We're saved! We can get out!"

"Thank God! Oh, thank God!"

I got the flats of both hands against the cover, heaved. Superhuman strength must have flowed into me then; the heavy disc lifted at once, slid sidewise. Blessed sunlight struck down!

"Up with you, Nan—up!"

I grabbed her, literally threw her out of that damned pipe. And just as I did so a scream shrilled to me, a strong man's scream. I looked back. The gas had reached the pit where

Thorndal was, was folding over its edge in a lazy, slow settling of doom.

I got my hands on the manhole rim, chinned, scrambled out. The oozy, scummed surface of the swamp was Eden to my eyes. Nan had slid down the tube's surface, was ankle-deep in mud.

"Father!" Her eyes widened in sudden realization. "Where's father?"

How could I tell her? I pretended breathlessness, pretended I could not speak. The great pipe was covered with wooden slats here—bound to it by wires that were rusted by the moisture of the morass. One was right at hand.

Perhaps—my brain was working lightning fast—perhaps I could get the wire off. I jerked at it—it snapped. And I was down again in the pipe, the wire coiling after me.

The sump-hole was half-filled with green vapor when I reached it. But Thorndal—a shrieking, fear-gibbering wretch—was still alive. The wire held, I got him out, just as the gas filled the pit and eddied over its edge.

I had to guide him to the manhole, to lift his hands to the rim. I thought it was because he was numbed with fear. But when he was in the light again I saw that the eyes in his blackened face were burned white. He was blind!

~ ~ ~ ~ ~

Soap and hot water saved his skin. But he is a sightless, doddering old man in our home now, Nan's and mine. Our children love their grandfather, he plays with them so gently, tells such nice stories in this thin, quavering voice.

A LODGING IN HELL

Chapter 1

THE STRANGLER

THE RAUCOUS TONES of the radio flooded the room:

"—the saturnalia of extortion and murder that has so long ravaged Halesburg must stop," it was blaring. "It shall stop, if the decent people of one fair city will aid me. The sadistic, ruthless racketeer who masks himself under the name of the Strangler trembled when an aroused citizenry swept me into office with the command, *free us from terror!* He saw the imminence of his doom when the legislature of Massikota placed in my hands the one weapon I need to defeat him. He cowers now in his lair, shaking, afraid. Mr. Strangler: whoever you are, wherever you may be, your end is at hand!"

A gasp of indrawn breath ended the speech, but the odd quiver of fear that had underlain its orotund bravado lingered in Kitty Brian's ears. That fear seemed to have seeped into the very house, seemed to hang about the girl; a chill, miasmic shadow which the living room lights could not dispel . . .

"You have been listening to an address by G. Harold Corbett, district attorney of Hale County. This is WKUP, the voice of the Halesburg Courier. A short interlude of organ . . ."

Switch-click cut off the announcer's unctuous accents and silence smashed down, a brooding silence somehow pregnant with threat. Kitty's fingers tightened on the embroidery hoop they held. This was silly, this nervousness, this mood of chill apprehension that tortured her. Childish! Just because she was alone in the house for the first time since Dad's death. She'd have to learn to live alone. She couldn't stay in Uncle Frank's house forever, kindly solicitous as he was . . .

Sudden auto brakes, shrieking, pulled her startled glance to the shaded window. Skidding tires squealed. Running footfalls crunched on the gravel path and the frantic pound of the knocker on the entrance door echoed through the house.

Apprehension of midnight disaster struck color and warmth from Kitty's cheeks. Uncle Frank! Had the Strangler's killers . . .? But he wasn't mayor any longer. The futile fight had been taken from him . . . She was out in the hall, was unbolting the great oak portal.

The man's face was livid, contorted, his slight body taut, quivering. Words spewed from him in a thin terror-squeal. "Mr. Brian. I got to see him. Do you hear me? I got to . . ."

"But he isn't here," the girl gasped. "He went to New York . . ."

Her words jolted him back, as though they had been physical blows. "Then I'm done for," he groaned, "The Strangler . . ."

The rest was lost as he whirled, and catapulted down the path between black masses of shrubbery, toward the vague shape of a curb-parked roadster.

Motor-roar thundered, drowning the pound of his footfalls. As he reached the sidewalk a dark sedan hurtled around the corner. Something snakelike writhed from the careening vehicle's open window, flicked to the fleeing man's neck. He leaped—was jerked—into mid-air, soared grotesquely to crash on the roadway. He was a thudding black bundle bouncing, skidding, plunging horribly in the wake of the rushing murder-car.

The horror vanished, far up the glimmering midnight stretch of Halesburg's Pershing Boulevard. Kitty Brian's fingers tore at her neck as if the Strangler's noose were clamped about its whiteness to choke off the scream that sliced her chest, rasped her throat, and would not come. It had not happened! It could not have happened!

Could not? How many times had it happened already, in the past terrible year? How many times had the noose of the

Strangler's killers garotted the throats of those who had refused his extortionate demands, of members of his own gang who had obscurely offended him, of witnesses to the flicking, lethal swoop of his executioner's loops . . .

Terror surged, a nightmare flood in Kitty Brian's veins. Was she marked now for the inevitable death that had terrorized Halesburg so long? In the instant the black sedan had swept around the corner, the roadster's headlights had sprayed through its windshield and spotlighted the visage of the killer. The brutal, apelike countenance was ineradicably limned on the screen of her memory—and she had recognized it!

But Martin Glatow could not know it! Engrossed in his crime he could not have seen her. If Kitty kept silent the Strangler would never know what she had seen. If she shut the door, and went to bed, and was surprised in the morning to read of another body found, somewhere, with the red mark of the lethal noose around its neck, she would be safe.

But if she told? No one had ever lived to appear in court against a servant of the Strangler. No one at all—no matter how the police had tried to protect them, how secret their identity had been kept . . .

" . . . It shall stop if the decent people of our fair city will aid me!" It seemed as if the radio had spoken again, with Hal Corbett's shaken, earnest appeal. Kitty Brian turned. An invisible viscid fluid seemed to cling to her limbs so that she had to use all her strength to reach the telephone. But her voice was clear and firm as she spoke into the transmitter's black maw.

"Give me Harold Corbett's home, operator. And hurry. *Hurry!*"

Light, its source artfully concealed, glinted cheerfully from the chromium fittings of the air-conditioned car. The staccato clacking of track joints, underneath, did its best to tell Kitty Brian that each minute of the train's smooth speed added another to the thousand miles stretching between her and terror. A thousand miles—but dread was still a hard, cold lump in the girl's chest, a queasy, slow creep of febrile chill in her veins. Dread that had accompanied her furtive flight across dawn-dreary fields, that had ridden with her the eternal, fearful day, that whispered now in the rush of speed-wind against the night-darkened panel of the window beside her.

She shrugged lower in her seat, tried to focus her attention on the magazine the news-dealer had sold her, but the print blurred into a mass of illegible grey as the nape of Kitty's neck prickled with the eerie, frightening feel of eyes upon her, of watching, inimical eyes.

But she did not again spin around in a futile attempt to trap the watcher. Each such attempt had been met by rows of inscrutable faces utterly disinterested in her. This time she caught herself in time. Yawning, she picked up her pocketbook from the seat, fumbled in it, pushed aside a tiny, pearl-handled pistol, extracted a red-enamelled powder compact.

The girl snapped open its lid. Her face in the small mirror was pert, downy-skinned. The chestnut nimbus of her hair softly fringed a high, white brow. But beneath it apprehension, unforgettable horror, peered from the tawny lambency of her long-lashed eyes. Lifting the glass as though to inspect the results of her ministrations she captured a reflection of the passengers behind her.

They swayed slightly, keeping time in a queer jiggling sway with the motion of the speeding train. The shoulder of a tired-looking mother supported her small daughter's blonde curls. A broker's billowing rotundity crushed his pince-nezed, professorial-looking seatmate, and their contrasting countenances were both dazed with the half-stupor of the long journey. Kitty's hand moved a bit. Across the aisle two schoolgirls chattered and behind them a man in a navy-blue suit was absorbed in a book . . .

Or was he just pretending to be absorbed? A pulse pounded in Kitty's temples and the compact dropped from nerveless fingers into her lap. From under the man's drooped eyelids she had caught the glint of a covert gaze fastened on her, of a steel-grey, baleful scrutiny stealthily sinister.

Breath hissed from between the girl's teeth and despair squeezed her heart with cold fingers. She'd been a fool to think that she could escape the Strangler. A pitiable fool. The grim, inevitable doom, through which he had fastened his tentacles on terror-haunted Halesburg to drain it dry, reached out a thousand miles to close upon her. Nowhere was there any safety for her. Truce for the moment, perhaps, in the train; but when the turbulent, terrifying immensity of New York had swallowed her his emissary would strike . . .!

How? With the noose that was the Strangler's favorite weapon? Or with a hail of lead that on occasion his underworld retainers had felled their victims with? Chattering machine-gun lead—there had been that massacre in Courthouse Square when a dozen policemen had been mowed down so that the one cringing youth they guarded might be kept from the witness stand . . . No use to appeal to the police. Even if they believed her . . .

"Stamford," a brakeman bellowed. "Stamford. Next stop New York."

Next stop—only a half-hour more and then—what? Only a half-hour to think. To devise some way of escape. Not for nothing did she bear that name, Brian, proud heritage of an ancestry whose fighting fame still lived in the sagas of old Ireland. Her pallid countenance frozen into an expressionless mask, she racked her brain for some plan, some inkling of a plan . . .

"Papers!" The train was moving again and the newsvendor's raucous shout echoed from behind her. "Late New York papers. Last chance for California and Massikota papers, delivered by airplane. Find out what's happened in your hometown since you left."

Kitty twisted about. "Have you got the *Halesburg Courier?*" she called, her clear voice flinging impulsive defiance at the man in the blue suit.

His head came up. His slitted stare sought her face, flickered away. He was a stranger to her, and some queer feminine quirk darted the thought through Kitty that under other

circumstances she might have regretted that. There was
strength in his flat-planed, youthful visage; an intriguing hint
of the out-of-doors in his bronzed skin, in the tiny weather-
wrinkles raying from the corners of his eyes. Then a puckered scar; a blue, healed bullet-furrow slanting from nose-
bridge to his ebony hair, to remind her that he was a hired
killer of the underworld, a paid dispenser of murder . . .

The train-vendor's bulk came between them. "Here's your
Courier, miss. Fi' cents." . . .

Her own picture was boxed on the paper's front page and
above it black headlines screamed:

THE STRANGLER STRIKES ONCE MORE; ROPE MURDER WITNESS VANISHES

Kitty's burning glance stabbed along the swollen, bold-
faced type-lines.

"Servants returning from holiday find empty house . . .
No marks of forcible entry.
. . . No clues . . . Ex-mayor Francis Brian, uncle of kid-
napped girl, is in New York, cannot be reached . . . Police
net thrown out, radio cars patrol all roads."

And then:

"This time the Strangler has overreached himself," District Attorney G. Harold Corbett stated to a COURIER in-
terviewer. "His dastardly crime will not save his creature,
Martin Glatow. Catherine Brian's eye-witness account of
the brutal killing is in my safe, and under the new law it is
admissible evidence against the prisoner if the person who
swore to it is dead or otherwise unavailable to give verbal
testimony.
"Confronted by the inevitability of his conviction, the
murderer will break and reveal the identity of the mysterious Underworld King who has so long terrorized Halesburg. The Strangler is at the end of his rope, and his useless attack on Miss Brian shows that, facing defeat, he has
lost his head.

"I regret, however, that overestimating the terrorist's shrewdness, I advised Miss Brian that she had nothing to fear from him . . ."

Nothing to fear! Kitty's mouth twisted bitterly as the threatening, ominous gaze of the Strangler's slayer bored into her back. Corbett had been terribly wrong, and even Uncle Frank only half right. His letter was in her bag, but its phrases, which had ignited the flaming terror that seared her now, were burned into her throbbing brain.

"Corbett's a criminal ass if he thinks the Strangler can't get around the fool law he raves about in the *Courier*. Documents have disappeared from the City Hall vault before now, as I know to my cost, and this one will go too. Then he will silence you . . ."

"Your only chance, my dear niece, is to flee Halesburg. Don't say a word, even to Corbett, for fear of some leak. Come to New York. I'll hide you here till the trial is over . . . I've made arrangements . . ."

"New York!" The brakeman's shout was a knell of doom. "New York. All out." Panic clawed the girl's breast as brakes screamed, as the terminal's clangor beat about her. "All out. All out." Down the car's long aisle people rustled to their feet, lifted valises from the baggage rack, their faces beaming. For them that cry meant homecoming, for her . . .?

She shot a glance over her shoulder. The scar-faced man was buttoning his jacket, was going back to the rear exit. Was she mistaken? After all her perturbation was he innocent of connection with the Strangler? He turned, darted a swift look at her, turned away. The glimmer of hope died as quickly as it had been born. She could take only one passage from the train and he would be waiting there for her.

Kitty choked down a sob. She rose, swung down her little week-end case, tailed on to the end of the line of passengers slowly vanishing through the front end of the car. Desperation hammered the chaos within her skull. Somehow she must evade him before she reached the appalling open of the city streets and he put the finger of death upon her.

Chapter 2

The Phantom Who Laughed

Kitty Brian hesitated in the vestibule. Below her, the arrival platform was filled with a scurrying throng, with sweating, red-capped porters plying their trade, with lumbering, high-piled baggage trucks. The blue-suited man came past, his grey eyes searching for her.

Kitty was certain he saw her leaving the car as the crowd shoved him by. He didn't have to keep behind her, she must go along this platform to the brass-railed exit far up there. That was where he would lie in wait for her.

A luggage elevator came down through the train-shed's vaulted ceiling and alongside her a waiting truck lumbered onto its small platform. Yards ahead Kitty's pursuer was framed in a square of white light from Grand Central's domed concourse. He turned to make sure she was following, went through. He could wait, out there, but he would not be permitted to return without at least momentary delay for expostulation and argument.

The girl's heart pounded and she snatched at the baggageman's overall-sleeved arm. "Take me up with you. Please take me up. Please."

"No, lady," the fellow grunted, pulling away. "It's against the rules."

Her eyes pleaded with him, desperately. "My husband— he's sent a detective after me." Kitty's hand slid to the workman's wrist and she pressed a crisp bill into his callused palm. "Can't you forget the rules . . ." Her fearful gaze fled to the open door through which the last of the crowd dribbled.

"Hell! Old man gettin' leery, eh? Well I'm a sport, hop on."

She was on the lift and it was slowly climbing the open shaft—*too slowly!* A confused, shouting swirl at the exit spewed out a lithe, blue-clad form. It catapulted down the platform, hunched, leaped without perceptible pause, cleared the barred, man-high gate. Hands clutched the edge of the elevator-floor, pulled their owner breast high of it.

Kitty whimpered, slammed her small valise full into the scarred face . . . It was gone, she heard a sickening thud from the concrete below, and the ceiling line cut off her vision.

A scream fighting for utterance, she rose into the bustle of the terminal's baggage room. "Gees, you've got guts," the laborer exploded. "Wisht I wuz the boyfriend you're meetin'."

Curious faces gaped at the girl and the seamed visage of a walrus-mustached old man purpled as he started out from behind a brass-topped counter. "Beat it, kid," her companion blurted, starting her off with a hearty push. "Grab that taxi that's just unloaded out there. I got to do some fast talking to get outta this."

The hackman leered knowingly at Kitty Brian as she paid him off, and then his gaudily painted cab roared away. It left behind a stench of burned gas and a dim silence. sinisterly emphasized by the far-off, unsleeping murmur of the giant city. The street was a narrow, dead ravine between looming, dark loft-buildings whose iron-shuttered windows were oddly blind in the pale glimmer of wide-spaced lamps.

A terrible loneliness invested the girl, and the dread of which her triumph at Grand Central had for a while relieved her was again an almost tangible pall oppressing her. She stared at the bleary façade of the low structure before which she stood. Could this be the hotel to which Uncle Frank's letter had directed her?

"At one of the better places you would be sure to be recognized," he had written, "so you will have to be content with a second-rate establishment." Reasonable enough. But could he have meant this battered wreck crushed between its towering, gloom-shrouded neighbors! Had the driver made a mistake?

Once-gilt lettering, tarnished now and flaking off, blotched the glass panel of a door through which grimed luminance struggled. Kitty moved closer, peering.

Hotel Hades, the letters spelled. *Hotel Hades!* Her heart thumped, and then hysteric laughter quivered in her throat. Hotel Hardesty, it should be. That was the name in the letter. Hotel Hardesty. A gruesome accident of erosion had made of it that other, ominous title.

Fury at the panic into which her frayed nerves had tricked her flared up in Kitty and she fairly threw herself up the short steps leading to that door. She reached for its knob . . .

She spun around to a sudden shrill cackle of weird laughter, a high-pitched, mindless cachinnation tearing to shreds the street's sepulchral hush . . . Where had she come from, that straggle-haired, age-bent harridan who spewed mad laughter from across the narrow gutter? From which of the haunted, stygian shadows had she materialized to stand there, shaken with gibbering mirth, flinging at the girl a bony arm whose fleshless, gnarled fingers were curled to the ghastly similitude of a skeleton claw? An instant ago there had been no one there. Kitty was certain of that. No one.

The girl's skin was an icy sheath for her shrinking body, and fear crawled her spine.

"What—what are you laughing at? Who are you?"

She had managed only to whisper. But somehow the hag had heard. Her eerie laugh cut off, as if a faucet had turned to stop it, and her answer came to Kitty across the murk. "Ask him." A toneless, intonationless voice, like the voice of a phantom risen from some mouldering grave. "Ask him in there. Maybe he'll tell you. Or maybe he'll let you find out for yourself."

The weird accents soared to shrillness, to the humorless shrill cackle that had first announced the macabre apparition's presence—and ended abruptly as it had begun. Ended—*because the woman who made it was gone!* As if a nightmare had blinked out she had vanished, and there was only the pale glimmer of the dim sidewalk for Kitty to stare at, and the sightless, mocking gaze of the shuttered windows, and the flat, dark pools of shadow the street-lamps' feeble radiance could not disperse.

But she had been there, the shaken, trembling girl told herself. She had been there. She knew that she must convince herself that the laugher had really been there, that the hag had, perhaps, only jumped back into the deep blackness of that building entrance just in front of which she had appeared. The alternative was . . .

"Well, lady—are you coming in?" Kitty jumped at the impact of the dry, querulous question from behind her. She twisted about. The hotel door was open, held by a weazened, hunch-backed gnome of a man from whose knifelike shoulders a threadbare, gray alpaca hung loosely.

"Who was she?" Kitty blurted. "Tell me! Who was she?"

His head was grotesquely too big for his shrunken body. "Who was who?" His speech rustled as dead leaves rustle, stirred by a November wind. "What're you talkin' about?"

"That woman. That old woman across the street. She said you knew her."

He peered at her, and a curious look came into his eyes that were rheumy, bloodshot about tiny, colorless pupils. "I don't know what you mean. I've been here five minutes an' I ain't seen nobody but you, standin' there an' mumblin' to yourself."

The night, dank, damply chill, shut in on Kitty with the oppression of a nameless fear. "But—but you must have seen her. You must have heard her laugh . . ." She didn't recognize her own voice, so thin, so shrill it was.

"I ain't seen nobody and I ain't heard nothin'," the fellow spat at her venomously. "An' what's more I don't want no hopheads nor nuts in here. Jim Hardesty don't run no looney house. Good night!" He started to close the door.

Kitty threw her slight form against it, bore it backward. "You can't do that. You can't shut me out." Where could she go at this hour? How would Uncle Frank find her? "Someone's meeting me here . . . Let me in!"

She was inside, by the time she had finished, and the door had creaked shut behind her. "Meetin' you? What you say your name was?"

Dust choked her, and stagnant, vitiated air. "Catherine Brian."

Where was Uncle—Frank? He had written that he would be here, waiting for her, but there was no one in the small, unswept lobby around which her glance darted, except the two of them.

"Brian," mused the man. "Brian. Oh yes. There's a message here for you." He shambled past worn, decrepit chairs, past pot-bellied cuspidors whose verdigrised metal might once have been gleaming brass, went behind a paint-peeled small counter and poked a yellow envelope out of one of a set of nicked pigeonholes that covered the wall behind it. "Here."

The high counter came up to the man's chin, so that Kitty could see only his head. The raw glare of a single, unshaded bulb, high up, showed her that despite its uncanny disproportion the yellow skin was drawn tightly over its bones, so that it seemed almost as if a jaundiced false-face rested on the drab shelf. He seemed to have forgotten about what had happened at the door, or was willing to ignore it. She was grateful for that.

She put her small valise down at her feet, picked up the envelope. It rattled in her shaking hands but she managed to get it open. "My dear," the note ran. "I've been delayed but I'll come to you as soon as I can. Your room's reserved. Don't leave it till I come. Uncle."

Kitty licked dry lips. She couldn't stay here alone. The musty atmosphere of the ancient hostelry was loaded with brooding threat, was creepily alive with elusive terror. She couldn't . . . But she must. She had no choice.

"You—you have a room for me?"

"Yes," Hardesty's sere tones rustled. "Yes. Upstairs." A tagged key clanked on the wood. "Jane! Jane! You've been sleeping there long enough. Wake up. Take the lady to one-one-nine!"

Whom was he calling? There had been no one in the lobby. The whisper of shuffling feet sounded behind. Kitty turned, wondering. Across the dreary space someone came toward her, moving with the weary decrepitude that imbued everything, animate or inanimate, within this gloomy inn. It was a bent, scrawny female, her emaciated form tight-buttoned in a black and threadbare travesty of a bellboy's uniform, skirted in concession to the sex of its wearer. The shadow of a pillar obscured her face, slid away—and incredibly it was the raddled countenance of the hag who had laughed at the girl—who had laughed and vanished!

"Oh no-o-o!", Kitty moaned, staggering back against the desk. "No-o-o!" The touch of the wood threw her away from it, threw her to the entrance. Her icy fingers clawed at the rot-pitted knob, twisted.

Half perceived movement in the gloom-ridden street pulled her dilated, frantic stare through the smeared glass of the opening door . . . She flung back into the lobby, the fiery blaze of an earlier terror searing to inconsequence the panic that had driven her to unthinking, wild flight.

She staggered with outstretched shaking arms to the leering hunchback, to the glazed-eyed, gaping hag. "Hide me!" she mouthed. "Please hide me."

In the shadows, out there, she had glimpsed the lithe, pantherine form of the blue-suited, scar-faced man whom the Strangler had dispatched to destroy her! He was angling across the street, was coming straight to this door to rout her out of the sanctuary where she had sought to conceal herself from him.

Chapter 3

DEATH ENTERS BY LOCKED DOOR

"IN THERE. QUICK!" Hardesty snapped. "Jane will show you . . ." At Kitty's gasped appeal the woman had grabbed up her luggage, was scuttling, with a speed uncanny by contrast to her apparent senility, through an arched doorway, and disappeared up an uncarpeted stairway that rose to obscurity behind it. The terrified girl dashed after her, darted up the murky ascent, came out into a long drab corridor, door-lined and musty with the same brooding threat that had filled the lobby below.

But here there was a sense of presences behind the shut, paint-peeled doors that were numbered by scabrous small plaques. Of a lurking life somehow not altogether human, tinged somehow with ineffable evil.

A premonition of dread leaped to frigid life in the girl's bosom. She slowed, half twisted around to flee from this macabre gloom. Below rusted hinges creaked, the hinges of the lobby-door. *He* was coming in, the Strangler's emissary! She flung around again, launched again into headlong pursuit of her weird guide.

Down there was concrete, real peril, the revulsion from this gloomy vista was only born of her shredded, quivering nerves. To have gone down there again would have been madness! Kitty gulped, grabbed at a door-jamb, swung herself through the door, far down the passage, that had opened to Jane's clanking key. Her frigid, shaking hands slammed shut the portal. She leaned against it, pulling dusty air into her laboring lungs, fighting for breath, fighting a glacial quiver of fear that jelled her blood.

She must get a grip on herself. There was nothing uncanny, nothing supernatural about the black-garbed woman who had pulled down its shade over the sleazy room's single window and removed the threadbare but clean-looking spread of an iron-posted bed. The bracketed light she had switched on threw her shadow across the counterpane, her movements made small sounds in the little chamber. Queer, Kitty thought, that she should be surprised at such signs of naturalness. It was beyond reason that this was the hag who so horribly had laughed at her. That had been some mind-shattered waif of the streets, Hardesty's disclaimer of whose presence was explicable enough. She herself had stood in front of him, hiding his view of the street, and he was, perhaps, hard of hearing.

That other though, the man who had pursued her from Halesburg, who had traced her here! He was no phantom of a distraught imagination. "He'll find me," she spoke her thought aloud. "The old man can't keep him from finding me . . .

Jane turned to the girl. "No one gets by Jim Hardesty that he don't want to," the woman cackled. "He's too old a bird at this game not to know how to get rid of them as he wants to get rid of." The wrinkled, saffron parchment of her visage was spasmodically distorted by what might have been meant to be a grin. "You needn't be afeared o' that."

Kitty pushed herself away from the wall. "Do you think so?" she quavered. The need for companionship, for reassurance, made her forget her queasy fear of the old servitor. She seized a dry, bony hand in her trembling fingers, held on to it as a frightened child might clutch its mother. "I've been so terrified for days. Do you really think I needn't be afraid any more?"

Jane made no effort to release herself, but peered at the tremulous girl for a long moment. "Why," she muttered. "You're a dear little thing. You're not . . ." Some obscure emotion silenced her, some impulse against which she appeared to be battling. Her whole scrawny frame was shaken by a strange wavering; was rigid, abruptly, with decision. "Afeared!" she flung at Kitty. "I don't know what 'tis that's scared you till now, but it don't hold a candle to what there really is to fear in this hellhole. Don't stay here another minute. Get out! Get out, I tell you, afore . . ."

Then she choked off, her hand tightening convulsively on Kitty's. Her old eyes darted to the door, the faded pupils dilating, and a sudden, fearful silence was brittle in the dreary room.

A silence in which a faint, furtive whisper of sound was terribly distinct, the hiss of fabric, of someone's clothing, rubbing against plaster in the corridor. "I'll bring you towels right away, miss," Jane said, somewhat more loudly than necessary. "Is there anything else what you need?"

"No, thank you." Kitty took the cue. It was hard, terribly hard to speak naturally while fear twisted at the pit of her stomach. "This is very nice.'

Fierce entreaty in the woman's eyes warned her to inaction. It was as if Jane was saying, "My only hope is that he did not hear me." The withered hand shook as it reached for the doorknob. The grimy panel started to open and Kitty's heart contracted with dread.

The slit between door-edge and door-jamb grew, slowly. It seemed to Kitty that she saw the flicker of a shadow, moving away. Then the aperture was wide enough for her burning eyes to stare past Jane, and there was nothing outside but the gloom of the passage and the blank face of the opposite door.

A muscle twitched in her cheek. She thought, "Of course he got away. You were so slow about opening the door." But Jane was leaving the doorway.

Kitty grasped the key with numbed fingers, twisted it and heard the bolt click into its socket. Then something caused her eyes to fly to the window.

Something was on its sill! A bit of white paper! Only a jagged-edged piece of torn paper, but Kitty whimpered at the sight of it. It had not been there—she was certain it had not been there—when she had watched the old woman pull down that shade.

How had it gotten there? What was its meaning? Had Jane, perhaps, left it there unnoticed while her own attention had been concentrated on the sound betraying the prowler at the door?

Words were scrawled on it. *"I'll be back,"* they said. *"When you're alone."* There was no signature. There didn't need to be a signature. Kitty knew who had written that threat. Hardesty had not admitted him but the man from Halesburg had reached her in spite of him.

The girl's flesh crawled at the thought of what Jane's presence had saved her from. Saved her only for the moment, his threat . . . He might be out there now . . .

She snatched her tiny gun from the pocketbook still clutched in her hand by ingrained habit, snapped up the shade, flung up the window sash . . .

Across a narrow area the high, windowless bricks soared. The hotel wall dropped sheer to the gloom of a malodorous alley. To one side a fire escape clung to the clifflike façade— and a shadow moved on its spidery ladder!

Kitty's teeth bit into her under lip. Her gun jerked up, at the approaching prowler. Her trigger finger hesitated an instant as the blurred climber was obscured by something hung over a landing rail—and behind her the light went out, flooding the room with darkness!

A rolling sound whirled the girl about. Intense gloom blinded her eyes but she sensed stealthy movement somewhere within it. She crouched, striving to penetrate the obscurity, striving to locate this new menace while the imminence of that other threatened her from behind. Something thudded, meatily, as though a limp body had struck the floor.

Her finger jerked, involuntarily. Orange-red flash jetted from her gun, the small butt jumped in her palm. The momentary light left an impression on Kitty's retina of a huge, dark phantasm looming just ahead of her, a shapeless, batlike form about to swoop down upon her. A fetid, graveyard stench assailed her nostrils. She was enveloped suddenly by a whirl of voluminous, musty cloth. Before she could fire again the pistol was jerked from her hand.

A soundless scream rasping her throat, Kitty flailed out at the stuff in which she was tangled. Her fists battered unavailingly at the whirling, suffocating fabric. They met with nothing tangible beneath it, nothing to assure her that it was other than the creature of a nightmare with which she battled.

Eerie panic stabbed her, ran livid in her veins. An incoherent shout impacted against her ears. Incredibly she was free of the tangling, horrible maelstrom.

A concatenation of animal howls, of bestial snarling, burst out alongside her. Kitty was conscious that it came from the window whose grey rectangle heaved; with a black, tumultuous mass. Realization pounded in her brain that this was her chance . . . She whirled, hurled herself to the door, her frantic fingers found and closed on the knob, twisted, jerked. The door resisted her efforts, would not open. Her other hand, automatically thrusting against the panel, was bruised by the key, just where she had left it! *The door was locked from inside!* How then, had the—whatever it was that had attacked her—managed entrance?

The noise of the macabre struggle at the window battered the appalling query from her reeling mind. She thrust over the key, the door jerked open. She plunged out.

Light, returning suddenly as it had gone, pulled Kitty around. Something on the room's floor leaped at her, photographed itself on the quivering screen of her brain. A body sprawled there, awkwardly contorted. The death-etched face of Jane stared at Kitty with mute reproach. A knife-haft jutted from the scrawny, pinched breast, and around the depression it made, the black uniform glistened wet with a gruesome seepage. The old woman had been overheard then, by the eavesdropper, as she was trying to warn Kitty of some terror that prowled the corridors of the hotel and swift punishment had overtaken her.

A muffled shriek jerked the girl's burning gaze to the window. A black bulk vanished through it. The rectangle gaped vacant, terribly vacant, but the shriek came again. Fainter. From below a vague thud sickened Kitty. The thud of human flesh fallen three high stories to concrete.

They had both done for themselves. Both the attackers who so terribly had menaced her. Fighting over her they had both fallen . . .

But—the edge of the window-frame was jagged by clutching fingers, and then a face appeared in the opening, a face across whose forehead a puckered, livid scar ran from nose-bridge to ebony hair.

The girl slammed the door and ran screaming down the passage.

Chapter 4

THE CORPSE THAT WALKED

A WOMAN SCREAMED some incomprehensible phrase, a doorway suddenly open, was filled with a portly, pajamaed figure whose fat-drowned little eyes blinked sleepily. Kitty Brian shot past, winged by terror, reached the staircase, half-ran, half-fell down it. On the last step she lost her footing, catapulted out into the lobby, crashed, face down, on its splintered floor.

The girl lay there, the wind knocked out of her, half-stunned. Lay there and cringed, her flesh prickling with anticipation of a bullet blasting into her, of a noose settling about her neck.

"Kitty!" someone exclaimed. "Kitty! What in Jehosaphat . . .!"

She shrank closer to the floor, whimpering, not daring to look up. "Kitty," the voice said again, Francis Brian's voice, and his hand was on her shoulder. "Are you hurt? What's the matter?"

The girl pushed her palms against the floor, thrust herself up. Faded blue eyes peered anxiously at her out of a sunken-cheeked face pointed by a familiar iron-grey vandyke.

"Uncle Frank! Take me out of here! Take me out of here quick." She rolled over so that she could face the stairs, gazed fearfully at them.

"Why?" Brian exclaimed sharply. "What were you running from?" A muted clamor of voices from above came out of the arched opening, of questioning voices from a huddle she sensed at the head of the stairs.

"Dead," Kitty moaned. "Murdered, on the floor." There were limits to the audacity of the Strangler's minion, he had not dared follow her past the roomers whom her screams had aroused and brought streaming into that corridor. But he was still somewhere near. She knew now he would never give up till he had accomplished his sinister mission.

"Murdered!" said Hardesty. The girl had not noticed the hunchback hovering over them. "Who? Where?"

"Jane! In my room!" Hysteria pumping in her veins made speech almost impossible. "And he's there too, the killer."

"Yes?" Hardesty whispered. "Yes?" Curiously his gargoylesque face seemed to harden, to change into a mask of brutal ferocity. "In my hotel?" There was a gun in his hand and he went up the stairs, stiff-legged, passed out of sight. "Keep back." His command reached her, rustling against a murmurous background. "Keep back, folks, if you don't want to get hurt. The girl says there's someone been killed in her room."

Brian lifted her to her feet. She clung to him. "Take me away from here," she moaned. "Take me away from this terrible place."

He looked troubled. "I can't, honey. It's two o'clock in the morning. There isn't another hotel in town that would take us in, without baggage, at this hour. Hardesty has known me a long time and . . ."

"Mr. Brian," the hotel man called from above. "Will you come up here, please, with your niece."

"Come, Kitty," Brian said. "Come."

The girl shuddered, started to refuse, then realized that with all those people up there there wasn't any danger. When Uncle Frank saw that corpse on the floor he'd know why she couldn't stay here.

They went up the stairs together, Kitty holding her uncle's hand as she used to when she was a child and he came to visit her motherless home. "Why doesn't he call the police?" she quavered.

"He boasts that no policeman has entered here, on business, in forty years. He won't break that record now unless he has to."

A knot of people clustered around the door of her room, dishevelled, in pajamas, nightgowns, the women with curlers making grotesque halos round their heads.

Except for Hardesty, standing in the center of the floor with his revolver still in his hand, it was empty! Starkly empty. The corpse, Jane's corpse, had vanished!

"Miss Brian," the man greeted her. "Where's this person you said was murdered here?"

Kitty was rigid in the grip of a nightmare paralysis, staring at the place on the worn carpet where she had seen Jane's knifed body. What had become of it? Had the scar-faced man . . .? But that was absurd!

"Is this the room?" Uncle Frank said. "Are you sure this is the room you were in?"

"That's it, of course . . ." But, looking up, she saw her bag on the dresser, saw the plaque on the door with the number, 119. An icy tide rose within her throbbing skull, the tide of a ghastly fear. Reason could not explain what had happened to her, what she *thought* had happened. Reason could not—she snatched at a saving hint flung up from something in her subconscious, something she'd read. Murders in hotels were bad for business, were covered up . . .

She wheeled to Hardesty, her small fists lifting, her eyes blazing. "She was right here, your servant Jane, right there where you're standing, with a knife in her breast. You've taken the corpse away, you're hiding it!"

"I looked in here right after you came flying out, miss," the obese man who had gaped at her interrupted. "There wasn't nothin' in here that ain't here now."

"You lie!" Kitty swung on him. "You . . ." Then she was stricken dumb. Shoving through the gathering, towels over her arm and her fleshless lips mumbling some inarticulate apology, came the old woman she had seen, a knifed and lifeless corpse, lying on this floor!

A woman laughed. It was she herself who was laughing, who was squealing a wild, writhing thread of laughter from a twisting throat while dark phantasmal shapes formed on the walls, the ceiling, swooped upon her, merged, and swallowed her in a dreadful night of madness . . .

Chapter 5

Terrible Heritage

Madness! Kitty kept her eyes tight shut against terror. How could it be anything else but that? Such things could simply not be real. The horrible woman who had laughed at her in the street; the scar-faced man closing in on her, always closing in; the eerie attack upon her in the suddenly darkened room; Jane's corpse that was alive—they were all phantasms of a mind that had given way from the strain of long fear. Paranoia, they called it, she remembered, delusions of persecution.

No! Her whole being revolted from the thought. She was not mad! Not she. Not Kitty Brian. There was some other explanation . . . The silk of her nightgown was cool against her fevered skin. Her weary body was cushioned on a bed, sheets covered her. She had been asleep, had just awakened. That was it! She had dreamed it all. Was ever nightmare so real, so terribly, appallingly real? What would she see if she opened her eyes? The quilted walls of a padded cell? Or the room in Francis Brian's house where he had made her so warmly welcome?

She was afraid to look. Afraid . . . But she must. She must know. Now. Now!

Vague light danced, flickered on a dingy, cracked ceiling. A shadow moved across it—gigantic, awesome. The shadow of a thin head, horned and pointed-chinned. *The shadow of Satan!* Clawlike hands were silhouetted against the grey-white, swooped down at her clutching . . .!

"Are you awake, Kitty dear? How do you feel now?"

Uncle Frank's familiar, kindly face hovered above her, blotting out the fearsome shadow. "Where—where am I?" Kitty murmured. "Where . . .?"

"Still in Hardesty's Hotel, honey, but in a different room. You've nothing to be afraid of any more. Nothing at all."

There was tenderness in the way he said it and strength. Calming strength. "It—it was a dream, Uncle Frank. Tell me it was only a dream."

He hesitated, his look clouded. "It didn't happen, Kitty. But don't worry about that. You'll be . . ."

The girl sat up in bed,. "Uncle Frank! Then it wasn't a . . . Then I *am* . . ."

"Hush, child. Don't excite yourself again. Just remember that I'm, here now and that nothing's going to happen to you. Sleep. You've got to get some sleep so that when the doctor comes in the morning . . ."

"The doctor! But I'm not sick." She knew what he meant. She knew what kind of doctor he meant. "I'm not . . .!"

"I'm afraid you are, my dear." Brian hitched closer and the girl saw now that he was seated at her bedside; that the flickering radiance came from a wick floating in a glass of oil, a nightlight such as she had lit many times in her father's sickroom. "I'm afraid that you have inherited a terrible illness— from your mother."

"My—mother—!" Her lips were numbed, frozen. She could hardly move them to speak. "But—but there was nothing wrong with her. She died in childbirth!"

A spasm of pain contorted her uncle's face. "Kitty," he said. "Ralph—your father—made me promise never to tell you." He took her hand in his. "But I'm afraid that you must know. If you are to make the best of the ordeal awaiting you in the morning, I must tell you. Ralph, if he were here, would agree with me. My dear, the mother you have never known, the mother they told you died when you were born, is still alive."

"Alive!" The word was a whisper of sound falling flatly on the air. "Alive! What do you mean?" She knew. She knew the terrible truth before he answered. The pound of her heart against her ribs told her, the aching throb in her temples.

"It wasn't death you brought her, Kitty." His fingers had slipped to her wrist, were tightening there as if to hold her down. "It was something far more dreadful. A life in death. A never-ending darkness. Fear incarnate shrilling through eternal night." His eyes bored into her ears, seemed to pierce, knifelike to the shrieking horror that was her brain. "Insanity, Kitty. Insanity. The day they took you home they took her to an insane asylum, a raving maniac. That is your inheritance my dear. That is the fate that has hovered over you from your natal day. That is the doom that has overtaken you at last!"

Comprehension exploded in her brain, shattering hope; exploded with physical violence in her whole slim body, constricting its muscles, seizing her with a writhing convulsion that save for Brian's steely grip would have thrown her out of the bed. He held her down, with a strength unsuspected in his aged frame, held her as she tossed and fought to free herself while the uttermost terror that man can know seethed through her, ran riot through the giddy vortex of her consciousness, howled through the black and lonely aisles of her hopeless soul . . .

At last Kitty fell back exhausted, great sobs shaking her dry, tearless eyes staring at the man who suffered with her in her Gethsemane. "Mad," she whispered. "Mad!" And somewhere within her a hollow voice echoed, "Mad. Forever mad."

"That's better," Francis Brian said, releasing her. "That's a good girl. If we face it calmly we can make the best of it."

The corners of her mouth quirked with the laughter, with mindless laughter that fluttered in her corded neck but she choked it down. "The best of it," she parroted. She must not give way again. She must not. "Let me think." He was right, she must make the best of it. A sly, crafty cunning was born within her. "Look," she said. "Look, uncle. I can fool the doctors. I can fool them yet."

"What do you mean?" he questioned sharply.

She sat up, excitement pounding in her temples. "Look. I'll say I fell asleep in my clothes and had a bad dream."

A veil seemed to drop across Brian's eyes. "I'm afraid we can't get away with that," he said musingly. Kitty had never noticed before how much like a vulture he was . . . But it wasn't true, it was her madness making her fear even him.

"All those people saw your antics, heard you say that you had seen the corpse of a woman who was alive and knew nothing about any attack."

"I'll say that I was so tired I fell asleep in my clothes. And you'll tell them that I've always walked in my sleep, that I've frequently waked up from nightmares screaming. It's natural that I should tonight with that man following me from Halesburg . . ."

"What man!" Brian's exclamation cut across her speech. "What man are you talking about?"

Kitty remembered that she had not told him. "I noticed him in the train, slipped away from him at Grand Central—a young man, nice looking except for a scar across his forehead, like this." Her forefinger stroked her temple, descriptively. "He—what's the matter?"

Brian had jumped up, his face a mask of livid fury for a moment. Then it cleared, was expressionless once more. "I thought that was one of your hallucinations, but . . . Kitty! I didn't come to New York to see my bankers, as I told you. Even though they defeated me for re-election, the people of Halesburg are my people and I was determined to spend my private funds to rid them of the Strangler. I hired investigators—they called me here because they had finally discovered his identity. His name is Allan Ford, they told me. And they described him to me. Kitty! *The man with that scar is the Strangler himself.*"

"The . . . Strangler!" Despite all the horror into which she had plunged since her attempt to flee from them had begun, that name still had power to jell her blood. "He's here now! That's real anyway. He's here . . .!"

Brian's fingers were on her shoulders, were digging in. "Here!" he snapped. "What are you saying? I thought you'd gotten rid of him."

"I thought so too! But I saw him coming across the street. I saw him at my window. I didn't imagine that . . ."

Brian's thin lips writhed. "No! You didn't . . . We didn't figure on . . ." He was stammering, broken phrases that seemed to have no intelligible meaning. "I've got to tell

Hardesty, he'll know what to do about it." He started for the door, turned again as a thought seemed to strike him.

"Listen, Kitty," he said. "I'll take care of Allan Ford. Go to sleep and don't worry about him. But get it firmly fixed in your mind that the best place for you is a sanitarium. The less you fight against commitment, the easier it will be for you. Admit your delusions and . . ."

"No," the girl flared. "I won't." From somewhere had come sudden strength to defy the horror to which she seemed doomed. "I'm not crazy. I'm not . . ." She couldn't keep her voice down, couldn't keep the shrillness out of it.

The Brian temper blazed in the old man's eyes. For an instant Kitty thought that he was about to strike her. Then, with evident effort, he gained control of himself, cloaked himself with an icy calm. "Perhaps you're not," he said soothingly. "Perhaps you're not. We'll see by morning."

The door closed on his spare form, Kitty heard his footsteps moving away, stumbling, weary. He was exhausted, she thought, tenderness welling up in her, by loss of sleep, by the distressing scene she had made. He wasn't young any more. He was all she had, now that Dad was gone, and he was trying to do his best for her. For Halesburg too! That was so like him, keeping up the fight against the Strangler even after the city had repudiated him. He had been hit hard by that, poor Uncle Frank . . .

What was that? Uncle Frank's footfalls had died away, but the corridor wasn't silent. Something had brushed against the door panel, was slithering away. Rapidly but covertly, as though someone was following the old man, was stalking him . . .! Could the Strangler have overheard? If he had been lurking out there, if he had been listening, Brian was in terrible danger. Knowing that he knew him as Allan Ford the Strangler must silence him.

Kitty leaped to the floor. She flicked out the nightlight that it might not betray her by shining out into the passage, padded to the door. She forced herself to open it slowly, silently, though her pulses hammered and the need for haste twisted in her breast. She slid out into the corridor. It stretched away on either side, dim, empty . . .

This room was nearer, much nearer the stairhead than one-nineteen. Uncle Frank and the man who hunted him, had gone to the left, toward those stairs. To the right was room one-nineteen, where terror had first assailed her. Kitty recalled the fire escape outside its window. The Strangler, Ford, had only momentarily abandoned his designs on her. Brian disposed of, he would return to kill her! Through that room, out of that window, lay the road to safety for herself.

If she screamed a warning, aroused the people . . . but they would think her again seized by a fit of madness. They wouldn't believe her, would try to restrain her. While that was happening Ford would blast down Brian . . . She couldn't save Uncle Frank. She could save only herself, by turning to the right . . .

Kitty turned to the left. Her bare feet made no sound at all as she glided, her heart pounding, down the hall. She reached the stairs, held her breath as she peered below.

The opening into the lobby was an arch of pallid light. Silhouetted against it was a crouching form. A vagrant beam glinted from metal in Ford's hand, from a gun. It was rising, slowly rising, somehow more deadly because of its leisurely certitude.

If she could get within striking distance before the murder-gun brought to bear on its target! Kitty moved cautiously down the long stairs. A murmur of indistinguishable voices came from beyond the killer and he seemed intent on listening to them, holding his fire while he eavesdropped on plans for his capture. The girl's blood was a dark surge in her veins. Fear dropped away from her, she was conscious only of the clawing of her hands, of the quivering of sinews across the back of her shoulders, in her thighs as they tensed for a pounce.

Her toe caught in a hole in the carpet, made a tiny ripping sound. It was enough! The killer heard it, whirled. His gun snouted at her.

Kitty froze. Ford didn't shoot. He came up towards her,
pantherine, his baneful gaze upon her, hypnotic, holding her
rigid and voiceless, his free hand fumbling under the happing
fold of his coat. Why didn't he shoot and get it over with? Of
course! It was to be the noose for her, the silent, strangling-
noose!

Chapter 6

PARADE OF THE HANGED

THE NOOSE! A black filament coiled against the lobby-light,
writhed snakelike, flailed down! Tightened—on the killer's
throat! His gun arced away. Ford sprawled backward, thudded down at Hardesty's feet, at the feet of the big-headed
hunchback who had suddenly appeared behind him and las-
soed him. A terror-quenched gasp from Kitty Brian had
warned Hardesty, in that last moment, and the Strangler was
defeated by his own weird weapon!

Not yet! Kitty realized abruptly that he had *thrown* himself
backward, at the first touch of the rope; in the only possible
counter; had thrown himself toward the garroter to keep the
noose from tightening. He rolled over now. His hands
flashed out, gripped Hardesty's ankles. The cripple pounded
down on top of him. The two heaved in a flashing moment of
terrific combat. A fist rose and fell, there was the crunch of
knuckles against bone. Ford sprang erect. He was tearing the
lasso from his neck and Hardesty was a flaccid, motionless
bundle at his feet
    Pent breath gusted from between Kitty's lips; the same
breath the sight of Hardesty had stopped in her throat, so
short had the combat been. The Strangler flung the rope from
him, wheeled to come at her once more.
    She whirled, hurled herself up the stairs. Ford's feet
pounded behind her, and he shouted, amazingly, "Wait!
Wait, Miss Brian!"

He thought, too, that she was insane. He couldn't catch her. He didn't have his gun to fling lead after her and he thought she would stop when he told her. She wasn't as crazy as all that.

She plunged out into the corridor again. It wasn't empty any longer. Thank God it wasn't empty. There were people here, dim forms clustered around the door of the room from which she had come. She sped toward them.

"Help!" she cried. "Help me."

"Here she comes," a strange, high voice sounded. "Get her." Terror clawed at Kitty as the figures turned, as she saw that they were cloaked in the white of hospital attendants, that their faces were concealed by the white half-masks of surgeons. Trying to stop herself she stumbled, catapulted right into their midst

Hands grabbed at her, lifted her from her feet. A wet cloth smacked across her mouth, gagging her. Weird, bulging eyes stared at her. She tossed, struggling. The smell of ether was sickly sweet in her nostrils, in the back of her throat. A nauseous giddiness whirred inside her skull. The faces, the eyes, ballooned till they were large as half the world . . .

Her own head was a swollen balloon within which a sick miasma billowed in a vast vacancy. The vertiginous odor of ether permeated that aching void and twisted with impalpable fingers at the girl's stomach. The very wretchedness in which she was sunk brought her up out of weltering oblivion.

Kitty Brian opened her eyes and was not quite certain that she had opened them! For a nubian darkness pressed against them, a terrible absence of light so dense it seemed to have tangible weight. An utter, palpitant soundlessness rendered the awful gloom even more fearful. Except for a vague impression of limiting boundaries, near or far she could not tell, Kitty might have been buried erect in her grave . . .

Was she dead? Was death like this? Had they killed her, those specters in the white garb of mercy who had had no mercy for her? . . . Agony stabbed her temples, sent jagged streamers of fierce torture down through her rigid body . . .

Kitty tried to lift a hand to still the agony in her head. Her brain commanded, her muscles responded, but her arm did not move! It was awkwardly twisted, held in a long sleeve and pressed tight against her body. Her other arm was held in such a sleeve, and her legs were clamped immovably by a rigid, unyielding constriction that corseted her body from agonizingly squeezed breasts to ague-shaken calves! The sheer silk of her nightdress was no bar to the harsh pressure of some rough-surfaced, strong fabric that bruised her soft flesh, that rasped it to anguished rawness. Something like a jacket of canvas . . .

A jacket of canvas. A tight canvas jacket with sleeves tremendously long to bind one's arms! A straitjacket. That was what it was! *A straitjacket!*

A straitjacket! Kitty knew now, terribly she knew, what they had done to her, where they had taken her. Straitjackets are for the insane, the howling, violent wretches whose souls have gone down into the shrieking, hopeless depths of Bedlam!

And out of the darkness a voice spoke the word that quivered on the brink of her mind. "Mad!" A hushed voice pregnant with despair. "Mad!"

An arctic tremor thrilled through the girl.

"My baby. I've waited for her so long, so terribly long." Impossible to tell where it came from, whether from within the whirling hell of her distrait mind or from somewhere in the palpitant black. "But I have my Kitty at last. Mad—and mine at last." The voice streaked higher, shrill with gibbering triumph. "All mine forever!"

It wasn't her mother. It couldn't be her mother . . . The insane hear voices that do not exist. If she didn't hear it, if she could keep herself from believing she heard it, she was not insane . . .

There. That was better. She wasn't mad. She didn't hear the voice any more. That proved it, didn't it . . .?

A hazy, green-tinged glow assumed existence in front of Kitty, a shimmering vapor oddly luminous that did not so much dissipate the darkness as make visible a part of it.

Make visible a seated woman cloaked in sombre black whose head was bent to the babe cradled in her arms. Kitty could not see the woman's face, could only vaguely distinguish her form, but there was something dimly familiar about her, some elusive reminiscence buried so deep in the mists of time memory could not evoke it . . .

The woman's black cloak was a little open to expose the ivory round of a breast the babe's head dented . . . A gasp of horror gusted from the staring girl. That was not the head of an infant. *It was the lifeless, crudely modeled head of a doll!*

And she was staring at nothing but impenetrable murk . . . The insane see things that are not. The insane . . .

The light returned, this time over her. Kitty threw her head back so that she could see it. It hung there, a viridescent cloud jagged by a black, foot-thick beam that jutted into it from an unseen support. The end of that beam was just over the girl and from it a rope dangled, a rope whose nearer end was a noose. The new hemp was stiff and held that loop open so that it was just large enough to slip over her head, to slip and tighten . . . But it was too short, by two feet at least. It was too short to reach her, to settle about her neck . . . Was it lower, imperceptibly lower? Was it coming slowly down?

The darkness blotted it out, and Kitty could not be sure. But it still was there.

"The only release from madness is death."

Who had said that? Who . . .?

A hand, a naked arm, was struck out of the darkness by green light that illuminated it and nothing else. The hand twisted, its fingers writhing with some demoniac anguish that meshed the arm with a network of swollen veins. The arm folded at the elbow. The fingers clawed at something, at a neck about which a rope was knotted, cutting in! Bulging eyes leaped out of the gloom, an engorged face darkened by the purple of suffocation . . . It vanished. The flitting green spotlight of her hallucination pulled the girl's dilated gaze back to the noose over her head. *It was lower!* It was lower by six inches at least. It was descending, slow as the minute hand of a clock, as slow and as inexorable. The noose of the Strangler was descending, the noose of the terror that had made Halesburg a haunted city.

There was no more darkness. The light had expanded till it filled a cavern that to the distrait girl seemed huge as space itself. Shadows dashed soundlessly across a vague floor, gigantic shadows of beings grotesquely human. They were convulsed by a strange, appalling agony, by a torture against which they struggled unavailingly as Kitty herself struggled against madness that clamored for the last shred of reason she retained. They seemed to leap up from the floor, to take more solid form.

Over there, to one side, one of the shadows attained a spectral reality. It was the twitching form of a woman, and about her throat there was the red mark of the strangler's noose. The woman was Jane!

A feathery touch brushed Kitty's hair. It jerked her wild, staring eyes upward again. That which had touched her was the hangman's rope. It had come still lower. It was settling down over her head. In instants now it would reach the level of her throat and then it would tighten . . .

A scream pulled her gaze away from the creeping death. Another shadow had taken gruesome life. It had the contorted, fear-struck features of the man whose murder she had witnessed. In the moment she glimpsed it something snakelike writhed out of darkness, flicked to the man's neck. He was jerked into the air . . .

Blackness smashed in, blackness through which Kitty heard the roar of a motor surging away, the horrible bump, bump of a strangled corpse it dragged in its wake. Had that been a hallucination, too, the first terrible illusion of her madness?

"Come to me, Kitty," her mother's voice shrieked out of the ambient dark. "I can save you from it. Only I can save you from the Strangler. Come to me! Scream!"

That scream took shape in Kitty's throat, fought for utterance. She fought to hold it in. The noose was on her throat now, was tightening. Death was tightening on her throat.

Death or madness. Death or madness. The rope constricted. Gibbering lunacy or the awful mystery of extinction. A pulse now, the space of a heart beat, and she could scream no more.

Terror of death, terror of lunacy, fought for possession of Kitty's soul. Now! Now she must choose or forever after . . .

Chapter 7

STRANGLER'S END

KITTY PITCHED FORWARD, crashed to the floor. The impact jarred her, but even as pain darted through her she realized that at that last moment of ineffable terror whatever bonds had held her erect had given way, had loosed her from the threat of the lethal noose. It was still about her neck but it hung limp, merely a rope now, not the throttling finger of death.

She was saved—or was this another trick her wrecked mind was playing upon her? For pandemonium burst loose all about her, an eldritch shrieking, the trample of many running feet, shouts, the thunder of blasting guns.

She rolled, was aware that light—real light and not the weird viridescence that had exposed horror to her—filled a large, beam-ceiled chamber walled by dirt-encrusted brick. Just over her was a gallows tree, a cut rope dangling over a waist-high post—behind it ladderlike stairs.

A maelstrom of fleeing figures surged near the opposite end of the basement. A half-dozen dark-clad men were advancing in a crouching crescent upon them. Kitty's light-dazed vision cleared, she recognized Hardesty among those who, reaching the impasse of the wall, had turned now, were firing back at their attackers. She saw the portly man who had tried to stop her first frantic flight, others who had been in the curious crowd awakened by her screams. She saw Hardesty go down, his grotesque countenance suddenly a bloody mask.

She half-understood now. The Strangler had captured her, had brought her down here to kill her. Because she had defied him so long he had devised the cruel, lingering torture of the leisurely descending noose. The voices, the visions— perhaps she had been temporarily crazed by her plight. Hardesty had led a band to her rescue . . .

But he had failed. The others from the hotel, their leader down, were throwing up hands in surrender.

Someone was coming down the stairs, moving silently. Long legs came into view, a gnarled hand in which a gleaming knife was clutched. A thin torso. The pallid, vandyked countenance of Uncle Frank! The knife in the old man's hand told the story. It was he who had cut her free to save her from the noose. He had had to flee the Strangler's descent, but now, with infinite courage, he was returning to complete the rescue.

Crisp footsteps detached themselves from the mutter. Ford was coming toward her, his gun still in his hand. Too late! He would see Uncle Frank . . .!

"Uncle Frank," she screamed. "Run. He's coming. Run. Save yourself."

The old man heard her, but valiantly he came on, leaping to her in a frantic but hopeless effort to still save her from the Strangler. He reached her, knelt, his eyes glittering strangely. His knife lifted, started to slash the strait jacket . . .

Ford's gun crashed. Brian jolted away from Kitty, slammed down, sprawled, twitching. Ford was bending over her, his smoking gun snouting at her. Kitty gathered herself to receive the tearing lead.

It did not come. The Strangler thrust the weapon into his pocket, his hands, closed on her shoulders.

"Shoot me," Kitty mouthed. "Please shoot me. Don't hang me. Kill me with a bullet."

Peculiarly, her plea seemed to stun the killer. His mouth worked. "I'll be damned!" he ejaculated. "Who do you think I am?"

"Who? The Strangler, of course."

He whirled away from her, was lifting Uncle Frank. Death's grey pallor already spread over his seamed countenance, a scarlet dribble oozed from the corner of his mouth. A burned hole over his breast, a crimson stain, told where he had been hit.

"Brian," Ford yelled. "Brian! You are done for. You're finished. Tell her, for God's sake before you pass out."

Brian stared glassily, unseeingly. But his lips writhed. "Kit—ty." It wasn't his voice any more. "I—am the Strangler. I—fooled everybody except—" A red bubble popped from his lips, burst. He didn't say any more. He never would say anything any more.

"Uncle Frank," Kitty moaned. "The Strangler. Then—then who are you?"

"Allan Ford. Department of Justice." He laid the old man's body carefully down, turned to her and started tugging at the straitjacket straps.

"Corbett's an old college chum of mine. He asked me for help. I went to Halesburg, uncovered various traces that made me suspect your precious uncle. But they weren't evidence, and I couldn't do anything officially as long as he confined his activities to Halesburg. I did watch his mail however, steamed open his letter that brought you here.

"That stuff about your affidavit being stolen was pure bunk, and we thought he was simply getting you here to persuade you to repudiate it. His use of the mails might bring the D.J. into the picture if that was true.

"That little fracas at Grand Central delayed me, but of course I knew where you were going. I came here, started to enter the lobby when it occurred to me that maybe the hotel man was part of his gang. As it turned out he was.

"I located your room by the light coming on, climbed the fire escape to see if I could manage to listen in. That hag's talk got me worried about you. I slipped a note under the window, went down to take a look around. When I came back you were fighting with a fellow dressed in a lot of black draperies.

"He saw me at the window, hopped me. I thought I was a goner for a minute but I managed to pull him through, sling him down to the walk. You saw me from the door, and screamed.

"I pulled back, but kept watching. The hag jumped up from the floor, pushed the dresser and went out through a door to the next room that it hid, pulling it back in place—"

"That was how they got in," Kitty gasped. "But why didn't they kill me? They could have . . ."

"Wait a minute, girl. I couldn't do anything—just then. You had the whole place in an uproar. I ducked down to the street again, 'phoned for help from the local office of the D.J., poked around, found there was a way in from the street that didn't lead to the lobby and used that."

"She used it too, after she laughed at me."

"Huh?"

Kitty explained, Ford grimaced. "So they'd started right in, eh? Well, you weren't in room 119. I didn't find out where they had moved you till Brian came out of another room. I followed him, was getting an earful of his talk with Hardesty that pretty well completed my case when you showed up.

"I thought that was my chance to put you wise, but Hardesty noosed me, and by the time I got rid of him you'd jammed the works. I got out of the place by the skin of my teeth. Your uncle chased me, I ducked him, met my men and posted them. But I wanted to get you out before the fireworks started. Once more you had vanished and the damned place was deserted. I nearly went nuts tracking you down. Finally I uncovered a concealed hatchway.

"I crept down here, found them going through a lot of hocus-pocus with a green spot-light, black-out skits, hidden voices and so on. There's a half-dozen broken-down old actors been staying here."

The straitjacket came free. Kitty was free to move again, but she lay there staring up at him. "Why," she sobbed. "Tell me why they did all that to me?"

"Don't you understand? That affidavit had Glatow on the way to the chair and he would have spilled the whole works to save himself. Brian was on the spot. He didn't dare kill you; that would have only made matters worse because then the deposition couldn't have been shaken. But if you were insane it wouldn't be worth the paper it was written on. So he got you here to make you that way. You fought back, but the more you fought the more determined he was to succeed. This business down here was his final resort . . ."

"And except for you, it almost succeeded." Again a long shudder ran through the girl. "Then—then none of it was true. Not even that my mother was—was . . ."

"I hope not." Something warm, bold, came into Ford's gaze upon her, and for the first time Kitty realized that the flimsy sheerness of her nightdress was all too revealing. A hot flush mounted to her cheeks. "I don't mind marrying the niece of a murderer but I wouldn't want my children to have any insanity in their blood. Not any, that is, except this kind."

And then he had lifted her in his arms, was holding her close to him while his lips sought hers in a long kiss.

DEATH LANDS A CARGO

Chapter 1

MARK OF THE DEVIL'S HOOF

THEY HAD TAKEN away the rude wooden trestles on which the coffin had lain, and the room to which tragedy had called back Ruth Adair was just the same as it had been two years ago when she had left it—except for the heavy, cloying scent of funeral flowers mingling with the salt tang of the sea.

"Jim!" The girl's speech was muted, tight with a queer dread. "Why didn't they let me look at my father before they took him away?"

The driftwood fire within the deep embrasure of the stone-smudged fireplace was shot through with darts of green and scarlet. Shadows overhung the two—dark shadows brooding between the adze-hewn, time-blackened rafters of the low ceiling. Against the firelight Jim Horne's stalwart figure was a tall silhouette, somehow ungainly in the suit of Sunday best he had worn to Cap'n Eli's obsequies. His wind-reddened, broad-planed features were expressionless, mask-like.

"You were late." The words boomed from his deep chest. "If we had been any longer, the dark would have caught us out on Dead Man's Arm."

"But it was my father, Jim. My father! I had a right to say good-bye to him."

The man's big fists knotted at his sides. "You had a right to stay here with your father and your old mother and not go off to New York, draining them of their little savings while you studied singing." There was almost savage rebuke in his tone, and bitterness. "If you had stayed here—"

"Jim!" Her sharp cry cut him short. "My life is none of your affair. I told you that—"

"—two years ago, yes. You have not changed." A tiny muscle pulsed in his cheek. "Then I have no business here." He turned abruptly away, was across to the door in three stiff-legged strides. But he twisted around just as he reached it, and there was tortured urgency in his voice. "I came back to say one thing, and I will say it. You must go back. You must go back to the city tonight. You must not stay here."

An old anger flared within the girl. "I must not! Who are you to tell me when to come or go? When I take orders from any man it will not be a slow-minded fisherman, a great hulking clod good for nothing but to heave a net and pull an oar."

Jim's eyes blazed, then suddenly were bleak. "All right," he mumbled thickly. "It'll be your fault . . ." He pulled the door open—was gone.

Ruth stared at the drab, fitfully lighted oak, and the dull ache beating in her brain was not all because of her loss. Behind her the fire crackled, and slow feet thudded.

"Some tea mak' yoh feel better, Miss Ruth." The corpulent negress coming in from the kitchen had a cup and saucer in her lumpish, black hands. She set them down on the slab-topped chartroom table at which Cap'n Eli would never sit again, conning his maps and sailing in fancy remembered voyages. "Yoh ain't had a mite t'eat since yoh come home."

"No, Lidy," the girl said drearily. "No, thank you. It would choke me."

"Then stir it. Please, Miss Ruth, stir it for me."

"You're still at that foolishness, Lidy? I . . ."

"Please." There was an odd insistence in the way her old nurse said it. Ruth shrugged. She was too tired to argue, too dreadfully tired. She swirled a spoon in the streaming liquid, laid it down. The black woman leaned heavily on the table, peering at the circling of leaves on the tea's surface, and she seemed cloaked with an eerie shadow, blacker than the mourning garments in which she was clothed. For a long moment there was no sound save for the dully booming advance of the sea that the ancient walls could not keep out, the surge of the sea coming up close to the house and the swishing hiss of its retreat.

Ruth's finely chiseled nostrils flared a bit, and her chin quivered. "Lidy." Anguish edged the girl's tones, though her eyes were dry. "What was the matter with everyone at the funeral? Why didn't they talk to me or to mother? Why did they run away right after father was—was buried, as though they were afraid of something?"

Afraid! Voicing it, Ruth suddenly knew what the strangeness was that had overlain the heavy-bodied, bony-visaged fisherfolk from the village beyond the dunes. It was fear that lurked in their eyes, some crawling, inexplicable fear that had hurried them along the sandy spit and away as soon as that which had to be done was done, and Cap'n Eli lay couched at the very tip of Dead Man's Arm. Fear had been a tangible presence under the scrub pines that grew only on that narrow peninsula jutting into the water, was inexplicably even now a chill warning in her veins. In God's name what was this aura of fear to which she had returned?

"Lawd a-massy!" Lidy's exclamation jerked Ruth's startled glance to her. "De good Lawd p'eserve us!" It was half prayer, half groan. The woman's work-callused fingers clutched the table edge and shook with an uncontrollable ague. She was staring into the tea-cup. Grayness filmed her face so that it was like chocolate that has been alternately heated and cooled.

A cold prickle chilled Ruth's spine. "What is it," she cried, momentarily back in her childhood. "What is it you see, Lidy?"

"Ah sees mo' trouble a-comin' to dis house," Lidy chanted in a hushed, rapt monotone. "Ah sees de debbil hisself a-comin' outta de sea." She was looking at Ruth now, and in the black depths of her distended eyes light-worms crawled. "Dis very night—"

Ruth fought herself out of a billowing miasma of unaccountable dread. "Nonsense," she cried. "You can't frighten me with your silly nonsense any more. I'm grown up, Lidy. I'm no longer a little girl."

Protruding, thick lips, a leaden blue, writhed. "No, Miss Ruth. Yoh is no little girl. Yoh is ripe foh Satan an he comin' foh yoh. De leaves say it an' de leaves doan lie. De debbil boat sail on de bosom o' de ocean, an' de fingers o' Dead Man's Arm beckon it. Yoh got to go away. Yoh got to flee right now befoh de moon rise to mak' a path foh de ship f'om Hell. Yoh got to go away."

A queasy dread twisted at the pit of Ruth's stomach. Had Jim's words been a warning then? Was the negress reechoing that warning? "Go away? Lidy, how can I go away and leave my poor mother alone in this lonely house? She is so old, so feeble—"

"How yoh think yoh mother gwine feel when she see yoh wid you pretty haid stomped to bits by de debbil's hoofs like yoh daddy . . ." The negress' hand flew to her twitching mouth, but Ruth saw only the affrighted, staring eyes, saw only the horror that had leaped to their surface.

"Stamped!" The girl's skin was an icy sheath for her body. "Oh God! That was why the coffin's lid was screwed down so tightly! That was why they wouldn't let me kiss his dead lips! What was it that happened, Lidy? What was it that killed him?"

Lidy's terrified glance crept to the teacup, to the black oblong of the window beyond which the sea surged, came back to Ruth. "De same thing dat killed Otis Blake. De debbil . . ."

"Shut up, yoh ol' fool!" The hoarse roar from behind pulled Ruth around to the kitchen doorway. "Shut up yoh fool talk o' de debbil." A huge negro filled the aperture, his shoulders touching the jamb on either side. The firelight slid silkily over the brown gleam of his big-muscled arms, over his columnar neck, was quenched by the sleeveless shirt tight over his barrel chest. "I done tol' yoh I done had enough o' dat." In the dimness Lidy's son was a simian brute; half crouched, prognathous jaw outthrust, corrugated black brow receding from bony eye-ridges.

"William! What does she mean?" Ruth gasped the question at him, forcing the sounds past cold fingers that seemed to clutch her throat. "What—How did my father die?"

The negro's gaze shifted to her, his small eyes red-lit with smoldering, bestial hate. Just for an instant, then a veil seemed to drop over them, and there was only an emotionless black face looking at her. "Doan yoh pay mammy no never min', Miss Ruth."

"Answer me!"

"He walk on de breakwater an' de rocks give way. Big stone fall on his haid. He daid w'en Misteh Hohne fin' him." He was mumbling, evasive. Ruth caught herself up. Lidy's wild words, her own grief, were clouding her reason. "Mammy gettin' weak in de haid, cryin' de debbil done it."

The woman whimpered, "Stones doan' kill Mist' Blake. He lie under de pines an' blood pour outta he t'roat dat's tore open by de sea-debbil's claws."

"By de knife he kill hisself wid."

Lidy's voice rose. "Whah de knife? Dey ain' foun' no knife . . ."

"Hush." Ruth swayed, clutched at a chair-back for support. "Hush, both of you. You'll wake up mother with your wrangling." Weariness dragged at her, was an aching flood torturing her body.

"Get me a candle. I'll talk to you tomorrow."

Would Jim Horne come to her tomorrow, realizing she had not meant her harsh words?

"Yoh heah dat, mammy. Get Miss Ruth her candle an' den come along to de village."

"To the village? You—aren't you sleeping in your room behind the kitchen, Lidy? Aren't you . . .?"

"De las' year Cap'n Eli mak' me leave de house w'en I get troo my work. He say he doan wan' nobody in de house at night. But I stay here tonight. I sleep in my ol' baid."

"Yoh will not!" William's protest was harsh-voiced. "Yoh'll come home . . ."

The black woman turned on him, and suddenly her cringing was gone and she was erect, determined. "I sleeps heah, an' I watches ober Miss Ruth. Remembeh dat, Willyum. I watches dat no harm come to huh, like I done watched foh sebenteen year ontell she went to de city." Ruth was aware that the glances of mother and son had tangled, that a silent, meaningful conflict raged between them. And this time it was the man who gave way.

"Yoh suits yohself," he mumbled.

"I want you, Lidy," the girl put in. "I want you to stay here. It's bad enough that father will not be here tonight."

"Good night, den." The negro growled. "Ah's gwine home befoh de moon rises."

Climbing the partition-enclosed stairwell, shadows retreated from the flickering flame of Ruth's candle and formed again behind her. The worn wood treads vibrated vaguely with the beat of the sea as though the old structure itself were shivering at some dim threat. A sense of foreboding brooded about her, a sense of impending evil. In the hallway Ruth stopped at the door of her mother's room, listened. There was no sound from within, no sound at all.

Her cold hand crept to the knob, closed on it. She was afraid—she was almost afraid to open the door. She turned the knob, noiselessly, pushed against the seamed wood to swing it open, slowly, without a sound.

Candlelight filtered into the slant-ceiled, papered room. It painted with luminance a pinched, worn face that was as white as the pillow on which it lay, as white as the hair that was a wraithlike aureole about the wrinkled brow. One thin, almost transparent hand lay curled, flaccid on the coverlet.

Flaccid—there was utterly no movement in that bed. Janet Adair was ghastly still. Dread squeezed Ruth's heart—and then her held breath hissed softly from between her teeth. Her mother had sighed in her sleep, tremulously. The pale lips moved.

"No, Eli. Don't do it." The breathed words were just audible. "Don't betray the sea you love." So low the muttered speech was that the girl was not quite sure she heard. "Not even for Ruth. The sea's vengeance is terrible. It will take us all before it is through."

The girl waited, but the sleeping woman said no more. After awhile Ruth closed the door and stumbled down the hall to her own old room.

Chapter 2

THE HELL SHIP LANDS

RUTH ADAIR came awake with a start. Dread squeezed her heart, lay heavily upon her, more heavily than the coverlet that seemed to stifle her breathing. The voice of the sea beat against stillness. From outside a sharp sound came, and Ruth knew what it was that had awakened her. There was nothing ominous about the sound. It was only the flap of a sail, of a wet sail spilling the wind. Yet somehow the girl was afraid.

The window was a grey oblong, glowing with the luminance that is forerunner of the moon. Ruth stared at it, chill little shivers running through her. Beyond the window was a sandy beach, running down to the breakwater that defied the nibbling of the waves, and beyond that was the sea. It was all as it had been as long as she could remember, she told herself. Just as it had been—there was nothing out there to fear. Nothing. If she looked out of the window she would see nothing but the beach and the sea.

If she looked out! She dared not look out, and yet she knew she must. She could not lie here, cowering with a nameless terror. She could not lie here watching the shadows move across the ceiling as the moon rose, watching the shadows and waiting, waiting with bated breath for the doom that was creeping upon her, to strike—the doom against which Jim Horne had warned her, the evil Lidy had seen in the Sibylline cup. Her bare feet thumped on the floor, and slowly, step by step, she forced her reluctant legs to carry her to the window.

Water swished, rippling against a long keel. A ship was coming into the cove and the moon was rising. The moon . . .

The sea was a long, oily heave, and to the right it was blotched by a black bar that was Dead Man's Arm. The cape angled, halfway out, like a bent elbow, and its farther end split into five curled fingers of bleached rock that looked for all the world like a beckoning, skeleton hand. A thicket of dwarfed evergreens made a loose, shaggy sleeve for the arm, ended abruptly at the wrist of that bony hand. It was just there Cap'n Eli had asked to be buried . . .

There was nothing in the little bay before the house. The vast, darkly undulant expanse to the far horizon was utterly empty . . . A light showed above and beyond the pines, a point of yellow light. Even as Ruth glimpsed it, it grew, became a crescent whose lower edge the pine-tips jagged. A silvery shimmer glinted on the water, became a lane of golden radiance lying on the bay's surface. From the skeleton wrist it made a path of light to the breakwater—to the gap in the breakwater that must be the very spot her father had lain, pulped by falling rocks the sea had loosened.

A path! The moon was making a path . . . The girl's throat was suddenly dry and her scalp prickled with eerie fear. A shadow was forming, there in the crook of Dead Man's Arm. It darkened the bosom of the sea—was sweeping along the luminous lane with silent swiftness. Ruth gulped. It was only a catspaw of wind, she tried to tell herself, roughening the water. She had seen it a thousand times . . . Oh God! *It was the shadow of a full-rigged schooner sliding over the cove's surface!* Clearly, unmistakably, it was the shadow of a ship close-hauled—but there was no ship to cast the shadow. There was only that ominous silhouette darting toward the shore, toward the house, with a grisly soundlessness . . .

The shadow of the breakwater swallowed it, and it was gone. But somewhere a pulley creaked, and furling canvas slatted. Somewhere a phantom rope screeched, reeving through protesting sheaves. Ruth moved icy hands, thrusting them at nothingness as if to ward off the approach of ter-ror . . .

A footfall thudded just below.

Fear slowed, then shook Ruth's pulse, so that her heart jerked like a live creature in her breast. The beach was silvery with moonlight, but the glow had not yet reached the house and a murky gloom lay along the stone foundation walls. Within that pall of shadow something moved, a pallid something, wraithlike, without form.

The little hairs at the back of her neck bristled, and her throat contracted in a low whimper.

A voice rang out. "Who dat?" Lidy's voice, challenging, a-thrill with terror. "Who dat climbin' oveh de breakwater?"

Ruth's gaze darted to the retaining wall of piled, loose stone. The blue lunar glow lay clear along its tumbled disorder, and there was nothing there, nothing except a vague shimmer that might have been the quiver of air rising from the sun-heated rock. Nothing. But a hissing whisper came from the sands as though someone moved across it.

"Who dat a-comin?" The black woman surged out into the light, crouched, staring at nothingness. She was a hulking shape at the edge of the shadow, a white cotton nightgown enveloping her rotund form, flapping against her black shins. "Stop! Stop dah!" Lidy's arm lifted and Ruth saw that a carving knife was clenched in her fist. "Yoh cain't have Miss Ruth whilst I lives. Keep back!"

The knife flickered as if Lidy were slashing at some attacker. It stabbed out and down into empty air, but there was a gruesome chunk as if it had plunged into flesh. The negress tugged it back—its polished blade was oddly dull now, swallowing the light—and slashed again. Then, suddenly, the weapon flew from her hand, arced, thudding to the sand, and she was clutching at her throat, was clawing at it. She was being forced backward, was being driven down to her knees—by what? Mother of Mercy! What grisly invisible power was it that had Lidy by the neck, that was overpowering the old servant?

A horrible, choking gurgle came up to Ruth. It was grotesque, unbelievable. The colored woman was alone out there, absolutely alone, and yet she had fought an invisible someone and had been conquered, was swaying on her knees, was battling unseen fingers that squeezed her throat, cutting off breath, life itself.

A scream rasped Ruth's throat. Lidy was down. She was a convulsed hulk, writhing on the sand. Her head twisted around in the spasm of her anguish, and the girl could see her bulging eyes, her contorted face, the tongue protruding from her mouth. Life was being choked from her, and still Ruth could see nothing of her attacker, could see that there was no attacker.

It was over. Lidy Nore was a still, black heap on the sands, an almost naked corpse, flaccid, pitiful. Lidy was dead on the sands, killed by some dread presence from beyond the pale. Was it thus that death had come to Otis Blake? To Cap'n Eli? Death striking unseen out of the moonlight?

Was that death stalking Ruth now? *"Yoh is ripe foh Satan an' he comin' foh yoh."* The slain woman's warning sounded in her ears, and horror gibbered at her from the moonlight. "Keep back," Lidy had defied the invisible. "Yoh cain't have Miss Ruth whilst I live." And now she no longer lived.

Lidy had given her life to protect her and she could not leave the old woman's body out there for the crabs and the sand-worms. She pulled herself around from the window, padded to the door. She was out in the musty, lightless passage and its murk was alive with a dark malevolence that had infested all the house. Against the pound of terror in her breast, by sheer force of will compelling her strength-drained limbs to function, she forged through the gloom to the stair-case, groped for the banister and went down until she was crouched, trembling and weak, against the rough wood of the entrance door.

Through the panel the sound of movement came, of something dragging through the sand, the whispering sound of furtive movement across the hissing sand. Ruth's hand froze on the door knob. Her whole body was rigid, icy in the grip of a crawling nightmare paralysis that was the acme of fear. The phantom killer was outside. He was coming for her.

Why had she not heeded Jim's warnings, and Lidy's? Why had she not fled from this accursed place while yet there was time? . . . She had stayed because of her mother, and now the doom from the sea was coming to finish its work, to slay her and her mother and leave the house an empty, lifeless shell, staring out at the waters from windows through which there would be none left to look.

No! A sudden, desperate courage surged up in her, broke the impalpable thongs by which terror bound her. It was she for whom the invisible presence came—Lidy's vision had warned that—and if it did not enter the house her mother would be safe . . .

Ruth jerked open the door, lurched out to meet her doom, lurched down high steps to the sand. Then she stopped, tensed for the leap of the killer, for the pounce of the slayer from the sea.

The roar of the tide beat about her, and damp cold of the shore night struck through the sheerness of her nightdress to chill her body. Moonlight lay, a pallid blue film on the sands, mounded over Lidy's contorted corpse like a shimmering, winding sheet. Dead Man's Arm held the ripple of the cove in its crook, and its skeleton fingers lay beckoning under the gibbous moon. Otherwise there was nothing—appallingly nothing. No living thing moved on the deserted beach.

Ruth moaned, got somehow to the dead negress, knelt to her. The sand here was trampled, torn up by Lidy's struggles. But there were only the tracks of the devoted servant, coming from the steps to the place where she had died in futile sacrifice. There were no footprints, no spoor of whatever it was she had challenged and fought, between here and the breakwater. No sign of any other presence. No sign of how death had approached.

Breath hissed from between Ruth's teeth, and the pounding of her heart slowed. The clean, briny redolence of the onshore wind was blowing the cobwebs from her throbbing brain. Sanity returned, seeping slowly back to her bewildered soul. Smatterings of things she had read came back to her.

Lidy had challenged something invisible, had fought with an apparition unseen, had been slain by it. Impossible. Was there not some reasonable explanation? Might it not be that the woman had been self-hypnotized, driven half-mad perhaps by her adventurings into the occult, her heritage of superstition? That she had imagined the menace approaching from the breakwater, imagined his attack, and fighting a creation of her imagining died through the collapse of a diseased heart? That was it, of course. She had had a weak heart. Ruth remembered her sinking spells, her distress on occasions of excitement or stress. That was it! The girl gasped with relief grasping reality once more.

The negress' hands were still clutched at her throat, as they had been in her final paroxysm. Ruth reached for them, pulled them gently away.

An eerie dread closed in on her once more. Livid across the folds of the brown skin, a puckered weal ran, and tiny drops of blood oozed where a strangling cord had cut deep. Where a noose had cut——but there was no noose! There was no cord—it had vanished like the garroter who had used it. It had vanished—or never been visible.

Ruth stared at the telltale mark while horror crawled her spine. No phantasm of the mind, no weakness of the heart, had killed Lidy. There was the evidence, clear, unmistakable. The woman had been murdered, cruelly murdered, by a thing unseen, invisible. By a horror fashioned of the moonlight and sea-spume, a slayer visible only to his victim in the final, fatal moment . . .

A footfall thudded behind Ruth, and a shadow fell across her. The bulking shadow of something man-formed, compact of imminent threat, lay on her, and on the dead woman, and on the sand beyond. She felt the appalling loom of that which cast the shadow towering above her. The shadow's arm moved, and something lengthened the silhouetted arm. Something that must be a thick, gnarled club. Terror blazed across the girl's mind like a bolt of lightning.

Chapter 3

DEATH IS BETTER

RUTH COWERED, bent over, waiting for the blow to smash down on her, crushing her skull, pounding her into oblivion. It did not come. Time stretched into infinity, and the club did not fall, and the waiting was more dreadful than imminent death. The waiting, and the slow, cold realization that it was not death with which she was threatened. Not death . . .

Then—what? . . .

The question pronged white-hot fingers into her brain, twisted her around. Her staring eyes found columnar, spraddled legs, traveled up to a thick torso, to a ridged, outthrust jaw, and baleful, threatening eyes glaring down at her. To Jim Horne's eyes! It was Jim Horne who stood over her, clad again in dungarees. It was Jim Horne's great arm that hung over her, his raised fist clutched about the butt-end of a stout club!

"Jim!" Ruth heard the name, was aware only after a moment that it had come from her own cold lips. "Jim. You."

His mouth twisted across his colorless face, the only life in that grim mask. "You stayed." His voice was a husked growl. "You stayed here—tonight."

Somehow the girl tottered to her feet. She faced him in white-faced silence.

Home's club dropped slowly, as though some force outside himself had held it aloft, and now was relaxing its grip. Ruth saw that a long shudder was racking his great body, that the stony composure of his countenance was breaking, that his rough-modeled features were working, were tortured as with some obscure, terrific struggle going on within him. His mouth opened, closed . . .

And suddenly he was shouting at her, "Get in there!" His blunt thumb stabbed at the house. "Get inside, quick, and bolt the door. Don't open it for anyone. Not even for me. Do you understand? Not even for me."

"Jim. Why . . ."

"Get in there." His club was coming up again, she could see his knuckles whiten with the strength of his clutch on it, could see his biceps swelling. "For God's sake go, before . . . *Go!*"

The impact of his voice whirled her around, hurled her willy-nilly to the house door, through it. She slammed the oak leaf shut behind her, rattled a sturdy bolt into its socket. Leaned against the wood, whimpering. The echo of Jim's thick shout was still in her ears. "Go, before . . ." Before what? What was the emotion, the madness against which he had seemed to fight? Why had his weapon been raised over her? Why had he warned her against himself? *Where had he come from, so silently, so mysteriously, out of nothingness?*

It was Jim Horne, she remembered William saying, who had found her father's dead body. Found it? That club, the heavy club his hand had clutched, could smash an old man's head so that it might *seem* that a rock had pulped it . . . A grisly speculation trailed across the morass of her pulsing mind.

Oh God, what was she thinking? Jim Horne couldn't be a murderer. Not Jim. Not the boy with whom she had played along the beach and out on the water. Not the youth who had taught her to swim, who had given her her first, clumsy kiss . . .

But might not some alien being have taken possession of him? Some disembodied spirit brought from out of a watery hell by the ghost ship that, itself unseen, had darkened the sea's bosom with its uncanny shadow . . .

Ruth jumped, whirled around in response to a sudden, sharp sound. Embers of the driftwood fire glowed fitfully on the hearth, light shimmering through them in glimmering waves . . . A pine knot must have crackled, burst by the dying heat. That was all.

Ruth's mind flew back to Jim. Her spine prickled to the sensation of a gaze upon her, a hostile, inimical gaze. And then fabric slithered against fabric, far back in the room's vagueness. Stone grated, and in the obscurity under the chartroom table something bulked. Its shadow elongated, a hand came out into the light, a taloned *yellow* hand. It curved, clawed at the rug, tugged. A head appeared, high-cheek-boned, slant-eyed, thin lips curled over a wide-bladed, cruel knife. Even in that frantic moment Ruth rocked to redoubled horror as she saw it was the futile weapon Lidy had wielded . . .

The Chinese writhed out from under the table in a single lithe movement, was on his feet. His beady eyes went straight to Ruth, he snatched the dagger from his mouth, leaped for her. She screamed, hurled herself away from the door. Her feet struck the first step of the staircase. She fairly threw herself upward, into the weltering, tar-barrel murk to which it rose. Slippered feet thudded on the stairs behind her, and her heart pounded against its caging ribs, pounded as if it would burst through. She reached the upper landing, whirled to the passage.

The silent pursuer was close behind. Ruth snatched for the knob of her mother's door, twisted, flung the door in, slammed it shut behind her, and twisted the key in the lock . . . Just in time. A body thudded against the wood, the frail portal shook to the impact.

The girl whirled to look for something, anything, to shove against the door to strengthen it against the attack of the saffron specter that had so weirdly appeared to terrify her with a new menace. She saw a dresser, rolled it against the portal. Rolled it! It wouldn't be of much use when the lock was smashed . . .

The bed! The great four-poster would make a barricade. She turned to it—and froze motionless, aghast.

The bed was empty! There was the imprint of her mother's head on the pillow. The tumbled sheets still held the mold of her old body. But she wasn't there. She wasn't anywhere in the room. She had vanished, as mysteriously, as unaccountably, as Lidy had died; as Jim Horne had come to order Ruth back into the house.

To order her—not to safety, to the clutches of the Chinese, whose knife was scraping now at the wood of the door, slowly, methodically cutting away the fibers that held its lock! The steel point came through, sliced downward. In minutes the thin panel would give way and he would come in.

He would come in—to sink that steel into her quivering flesh. To tear at her with his pointed talons! Terror engulfed Ruth—all the eerie, incredible terror of the dreadful night that had turned the home in which she was born to a pest-house of mad menace. Her father, her old servant, mysteriously murdered. Her childhood friend, the man who had not been out of her thoughts in all the long months of her absence, metamorphosed into an avatar of strange threat. An impossible, blood-lusting Oriental impossibly materialized into a vacant room, pursuing her with a curious, silent fury. Her aged, feeble mother weirdly vanished, and the scrape, scrape of cutting steel paring away her own last defense. The doom the black seeress had predicted was closing relentlessly in on the helpless girl!

Mind-shattering, livid fear, voiced at her from the obscurity of the moonlit chamber. Fear was a blaze of black fire in her blood, of madness in her brain. Her wide, staring eyes flickered to the bed where her mother had reposed . . .

Then the dark mantle of her terror dropped away, and cold rage replaced it. She was no longer a soft, civilized maid. She became a primitive woman, fighting for life, for sanity. Fighting for a loved one. She would find out where they had taken her mother. She would make the yellow devil tell. And then she would wrest their captive from his fellows, if she had to go down to Hell itself to find them, if she had to battle every fiend in Hades.

Ruth crossed to the dresser, pulled out a drawer. Her groping hand touched chill metal, came out with a long scissors, the scissors with which her mother had laboriously cut out little dresses for her, long ago. Razor-edged with many sharpenings, its blades were narrow, their ends, where they joined in a point, paper-thin. The girl clutched her weapon,

slid around the dresser and crouched against the wall beside
it . . .

A screech of metal against metal sliced through the swirling
chaos of her brain. The carved-out door-lock fell to the floor.
The panel banged inward, crashed against the dresser. Something thumped against the portal with a meaty thud and the
piece of furniture rolled in on its oiled casters. Ruth glimpsed
an emaciated body in the widening aperture, a ribbed, jaundiced torso naked to the waist, crisscrossed by curious, raised
lines, its back to her, its sharp shoulder against the wood.
Then the muscles in her straining thighs exploded like
unleashed springs, catapulting her at the intruder, the scissors
in her hand flailing, unsheathed claws of the enraged tigress
she had become.

The scissors point struck flesh, at the base of the Mongol's
neck, met gruesome resistance, ripped a jagged gash, came
away. The Asiatic whirled, his scrawny arm darting up, slicing his knife down at Ruth. Her fingers caught the bony wrist
in mid-air, halted its lethal swoop.

In the same instant she felt her own right wrist clutched.
She strained to get free from the steely grip that held her im-
provised weapon powerless. She tightened her own grasp on
the Chinese's arm. The two froze in a ghastly, heaving dead-
lock, their feet planted on the floor, quivering muscles battling for mastery. Fetid breath gusted in Ruth's face. Almond
eyes glittered malevolently at her from deep-sunk sockets.
The Mongolian was hairless, and his skin so tightly drawn
over the bones of his head that it was a skull that leered at
her, a saffron tinted skull.

Ruth could see the gash she had made in the Asiatic's
shoulder, and though it was so deep that the bone showed,
grayish in the slit, no blood flowed from the wound!

No blood flowed, and no sound came from between the
greenish, pointed fangs exposed by writhing, fleshless lips.
Eerie terror was back, netting Ruth's form with an icy, prickling mesh. Terror clawed at her, more poignant than the excruciating agony tearing her back and the sinews of her legs

and arms. Agony pierced her lungs with each labored, hissing breath as the strength of her first mad onslaught seeped away and she bent back, ever back under the increasing, terrible pressure of her ghastly antagonist.

She was beaten! She gave way, suddenly, toppling backward. The Chinese's own straining effort threw him forward, against Ruth, as the resistance against which he fought unexpectedly vanished. A final despairing instinct jerked the girl's knees up as she fell, they pounded into the yellow man's groin. Even then no sound came from him, but his gaunt features twisted with pain, and his grip on Ruth's right wrist relaxed. She twisted it free, drove the point of her scissors into the corded, yellow neck.

The metal sank in, nauseating her with the sliding sough of its stab. Her fingers touched skin that was clammy, cold, and the weight lying on her was suddenly limp. The deathly chill of it was damp against her nearly nude body. Revulsion galvanized her into a last fury of action. She thrust at the flaccid corpse, beat her shaking fists against it, until she had forced it from her. She rolled away from the horrible cadaver, and lay panting, face down on the polished floor. The flooring vibrated beneath her with a monotonous rhythm in time to the long, dull boom of the sea. She lifted and fell on a weltering tide of dark horror.

"Thank you," a toneless voice grated from above. "You saved me the trouble of disposing of this carrion."

Ruth looked up. Water splashed into her face, a drop of water, stinging, and she stared up into a narrow, grey countenance. In a single frantic flash she saw glittering eyes, a hooked nose and pointed chin, a thin-lipped Satanic grin. She saw dark, stringy hair wet pasted like clinging seaweed to a livid brow, and drenched garments tight on an incredibly thin body, tight and shimmering with a ripple of emerald light like moonlight on windless, stagnant water. She saw long nailed, curved fingers, dripping water, reaching down for her.

Realization rocketed through her. This was the Master of Horror, the fiend come up out of the sea to take her to his dread domain. One reaching claw touched her arm, and its touch was a frigid burning, an electric shock that galvanized her body, so that she sprang to her feet.

The apparition laughed gloatingly, came toward her with appalling surety that she could not escape. He was between her and the door. Ruth whirled, her frantic glance found the open window. Death, any clean death, were better than capture by this sinister creature. She catapulted to the opening. The soles of her bare feet felt the sill as she sprang. She flung herself headlong out, and fell toward the silver glimmer of the moonlit sands.

Chapter 4

ON DEAD MAN'S ARM

IT SEEMED to Ruth that the air was viscid, strangely buoyant, that her fall to death on the glistening sand was weirdly slow as a dive sometimes is from a great height. She did not want to die, terror of oblivion suffocated her even as she fell. She was a child of the sea, and in her extremity the lessons the sea had taught her flashed to her aid. She brought knees up, tucked her arms between them and the soft warmth of her body. Made of herself a flaccid bundle dropping down, every muscle relaxed. The impact of her landing pounded breath out of her, half-stunned her; but her limpness, the shock-absorbers she had made of her limbs, took the blow of the landing and no bones were broken.

She toppled sidewise. Her cheek fell against something, cold, clammy. It was the thigh of Lidy's corpse, and a crab scuttled away. Ruth pulled briny air into agonized lungs, jerked her head away from the grisly touch of the cadaver. Brown-skinned flesh hung in strips where already the beach-scavengers had been at their loathly feeding.

Her glance recoiled from gruesomeness, swung to the wall of the house. She saw the somber roughness of the house's stone foundation, the paint-peeled frame of a tiny cellar window. A spectral something moved vaguely across the black square.

The girl twisted over and attempted to rise from the sand. She had to get up and run over the dunes to the left, over the dunes and away from this outpost of hell. If she ran fast enough she could get away, she could get to the village where people were, human beings who would take her in, who would shelter her against the grisly evil that pursued her. Behind her a hinge squealed, and feet thudded on wood of the threshold.

Ruth sprang erect. A swift, terrified backward glance showed the brine-soaked apparition plunging out, the water-devil with the visage of Satan. Her heels dug into the sand. And then, in an instant before her muscles responded to the frenzied command of her brain, a moving something caught her gaze, something moving at the angle where Dead Man's Arm jutted out from the shore. It vanished under the trees clothing the cape, but Ruth knew what she had seen was the bulking form of William Nore, Lidy's son—and over his shoulders had been the thin, white clad figure of her mother.

She leaped into a frantic, staggering run. She twisted, not to the left, where chance of safety lay, but to the right, to the grisly spit whose skeleton hand had beckoned the hell ship from the sea. The cape cloaked with ominous pines into whose gloom the black man had carried her mother.

Sand spurted from under the girl's flying feet, and the thud, thud of the pursuing fiend pounded after her. The dark thicket flashed nearer, nearer, but the sound of the phantom hunter drew up on her. Terror spurred her to incredible speed, terror of the foul thing stalking her, of the fate to which her mother was being borne. Oh God!—What fate was it to which the negro was bearing the aged woman?

The pines were closed ahead, their lightless obscurity opening to swallow her. And then, suddenly Jim Horne came running from behind the house to intercept her, his club upraised. "Ruth!" he called. "Ruth—stop . . ."

She did not hear the rest; a final, desperate leap had launched her into the blackness of the pine thicket, and as it swallowed her it blotted out the sound of pursuit, of the two grim antagonists who had joined forces for her destruction.

Ruth plunged through underbrush that tore her flesh, that whipped stinging lashes across her face and body. Brambles caught her nightdress, ripped the filmy stuff from her, so that only a few shreds remained to flutter about her flanks, her breasts. She was following the vague sound of a huge body threshing through the thicket ahead; she was fleeing from the servants of evil who hurtled after her.

Once she heard Jim's voice, distance-muffled, shouting: "Ruth! Wait . . ." Calling to her as if he thought she was still blind to his betrayal, to his oneness with the fiends evolved from the sea and the moon's lifeless beams. Once she heard a scream from far ahead, a thin, quavering scream that could come only from the throat of her mother. Panic swept her at that sound—and was followed by despair. And then there were no more sounds except those she made herself, crashing through the thicket. That, and the unceasing mutter of the ocean, unseen but close now on either hand . . .

It seemed that she ran forever, fighting the battering of the dark woods that were in league with her enemies; fighting the weariness that tugged at her muscles, the pain that was a garment for her naked body. She was a wild, mad creature hurtling through an unreal, cruel purgatory . . .

Light glimmered through the tree-trunks before her, a vine caught her ankles. She staggered, the impetus of her headlong flight carrying her out into a clearing. She pitched to her knees. Stayed there, moaning, not feeling pain any longer, feeling nothing but a renewed burst of horror within her as she stared at something that swayed back and forth, penduluming against the yellow round of the full moon, which rode high now in a lowering sky.

It was a body, it was a woman's body, swinging at the end of a rope, and that rope hung down, straight down from the yardarm of a mast. There were other masts, their yards thickened by furled canvas, their rigging a tangle of black meshing the lunar grow. They sprang from a long, low keel; a black keel that slowly rose and fell on the oily heave of an unreal sea. A sea that shimmered greenly like the shimmer of the garments the fiend wore, who was the captain of the schooner from hell at which she gazed.

Ruth Adair's body twitched and a great wave of terror-spawned hysteria suddenly shook it. Abruptly the girl burst into loud, crazed laughter. Her hold on reason slipped, and an illusory clairvoyance seemed now to reveal the sinister plan of her persecutors. They had played with her. They had let her go, not bothering to overtake her. Of course they had let her go, she was going just where they wanted her to go—to the landing place of their ship, of their schooner from Hades. How they must have laughed, watching her struggle through the woods, watching her running. She could laugh with them. It was funny. Oh how funny it was.

And the funniest of all was that they had used the phantom of her mother to lure her on. The *phantom* of her mother!

Suddenly the girl's mad laughter ceased. They were coming for her now. A splash in the water was followed by a shadow jutting out from the penumbra of the hellship's keel, and a longboat was riding the water, its oars skimming the waves, dipping and skimming again, like a monstrous water-spider scuttling toward her. It was a spider, and she the fly, and there was no escape for her. She no longer wanted to escape. She wanted them to take her aboard the schooner. She wanted to see her body hang from the other end of that yardarm. And then she would take the spokes of the wheel and steer the vessel back to hell. She knew how to steer, Jim Horne had taught her how to steer. She would sing as they sailed, and Jim would be on the bridge too. Jim Horne, Captain Satan's first mate. And then she saw that Jim was standing above her.

"Jim," she said to him. "Jim, I will steer the ship for you." It was not strange that he was here in the clearing, that he was bending down to her, not strange at all. "When we get to hell Satan will wed us." She could say it now that they were both dead. She couldn't say it in life. She could only mouth bitter words at him, words bitter because he would not love her as she had always loved him. "And then because of our love hell will be heaven."

Then a form came up out of a dark rock pile behind Jim. His grey face was furious, and he bounded toward Jim, a rock upraised in his taloned hand. "Jim!" the girl screamed. "Behind you!"

Chapter 5

GRISLY CARGO

HORNE WHIRLED, grating an oath. The stone flew at him, bounced off his shoulder. His leap carried him yards across the clearing, his fist slapped into Satan's face. There was a squashing sound, and that gaunt visage was splotched with red. Then two forms were locked in a snarling, growling combat, and Ruth was aghast as the madness died within her and she was aware that Jim Horne was fighting for her, had all through the ghastly night been fighting to protect her.

The girl staggered to her feet. Against any human antagonist Jim could hold his own. But was it a human being he was fighting? And even if it were, even if Jim could defeat him, his confederates were coming from the black-hulled schooner, were coming fast in the longboat that skimmed the water under the drive of powerful oars.

Ruth twisted around. The dory was very close, and she could see its occupants, their swinging backs, their white fists tugging at the oar handles. She could see that there were others in the boat who were not rowing, bent forms squatting between the thwarts. Now a hand lifted and she caught the glint of metal on a yellow wrist, could hear the clank of chains.

Oh God! What was this grisly small craft oaring in, who were the chained beings that made its living cargo? The terror of the night closed in again on her. The keel of the rowboat grated on rock, the bow oarsman turned. It was the negro, William Nore!

Ruth whirled again, just in time to see Jim's great arms lift the struggling, writhing, reptilian form of his opponent high in the air, to see Jim pound him crashing down. "Jim," she screamed. "Watch out! The others . . ."

Jim came around, a scarlet weal across his cheek, his mouth awry. "It's all right, Ruth. It's all right. They're friends."

He was striding toward her, was tearing the straps of his overalls from his shoulders, and stripping the dungarees down. He stopped to pull them off. "Put these on, darling." He tossed them to her.

The girl caught the garment, started toward the curtaining shrubbery. But a cry halted her, a thin, piping cry from the longboat. "Ruth. Ruth. Are you all right?"

She turned. Her mother was standing up, her old arms outstretched. Her mother!—But the woman's form still hung, a ghastly pendulum swinging against the moon.

The blaze from the driftwood fire on the hearth in the living room of the old Adair house reached high between the age-blackened rafters of its low ceiling, driving away the shadows. "Jim," Ruth said. "I can't understand any of it. Did I dream it all?"

Horne turned from the fire, looked moodily at her. "No. It wasn't a dream. I—I hate to explain it, but I suppose I'll have to . . . Look, Ruth, you didn't realize how little your father really had when you wrote him for more money. He couldn't deny you. And when William Nore came to him with a proposition that they handle live contraband, he said yes, even though it must have gone against his grain."

"Live contraband?"

"Chinese, smuggled into the country to evade the law. Cap'n Eli didn't realize what he was letting himself in for. The men in that trade aren't human, they're fiends. And this particular crew was the worst of the lot.

"The government realized the Chinks were coming in somewhere along this coast. They couldn't send strangers in, and I was appointed an undercover agent, to try and stop it. Otis Blake was selected to help me, and we were thunderstruck when we discovered that the smugglers were landing their living merchandise on Dead Man's Arm.

"It still didn't occur to us that Cap'n Eli was mixed up in the thing, though we did suspect the negro. However, we couldn't make out how they were being taken away from the spit. From out at sea we could see only that they were being taken into the pines, and they weren't there in the morning. Otis volunteered to hide out there, spy on them. The next day he didn't show up—poor fellow, we found his body on the skeleton hand, his throat cut.

"Lidy started a lot of talk about the devil haunting the cape. A lot of damned fools in the village believed her.

"This was last week. I kept snooping around—and found out that a tunnel had been dug from the woods, along behind the breakwater, then into the cellar of this house. I came to Cap'n Eli with my discovery—and he told me he knew all about it, that he was in on the thing. He showed me a trap-door under the table, that had been arranged for the Chinks to be brought up and out of if the cellar exit out back were being watched.

"Ruth! I couldn't arrest your father. I gave him a chance to get out of it. He promised me that he would tell the gang he was quitting. He did tell them—I imagine that was the reason they bashed his head in with a rock, out there.

"This morning I got word from our operative in Halifax that a shipment was going out, and I knew they would be landed tonight. With your father gone, I didn't hesitate to have a Coast Guard boat sent down here, had it waiting down the coast, hidden in a cove. I tried to warn you . . ."

"Lidy tried to warn me too. She must have sensed something coming, and she tried to frighten me away with her talk of a hell ship sailing a moon path on the water."

"I've seen that eerie effect myself. When the schooner came in the other side of the point the just rising moon threw its shadow on the cove out here . . . Well, I was out behind the house, signaling the coast guard launch when I heard Lidy yelling her defiance of the devil—perhaps that was to frighten you some more, drive you away, perhaps her mind

had really given way and she believed the story she had herself invented. At any rate, there was a Chinese in the cellar
who was left from the last shipment. He hadn't paid his passage and the devils had been torturing him to get even. The
window was too small for him to get out, but when he saw
Lidy's knife, he wanted it. He unraveled an old net down
there, made a noose which he flipped out through it, got it
around her neck. He had a long pole by which he fished the
knife in, and somehow he managed to get the strangling cord
loose and pull that back in too. He started working at the fas-
tenings of the trapdoor—"

"And got through just in time to attack me," said Ruth,
shuddering.

"The poor fellow thought you were one of his tormentors,
was wild for revenge. In the meantime William Nore, who
had never really gone to the village, had looked out and seen
his dead mother. He thought that had been done by the
smugglers, scuttled up the backstairs to warn you and your
mother. You were not in your room. Again he thought the
contraband runners were responsible, he went to your
mother. Warning her to be silent he carried her out and down
the way he had come. I saw him coming out with her, and by
that time had gotten a message that the ship was captured but
that Grange, the leader of the gang, had dived overboard and
gotten away. I thought that perhaps Grange might make for
the house, that the safest place was the ship, sent Nore out
there . . . started around to look for you. As I came out from
the corner of the house I saw you running, and Grange after
you. I threw my club at him, he dodged it, made the woods.
Then I lost him in the underbrush . . . You know the rest."

"Who—who was the woman they hung?"

"Our operative in Halifax. They discovered she was a spy,
took her along and killed her when they landed here, just before the coast guard boat came into sight. They were too late
to save her."

"Oh, the poor girl!" Ruth blinked away tears.

"Ruth." The new authority was suddenly gone from Jim, he was again gawky, awkward. "Ruth. I—I want to ask you something."

"What is it?" A pulse beat in her wrists, and suddenly she too was very shy.

"You—you said out there—hell would be heaven because of our love. You—didn't mean that—you . . ." He bogged down.

"I meant that I love you," she said, and then she was in his arms. "Oh my dear, with all my heart and soul." Hot lips were crushed against hers . . . After awhile she pulled away, smiled tremulously. "This isn't hell, Jim," she whispered. "But that was a good imitation of heaven."

DEATH'S MISTRESS

OFFICER JOHN HAYDEN shrugged big shoulders as if the stiff cloth of his tunic bothered him, but his uneasiness had nothing to do with the fit of his uniform. Something in the wee-hour stillness of Exterior Street was getting him, something ominous in the black loom of the freighters squeezed between pier sides, in the continual lap-lap of greasy water against their hulls, distinct in the silence. The bay seemed to have a million tongues tonight, and each one whispered a warning.

A warning of what? Hayden's narrowed eyes slid along the deserted expanse of cobbles he patrolled. Illuminated patches hugged the wide-spaced street lamps closely. Between them shadows lay heavily . . .

The officer's unquiet glance roved to the right, skimmed blank façades of dingy warehouses, paused hesitantly at the black maw of an alley. He knew he ought to take a look in there, yet a curious reluctance restrained him. Anything, almost anything might be hidden in that tar-barrel murk!

Hayden shrugged again. "Hell of a cop I am," he muttered half-aloud. "Ye'd think I was a rookie doin' his first twelve-to-eight tour." He swerved toward the alley mouth, digging into a pocket for his flashlight; but his other hand took a tighter grip on his nightstick . . . There was a prickle of cold across the back of his neck as he sensed, rather than saw, a flicker of movement within the alley toward which he slowly thudded.

His torch-beam shot out. Crazily-leaning wooden walls leapt into being. The light-disk danced along scummed flagstones, broken and up-ended, probed a pile of heaped refuse, moved further back—and was suddenly notched by a heavy-soled shoe, the blue hem of a trouser-leg. It stopped, quivered a bit, moved again, held in the center of its luminance a prostrate, oddly twisted form in a police uniform! The body lay face down in the alley filth; one arm was flung over the sprawled figure's head, and at its end a revolver barrel snouted.

Hayden's jaw hardened. His stick beat a rapid tattoo on the sidewalk, then he was plunging forward, cat-footed, toward the thing in there while his flash-beam stabbed into emptiness beyond.

The cop reached the unmoving form of his comrade, stood half-crouched above it. His eyes followed the lance of his light. Neither sight nor sound betrayed any living presence in the alley, but through the multifarious salty odors of the sea-breeze a faintly acrid tang stung his nostrils, a pungency that was somehow alien, exotic. It pulled his gaze down again to the body at his feet, and something he had been unable to see from the alley mouth struck the blood from his lips.

The fallen cop's hand, the fingers that gripped the butt of his useless gun, were brown, shriveled—had the texture and sheen of old parchment! The nails were blackened, curled oddly outward.

"God!" Hayden groaned, and dropped to his knees in the slime. He touched the strangely discolored hand with a tentative thumb, snatched it away as a crackle like that of dried tissue paper came startlingly loud in the silence. But the sere feel of withered skin clung to his fingertips, and the hardness of bone beneath. "God," the cop said again, in a hushed, shocked voice.

A hot spot of wrath burned in Hayden's skull at the same time that his skin crawled with unacknowledged fear. There was no whisper of sound in the alley as he pulled air into tightened lungs; but he felt eyes upon him—hot, inimical eyes. His light toured the narrow passage; slid along blank, windowless walls; skimmed mildewed, debris-strewn paving. There was nothing there, nothing!

"Good Lord," he grunted. "Why in hell don't Fred come? He oughta heard my raps and snapped into it pronto." Officer Fred Kane's beat ended only half a block from here and the two always timed themselves to relieve the tedium of the dawn patrol with mumbling talk. Hayden fumbled for his whistle; his dropping glance went almost furtively to the body's shriveled hand. And he gasped!

A tiny movement, when he had touched it perhaps, had pulled back the sleeve, revealing flat silver links of a wrist-watch band and the watch itself. Hayden stared pop-eyed at the odd, octagonal timepiece and his mouth worked. He knew that watch, had compared it numberless times with his own. It belonged to Fred Kane, to his buddy, his side-partner through half a decade of sidewalk pounding! But only an hour ago he had been chatting with Fred . . .

The policeman forced his arm to move, his hand to touch the flattened shoulder of the corpse, pressing it so that the head rolled limply and he could see its face. Its face! Good God! That which stared sightlessly at him was the face of no human thing!

The skin, brown and shriveled like that of a long-dried apple, had fallen into cheek-hollows, as if there were no flesh beneath. Blackened lips were retracted from stained teeth. The nose-tip was gone, the nostrils had vanished and their cartilage had shrunk tightly closed. Lidless eyes were glazed white marbles in deep black pits. This was the face of a mummy, long dead, of a cadaver exhumed from an age-eroded tomb! Horror rocked the stalwart policeman back on his heels. He whimpered in his throat, fought nausea.

At that moment voices sounded behind him. He exploded to his feet, whirling as his free hand plunged to the holster for his gun! From the darkness of the alley, came the gruff rumble of a man's voice, the shrillness of a woman's.

The woman's: "No! No! Not again! Don't make me . . ."

Hayden's flash-beam searched for the voices, lashed into a billow of blackness, a swirling cloud of black vapor rolling toward him. Tendrils, reached out for him, coiling ebony tendrils, monstrously alive! The cop's scalp tightened, the cold breath of fear beat on him, and the woman screamed, "Help!" Screamed shrilly, agonizingly from beyond the cloud!

Hayden swayed a lightning instant, terror of the black mystery clamping his limbs. Then, snarling, white-faced, he plunged into the impenetrable mist.

He plunged, and his skin was suddenly a living flame that seared. Black fire scorched his face. A lightless blaze charred his eyes, nostrils, mouth! He drew flame into bursting lungs, his trigger-finger jerked spasmodically. Shot-Shot-crash pounded within the lethal cloud. And the flare of his gun was drowned in black vapor that swirled, thinned, and was gone.

Somewhere a woman laughed stridently, hysterically. Laughed till the sound of her mad cachinnation was drowned in the roar of a motor leaping away from the dark alley where two mummies lay—two horror-faced mummies in the blue uniform of the Granport police force.

Grim-visaged young Dan Lorraine, captain of the freighter *Lomand,* twisted with a weather-reddened hand the doorknob of Praying Joe's, hottest spot on Granport's waterfront. Erstwhile hot-spot, that is—for the usual tumult was silent behind the portal he was opening and the flaring neon sign above him lit with its red glare a deserted, eerily hushed street. Dan's yellow eyebrows knitted in puzzlement.

The door came open on a cavernous, dim-lit, low-ceilinged hall. The sailor's footfall thudded loudly, echoing, and a white-aproned bartender pounded across the floor toward him, a bulldog automatic jumping from a hip pocket. The man's face was a hard mask, but his little eyes glittered oddly, and his ordinarily florid features were filmed with a sickly green cast. Were it not for the thick-necked, jutting-jawed bull's head topping gorilla-like shoulders, Dan would have thought that fear lurked in Praying Joe's tiny orbs. Then recognition dawned on the dive-owner's face.

"Hell!" Joe grunted. "Dan Lorraine. Didn't know you was in."

The ship-captain watched Joe slide his gat back to its covert. "Yes," he growled. "I'm in, and I'm going out again on the dawn tide." He rolled past the saloon-man to the bar, got a foot up on the brass rail. "Whisky sour, Joe, and be damn quick about it."

In seconds the concoction slid across the mahogany, and Dan had gulped it down with a shudder. "Lousy as ever," he grunted. He let his eyes wander through the big cafe and came back to Praying Joe. "What," he said heavily, "is the matter with you and this whole rotten town?"

Joe swiped a foul-smelling rag across the wood-top, leaving a greasy film of dampness. His heavy face glowered. "What's eatin' yuh, pal?" he said at last. "What makes yuh think anything's wrong wid Granport?"

"Think!" the seaman exclaimed. "I damn well know it." He threw a big-thewed arm out in a sweeping gesture, indicating the dim-lit, nearly empty room, the few furtively whispering, tight-mouthed men who were its only other occupants, the vacant stage beyond the long bar. "Nice, lively spot this after ten months slogging the waves with the everlasting stink of Patagonian hides in your nose. Praying Joe's, the rip-roaringest dive on the waterfront, gloomy as a funeral parlor—and the rest of the port just like this. Nobody on the streets except the cops, and they going around in pairs with their hands on their gun butts, eyeing a fellow like he was a public enemy number one. Half the theaters closed, the rest empty. Hell—when I came in you went green-gilled and grabbed out your gun as if you thought I was Stan Kanio himself prowling for a stick-up."

The aproned one's eyes jerked to the tables and back. "Stan Kanio's not stickin' this joint up, nor any other. He's six foot under."

Lorraine straightened, interest momentarily brightening his broad-planed, wind-wrinkled features. "Oh, yes? Your dumb police force got him finally, did they?"

The bartender spat into the sawdust on the floor. "Not so dumb, Dan, not so dumb. They blasted him at the docks, caught him flat-footed wid a bag in each hand."

"Uh-huh." Lorraine's mouth twisted wryly. "Never gave him a chance, I suppose. Shot him like a dog when he couldn't pull his gat."

"Well," Joe shrugged, "they wasn't takin' no chances." He seemed relieved at the turn of the conversation. "His moll got away, somehow, in the rumpus. She—"

"So it isn't Kanio that's scared Granport gutless," Dan interrupted. He pushed thick fingers through his shock of yellow, rumpled hair. "What is it then? What are you afraid of, you and the rest of the burg?" His fingers were magically around the saloon-man's wrist, jamming him up against the counter. "Spit it out or, by God, I'll break your arm." The captain's narrowed eyes burned with a cold blue flame as they probed the other's tiny orbs.

Joe gulped and licked white lips. "Cripes," he whined. "No call for yuh gettin' tough. I thought yuh knew. Dere ain't nuttin' else in de papers but de mummy death."

"The what?" Dan leaned forward, his eyes glowing. "I've just landed, haven't seen a paper. What's that you said?"

"De mummy death. Two weeks it's been goin' on now, cops bein' found all over town all dried up like dem mummies in de museum. Dey ain't got no noses, deir ears is all dried up, deir faces—cripes—I seen one an' I ain't slep' fer t'ree nights with it lookin' at me in de dark." The saloon-man spilled whisky into a glass and threw the fiery liquid down his throat.

"You saw one. How—?"

"Yeah! I seen one an' I wish I hadn't. Tim Rollins it wuz, he wuz at me side door slucin' his t'roat wid a schooner o' lager when a dame steps up ter him. 'Officer,' she sez t'rough her veil. 'Officer, dere's a man in de hallway o' Number Twenty-six. I t'ink he's dead.' Her voice wuz soft an' she talked like a toff.

" 'Dead drunk, more likely,' Tim sez an' he finishes his drink before goin' over. I watched him go up the stoop, an' inside de hall. Sudden-like I hears a yowl like nuttin' human. I wuz too damn scared ter do anythin' fer a minute, den I grabs me gat an' beats it over. Dere he wuz—Oh Gawd—don't ast me ter tell yuh what he looked like! . . . ."

"And the woman?"

"She wuzn't anywhere aroun'. I didn't see her go, an' no-body else did." The narrator's voice was a husky whisper now, a whisper in which ancestral terror quivered. "An' I didn't see her come neither, dough I wuz standin' right next to Tim, lookin' out. She wuz dere one minute, nowheres de next." His next words were barely audible. "If yuh wuz ter ast me, I t'ink she wuzn't no woman at all."

"A man? But you said—"

"Nor no man, neither." Save for its network of wormlike red capillaries, Joe's face had gone fish-belly gray and his eyes were livid. He looked past Dan, seeing things that were not of the real world. "Nor no man," he repeated solemnly.

The sailor was all alive now, his big frame athrill with a tremor of excitement. His grip on the other man's wrist re-laxed. "Wait," he said. "Wait. You said this mummy death takes only cops. What's everybody else scared about then?"

"Gees, guy, don't yuh get it? Here's a harness-bull paradin' his beat. Dere's a holler fer help somewheres, er someone comes runnin' up tellin' him about a prowler climbin' a fire-escape. Eight chances outen ten it's straight enough, but de udder two chances is dat it's de mummy death baitin' him. W'addya t'ink de cop's gonna do?"

"He's not going to be in any too great hurry to go looking for trouble," Lorraine answered, musingly. "He'll stop to think it over, to question his informant."

"Uh-huh. An' in de meantime de prowler gets away, or de stick-up's finished. Dat's what's happenin' in Granport de last two weeks, an' dere's plenty takin' advantage o' de set-up. Dey've even cleaned two banks, wid de squad-cars showin' up a half hour late."

"So that's it," Dan said softly. "So that's the layout. The police force paralyzed by fear, and the crooks running wild."

Chapter 2

THE MURDER GUN

THE PALL OF FEAR lying over Granport was almost tangible as Dan Lorraine, somewhat later, rolled through gloomy, vacant streets on sea-legs that were only a trifle unsteady. He was on his may back to the *Lomand*, a bare three hours' shut-eye ahead of him before he must turn out to sail on the dawn tide. This morning he had swallowed wrath as he read the radio that would take the freighter down to New Scotia with not twenty-four hours' lay-over. He had raged at the stevedores emptying her holds, had glowered through the business of obtaining clearance at the Barge Office. But the port toward which he had strained his weather-worn eyes all through the long coastal trip was a place accursed, a city shuddering under the threat of a nameless horror. He was glad, now, that everything was ready for a speedy departure.

A high board fence loomed at his right, huge white letters proclaiming that behind it lay Morrison's Ship Chandlery Yards. Dan glanced up and down the street. No one was in sight. He wheeled swiftly, pulled aside a loose board whose location he had discovered earlier in the evening, and squeezed through. Trespass or not, this was a short cut to the *Lomand's* berth and he was in no mood to take the long trek around. Dan was fed up on Granport.

Piled anchors, huge mounds of rope, all the various appurtenances of the seafaring trade, were shadowy in the dimness. The captain sniffed the tarry, familiar odors luxuriously. He was through the store yard. Behind this other fence was Exterior Street, and across its cobbles were Pier Nine and the *Lomand*. With the surefootedness of the sailor, Dan ran up a leaning scantling that braced the barrier, swung a leg over— and froze to the spot.

Approaching footsteps thudded along the sidewalk beyond the fence. He was a trespasser, and it would be troublesome if his unauthorized presence in the store-yard were discovered.

In Granport's present state of mind it might be worse. Dan pulled his leg back, crouched so that only the top of his head and his eyes were above the fence-top.

There they were, two policemen flat-footedly pounding pavement toward him about half a block away. They were on either side of the roadway, hugging the curbs well away from the shadows that lay along the pier entrances and the chandlery-yard fence. Dan could see their grim-set faces distinctly, their hands hovering near holsters buckled outside their uniform coats rather than within as was the usual custom. Their heads jerked ceaselessly from side to side in quick, fearful scrutiny of every possibly source of lurking peril. Lorraine's scalp tightened as the tensity of their bodies, their stiff-legged walk, conveyed to him across intervening space a contagion of the icy fear quivering within them. He knew, without being told, the terror that animated them, the depths of courage they were dragging to be here at all. Death—violent death— was a commonplace to them; their business was to face it. But the mummy death . . .

If they spied him up here those ready guns would leap from their holsters, unquestioning, and crash leaden death into him. Any movement to retreat would make sound enough to bring them after him on the jump. His only safety lay in their passing him unnoticing. Dan crouched lower, holding his breath. The thump of the patrolmen's brogans came nearer, nearer . . .

Dan's left foot started to slip, skidded off the narrow scantling!

His fingers dug into their hold on the fence-top. The toes of his right foot worked in their shoe, ape-instinct striving for a prehensile grip that civilized leather defeated. If they'd only walk faster! He could hold on only seconds longer. Then he'd have to twist, to drop, and . . .

The distant thrum of a speeding motor shocked the night silence. Even as Lorraine's remaining foothold gave way the sound crescendoed, was a roar of thunder beyond the fence. The sailor dared a contortion that banged his toe-caps alarmingly against wood, but brought his legs up and under him again. The sound was like artillery fire in his ears. A shout from the unseen street heralded it, and the blast of a police gun.

Dan held on grimly. That bullet had missed. He waited for another. It would be useless now to jump and try to run . . .

But the second shot did not come. There was instead the squeal of brakes, the scrape of skidding rubber, and a bellowed, "Stop, damn you! Stop!"

The *Lomand's* captain pulled his head above the fence-top. A big gray sedan was halted fifty feet from his vantage point, nosing toward him, so that it was evident to him that it had been roaring along the wrong side of the street. The near officer was just putting a thick-soled boot on its running board, the other was turning, starting to come across.

"Where's the fire?" the cop began. "Want the whole street for yourself? Whatcha doin' here this time o' night anyway? Gimme yer license."

"Oh, officer," a girl's fresh voice came from the front of the sedan. "I was just—"

Black smoke belched from the open rear window, enveloped the officer in a mushroom of murky haze! The engine roared into action, the car leaped out of the ebony cloud. Smoke belched from it again, billowing toward the second cop. Dan saw a form catapult out of the first cloud, thrown from the outleaping running-board, a sprawling form whose face, instantaneously, was brown-charred, shriveled like a dried apple!

Then Dan had leaped from the fence-top, had crashed down on the car roof and was sliding off, sliding down over the side and toward the cobbles that reeled past as the auto gathered speed in a swift surge of power.

The captain's leap had been instinctive, automatic, an explosion of his muscles undirected by his brain, touched off by the horror he had witnessed. But now he was clawing at smooth metal that gave no grip, was squirming overside and down—down to be dashed against leaping rock by the swift speed the death-car had attained in seconds . . .

The wind of its passage beat at him, whistled a doom-message in his ears. His feet went over the edge, his legs were following, slowly but inevitably. The rain-gutter caught at his belt for an instant, let go. He slid further as the auto twisted, and roared into some quiet street leading away from the water-front. Its speed slackened, and with that slackening his toes found purchase on a door handle, purchase enough for the sea-trained man to clamp knees on a doorpost, hold himself tight against the car side, and dip, finally, to firm footing on the running-board of the gray sedan.

He clung to sill and fender of the still fast-moving motor, and brought his head down to peer through its front window. A woman was driving the murder-machine. He glimpsed her reddish, luxuriant hair, her up-tilted nose, mouth muffled by the turned-up fur of her coat. She was turning to look at him, her eyes startled . . .

Dan's gaze was jerked away from her by the sound of a rear window opening.

The window was down, and a hand was pushing through it. A hand that held—not a gun, but something gun-like, with a three-inch barrel that seemed to swallow light!

"The black-gas projector!" Dan thought. "The mummy death!" Terror flared in him.

The woman's voice screamed through his terror, "No, Pete. No! He's not a cop! No! Please!"

"Hell," a man's voice growled, irresolute. "You can't let him go, he—"

"I'm not letting him go." She whirled to Dan. "Here you!" she snapped, her voice crackling as no woman's voice should, virulently. "Get in here or I'll let him blast you!"

There was nothing to do but obey. Lorraine managed to get the front door open, to crawl into the car, beside the woman. The sedan leaped into high speed, flinging him backwards into the seat. Hands clutched from behind, forcing him down, forcing his cap down over his eyes so that he could not see. Rough hands fumbled rope around him, bound his arms to his sides, pulled cloth tight over his eyes. The thrumming roar of the motor in front of him crescendoed ever higher as the murder car sped through streets he knew to be night-bound and deserted, sped to a fate he could only imagine. He shuddered . . .

Dan felt the car sway as it swerved, swerved again. The cold night air of open country came in to him now, but his throat was parched dry with fear. The fearful speed of the sedan slackened; he could hear rustling foliage scrape as it pushed its way through some narrow country lane, bumping and swaying. His eyes ached under the pressure of their blindfold, and the fur of the woman's coat irritated his cheek, his hand. But he sensed the warmth of her body, and a little of his fear seeped away.

The car slowed. A hand groped along his side. A throbbing contralto voice said in his ear, "No gun, Pete! He has no gun." The hand slipped inside the flap of his pea-jacket, pulled the ship's papers out of his pocket. He heard them rustle. Then, "Captain of the *Lomand,* are you?"

"Yes," Lorraine muttered. "Yes."

"Seventy-five-foot freighter, Diesel engined." She was evidently reading from the documents. "Five men in the crew. All cleared to sail."

There was a snort from the back. The man's voice husked, chuckled evilly, "Too bad her captain won't sail with her . . ."

"I wonder . . ." the feminine voice mused. "I wonder . . ."

The voice in the rear hardened to cold threat. "What's the idea, Marge? Thinking of letting the mutt go?"

"Well, Pete,"—tentatively—"he's not a cop."

"Forget it. He knows too much; he's seen your face, and the car. I'm not taking any chances, and don't you forget it."

"Hell!" She laughed abruptly, and there was something in the sound of it that made Dan shudder. "That's the last thing I'd do. Only reason I didn't let you blast him back there was because I've never really seen how the mummy death worked. We've always had to beat it before the smoke cleared away. I've only been able to read about it in the papers afterwards and—and I'm curious."

"Oh." Pete's tone was relieved. "I was beginning to think—"

"Nothing like that. Look . . . Here's a good spot—let's do it here." Brakes squealed, the car skidded, stopped.

"Oke. I'd like to work it right, just once, myself." Sadistic eagerness quivered in the gruff tones of the man. The door behind grated, then the one at Dan's right. His scalp tightened and he was cold all over. The sound of peepers crashed in to him from countryside stillness, and the far-off, melancholy hoot of a train. There were people on that train, he thought, for whom there would be a tomorrow . . .

"Come out of there," Pete growled. Dan felt steely fingers clutch his arm, lurched out under the impulsion of their pull. His foot caught in the running board and he crashed down into slimy mud. The woman laughed and a heavy shoe thudded into his side. "Get up, you dog. Get up and take it."

The seaman's arm struck fender-metal. He pulled himself erect, stood swaying. His throat worked, but the sound that squeaked out was not what he was trying to say. He bit his lips. Nothing he could say would do any good—they wouldn't listen. He heard the click of a cocked trigger . . .

"Wait, Pete. Wait," said the woman harshly. "Let him see what's coming. It'll be funnier that way."

"Cripes," the other protested. "You're nuts." But a hand worked at the knot back of Dan's skull and the blinding cloth pulled off. The seaman blinked; sight came back and he saw light from the car-roof tangle in the auburn net of the woman's hair. She had slid over to the seat he had occupied. Dan saw an oval, piquant face, a tiny mouth parted minutely, scarlet as a flower of evil. Avidity quivered in that white face, excitement danced in gray eyes wherein little lights flickered.

"Walk up the road, ten paces, then turn around." White teeth gleamed between ruby lips as she said it. A sense of unreality flooded Dan. Impossible that this girl—she seemed no more—was staging his end in the black death that would blast him to a charred, faceless mummy.

"Get busy. We can't wait here all night."

Dan shrugged, turned away and started off. As he did so he glimpsed at his feet a huge, apelike shadow from which jutted a thick arm and the silhouette of a grotesquely enlarged gun.

"One . . . two . . . three . . ." Meticulously he counted the steps of his death march. "Four . . . five . . . six . . ." Headlight glare made the thick foliage on either side of the road seem artificial, stagey. This was all stagey, unreal. His numbed brain hadn't fully grasped, yet, that it was he, Dan Lorraine, who was about to die. "Seven . . . eight . . ."

If he jumped sidewise, into that thicket . . . an honest-to-God revolver might miss, but the gas-gun would belch its cloud about him before he could reach concealment. Why make further sport for the fiends who played with him? "Nine . . ." The last step. Despair dropped its black pall over Dan. "Ten." He whirled to meet the black death smoke . . .

The scene before him photographed itself on his mind. Pete—half-crouched at the car side, his head monumental on tremendous shoulders, his nose a blob of unshaped dough on a pallid, dead-white face, his shaggy eyebrows penthouse eaves over tiny, glittering black eyes—was stabbing the club-like gas-gun at him for the kill. Dan tensed to take it.

But above the snarling killer a white arm arched abruptly out. Metal gleamed, vanished into the man's back. Blood spurted from between thick lips, burbled over yellow fangs! Pete crumpled. Marge's quick hand flashed out, caught the gas-gun from him as he thudded to the earth. The girl slid lithely out.

"God!" Dan grunted. "God!" Had she been acting a part, playing for a chance to save him . . .?

But her eyes blazed at him, a vulpine fury banished beauty from her countenance. "You," she snapped. "You! Get back here. Quick. Or . . ." The weapon lifted, was steady in a slim hand. "Or I'll finish you myself."

Her voice was thinned by excitement, shrill. Dan started back toward her. The elation that had pounded in his veins when he saw Pete go down under the girl's knife was replaced by a new fear as he drew closer and saw the lines of cruelty at her mouth corners, the shadows lurking beneath her eyes. He recalled how swiftly, how surely, her dagger had gone to its mark, remembered that this was the woman who had acted as lure for the mummy death, and shuddered. It was not for his sake that she had intervened to save him, not for his sake that she had plunged the knife into Pete's back!

"Can you drive?" she asked as he reached her. "Can you drive a car, sailor?"

"Yes." He could scarcely get it out. "Yes." He fancied that the red on her lips was the stain of blood.

"Then get under the wheel. Hurry." Some urgent need for haste crackled in her voice, and the black nose of the murder-gun snouted at his midriff.

Dan fought for control. "I can't drive with my arms tied."

"We'll fix that," she murmured. She glanced swiftly down at her victim, sprawled face down in the mud. Dan started to move; her eyes flashed warningly back to him and he froze.

Her knees bent, the fingers of her free hand closed about the knife-handle projecting from Pete's blood-soaked back, jerked at it. It resisted her pull. Her little foot lifted; one sharp heel was planted between the shoulder-blades of her victim, and she tugged again. The knife came free, sliced through the ropes binding Lorraine's arms.

"Now get busy," Marge said, without a quiver in her even voice. "Hop to it."

Somehow, Dan got into the car, though his limbs were water-weak and his brain quivered with revulsion. The girl, Marge, slid in after him, supple as a panther. The door slammed, the light behind clicked out.

"Go," her voice lashed in the sudden darkness. "Straight ahead." Dan felt the hard muzzle of the gas-gun pressing against his side. The car leaped into motion, almost of itself.

Close-planted trees flicked by as the gray sedan's headlights bored a tunnel through darkness. Almost at once—they couldn't have gone more than a quarter-mile—the girl snapped out, "Slow." Her hand darted to the dashboard and the headlamps clicked off, on, off, on, and off again.

"To the right," she whispered. "Here."

A darker opening loomed against the dark of the bordering trees. Dan tooled the sedan into it, feeling as if he were driving through the gate of his own tomb. Gravel crunched under the wheels, and a curving driveway glimmered palely in starlight.

Something showed in the driveway ahead, the dark figure of a man. Dan braked. The fellow held a stubby shotgun at ready; a vagrant light-gleam showed his gash of a mouth and his prognathous jaw. "Marge?" he called.

"Yes, Sam." The woman's tone was light, pleasant. "The boys been here yet?"

"Yeah, and gone. The junk ought to pay twenty grand, I figger. But dey had to bump the watchman."

"Swell! Come here a minute."

"What . . .?"

"I've got something for you. Come here, will you?"

The man lowered his weapon, strode forward, swerving to the right.

Then abruptly the guard vanished in a swirling black cloud that billowed over him, over the car-front! Marge laughed, and the gun-pressure was back in Dan's side. "Hope he likes that present," the woman giggled. "But I'm afraid he won't thank me for it."

The wheel-rim was hot to Dan's hands and his skin crawled. "Good Lord!" he grunted. "You didn't give him a chance."

Marge laughed again. "No. I didn't," she agreed. "No more than I'll give you if you try any tricks."

The death cloud thinned rapidly, was gone. A shape of horror was draped over the sedan's hood, a faceless thing whose cavernous eye-pits stared with sightless reproach at the windshield.

"Drive on!" the woman snapped.

"But—" Dan yammered. "But—"

"Drive on!" Her voice was relentless, urgent, and the evil weapon stabbed meaningly into the seaman's ribs.

Dan's foot went down on the pedal. The car jerked forward, and the shriveled mummy slid from its perch. The rear wheels of the sedan bumped over something and Dan heard the crunch of bone.

The driveway curved again, a vague structure loomed blackly to the left. "All right," Marge whispered. "Here." Dan braked, switched off the ignition.

"Now listen, sailor," Marge said. "We're going in there and we're going to attend to some things. Remember I'm not taking my eyes off you or my hand from this gun. If you behave you'll be all right; if you don't you'll get the same dose Sam did. It doesn't matter to me, either way. Understand?"

There was no mistaking her earnestness, her intent to do that which she threatened. Dan knew he was helpless, was in the power of an implacable captor who thrilled with the lust to kill, to kill horribly with her over-sized weapon that belched a noiseless black cloud and stripped its victim of all human semblance. She had the face of a woman, beautiful, infinitely desirable, but her soul was that of a devil incarnate. He had seen her kill ruthlessly, horribly, had heard her laugh as she killed.

Dan nodded. "I understand," he muttered. "Perfectly."

"Come on, then." She slipped something metallic into his hand. "Here's the key. You'll walk ahead and open up."

Chapter 3

KILLER'S KISS

The door to the house slammed to behind Dan Lorraine, shutting out even the vague starlight, and the sound reverberated in hollow emptiness. The air here was heavy with dust, with darkness. Dan hesitated, heard the scrape of fabric against fabric behind him.

Suddenly a warm, soft body was pressed against his, moist palms were against his cheeks, pulling his head down. Lips brushed his lightly, tingling! Then, almost before he was aware of her, Marge had slipped away, and her light laugh rang out. "You're a dear boy," she thrilled. "You're just like—" Her voice broke, queerly, into a sob.

Blood pounded in Dan's temples. He was a sailor, just in from a long voyage. And he was young, virile. For an instant he forgot—many things—flung out an arm, groping for her. Then he dashed the back of his palm across his mouth to erase the taste of that kiss, swore under his breath.

A switch clicked and a single bulb spilled dingy yellow light over drab, damp-streaked walls; a splintered, bare floor. A window was covered by black cloth, clumsily nailed. On a wooden kitchen table there were chipped plates, a half-cut loaf of bread, some slices of ham on greasy paper. Dan looked at these and his spine prickled as he realized that the man for whom it had been intended would never finish that meal.

Marge was at the further wall, facing him. Her fur coat was gone and a filmy, gossamer frock only half concealed the rounded, voluptuous curves of a youthful body. Long lashes drooped sensuously over her lustrous gray eyes, and a tiny smile just touched the wings of her lips. But the grim gas-gun was firmly gripped in one hand, while the other fumbled, oddly, behind her back.

Something grated, and Dan was startled to see the solid-seeming wall move. A panel lifted like the curtain of a marionette theater, and a square black hole gaped behind the woman.

Light filtered into the wall-hole, edged a trunk-like box, steel bound. Marge gestured to it with her weapon. "Get it out. Quickly. We haven't much time . . . tide's full in an hour."

The box was heavier than Dan had thought. It scraped out and thudded to the floor. He turned to her. Her under-lip was caught by pointed little teeth, her eyes glared feverishly. "Take it out to the car." She snapped the command.

Dan heaved the case to his shoulder, staggered out. What was she up to, where was she taking him, taking the chest? What was in store for him when she no longer needed him? The black gas? Why go all through this if that were so. Why not drop the thing, turn on her, take a chance on one good blow before the mummy death claimed him? Yes . . . His muscles knotted.

"Put it in the back seat." No, not now . . . It would be suicide, and Dan didn't want to die. Not like that, anyway—not as those policemen had died, and the guard out here . . . He'd get a break later. He'd wait for it.

"And now, Dan darling, for our honeymoon." Saccharine sentiment, mocking, slurred her contralto. "Drive me to your ship, my dear."

Lorraine twisted, his fists clenching. "My ship!" He had been overawed, powerless under the incongruous threat of her somehow reptilian beauty and the doomful omen of the gas-gun. But when she menaced his craft . . . "I'll be damned if I will!" he said.

Her face was a white mask, a Medusa's head that turned him to stone, and the black gun, lifted, was a tunnel of doom. Only her eyes were alive. Gazing into them Dan saw hell itself leering at him. Suddenly the strength went out of his limbs. "All right," he gulped.

Country roads ran under the wheels of the car, endlessly, and as endlessly the treadmill of his thoughts ran through the seaman's brain.

The small houses at the edge of Granport flicked past, then they were in the city. Two police officers on a corner looked at the gray car curiously, and never knew how near death had passed them by. The car vibrated to the cobbles of Exterior Street, curved into the shadows of the pier where the *Lomand* lay, slithered to a halt. Marge whispered, and Dan called, choking, "Ahoy the *Lomand!* Turn out the crew. We sail at once. And get down here for a trunk out of this car."

"Mister Carem's not aboard, sir."

The gun poked into Dan's side. "The mate's joining us at New Scotia," he said quickly. "My wife's taking his bunk till there."

His crew was well trained. In minutes Dan was moving along a dim deck to the after house, Marge close beside him.

Bill Hallam, the thick-necked boatswain, had peered curiously at the woman Dan introduced as his wife, had mumbled evasive congratulations. Then he had gotten the mysterious box out of the rear, had slung it easily to his shoulder. He was padding behind them now. Below deck, the Diesels thrummed.

Fine fellows, these men of his, shipmates for the five years he had owned and commanded the *Lomand*. Friends rather than subordinates. Dan felt oddly hopeful, despite the gas-gun that he knew still threatened him from the concealment of Marge's wrap. They'd sense something was wrong, he was sure, would soon realize that he was not master of his own ship. Only one familiar with the sea could prevent his giving some sign to them that he needed help.

That remark of his about New Scotia, for instance . . . Once out of the harbor the helmsman would become aware that the course he laid would not take them there. Lorraine grinned covertly. The she-devil had overreached herself by pirating his vessel. He had been wise to wait . . .

The *Lomand* was designed for compactness and a minimum crew. Perched on her high stern, the after house included the officer's cabins, the chartroom and, in a recess, jutting forward from the latter, the wheelhouse and bridge-telegraph. Midship was the single well-deck with its derricks, and forward the bow rose to the tiny fo'c'sle. Below were the cargo holds and the engine room. No bunkers were needed; the Diesel's fuel was carried in the skin of the ship's double bottom as ballast. A trim ship, well found . . .

Dan grimaced inwardly as Hallam thumped the heavy chest down on the floor of the chartroom.

"Send Hal Keegan forward to take the wheel, and prepare to cast off."

"Aye, aye sir." The sailor turned on his heels, went out into the dark. Dan turned to the woman.

"You're doing fine." She smiled slowly. "Get out of the harbor and I'll tell you what to do next. I'm going into this room." She indicated the mate's cabin—"but don't forget I'm keeping the door and my ears open, and the gun ready."

Grizzled Keegan came in, his weatherworn eyes devoted. Dan gestured him to the wheel, picked up his megaphone. "Stand by to cast off," he ordered.

His heart had lightened momentarily as the routine of leaving port proceeded along its familiar course. Then his eye fell on the chest, and he remembered the girl sitting in the darkened cabin, the gas-gun with its charge of horrible death clutched in her slim fingers. Fear tightened once more around his heart. What wild scheme was brewing in her distorted, evil brain? Where was she taking his ship, his crew?

Riding light, the *Lomand* pitched a bit to the swells as her prow cut across choppy water. The sky had thickened. Except for the channel lights the dark was impenetrable, velvety. Silver Head's white-green-white winked by.

"Hold her head Nor' nor'east," ordered Dan. He jerked away from Keegan's "Aye, sir," as he felt a touch on his arm.

"Where are we, darling?" Keegan would scarcely notice the mocking tone.

"Out of the harbor—on the open sea."

"Then you have time to talk to me. Come back here, please."

Her right hand was hidden under a long cape. Dan knew what it held. He stepped back into the gloom.

"What course do you want me to lay?" he whispered. Anywhere but south-by-east, he prayed, the direction of New Scotia. Keegan had gumption, would obey the orders without a word, but when he was relieved he'd carry the news forward of the captain's aberration. And then—maybe things would happen.

"Wait." Reflection from the binnacle-lamp just edged her face with luminance. Dan saw uneasily that she was looking at the helmsman, five feet away, and that her eyes glittered strangely. Her arm came out from under the cloak—and abruptly Lorraine knew what she was about to do. He started toward her . . .

Black smoke poured from the gun's orifice—not at him, but at old Hal, intent on the compass! It blotted out the light

there, billowed around the stalwart figure of the old tar. The
ship yawned as shriveled hands let the wheel twirl.

Feet pounded along the deck below and someone called, "Is
anything wrong, sir?"

Dan was voiceless with horror, staring at the prostrate, distorted form of his old shipmate sprawling out of the—death-
cloud. The gun swept around to him. "Tell him no. Quickly!"
Marge snapped, and her face twitched with fierce threat. "Or
I'll blast you, and him, and all the others!"

"No, Bill. Hal slipped, that's all. You can turn in now."

"Aye, aye, sir." The shadowy form turned away.

"Take hold of it, quick. Fix it!"

No denying the urgency in her command. Dan leaped to the
wheel, twirled it back till the swinging compass-card showed
the ship was back on the course he had set. "What did poor
Keegan ever do to you? Why did you do that?"

"Because I wanted to be alone with you . . ." Another ka-
leidoscopic change had come into the strange woman's tone.
It throbbed now with languor, with tingling promise.

Dan kept his gaze steadily ahead, while his brain raced. He
had been weak, a fool. He should have let her kill him back
there at the house. His great body shook to the pound of his
heart. He must find some way to circumvent her, to save his
crew from her murder-lust.

"I didn't want anyone else in here," she said. "Look, you
can do something to that thing so you don't have to hold it,
can't you?"

That suited him, it would leave him free for the desperate
attempt he meditated. Deftly he adjusted the requisite fasten-
ings and turned.

Marge had retreated to his cabin, had snapped on a light
within. She was just within the doorway. Her free hand went
to her neck, her fingers jerked at a collar fastening. The long,
dark cloak that had covered her slipped to the floor. Dan
gasped, his cheeks burned hotly.

Bared white shoulders sloped to a heaving chest that
swelled in turn to rounded breasts. An abbreviated, silken
garment made pretense of concealing deep, voluptuous hips,

and its lacy lower edge frilled along the tops of white thighs whose flat muscles pulsed . . .

The shaken man forced his eyes away, forced them up to the woman's face . . . Her perfect lips were half-parted with strange ecstasy; the pink membrane within her flaring nostrils was startling against the dead whiteness of her skin. Her eyes had darkened, were narrowed and slumberous, alight with promise.

Dan's fingernails cut into his palms, his tongue licked dryness. "God!" he groaned.

Triumph twitched minutely at the corners of Marge's mouth. "Dan," she husked. "Dan. Come . . ."

In his wrists, his temples, Lorraine's pulse throbbed painfully. At the inner bend of his great arms the very skin ached with longing for her. Step by step he went toward her, and desire blazed in his shaken soul, blotted out memory, fear . . .

One little cell in his reeling brain noted that the black gun still swung at the end of one nude arm, that one finger was still curled about its trigger.

He was within the warm aroma of her, the fire within him leaped to meet her fire. She was in his arms, pressed close to him. They were one flame, swirling . . .

For a single instant Dan's vision cleared. He was facing outward through the door of the cabin. Light lay in a broad band across the dark chart-room floor, just reached the prostrate form of Keegan. From the brown, parchment horror of that which had been the old sailor's face two black pits stared up at his captain, and shriveled lips seemed to move . . .

"Dan," the woman on his breast sobbed. "Dan, my love. You will take me far away—and I will make you rich. We will be so happy, Dan, together. So happy. Kiss me, Dan." Her head turned upward, he saw deep down into the depths of her eyes where passion burned. Her hot lips sought, found his . . .

Dan's palm drifted slowly down the coolness of her arm that hung loosely along her side, felt its skin quiver to his touch. Her wrist-pulse pounded . . .

Dan's fingers touched cold metal. They clenched and jerked . . . The barrel of the gun was in his hand, was free!

The muscles of his other arm exploded, flung the girl from him. She reeled across the cabin, stopped herself, twisting. She haunched and sprang at him, like a white panther, her hands clawing, her eyes a blaze of silent fury.

The leap was unexpected, lightning like. Dan had no time to reverse the gun, to use it if he could. He slashed it as a club at the woman's head. She twisted in mid-air, dodging it, and thudded against him. Her nails raked across his cheeks.

Dan staggered back, the gun jarred from his insecure grip by the impact. He glimpsed it skidding across the floor, out of the hatchway, and the woman swarmed over him, snarling, biting, scratching, a naked maelstrom of fury.

They crashed about the cabin. Dan recovered himself, got a grip on the woman, thrust her away from him.

"You fool," she snarled, gasping. "You damned fool!" Her face was contorted, fiendish. Her nails ripped for his eyes, and his jerked-back head barely avoided them. He rolled, bringing her under him, got his hands on her arms, holding her down, helpless.

"Fool!" she spat at him. "You're throwing away what a hundred men would have given their lives to get!" She writhed under his grip, but it held.

Dan's hand lifted, fisting, but murderous fiend as she was, he could not crash it down into a woman's face. Her head lifted, her teeth clicked viciously a half-inch from his arm. He slapped her cheek, open-handed. Her head thumped against board. She was motionless . . .

Lorraine lifted himself, glanced around. A coil of light sounding-line hung from a hook on the bulkhead. In seconds his deft sailor's hand had trussed her arms, her legs.

As he finished, her eyes opened. Tears glinted in them. Her voice was like a little child's grieving. "I thought," she sobbed, "you would take me away to peace—and love . . ."

Dan did not reply. Abruptly he realized that a strange silence brooded over the vessel, that the quiet thrum of the Diesels was stilled. Queer! He strode across the chartroom floor to the engine-room speaking tube, jerked its mouth-piece.

"Tom," he called. "What's wrong?"

He listened. No answering voice came from the tube. "Tom! Joe!" he yelled. "What the hell's the matter?"

Dead silence answered him.

The *Lomand* was drifting, no way on her. From somewhere in his subconscious Dan pulled recollection of a distant shout, sometime during his struggle with Marge—a shout of terror. He plunged to the after house entrance, looked out over the dark, silent deck, toward the black loom of the fore-castle.

"Hallam," he bawled. "Bill!"

He might have commanded a ship of the dead, for all the response he got. Icy fingers clutched his heart. What had occurred aboard while he had been engrossed with melodrama in his own quarters, what had happened to his crew?

Minute sound, an almost unhearable thud, came to his ears, pulled his eyes to the oblong of the engine-room hatch, somber against the glimmer of the deck.

Dan pounded down the after house companion, to that dim opening. He peered down into darkness, his scalp tightening.

"Tom," he bawled, and listened. Only the swash of bilge-water in the *Lomand's* scuppers answered him. The ship lurched drunkenly, and Dan heard the thump of something soft below.

The smell of grease stung his nostrils, of hot oil. And another odor, sweetish, vaguely familiar. The smell of blood. Dan swallowed, let himself down the ladder. There was a switch just here . . . He found it, clicked it on.

Dan was staring, white faced, at what lay on the grating at his feet. A stocky form in blue dungarees, supine, limp. A head pulped, smashed beyond human recognition as a human head. A bloodstained spanner, and a sloshing pool of gore in which lay all that was left of Tom Bailey, engineer!

Chapter 4

DEATH IN COMMAND

Dan Lorraine pulled the back of his hand across his forehead, but he didn't know it. An iron band was around his brow, and shivers ran through his stalwart frame. The woman, Marge, couldn't have done this—she had neither opportunity nor strength. Who, then . . .?

An eerie feeling that something lurked in the gloom, that someone was watching him warily, came dully through the murk of Dan's stunned brain. His eyes shifted, tried to probe the mystery. There was nothing to see back there but darkness. The captain half-crouched, moved forward around the corner of the motor.

A thin thread of yellow luminance sifted through crossbars, pistons of the Diesel. It fell across a black heap ominously motionless, slumped over a guard rail. Dan moved closer, his spine prickling. A white face looked up at him—the face of Joe Neill. But beneath its chin was the black-shirted *back* of the oiler! Lorraine rocked back on his heels. *Some tremendous force had twisted Joe's head clear around on his shoulders!*

In the dead man's unblinking eyes was mirrored horrors; soul-shattering fear. From the corner of his mouth saliva drooled . . .

What was that? Dan whirled to the scraping, furtive sound at his left.

He stared at the blank, sheer wall of the engine-room bulkhead. It was from there the sound had come! Whatever, whoever had slain these men thus brutally—must be in the cargo hold beyond!

There was an entrance to the hold right ahead, little used. Dan's eyes found its dim outline, stared at it. It was closed. His fingers opened, shut. He was weaponless; the killer was powerful, merciless . . .

Dan got the flat of his hand on the bulkhead panel, shoved sidewise. Dim luminance spilled only a little way into the hold ahead; beyond was Stygian gloom. Dan's hand came up, jutting to simulate the blunt barrel of an automatic.

"Come out of there," he boomed. "I've got you covered."

His voice plunged, reverberant, into emptiness. Its drum-thump ceased, and nothing happened. But far forward, where the hull of the vessel pinched in to its knifelike prow, something moved.

A chuckle came out of the blackness. "Come and get me," someone husked.

Distorted, strangely blurred, Dan knew that voice! It belonged to a man whom he had seen killed! His mind flung back to the two dead men behind him. Tom Bailey, an all but headless corpse! Joe Neill, his head twisted as nothing natural could have twisted it! In God's name, what was it that hid in the blackness?

Again that gruesome, grim chuckle! Dan lunged, suddenly, lunged through the open hatch and into blackness. Darted, at a lumbering run, toward that unearthly chuckle!

"I'll get you," he howled defiantly.

Crash! The heavy bulkhead door had crashed shut behind him, shutting off light! Dan whirled around.

A mocking, hoarse laugh sounded hollowly, like the laugh of a dead man, come back for vengeance!

Fiend from hell, or living madman, ghost or human, Dan was shut in with the killer, shut in a pitch-dark hold, closeted with weird and horrible death. For death was here—death turned pirate—death that had conquered the *Lomand,* all but its master, and hunted that master now. Panic seized Lorraine, swept through him like an icy flood, and ebbed.

Of course. His lips twisted, he almost shouted aloud. If he could not see the killer in that absolute darkness neither could the other see him. And this was his ship. He knew every inch of it. Craftiness born in utter fear came to the sailor's aid. If that which stalked him were human at all, the advantage was on his side. *This was his ship!*

Softly, softly, with never a sound, Dan moved through that darkness. Silently, though every nerve was taut, every muscle quivering.

At last his foot found the ladder rung that was his goal. He whirled, darted up the companion! His hands, lifting above his head, struck the hatch-cover he knew was there, thrust it up and over. A final lunge and he was out on the deck. The hatch-cover crashed down again and Lorraine's quick fingers had battened it down.

Now the other, the engine-room hatch, the only other way out for the killer. Dan lifted, whirled aft to dash to that. And saw a white form flick across the window of the after house.

Good Lord! Marge was on her feet, was free! Marge! Killer too! And the gun, the gas-gun was somewhere there, on cabin floor or companionway. If she found that! Dan swerved in his run, sprang up the bridge companionway, plunged through the door of the chart-room.

The woman, still unclothed, lifted to him from her searching stoop. "You," she snarled. She backed to the further wall. "You!"

Dan's eyes flicked around the cabin, saw cut rope on the floor, saw the sharp blade of Tom Keegan's knife.

He started in. He must overcome her, truss her up again, get back to the engine-room hatch and fasten that before the other killer could find his way up and out. "Come here, you she-devil."

Crash! Something thudded against his skull from behind. The world exploded in whirling stars. Dan tottered, sank to one knee, shook his head to clear it. He wasn't out, but he hang there, not up, not down, and his legs, his arms would not obey the frantic commands of his brain.

A shadow fell across him. Great Jupiter! It *was* Pete, huge, repellant, his face blood-bathed. Pete whom they had left, weltering in mud and gore, miles back across the tossing sea! His lips were drawn back in a bestial snarl, his eyes blood-shot. And in his hairy hand the thick black muzzle of the gas-gun snouted! The gas-gun—Pete, ghost or living man, had found it!

But Pete wasn't looking at him, the gun was not pointed at him. Its black muzzle was aimed at Marge; at Marge, standing statuesque in her near-nakedness.

Miraculously, the fear was gone from her face. She was smiling, actually smiling . . .

"Hello Pete," she said, quite calmly. "Where did you come from?"

"From hell." The man's voice was hoarse, pain-shot. "By way of the big trunk on the back of your car, and the stinking hold of this lousy ship. I came from hell, to take you back with me."

Oddly enough Dan found that he could think quite clearly, though his limbs were paralyzed. The man, sorely wounded, had dragged himself a quarter of a mile to the hangout, had gotten into the car-trunk while the two were inside! But Marge was talking . . .

"I'll go with you, Pete," she said, "but not there. Look . . ." Her movement, as always was lightning quick. She had bent, flung back the lid of the iron-bound chest, had lifted again. "Look, Pete, the loot's all here . . ."

The man's red eyes strayed to the chest, but the gun remained cocked, steady on Marge. Dan looked too, saw bundles of green bills, a coruscating heap of gems, flashing a blaze of color. "It's all here, Pete, all that your mob collected while we kept Granport dazed, and we won't have to split it."

The big man grunted. "No. *I* won't have to split it. You're through, double-crosser. You're through. You're going to get the mummy death you gave the cops."

"Wait!" Marge said sharply. "Wait!" Dan could see her breast heave, but her face was calm, steady. "That isn't for me, Pete. Not for me. It was for the cops that hauled me into their back room and gave me the third degree trying to get a line on Stan Kanio. For the cops that blasted down Stan when he was all through and going away with me to run straight. But it's not for me."

"Oh yes it is," Pete growled. "I'm going to use it on you and then I'll laugh while you lie there, your pretty skin brown paper, your eyes white marbles." His mouth twisted. "White marbles—they won't haunt my dreams any longer . . ."

Marge moved a little, and a sinuous wave ran through her body. Dan saw Pete's eyes flame. "Oh yes, they'll haunt you, Pete. They'll haunt you, and my lips that you might have kissed, and my body that might have been yours—if you hadn't destroyed it. Look!"

Her white arms rose and fell, her hair dropped, a cascade of red gold, snaked along her white, glorious shoulders, slid lower till it half-cloaked the glow of her body. The semi-concealment enhanced, somehow, the lure of her, the blood-heating aura that shimmered about her. "You can't destroy this . . ." she purred, and came closer to Pete. "Not this . . ."

Lorraine could see the terrible struggle in the blood-smeared visage above him, the killer-lust fighting with that other lust the white form of the woman engendered. "You can still have it, Pete. You can have me and the loot your mob gathered while the cops shivered for fear of us."

She moved slowly closer, while Pete's thick lips worked. "You'll double-cross me again," he growled.

"I won't!" She was very close to him now. "Wasn't I straight with Stan in those police back rooms? Wasn't I straight with Stan even after they murdered him? You wanted me, Pete—and"—her eyes were veiled—"I wanted you, but I told you you had to wait till I had avenged him, till I'd made them pay for what they did to me. And now"—her fingers touched the gun in his hand—"if you don't use this we can both have what we wanted . . ." Her hand closed around it. "Or you can pull the trigger and have only the loot. Go ahead, Pete." Her voice throbbed, challenging. "Pull it."

"I can't," Pete groaned. "I can't—God help me!" She had the gun now. "Marge—" His big-thewed arms spread wide. "Come to—"

She leaped back. "I'll come—like hell!" The fiend was in her eyes again. "You devil . . . I found out yesterday that it was you that tipped the police to Stan's getaway, so they'd kill him and leave me for you. Well . . . I did a bum job with the knife, but this won't fail."

"No, Marge. No!" the man shrieked.

The black discharge of the gun caught him as he jumped. A single scream came from within the ebony cloud, and the thud of a falling body.

The woman slipped around the edge of the thinning cloud. Her eyes darted to Dan, still half-crouched. "Now you!"

Dan exploded from his crouch. His fist flailed the gun from her hand, he crashed into her.

They catapulted across the cabin, crashed against the bunk. Dan heard the sickening snap of bone, felt the woman's form go limp beneath him. He pulled himself away, saw gray eyes glazing in a white face, saw blood dyeing red lips.

Those lips moved. "Stan," she whispered. "Stan dear. Wait for me . . . I'm coming to you. And the cops can't get us there . . ." The great glazing gray eyes looked up into Dan's face, a smile touched the pain-tortured mouth. "Stan! . . . You've come for me." A white arm swung up, swung around Dan's neck, pulled his head down. "Kiss me, Stan dear . . ."

And with pity strong within his heart, he kissed her . . .

The bloody lips against which his own were pressed went suddenly cold. The form within his arms quivered, was still.

Looking up, Dan Lorraine saw, through a porthole, drab dawn break in a clouded sky.

MADMAN'S BRIDE

A GOLDEN LIGHT bathed the great banks of glowing, varicolored flowers piled high on either side of the altar, and seemed to pulse in time to the happy throb within Ruth Kane. Dr. Forbes' vestmented figure was a vague blur against that glory, the majestic words he intoned a stately rumble. Somewhere at the rail with her were dad, and Jack Storm, awkward in the unaccustomed dignity of the best man's role; and behind her, indicated now by a low, reverent murmur, was the seated host of friends and neighbors come to wish her well. But the only reality to Ruth was Rand's tall form beside her, the strong clasp of his fingers on her hand that he had not released after placing on it the ring, and the ache of her love for him. She had never known that love could *hurt* so much . . .

"I pronounce you man and wife!" Pent breath gusted like a great sigh from the congregation. The organ's first deep note pealed triumphantly through the vaulted spaces of the old church.

In that instant a *smack,* loud and sharp as a pistol shot, exploded in front of Ruth!

She looked up with a start, saw a spread hand dropping from Dr. Forbes' face. The black-clothed arm to which it was attached was Rand's! *In the instant that had made them one he had leaned forward and viciously slapped the aged minister with all his big-thewed strength!*

An outraged roar surged from the nave. Someone thrust Ruth aside. Now Jack and her father had hold of Rand and he was wrestling with them, was tossing them about in a blasphemous struggle on the very steps of the altar. Above their bobbing heads she could see his countenance, engorged with blood, contorted with a strange, berserk rage. His eyes were ablaze with a lurid, uncanny fire—and, horribly, his lips were retracted from their gums in a bestial snarl. He was growling, grunting, like some wild, foul beast! . . . A scream tore at Ruth's throat. But before she could utter it Rand was suddenly limp, the color draining from his cheeks, the swelled veins receding, his look dazed, bewildered.

"All right," he gasped. "I'm all right now."

He staggered as they released him, pulled a shaking hand across his forehead. "Sick . . ." he groaned. "So sick . . ."

An angry buzz zoomed around the girl from the sea of pale, gaping faces below; but the organ had commenced again, chanting the noble strains of Meyerbeer's Coronation March.

Rand's mouth twitched. "All dark for a minute. Dizzy."

Then he was turning to her, was reaching out for her, smiling—somehow wistfully. Quite evidently he had no recollection of the thing he had done. But something was in his eyes that chilled Ruth, some lurking, awful fear.

"Ruth," he said. "My wife!"

She came within the circle of his arms, was pressed close against him. His lips, avidly seeking hers for their bridal kiss, were icy cold, clammy. When she should have thrilled in the ecstasy of union at last with the man she loved, a shudder of revulsion swept through her. Past Rand's shoulder her father's face was gaunt, drawn, his bushy iron-grey brows beetling over irate eyes. She felt Rand's body quiver like a frightened child's, felt the pound of his heart against her breast, and suddenly pity for his distress flooded her, poignant pity and love reborn. Love redoubled because of his need for her.

"My dear," she murmured. "My own. My—husband." And she clung to him, warming his lips with the fire of her own . . .

"Congratulations, Mrs. Parker."—"You are lovely, that gorgeous ivory-white is *so* becoming to you."—"Kiss the bride."—"Leaving right away? We'll miss you."—"Kiss the bride."

A nightmare crowding around her, of twittering females, of whisky-breathed males. Of thin lips, and slobbering thick ones, of smooth faces and prickly, mustached ones engaged in the barbaric custom of kissing the bride. Kind people acting just as if nothing had happened. Acting *almost* as if nothing had happened. Flickerings of repressed horror betraying them. Pitying whispers that she was not supposed to hear. Cluckings of dismay. And a glimpse of Dr. Forbes, statuesque, his pure-white hair a saintly aureole and the scarlet stain of Rand's fingers lurid on his pallid cheek. When would this be, over? Oh Lord, when would it be over? . . .

A murmur, and heads turning. Mouths forming little o's. A break in the crush. Down there, just reaching the door into the vestry room, Ruth's father and Rand, side by side but not looking at each other. Walking stiff-legged and rigid with anger, their faces set, carved out of white marble. What was happening? She must get to them. She must!

"Excuse me." Smile sweetly. Smile! "I'll be right back." Smile while dread squeezes your heart. "No, we're not going now. Not till after breakfast in the Sunday-school rooms."

Ruth's silk rustled down the plush aisle and she felt curious eyes on her, hundreds of eyes peering after her. But she saw only the little arched doorway in the shadows through which her father and her lover had vanished; she knew only that she must get there, that what was going on behind that door was vital to her.

A dim figure was inexplicably at her side, a hand touched her arm. "Wait, Ruth," Jack Storm's voice said. "Don't go in there."

She turned to him. His cheeks were hollow, his mouth a thin gash. Dear, faithful Jack! She had been cruel to make him act the part of best man at her wedding when he—

"Please, Jack. Don't keep me. Rand needs me."

"Rand! That—" He checked himself, veiled the quick blaze in his eyes.

"He's my husband now, don't forget that. My husband." She hadn't meant to say it so sharply. His lips twisted pitifully, and his hand dropped from her arm. Her mind slid away from him, slid to the muffled sound of high, angry voices from the vestry room.

"I'll be damned if you'll take my daughter away from me!" Was it the dark oak between that made dad's voice so thick, so threatening? Rand's, responding, was shrill, thin-edged with passion. "Your daughter! She's my wife. For better or for worse, my wife!"

For better or for worse! The girl had opened the door with an icy hand, was through it. It thudded shut with a curious, dull finality. Rand bulked before her opposing her shorter but thick-set and still powerful father. Although neither moved nor spoke in the instant of her first glimpse of them, their poses were electric with challenge and defiance, quivering with passion and almost tangible hate. The stone embrasure of another doorway framed them, the street door through which she had come a short hour before athrill with anticipation and happiness.

"Ruth!" Both had whirled to the sound of her entrance, and the agonized exclamation had burst simultaneously from both throats.

Rand surged to her, his broadly sculptured countenance purple with passion, his eyes steely dark orbs glittering with threat. His left arm encircled her waist, lifted her effortlessly from the floor. He swung around, and in his other hand a squat, dull-blue automatic snouted venomously.

"She's mine!" Once more Rand was snarling like a maddened beast. "Mine! Stand aside!"

He moved, was striding across the small chamber. Ruth's father was planted square in their path, big hands fisted, head thrust forward bull-like, ghost-pale but indomitable.

"Stand aside, I say, or by God . . ." Rand's knuckles whitened. A muscle twitched at the base of his trigger finger and the gun-muzzle thrust into Ruth's father's vest. A scream tore from her lips.

"Don't! Don't kill my father! Don't!" Her flailing hand struck his wrist, struck down the gun. Her father's fist arced upward.

Rand pounded the blow aside with a slash of his gun, thrust past, his big shoulder staggering the older man. They were through and out in the quiet side-street. Sun blazed whitely around her. The little door crashed behind them and he had flung her into the seat of his grey roadster at the curb, had darted around and was sliding under the wheel.

Someone shouted—her father. Halfway down the block a policeman started to turn. Motor-roar thundered, gears clashed and Ruth was thrust back against leather cushions by the fierce leap of the car.

Hedges, houses, blurred into greyness, streamed past. A screaming skid around a corner past the white, goggling face of a frantically braking truckdriver, then their long, gleaming hood was swallowing the drab ribbon of Middle Road.

It was still early; the highway was almost deserted. They were going north, and little traffic came from the spread of abandoned farms and drear pine-barrens up-state. Speed was permitted and Rand made the most of it.

Wind beat in on Ruth, snatching the breath from her, chilling her. But it chilled her no more than she was already chilled by the violence into which her wedding had exploded, by the tragic conflict between her father and her husband— by the ferocity, the animal fury that had twisted Rand's loved countenance into something utterly unfamiliar, utterly abhorrent. What had taken possession of him? What wild passion had transformed him to a rabid, brutal stranger, this man with whom her life was now merged—*"For better or for worse"* . . .?

Oh God! All her days, all the days of her life . . . She shuddered . . .

But now the strangeness was draining out of his face. Hawklike it still was, slicing the wind that swept back his brown hair from the high, straight rise of his forehead, hawklike and finely chiseled. His brow was creased and his nostrils expanded as to some poignant mental anguish. But he was again her Rand, the lover who had swirled like a whirlwind through her drowsy, nurtured life and swept her off to soar with him in unexplored, undreamed-of regions.

His sigh was dreary, despairing. The car slowed somewhat. "I had to do it, my dear," he said, brokenly. "I had to do it. He wanted to keep you from me."

Pity for him warmed within her—and then she remembered the gun in his hand, menacing her father. "But you would have shot him. You would have shot dad, if—"

"No." The monosyllable was a throb of pain. "I would not. I could not. Not your father. Not the father of my beloved."

She loved him. Oh, God forgive her, she loved him! How hard it was to pull away from him, to set her face in cold, forbidding lines, to say: "You don't expect me to believe that, do you? You were just about to shoot. If I hadn't screamed . . ." The scene was vivid again before her eyes, and terror of him again an icy stream in her blood.

His hands were clenched tight on the wheel. He was bolt upright, unmoving. But the lines of his face quivered with agony, and she sensed his spirit reaching out to her, pleading. His head turned, slightly, so that his eyes met hers, and they were bleak, tortured.

"I would not—have shot. Ruth—believe me, dear. And help me. Please—help me."

She feared him—her blood was cold for fear of him, of the beast she had seen him become. Then why did she love him so? Words trembled for utterance. She did not know what they were and she dared not let them come.

"Once—" Rand's tone was flat, dead—"once you said—you loved me. Ruth . . ."

Far back a *put-put-put* rattled in the stillness. Ruth twisted. A dust cloud raced along the road, its dark center was a motorcycle and the bent-forward form of its khaki-clad, begoggled driver.

As she saw it the roadster leaped forward under her, knives of the wind slashed her. She turned. Rand's gaze was tense on the road, his face livid.

Madly they careened between speed-hazed foliage. Rand's lip curled again to show gritted teeth, grey gums—while worms of green fire crawled in his eyes and sinews corded in his swelling neck. Once more fear tore at Ruth, fear not of speed but of this man, this stranger who was her husband. Her skin crawled with the fear, and she sobbed, cringing beneath the almost solid beat of the wind.

The car rocked, taking a curve, slicing around on two wheels as it roared down the wind, tooled by a madman. A madman! Oh God, was that it? Was that why Rand—?

The *put-put-put* of the following cycle was close behind, close alongside. A gauntleted hand gestured; light flashed abruptly from a gun that it held. Rand snarled, but slowed— slowed and stopped. The highway-patrolman vaulted from his wheel, lunged toward them, his gun blinding in the sunlight.

"Parker?" he growled. "Rand Parker?" He was on the running-board, and his gun was thrust into Rand's face. "Snatch artist, eh. But you're not gettin' far this time. Reach!"

Rand's hands left the wheel, lifted slowly above his head. Ruth's heart pounded. Here was rescue, safety!

Metal clinked and the officer's other hand came over the car-side, handcuffs dangling. "Gimme your wrists, bozo, while I slip these bracelets on."

The line of jaw that was all Ruth could see of her husband's face whitened, writhed with lumping muscles. His shoulders slumped pathetically.

"What is this, officer?" Ruth asked suddenly. "I didn't know there was a speed limit on Middle Road." And she was startled at what she had said, startled that she spoke at all!

The man's florid, grim face jerked to her, the weather-wrinkles about his eyes deepening. "What the . . .! This ain't no pinch for speedin'. This is—Hey! Ain't you Ruth Kane? Ain't you the dame this guy's snatching?"

"Snatching?" Her eyes went wide, puzzled. "I don't understand." What was she doing, what was she saying? The policeman was heaven-sent to her rescue and she was—

"Kidnaping. Ain't this Parker kidnaping you? I got a flash on the short-wave that—"

"Kidnaping!" Ruth's head went back and a laugh shrilled from her, a thin, hysteric laugh. "Rand! Dear!" she sputtered.

"Did you hear that? Jack and dad must have done it. I saw them whispering together just before we started."

Then, to the officer, "Mr. Parker is my husband. We were just married in St. James' Church at Midville and we're starting on our honeymoon. My father and our best man are playing a trick on us."

The patrolman glowered. "Well I'll be—damned." His revolver lowered slowly, and the handcuffs. "An' me near breaking my neck chasing you."

Rand's arms came down; he fumbled in his pocket. "Strikes me," he chuckled, "that the joke's on you rather than on us." Something green crisped between his hand and the policeman's. "Will you drink to our happiness?"

The man grinned. "That I will, and mean it. Good luck to you, sir. The best of luck."

"That I have already. The very best." There was exultation in Rand's voice, and gladness almost ecstatic, "Good-bye, officer."

"Good-bye, and good luck again."

The motorcycle *putted* away. Rand twisted to Ruth, had her in his arms. "Oh my dear. My sweetheart. My wife."

"Be good to me, Rand," Ruth murmured against his greedy lips. "Oh, be good to me. Don't frighten me any more. Please don't let me be frightened any more."

"I'll try, dear. I'll try not to. But you must help me."

Fatigue and the long monotony of the drive had lulled Ruth to sleep. She awoke with a start to grey dusk over which the inverted drab bowl of an overcast sky was clamped tightly down. The road still stretched unendingly ahead, a ribbon of lighter grey between flat, dun fields where no living thing seemed to move. Rand was a silent, carved image beside her, peering ahead with brooding eyes, and beneath her was the rolling hiss of the tires and tiny rattles as pebbles spurted up against the fenders. Otherwise there was no sound, utterly no sound to relieve the uncanny hush of the day's dying. So unchanging was the dreary landscape that almost it seemed to the girl that they were quite still, thrumming a treadmill that would wheel eternally beneath them till the end of time.

Midville was far behind, with its trim, white houses and its spic gardens. Her youth was far behind, her friends, and her stern-faced but kindly-eyed father. It was as if she were in an alien, distant land, wandering alone.

No, not alone. With this man, whom, queerly, she had given up all that was dear to follow. This stranger! Who was he? What was he?

The girl gulped with sudden panic as the realization swept in on her of how little she knew of Rand, of her—husband. Three weeks ago Jack Storm had phoned to ask her if he might bring around a client who would be in town for a while pending some litigation. And a tall, still-faced young man had come up with him through her garden at dusk. Waiting on the porch their eyes had met. Some intelligence had passed between them, and—there had been nobody, nobody in all the world for her but Rand Parker.

Nothing had deterred her, not her father's perturbation, not Jack's stricken pleading. Now she was Rand's wife, her life merged irretrievably with his . . . His life was hers. The dread that brooded in his eyes as they entered into the desolate land that was to be her land, as they neared his home that was to be her home, that dread had come into her eyes too.

It was a leaden lump in her bosom, a crawling fear in her blood, of some unknown menace that waited somewhere on this empty road. This road that lifted imperceptibly for long, grey miles till abruptly it ended against the sky—as if beyond were a void, a vast, horrible nothingness.

And suddenly, even as she felt these things, the road was no longer empty. Ahead, so far ahead that at first it was only a black blotch against the grey, a lonely figure plodded toward the ominous horizon. Even at that distance it seemed weary, terribly weary.

At the instant Ruth glimpsed it, an oath slid through Rand's tight lips and the car surged forward with a burst of speed. It pulled the trudging figure nearer. The girl saw now that it was a woman, black hooded, black cloaked, bent with age.

Motor-roar crescendoed, the roadster was a juggernaut hur-tling through the twilight—hurtling straight at the ancient, quite unaware of the death rushing upon her.

A nightmare paralysis held Ruth; she could not turn, she could not scream. The woman was only a hundred yards away, silhouetted at the top of the ridge. She turned momen-tarily and within the shadow of her hood her face was cadav-erous, skull-like, the yellowed, parchment skin drawn tight.

She dipped behind the crest of the road. The roadster roared over it. And a silent shriek ripped Ruth's throat . . .

There was no one on the road! Slowly descending now, and curving, the concrete stretched away, starkly tenant-less. There were flat, treeless fields on either side, and for a mile ahead the highway was visible. There was nowhere the woman could have gone, nowhere she could be hidden. There ahead, true enough, the trail curved behind a gaunt, straight screen of poplars, but she couldn't have reached it in the time that had elapsed . . .

Brakes squealed. The car slowed, coasted to the poplars and just beyond. Stopped.

Ruth heard a quivering sigh from beside her. But she was in the grip of a cold shudder that ran through her, and her scalp was tight with fear—of the road, and the old woman in black who had vanished, and of Rand. Most of all of Rand. Once again she was afraid of her husband. Her husband! Mad laughter quivered in her breast as she thought the word. *Her husband!*

What was he? In God's name what was he? What strange rage inflamed him that he had slapped Dr. Forbes, that he had threatened her father with a gun, that he had hurled the ton-weight death of his car at an inoffensive old woman alone on a lonely road? Was he a madman? A demon? Her lips twitched. She must be far gone in terror to think that . . . But he could be so tender, his adoration could fold her to him in ineffable warmth. His voice could thrill so with love for her. As so often before. As now!

"Here we are, dear. At last we are here!" Softly, with just a trace of pleasurable excitement.

Ruth's blurred vision cleared. On the right the level desolation through which they had been riding so long continued. On the left—Good Lord—on the left the dark, swaying poplars screened a graveyard! The ancient burial-ground sloped gently up from the road and its tombstones jutted from the matted weeds and vines that had overgrown it like rotted, defaced fangs from the scummed jaws of some impossibly gigantic monster.

One only of the gravestones was new. It was right at the roadside and Ruth read the inscription, at first mechanically, then with an uneasy stirring.

GRESHAM PARKER
1866-1934
Living he taught us how to live;
Dying how to die.
Is there another who can give
Such claim to immortality?
Pray not for him but for those he left behind

Beyond, gloomy shadows lay heavily in the tangle, black and ominous, and at the very center of the burial plot a deeper shadow blanketed the ground. This was the shadow of a towering mausoleum, still whole but smeared with slimy green, somehow decrepit, somehow more dead than the dead it had been raised to contain. Otherwise there was no sight of a house, no slightest hint of any human being..

An awful premonition froze Ruth's blood. "Here?" she squeezed from between rigid lips. "Here? Where?"

Rand gestured—to the gaunt tomb stark against the grisly sky! "Here, dear. Home. This—is your home."

Chapter 2

In the Tomb

Ruth stifled a scream. *Home!* Horror stunned her like a physical blow so that she sat rigid, her heart stilled as if in death, her body sheathed with ice. Horror's talons clawed her breast, her shrieking brain. She retched, and the grey, eerie world circled dizzily around her in a mad whirl wherein two things only were still. The monstrous sepulcher loomed, windowless and somehow blind with the awful blindness of the damned, its great bronze door greenly phosphorescent, slimed, corrupt. And Rand leaned over her, gigantic to her distorted vision, gigantic and dreadful, his teeth flashing a white, fearful grin as his arms slid around her. And, queerly, she did not feel their touch at all.

Words dripped from his smile, searing her. "You know the beautiful custom, my dear," he said. "Of the groom carrying his bride across the threshold of their future home?" She knew it. As every other girl she had dreamed of the time when she should pass through the door of happiness in the arms of her lover. And now . . . *He* had lifted her. She was in *his* arms and he was carrying her through the graveyard.

Shadows that were more and less than shadows slid silently through the rank growth that had nurtured on human bones. Tendrils greyed by the grey dusk coiled about Rand's legs, released them reluctantly. Night's black pall dropped silently down, but the approaching, towering tomb was pallidly luminant with an uncanny glow of putrescence and decay. Home! The gravestones were a ghostly host about her, and dark wings whispered overhead.

Rand reached steps, eroded steps once proudly white. His footfalls thudded dully on their carpeting of moss as he ascended them. Everything else was blotted out by the huge portal across whose ominous high loom a shadow flitted. Wings beat, and a bat wheeled out of the gloom, dropped straight for Ruth. Somehow it was the final, unbearable touch of horror. A scream of agony sliced the silence, a scream from her own throat—and blackness exploded within her skull, swallowed her in merciful oblivion.

~ ~ ~ ~ ~

As Ruth swung up out of weltering darkness the first sensation she knew was that with which she had descended into it. Her body throbbed with horror. Dread was a steely band constricting the pulse of her temples. Fear sent tiny tremors through her slight frame. Despair crawled in her veins.

What was it she had wedded? Was he human at all, this man who had brought her through grey desolation to a rotting tomb? Her husband! Oh God! He was her husband, and the home to which he had brought her was a decrepit sepulcher foul with corruption. What now? What grisly fate awaited her in this dwelling of the dead?

Strange. Warmth beat about her, seeping into the chill within her. That on which she lay was soft to her strength-drained quivering body, and there was no taint of corruption in the warm air she breathed. Warily, fearfully, she opened her eyes—and gasped.

She was lying on her side on a couch, a comfortable, almost luxurious couch. Across the big room she faced flames dancing cheerily in the deep embrasure of a graceful fireplace. Their light was caught in the glowing, ruby sheen of a sumptuous Sarouk rug covering the vast expanse of the floor. Before the hearth a small table was covered with white damask, set with a glittering service for two.

Impossible! No, the other was impossible, the nightmare that had encompassed a grey, endless road stretching into infinity, a black-garbed hag who had vanished, a graveyard and a sepulcher. Exhausted, she had fallen asleep on the long journey, had dreamed awfully. It had been a dream. Of course it had been a dream. But it had been so terribly real.

Ruth sighed in relief. Her lids closed again as the grateful warmth of the fire folded over her. A door opened and closed, somewhere. Footsteps whispered across the rug. She sensed Rand standing above her, sensed that he had knelt beside her. His arm was across her breasts, his hand slid under her armpit, beneath her shoulder. His lips were on hers in a long kiss, and hers responded. Fear, dread were gone in the ecstasy of that embrace. He was her husband, her lover, her other self . . .

"My sweet." His very voice was a caress. Ruth's eyes opened once more, looked into the fathomless depths of his where love glowed. But there was pain there, also, and suffering. And a lurking fear. A hand seemed to tighten about the girl's heart, and she yearned to assuage his inexplicable agony. Her arm stole up around his neck, pulled his head gently down to her breast. His head nestled there like a tired child's.

A new log caught flame in the fire, flared. Fingers of orange-red luminance reached higher on the walls of the room and Ruth saw that they were of damp-streaked, green-scummed marble, window-less, lifting to black impenetrable shadows brooding beneath an invisible roof! Saw that those sepulchral walls were unbroken except to one side where rough, verdigris-patinaed bronze was the inner surface of the door she had seen in her dream.

Then it had *not* been a dream! Horror gripped her throat once more, doubly poignant because of the brief relief, and a long shudder quivered through her. Rand's head lifted. His eyes bored into hers, eyes staring with haunting fear out of a livid face.

His mouth twitched and a whisper, husky with dread, slid from it. "Afraid? Are you also afraid, my dear, of death?"

"Of death?" It wasn't death Ruth feared in that moment. "Why should I be afraid of death?"

"Why?" It was a hysteric squeal. "How can you be otherwise? Inescapably to be completely blotted out—the *you* that thinks and dreams and loves—suddenly to be nothing, inevitably to be—ended—like a candle-flame is ended when one blows it out, how can you . . ."

Rand's wail of terror was more horrible than any the girl could conceive cut off. Now he was listening, intently listening. The muscles of his face writhed in a paroxysm of fear that flared in his eyes like twin pools of black flame . . .

His hand clawed on Ruth's breast. The fire-glow in this chamber for the dead seemed to lose its radiance. An invisible shadow filled the room, some awful presence manifest in neither sight nor sound. Ruth also was listening now, her spine prickling. And sound came to her. A tiny hiss, a minute, sourceless scratching. It was darker in the room. Uncannily it was growing darker though still the girl heard the crackle of the fire. Moving air passed chill fingers through her hair.

The scratching was coming from the bronze portal and it was moving! It was opening slowly, slowly . . . A great crack showed between its leaves from the threshold to the murk veiling their top. The fading light seeped into it. Ruth saw a vague dark bulk in the aperture, saw gnarled, hairy fingers jag the door edge. Saw a hand come in; a hand clenched, gripping the hilt of a rusted knife. And then the light was altogether gone!

Darkness swallowed Ruth. Metal clanged resoundingly. Rand whimpered. The pressure of him on her taut body was gone. Feet padded in the blackness. Heavy, panting breathing was everywhere. Rand was somewhere in the blackness, and someone, *something* else was there too.

Faint whisperings of fabric, the slither of furtive feet, the soft thud of flesh against some furnishing, peopled the Plutonian lightlessness for Ruth with prowling, fearful life. Death stalked the darkness in his own dwelling, hunting down her husband, hunting down her lover. And she might herself have been a corpse, so cold, so unbreathing, so rigid she lay.

But her throat was sore, rasped with unuttered screams, and fear writhed within her. Fear for herself, unutterable fear for Rand. It was not death alone that prowled the murk. It was something worse than death. It was a fate unspeakable. Lightlessness of the eternal grave was about her, and the dank cold of the grave, and in them horror stalked a pallid prey.

Her couch jarred as something came against it. Slimy, rotten fabric brushed across her face, leaving behind the stench of corruption in her flared nostrils. Right above her soft bodies impacted. Someone snarled. An unseen struggle swayed above her, the more awesome because of its grim quiet. There was only a rug-muffled thump of pounding feet, a muted grunting not human at all, a hiss of straining body against body, to betray its progress. But she knew that Rand and the—the whatever it was that had come to hunt him down—were locked in mortal combat.

If only this paralysis of terror did not chain her helpless to her couch. If only she could move, leap up, help Rand. Help Rand—but how? She could not see him, she was utterly blinded, she could not tell where he was, could not tell him from his antagonist. How could she help him?

The invisible battle was more noisy now. Animal sounds came from it, slaverings, gruntings, and again the marrow-chilling snarl that twice she had heard before. The combat whirled away . . .

Then Rand shrieked—once! Horribly. That single screech of awful agony sliced the darkness, sliced the psychic lashings that held her. Ruth heaved from the couch, lunged at the sound, her little fists flailing.

"Rand!" she screamed. "Rand! You—" Her fists found cold and clammy flesh in the darkness, flesh that had no firmness, that quivered under their impact, jelly-like and unresisting as though far gone in decay. Once. Twice. Then a noisome mass pounded across her head, pounded her down, smashed her to the floor, and left her there half-stunned, numbed, unable momentarily to move.

But she could still hear. She could hear a slow slither across the floor, the drag of a heavier body, a moan of pain. She heard the screech of bronze hinges flung wide, and the clang of the closing portal. And she knew then that Rand, her Rand, was not dead—not dead but injured and in the power of the gruesome Thing that had brought eerie darkness with it, and the stench of an unhallowed grave.

That stench was still foul on her breath, but the darkness was lifting. Uncannily as it had come the blackness was fading. Bulking things were taking form in a lurid glow that deepened to the light of the fire that had not gone out, that never had gone out though its radiance had been completely quenched. The returning light wavered across the incongruously furnished parlor within a sepulcher, and Ruth saw that she was alone, utterly alone.

The girl whimpered, lying there. At the edges of the fire-glow that now did not quite reach the walls of the room, formless shadows were ominous, veiling intangible fears. The fire faded and flared and that which they hid surged toward her, retreated, surged toward her once more.

The rug where she lay was the color of blood—was wetted, stained in a dark pool right at her side! Ruth's eyes widened as she stared at the glistening smear. Her hand crept to it, her fingers touched it. It was warm, still warm, and the tips of her fingers where they had touched it were scarlet. This *was* blood. His blood. Rand's blood!

The rusted knife a shaggy hand had thrust through the tomb's opening door had found its billet in Rand's flesh. Rand was wounded, terribly wounded, and that which had come to attack him had carried him away—to finish him! Yes! There were other stains on the rug, a trail of them, and that trail led straight to the door.

Ruth's small hands beat at the rug and a red burst of wrath seethed in her brain. Suddenly she was on her feet, was reeling to the great bronze barrier, her lips a tight gash across her set face, her eyes ablaze with anger. No! The damned Thing could not kill him. She wouldn't let it. She wouldn't let it kill her husband!

She reached the portal, stared at it. There was no knob, nothing by which she could open it. Good Lord! She couldn't get out. She couldn't get out to help Rand, to save him. Why was there no knob? Of course! *The dead need none. The dead never arise to leave their tomb!*

But she was not dead, she was alive. And she had to get out. She had to. Rand . . .

Thinly through the bronze a scream quivered from without. Oh God! Oh merciless God! That was Rand, it must be Rand. He was still alive! He was screaming for help!

Ruth threw herself at the unyielding metal, battered herself against it. It was immovable, ponderous as though embedded in rock. Shifting the attack, she dug nails into the threadlike crack between its huge leaves, broke her nails to the quick in that impenetrable crack, and did not notice the pain, did not notice the oozing blood.

Through her own whimpering, her baffled mewling, she heard Rand scream again, and the tenuous sound was edged with anguish. He was out there, crying for help, crying to her for help against the grisly Thing that he had dreaded and that had taken him, and she could not get to him. Maddeningly she was locked in here and could not get out to help him.

Wild-eyed, Ruth stared around the room, looking for something with which to pound down the bronze barrier, to smash through it.

And she saw another door, there beside the fireplace! A small door of wood—it must be through there that Rand had come while her eyes were closed. Was it another exit?

Ruth hurled herself across the room to it, colliding with a heavy chair, not feeling the shock of the collision. She clawed at the small door's knob, twisted it, pulled it toward her. The door opened, she was through it. She was in a musty-smelling tunnel. Light filtered into it, and she saw its low roof, its damp-blackened walls, its earthen floor. Then the gallery twisted, cutting off light, and her running footsteps echoed hollowly from a vast, black distance.

The passage twisted, twisted again. Stone rasped her face, her arms, rasped the skin from it as curving walls gave first notice of unseen turns. She lost all sense of direction, all count of time. She seemed to have been running for ages through impenetrable dark, through a meandering gallery that bored musty, dank earth. Grave-stench was foul in her nostrils, unseen creatures of the slime scuttered from before her, slithering and horrible. The thud of her footfalls were loud in that enclosed space.

She slipped, fell . . .

And as she lay gasping she heard pounding footfalls behind her, an onrushing thud of footsteps that the pound of her own mad dash had hidden. She was not alone! She was no longer alone. Something followed her through the foul dark. Something pursued her.

She choked down a shriek of pure terror, scrambled to get to her feet. Her hand slithered in slime. She rolled to get a better purchase.

The earth gave way beneath her! She was falling—falling . . . A few feet and she thudded to a stop in soft loam.

Gasping, spitting rank earth from her clogged mouth, Ruth knew that the thud of that which pursued her was close upon her. She tensed in the grip of new terror, tensed to meet its onslaught.

But the footfalls pounded right overhead, pounded past, thudded fainter and fainter in the distance.

That slip, that frightening slide had been fortunate. It had thrown her into some depression in the dark tunnel, thrown her out of the way of whatever it was that pursued her, and it had passed her in the blackness. If she turned back now, back to the tomb, she would be safe. She could lock the little door, bar the bronze one, and be safe.

But already she had tried to get out of that room to Rand, and failed. This tunnel must lead to the outer air somewhere, some time—to the outer air, unimaginable peril, and Rand. It could not go on forever underneath the earth. Backward lay comparative safety, ahead was danger, danger the more horrible because its nature was unknown.

Ruth scrambled out of the pit and turned—away from the sepulcher that now was a sanctuary. Toward the dark ahead and its unknown menace. Toward Rand.

A chill breeze fanned her face. Somewhere close ahead there must be an opening to the outer air. Ruth was running again, running though fear clogged her muscles, clamped her breath.

A curving wall swerved her again. Before her an oval of light showed, glimmering light that would have been darkness were it not for contrast with the Stygian gloom through which she had journeyed so long. Ruth spurted on . . .

Then she saw the glimmer blotted by a still, waiting figure, a black figure whose outlines firmed to those of a little old woman, cloaked and hooded, and bent with age. The little old woman at whom Rand had murderously hurled his car. The spectral old woman who had vanished, inexplicably, in the blinking moment she had been obscured by the dip in the road.

It was too late to stop. Ruth threw herself at the dark, affrighting shape, was tangled in fabric, sleazy, rotted, odorous with corruption, was blinded by enveloping cloth and thudded against a cadaverous, bony figure within it. She heard a muffled shriek like the cry of a screech-owl. The skeleton-like form collapsed under her, but its tangled draperies pulled her down with it, atop it, and bony fingers raked her face.

The girl's flesh burned with cold fire where those grisly fingers had touched. The vileness of corruption pulled into her lungs with each gasping breath. She tossed about, fighting the clogging cloth, fighting the emaciated body that squirmed beneath her, fighting terror that was a gelid stream in her blood, an icy blade stabbing her brain.

Fingers that were bones covered by dry skin clamped Ruth's throat, squeezed, squeezed till her lungs shrieked for air and a blackness that was not of the night welled up in her brain. Crackling laughter rattled through the roar in her ears. She tore at bony arms, clawed arms imbued with supernatural strength, arms that would not move.

A green and ghastly light flashed into being, striking in between Ruth and the ancient hag in whose arms there was such convulsive strength. The girl saw the face of her antagonist—its yellow skin like parchment drawn together, so tight that every curve, every roughness of the bone beneath showed through and she was staring at a hairless skull—yellow-fanged, sunken-eyed, marrow-melting. The ghastly horror of that face stabbed her with a new terror even through the pain of her extremity . . .

And abruptly arms shoved past her own head from behind; shaggy, brutal fingers clutched the bony wrists at her throat and ripped them away. Ruth pulled a gasping breath into her tortured lungs, twisted toward her rescuer.

The huge hairy hands moved swiftly. One slapped over her face, covering her eyes, her nose, her mouth—its leathery skin rasping, its stench foul, noisome. The other slid across her breasts, slid around her, and its arm constricted, holding her tight. She felt bulging muscles ripple against her body, felt herself lifted effortlessly from the emaciated form of the ancient, felt herself cradled in binding arms that were like gnarled tree-boughs come alive. A grating, triumphant laugh sounded in her ears . . .

Chapter 3

A Grave for Two

Ruth lay on a mound of loose earth. Ropes lashed her, cutting into her soft flesh, binding her helpless, and a filthy rag was stuffed into her mouth, gagging her. Pain was a living thing, tormenting her—streaks of pain across her face, where the hag's fleshless fingers had sliced, pain noosing her throat where those same fingers had clamped to choke. Pain throbbed in her body and her temples.

But the physical hurt was nothing to her mental agony, the torture of her grief and her despair. For in the wan green light coming from a torch stuck into the earth of the abandoned graveyard, another form lay next to hers.

Gruesomely still on the bed of fresh-dug, foul loam, Rand's fine-chiseled face was a ghastly green cameo against the black dirt, its features frozen to a mask of infinite terror. He was not bound—there was no need to bind him. His body did not stir; it crouched there flaccid, unmoving, and across his dark breast a darker stain was his own clotted blood that had

ceased to flow. She could see the gash through his jacket—
the gaping wound a rusty knife, slashing in the dark, had
made.

Dull sound impacted her hearing, the thud of a spade sinking into yielding soil.

The green luminance was blackened by a moving shadow
that passed over her, and flattened, momentarily still, on the
loam beyond. A twisted, grotesque thing that shadow was;
the umbra of an ape-man from the mists of prehistory; a jutting-jawed, barrel-chested, long-armed being one step above
the beast, the more foul because human passions tainted the
clean cruelty of the beast. The shadow moved again, the
thing that cast it grunted, and earth arced, spattered to add to
the pile where Ruth and her husband lay.

She had sworn not to look at him again, but the irresistible
fascination of infinite fear pulled her aching eyes away from
Rand and to the digger. The green torch was behind him, its
radiance hazed by the effluvium rising from the ancient
graves, and he bulked against it a black, formless silhouette.
But Ruth could make out a browless, prognathous-jawed
head, huge in itself but incongruously small to the vast spread
of shoulder on which it was pressed. She could see the
shaggy, enormous black body, the muscle-bulging, simian
arms, the short, thick legs spread to the tremendous weight of
his torso and curiously bent at the knees. And the green light
filtered into the hole the man-beast was digging, the square-
sided, rectangular hole the monstrous sexton was cutting in
the stinking black loam of the graveyard.

Granules of earth slithered away from her as a shudder
Ruth could not repress took her bound, slender form. That
hole was a grave—of that there could be no doubt. It was a
grave—but it was wide, too wide for one corpse. Too wide
for the corpse of her murdered husband alone. *Who else was
doomed to lie in that rapidly deepening mortuary pit?*

Once more the question pounded at her brain, and again
thought fled gibbering from the obvious answer. That horror,
that ultimate horror, could not be. There must be some other
corpse hidden somewhere in the sepulchral gloom of the ne-

cropolis, behind one or another of the leaning, decrepit gravestones so ghastly green in the torch's flickering luminance, some other victim of the midnight delver. The woman, perhaps, the old woman who was anyway half a corpse. That was it, he had killed the old woman too and he was going to bury her with Rand.

The spade struck deep. Something white gleamed in the load it brought up, a bone. There were others piled to one side, helter-skelter, the desecrated bones of those who were being dispossessed to make way for new tenants of the soil where so long they had slept undisturbed. Clawed, hairy fingers plucked the newest relic from the shovel-load, flung it to the pile. It rattled, and a skull rolled away, brought up against some roughness, rocked a bit so that some awful return of life seemed to have come to it as it grinned up at Ruth.

Something touched her side, fumbled at her lashings. Somehow the girl resisted the startled jerk of her muscles, kept herself rigid. She rolled her head slowly, neck muscles taut and quivering, icy with fear lest the motion attract the killer. No one was beside her but Rand, no one at all, and he was motionless, death-flaccid as before.

No, not quite as before. His arm had moved, the arm toward her, so stealthily that even she had not heard its slow creep. His arm was extended to reach her and it was his fingers that worked at the knots that bound her. He was not dead! Rand was alive!

Thank God! Oh thank God! Rand was alive! At the moment that was all that mattered. Her lover was not dead. And in minutes he would have her free so that she might fight for him, fight for him and herself. A surge of strength warmed her chill frame, a surge of determination heated her numb brain. Somehow they two would beat the shaggy killer, somehow they would escape the fate to which he had doomed them.

A change in the tempo of the chunking spade-strokes brought her head around again. The ape-man straightened. The long shovel-handle stuck upright from the earth-bank where he had thrust it. He was finished. Oh God! He had finished the double grave too soon!

From beneath the beetling bush of his eyebrows his little eyes slid to her, caught the light and were twin green orbs glittering menace, grim, reptilian menace. Thick words mumbled from between his protruding lips.

"Enough. Big enough."

His flat-topped, simian head canted a bit to one side, as though he were listening. Ruth heard no sound, but that gargoylesque head nodded gravely and the brute-formed half-man lumbered into motion, coming toward her.

The fumbling of Rand's fingers had ceased, and the ropes were tight, tight as before. Every cell in Ruth's body shrieked protest, her brain crawled with terror and despair. The killer was coming for Rand, was coming to deposit him in the grave he had dug. The killer was right over her, had paused, was stooping.

His great arms stabbed forward and his hairy hands closed on her. The retreating slope of his animal face writhed as yellowed fangs showed in a cruel grin and his fetid breath stank in her nostrils. He heaved. She came up in his grasp, twisting futilely in the grip of hands that clamped ankles and wrists with a clutch of steel. He half-turned, ignoring her feeble struggles, and threw her—straight into the gaping maw of the grave he had dug!

She thumped to its noisesome floor, but did not feel the pound of her body for the smash of realization that stunned her mind. *She* was the other destined for this earthly crypt. *She,* alive and conscious, was to be buried here. Buried alive!

Thump! Rand pounded down alongside her, threshed, groaned. Her husband lay next to her! A spasm contorted Ruth's body, mad laughter tore at her throat. God! Oh God! This was their wedding night! This grave was their couch, their nuptial bed! From church to sepulcher to grave—was ever honeymoon a nightmare such as this?

He was alive, and she was alive, and they were in a pit that was a grave, and the first clods of earth that were to bury them thumped down. Another!

Rand rolled. Concealment useless now, his fingers tore at the knots that bound her and his voice rattled in her ears. "Ruth. Pull. Try to loosen them." His voice was thin with terror. "Help me."

Useless. Worse than useless to struggle as earth rained down on them from the mad sexton above them. Mad? Of course he was mad, and she was mad, and this wasn't happening at all.

She could see the great, grotesque figure up there, could see the sweep of his spade over the aperture and see the earth slide off it, thud down. She saw misty light behind him.

Abruptly, then, there was a swirl of blackness behind him. A skinny arm darted out of folds of black fabric. A knife arced and suddenly vanished in the jointure between the bullet head and bulking shoulders. Blood spurted, sprayed over Ruth and Rand.

And in that moment the ropes came free! She twisted, clawed at Rand. The two lifted; their heads came up out of the grave as the ape-man slid past them down the grave-side. The gaunt figure of the hag was black against the pale loom of the mausoleum, and the knife in her hand dripped scarlet. Then she was twisting, turning to run.

Words burst from Rand, a great, sobbing cry. "Wait! Don't go away. Don't!"

He had scrambled from the grave, but the old woman was a flitting shadow among the tombstones. Rand plunged after her. Ruth got hands on the crumbling earth of the grave; her feet groped and found a lift in something that heaved under them, something she knew was the body of the ape-man not yet dead. Fingers clutched her ankle; she kicked viciously, leaped. She was out of the grave, was on her feet; she was running after Rand, already far off in the sepulchral vista of the burial ground.

She was running after Rand, and he after the flitting black shape of the woman.

"Rand!" Ruth screamed. "Rand!"

"Come on," he flung over his shoulder, not turning. "Come on." And suddenly the woman was gone.

She had vanished in an oval shadow near the road, and Rand plunged into that shadow, vanished too! Ruth skimmed past a leaning stone, twisted to the dark place where the two she followed had flicked into nothingness, saw that it was an arched opening in the earth. Ruth dived into it.

Musty blackness closed around the girl, earth thudded beneath her pounding footfalls and a stone wall scraped her arm. She was again in the tunnel along which she had fled from the tomb—and far ahead of her was Rand, and ahead of him the woman in black. The pound of their feet was a thunder in the passage—the pound of their feet, Rand's shout, and the woman's shrill scream.

It seemed to Ruth that there were fewer turnings in the black passage than when she had fled along it before, and that it was longer . . .

Then abruptly its floor lifted under her feet. Light burst on her, across which passed the two she pursued—Rand now close upon the black-cloaked woman. Then Ruth was out of the tunnel.

But not in the mausoleum. This was, queerly, an old-fashioned parlor with velour-draped windows, a dusty what-not crammed with gim-crackery, a fretted table at its center on which burned a round-globed lamp. And in the room's center Rand struggled with the old woman in black.

No! He held her in his arms! The hood was dropped back from her skull-like head, and—Good God!—he was kissing the fleshless lips!

The panting girl's eyes went wide with panic. Was he mad? Was her husband indeed a madman?

Rand's face lifted from the woman's, and it was alight with joy. "Mother! It's all right. I'm over it now. I shall never be afraid of death again."

"Your father was cruel, then, but he was right." The thin, quavering voice was wholly human, and Ruth saw now that her visage was tender somehow, and gentle—that only the tracing of years and suffering had made it seem so horrible.

"You will be the happier for this one dreadful night." Her thin, transparent fingers touched his cheek. "You understand and forgive him now, do you not?"

Rand's countenance hardened. "I understand and I forgive him for myself, but not for what he has done to—my wife. If I had known—" He turned, his arm reached for Ruth, and trembling, she slipped into its circle, felt it tighten—"what it would do to my brave and loyal wife . . ."

"Brave and loyal is right," his mother interrupted, "and very sweet." Her eyes were pleading. "So brave and loyal and sweet that I am sure she too will forgive us when she understands."

There was something so pathetic, so appealing in her tone and her expression that Ruth could not be harsh. "What is it," she asked, "that I am to understand and forgive?"

"The horrors you have passed through tonight." Rand's mother sighed. "The shock of being brought to a tomb to pass your bridal night. Perhaps Rand should not have done it. Perhaps he should have permitted himself to be disinherited . . ."

"It wasn't the money, Mother. If that were all . . ." Rand made a gesture of renunciation. "It was because it was father's last wish and I could not refuse."

Ruth looked from one to the other, bewildered. Her husband's cheeks were still waxen-pale, his eyes anxious. His mother smiled wistfully. "You see, my dear, what emotional strife he must have passed through."

"Yes," Rand croaked. "I think I was half-mad with resentment during the ceremony. I don't remember anything but the beginning, and kissing you at the end. Once, even, I thought I saw his face in front of me and that I slapped it . . ."

So that was why . . . But the old woman was talking. "My dear, we Parkers are a strange family. My husband Gresham was moody, perhaps eccentric. But a wise man. A very wise man. I had two sons. Paul, the oldest, was born—well, you saw him outside tonight . . ."

Ruth gasped. "That was your son! Rand, that was your brother . . . !"

"That was my son, and my cross." Tears showed in the old woman's eyes, and agony. "We were quite sure his deformity was only physical, though he was never very bright. Certainly he was never violent, until—" She stopped, shuddered. "But that comes later . . .

"Rand, while otherwise a normal boy, has been afflicted from earliest childhood with an abnormal fear of death. He used to awaken at night screaming, and sob in my arms that he did not want to die, to *stop*, as he put it. As he grew older the fear grew worse . . ."

"I suffered the tortures of the damned," Rand put in. "Sometimes I cursed my parents for bearing me so that I should know what it is to live and be aware that inevitably I must die . . ."

"Wait, Rand, let me tell Ruth. This omnipresent fear of his preyed on his mind till we were afraid that he would become insane. Gresham tried various schemes to cure him, but never successfully—until, on his dying bed he thought of something.

"He put it in his will. After setting aside a life income for me, his property was to be held in trust until Rand married. On his wedding night Rand was to bring his bride to the mausoleum in the graveyard over the hill, without giving her a word of explanation, and spend that first night there with her. You see, he wanted to tie up his son's happiest experience with the thought of death, and thus invest that thought with something of the glamor of the other.

"If Rand failed to obey, all the property was to go to Paul. If he went through with it Rand would get the estate."

"Oh horrible!" Ruth shuddered.

"Yes, very horrible. But wise, except that Gresham could not have foreseen that Paul would have gone violently insane while Rand was away discussing the trust with Mr. Storm, his lawyer . . ."

"Was he insane, Mother?" Rand broke in. "After all, if he drove me away from the tomb, or killed me, he would inherit—"

"He was insane, Rand." The old lady's response was peremptory, but Ruth wondered if she quite believed it. "My—my daughter—" Again that wistful smile—"If your experiences tonight were terrible, what do you think mine were, knowing that Rand was coming with his bride and that my other son was lurking somewhere to kill him? How do you think I felt, watching on the road to intercept Rand? What horror do you think was mine when I saw your car coming, and at the same moment saw Paul crouched in the mouth of the tunnel Rand had dug so that he could get in and out of the sepulcher unobserved—Paul with a knife in his hand that he meant for his brother? I chased my mad son . . ."

Rand stirred. "When I saw you out on the road I knew something was horribly wrong and speeded up to overtake you. But you were gone by the time I got over the ridge. The first I knew it must be Paul was when the screen I had rigged to cover the fire, whenever the tomb-door opened, began to drop—"

"I caught Paul and locked him in his room, but he got out again and—"

"Wait," Ruth cried. "Wait. I can imagine the rest. I don't want to hear about it. Not ever again."

"Ruth!" Rand's voice was husky, broken. "Then you cannot forgive me! But—I can't blame you . . . I'll take you home in the morning, and—"

Ruth's hand touched his lips, stopping him. "Silly. You will take me nowhere in the morning." A great wave of pity surged within her. "I *am* home. *This* is my home. And we'll forget all the horror and I shall try to make you very happy from now on, you—and Mother . . ."

Rand's exclamation was a great shout of joy as he gathered her into his arms. "Then you forgive me?"

"Of course. Of course, my husband, my lover. Of—"

The pressure of his lips against hers, choking off utterance, was so sweet, so sweet . . .

SATAN'S BEDCHAMBER

Chapter 1

TRAPPED BY THE CLOUDBURST

Elise Gornoff whirled as she glimpsed the sudden swoop of some black, phantasmal thing from the corner of her eyes. A soundless scream constricted her throat . . .

But there was nothing there! Nothing at all was in the huge, beamceilinged living room of the house on Phantom Island, save the black shadow-shapes that always lurked here, more fearsome now because of the approaching storm's lurid murk . . . Then for a single, searing instant, the age-darkened grain of an oaken wall seemed to writhe, as though something were melting into it!

A rumble of thunder from the leaden sky faded, and the black surge of terror in the girl's veins ebbed. Her delicately modeled mouth quirked in a brief smile of bitter self-mockery.

She was silly, childish, to be so startled. There were no evil wraiths on Phantom Island, despite the old wives' tales that had kept island and house uninhabited until Serge Gornoff had brought his bride here. Two hundred feet across the west branch of the River was Waterville, a bustling, congested city. There was nothing to fear . . .

Wood scraped against wood, beyond heavy portieres that cut off her view of the hall beyond. Elise's heart thumped. They were coming out of the mysterious room whose entrance was a secret panel in that hall's oak-lined wall. Serge was coming out of it, and Nikita and Pavel. Their dull footfalls broke the cowering stillness of the house.

In what dreadful ritual did they engage in that room she was forbidden to enter, forbidden even to mention? The old, futile indignation flared up in Elise. She was Serge's wife! Even though he were fifteen years older, she was his wife and had a right to share his secrets. A better right than the two servants, even though they had accompanied their Baronn on his flight from the vast, dim Russia that had rejected him and his class. She should long ago have demanded to know . . . But she was afraid to know.

The curtains swung apart, and Serge Gornoff came through them. "My dear," he said. He moved across to Elise, his feet whispering on the rug. The girl's throat pulsed at the sight of his tall, distinguished figure, and her love for him was a dull pain in her breast. "You are beautiful, here in the dimness. Like a white flame. A lonely flame." His ascetic face was lined with weariness, not of the body so much as of the soul, and pain dwelt deep in the dark wells of his eyes. At his temples a hint of white edged the iron lustrelessness of his hair.

"I am always lonely, Serge." Elise swayed toward her husband, gave him both her hands. His were icy, but they closed on her slim fingers and clung with a strange fierceness, as if he were afraid that she would be taken from him.

It was this savage possessiveness of his love that had made her marriage a long agony of loneliness. He had isolated her on this island, had cut her off from all her old friends in a semi-Oriental seclusion . . .

"Tonight it will not be so lonely here, when our guests come."

The girl's heart thumped suddenly with warm gratefulness. He was actually looking forward to their arrival. He was human, after all . . . Thunder, nearer, deeper, growled in the heavens.

Gornoff glanced at the lurid, glowering oblong of the window. "Or perhaps they will not come." He seemed disappointed. "This is no pleasant place in a storm."

"That isn't stopping them. I watched them cross the foot-bridge from the mainland, a while ago. They're climbing up the hill, through the woods. They are coming . . ."

A voice from the hallway interrupted her. "They come, panya." Elise turned to face the bent figure in the archway. Nikita's grey, stringy hair straggled across her hook-nosed, witch's face. "But they not go away . . ."

With an exclamation of sudden anger Elise sprang across the room. "You . . .!" Her fingers dug into fleshless bone of the woman's arm. "What do you mean?" Wrath choked her voice. Wrath and icy, sudden fear. "What . . .?"

"Elise." Gornoff s voice was suave, unexcited. "You forget yourself . . ."

The girl whirled to face him, her grip on the hag unrelaxed. "No, Serge. I've just remembered myself. I've just remembered that it is I who am mistress here—"

A vast, rumbling torrent of sound cut her off—a roaring that battered against the house from without. The stone-walled edifice, the very ground beneath it, shuddered under the tremendous detonation . . .

Gornoff, in the window bay, stood taut and quivering against the glare of blue lightning. "Bashe moi," he grunted. "Good Lord! The River . . ."

Elise, her passion suddenly puny against whatever cata-clysm had loosed that detonation, found herself standing be-side him. There was no rain as yet, but a roaring, solid gale pressed the forest down; and beyond it—beyond and be-low—a twenty-foot wall of water rushed down the river channel.

It thundered down on the footbridge. There was no longer any bridge, there were only a few tumbling sticks of timber harried by a chaos of rushing, foaming water. The base of the island was engulfed. The low river-bank streets of Waterville across the incredibly widened stream vanished.

"A cloudburst in the hills!" Gornoff exclaimed. "Look." Elise turned in the direction of his pointing finger. The north-ern sky was menacing midnight black. "We're cut off from the mainland. Your friends will have to stay here longer than they thought."

"Cut off!" The girl gasped. Was that what Nikita had meant? But how could she have known . . .? "Serge! They're in the woods. Will they . . .?"

"Here they are." A wind-tossed figure appeared at the edge of the clearing before the house, then another; but something in her husband's tone pulled Elise's gaze away from them, to his face. Fingers of icy fear squeezed her heart. That patrician face was darkened by virulent hatred. The eyes were red embers . . .

"Serge! I . . ."

No, she was mistaken. It was only that the black pall over the sky had thrown a shadow across Serge's countenance, only that his pupils had mirrored a lurid streamer of angry sunset that had broken through the clouds in the west.

"What, Elise? What were you saying?"

"I . . . I forgot to tell you. Beside my sister Naomi, the Falks, and Dick Tyler and May Bailey—I asked Hugh Rayne too."

They were struggling across the clearing, clinging to one another against the wind's blast, the girls shrieking with bewildered laughter at their own helplessness . . .

"Rayne . . . Oh yes, the young man who I displaced in your affections."

Why did Serge say it so slowly, so gloatingly . . .? "I thought perhaps that being here with Naomi, he would decide to like her as well as he once thought he liked me. I thought . . ."

Gornoff didn't seem to hear her. "That makes it perfect," he was saying. "Perfect."

What did he mean? Elise moistened her lips, and felt a weird, vague fear at her husband's words. Suddenly she knew she shouldn't have asked Hugh Rayne to come to this house. She shouldn't have asked any of them. It was a trap. It was a place of black menace—and Serge Gornoff . . .

"Elly. Elly dear." A small, slender girl burst through the drapes, pattered toward her sister. Naomi Wilson was blonde as Elise was dark, her red lips made for kissing. "Isn't it a shame. Hugh couldn't come with us. He said he'd get over later, but now he won't be able to . . . what? What's that you said?"

"Nothing, dear. Only that I am glad that you got here safely." But Elise lied. What she had said was, "Thank God—thank God."

Chapter 2

SOUVENIR OF MURDER

Dick Tyler and Wally Falk had wanted to go back to Waterville. The flood, they feared, had spread wide destruction in the low-lying slums along the riverfront, and help would be needed. But there was no boat on Phantom Island, and even if there had been it could not have lived in the seething torrent the river had become. So perforce they had to remain, to May Bailey's palpable relief.

"Maybe you're losing a chance to be a hero, Dick," she said, grinning impishly. "That's all right with me. I look swell in black, but grandma's wedding dress is a dream, and it would be a shame not to wear it."

Wally Falk laughed, curtly, bitterly, at that, and Elise Gornoff caught the flicker of a strange look in Ida's hazel eyes as, slitted between long, dark lashes, they had flitted from her husband to May. There had been rumors about those two, Elise had recalled . . .

After dinner, in the living room, Elise became poignantly conscious once more of gnawing, baseless dread. The night lay black against the window through which she stared, and the sound of rain on the glass was like pale, blind fingers fumbling at the pane. The wind rose, moaning . . .

"Like a woman waiting for her demon lover," Naomi quoted, pressing close to her. "That's how I feel tonight. I wish—oh Elly—I wish that Hugh had come."

"He's grand, isn't he," Elise murmured, "with his broad shoulders and his laughing eyes, and his tousled red hair one always wants to smooth?"

"Elly," Naomi laughed teasingly, her voice louder than she intended. "I believe you're still in love with Hugh. Is that why . . .?"

Elise didn't hear the rest. She had a sudden feeling of harsh, inimical eyes upon her, and whirled about to find her husband watching her, his face contorted into a mask of almost maniacal rage.

The girl gasped—and the look was gone. Had she imagined it? Had he heard . . . Pavel, simian-armed, barrel-chested bulked between the parted curtains. His clothes were wet with the rain.

Serge swung around, as if instinctively he knew the man was there. Pavel beckoned. Gornoff's feet whispered across the rug. The drapes swung shut behind the two.

Tiny chills scampered Elise's spine. Definitely there had been something furtive about the way Pavel had signaled Serge . . . Nonsense. He acted only as a well-trained menial should . . . But there was a sound of wood scraping on wood, out there in the hall.

They were going into the secret chamber! Even with guests in his house Serge couldn't keep out of there! Was it because there were guests in the house . . .?

"Elise," Ida Falk called from the floor where she was curled, a small bundle at Wally's feet. "I wish your husband would tell us some more stories about Russia's glorious past. He . . ."

"I'll do better than that." Serge's voice announced his return. "I'll bring you a voice from that past." He had a book with him, a tome so huge it took both his hands to carry it. The leather with which it was bound was scuffed, ragged, and greenish with age. "Perhaps it will tell us things the old Boyars knew, things that men have forgotten." His wife had never seen that volume before. Had it come from the hidden room?

Gornoff placed it on a table, carefully. "All the world has heard of Rasputin," he continued. "The last Tsar and his family were completely under his uncanny dominance; and it was because of him the dynasty ended in the scarlet of fire and of blood. All Russia called him the Mad Monk. He was not mad. He was a monk. But he did not serve God."

They were sitting up now, Ida, and May, and Hal, and Wally. Something in Serge's low accents, a green flicker of flame in his black eyes, was gripping them. Naomi moved closer, and Elise's hand went out, as if to snatch her baby sister back from the brink of some yawning, invisible chasm . . .

"Rasputin—his body at least—was killed one frosty midnight by a group of nobles more loyal to the Tsar than the Tsar himself." Gornoff's voice quivered with some obscure, remembered emotion. "Those who killed him, too late, were executioners—not assassins. Nor looters. There was only one thing missing from the contents of his house where so many men—and women—had lost their souls. This book."

He smiled. That smile was a grimace of nickering mockery, making almost satanic his thin, sardonic face. "There is one section that appears to be the basis of that modern pastime of numerology you have all played with and laughed at. Would it amuse you to test the ancient method?"

"Oh, what fun!" May exclaimed, her eyes sparkling. "Let's!"

But Elise wanted to scream, "No! . . . No!" And wondered distractedly why she felt such an impulse.

"We shall start with you." Pencil and paper lay on the table beside the book. "M-a-y—B-a-i-l-e-y." Serge was jotting down the letters, performing some abstruse calculation. "Your number is one-two-four." He opened the book, ran a finger down a crackling, parchment page. "Here it is."

Gornoff's fleshless lips moved silently, as though he were translating. Then: "Beneath a shimmer of sunlight on rippling waters, a warm spring wells, wherein love may find quiet nurture . . ."

"How in hell . . .!" Tyler ejaculated. "You couldn't know that." His arm was around his sweetheart, drawing her close to him. "I'm the only one who knows what this kidding little nuisance really is."

Again that flitting lip-movement of evasive irony. "The hand that wrote that is dead a thousand years. The truth is eternal if one only knows where to look for it. When Miss Bailey's mother named her, she fastened upon the babe her nature—and her fate. Her fate . . . There is more. Listen. 'But too soon death's frost will clutch the green-gleaming lake, and still its laughter forever.' "

"I told you I was a cold proposition Dick," May laughed. "Watch out." There was no humor in her laugh . . .

"I say," said Wally Falk, starting forward. "This thing's likely to make one or two of us damned uncomfortable. Why don't we try it on someone who isn't here. Someone we all know . . ."

"Hugh Rayne," Naomi breathed. "Please, Serge. Work it out for Hugh Rayne."

Gornoff shrugged. "Very well." His pencil was busy again. Elise could not be quite sure, but she thought a tiny muscle twitched in his sallow cheek. He finished his calculations, turned a page or two . . . read . . .

Suddenly he closed the book with a bang, his lined features bleak, his lips drained of blood. "Perhaps we had better do something else."

"What is it?" Naomi demanded. "What did it say, Serge?"

His hand was trembling. "I had rather not."

"Oh, I say," exclaimed Dick Tyler. "You can't leave us up in the air like that. Read it."

"There was very little there," said Ida Falk, peering over Gornoff's shoulder. "Only five words. All the other numbers had a lot after them."

"What did it say, Serge?" Elise bit her lip. She didn't want him to answer—but she had to know. She had to know what the esoteric volume had said about the man she was planning to mate with her sister. "Please."

"If you ask it," Gornoff bowed, "my dear." He opened the book again. Quickly, too quickly, he found the right page.

Almost as if he had kept a finger between the leaves to mark it. Was his reluctance only feigned?

He read the guttural, harsh syllables aloud, the meaningless Russian. And then he translated.

"Six—sixty-six—" he said, tonelessly. "The number of the beast."

The words were followed by a sudden, queer hush—a silence in which dread seeped into the very bones of the listeners, penetrating skepticism as the chill of an early spring rain pierces even the thickest clothing . . .

Naomi whimpered. "The beast. What . . . what . . .?"

Dick Tyler answered her. "I know. I remember it from comparative religions at college." His fresh, young voice seemed to affront the brittle silence. "The beast is the incarnation of the great antagonist, the avatar of evil. He roams the earth in the dark and the tempest, seeking those whom he must destroy. The old chiromancers had a word to evoke it. It—it's on the tip of my tongue. I've got it. It's . . ."

"Stop," Elise shrieked. "Don't say it. Don't . . ."

Nikita suddenly appeared beside Gornoff. She laughed her cackling, senseless laugh. It ended in some gibberish—a single word . . .

An earth-splitting, stunning thunderclap seemed to wipe out the lights in the room. Utter blackness fell solid-seeming in its impenetrability. A cold wind blasted past Elise, a draught from some frozen hell. An invisible form brushed against her arm, wet and shaggy, and an unshod foot thudded on the floor somewhere in front of her. A man cursed . . .

Then the scream rose out of the blank darkness, a livid crescendo of uttermost terror, of excruciating, unearthly anguish. It stabbed into Elise's quivering heart like a lance, rasped her taut nerves . . . It ended, abruptly.

Before the girl could move, before she could throw off the nightmare paralysis that held her, the thing brushed by her again. Its brief touch was revolting to her skin, the clammy touch of something long dead and mossy with rottenness. An odor of noisome putrescence trailed after it—and was gone as that icy draught shut off . . .

It had been a woman who screamed—a girl! Was it Naomi? Was it . . .? There was a bubbling sound in the darkness that was worse than the scream. There were no intelligible words, but its meaning was clear, too dreadfully clear . . .

"Light," a voice shrieked. "Light . . ."

A match sputtered. Its tiny flame flared, steadied. The darkness withdrew a little from white, staring faces—from a crumpled heap on the floor.

Elise could not make out the color of the shreds of flimsy fabric torn from a once-white, lacerated body. The same dark-glistening, viscid fluid that obscured it made the writhing face a gory mask. But the hair—it was close cropped, tawny! Relief, damnable, selfish relief caught in Elise's throat. It was not Naomi who lay there, contorted in incredible anguish. It was . . .

"May!" The name wrenched from Dick Tyler in a great sob, and he was down on his knees beside his sweetheart. "Almighty God! May!" His hands were suddenly gloved with red as he gathered her in his arms.

"What—" Wally choked—"What happened? Who . . .?" Rain lashed Elise, from behind. She realized that the window was open.

"Here," she called, not aware that her cry was a shrill, eldritch shriek. "Out here through this window—it went . . ."

They rushed at her, pell-mell, went past her, snarling like a pack of rabid hounds. Dick, with his scarlet, clawing hands, led them, his face a mask of death save for the eyes from which a terrible wrath blazed. They clambered out through the window, went pounding across the clearing.

"Keep together," Elise heard Serge command. "Keep together for protection . . ." The rest was lost in the threshing of heavy bodies in the wood's underbrush.

Nikita was standing in the archway, and there were two lit candles in her gnarled hands. Their radiance fluttered across her countenance. It was a face out of some delirium, a harpy's face . . .

May was not dead. Even that mercy was denied her. Red bubbles rose on her torn lips, as she tried to form words. She was saying something—but what it was no sane mind could have conceived!

Chapter 3

THE SECRET OF THE NIGHT

Elise Gornoff fought her way out of the cloak of black horror that enveloped her. "Stop the blood," she croaked. "We've got to stop it . . ."

Those ghastly wounds were jagged-edged, shredded . . . They had been made by no knife, by no conceivable weapon a human being would use. Fangs—claws—had torn May Bailey—mangled her. The fangs and claws of some ravening, giant animal whose presence on the island had hitherto been unsuspected . . . Some beast . . .

Beast . . . The words Gornoff had read from the ancient, occult book flooded back into Elise's numb brain: "The number of the beast!" The nape of her neck bristled with ancestral fear . . .

A shout from outside brought her whirling around to the window. A shout: "Here he is"—and the pound of running feet. Without conscious volition she went out through the doorway. The wind pounded her. The rain stung her. Blacker against black, figures were visible at the edge of the woods. Drenched, gasping, Elise reached them.

The men were stooped over a dark form, inert on a crushed bed of tall grass . . . The sky went blue with livid lightning . . .

"Rayne!" Wally Falk exclaimed. "It's Hugh Rayne!"

Incredibly it was Hugh Rayne! Sprawled there senseless, rain drenched.

"The beast," a voice squealed, unrecognizable, and Dick Tyler leaped at the prone man. His darting hands were red with May's blood, against the pale glimmer of Hugh's

face . . . Snatching fists grabbed Dick, were dragging him
away . . .

"He's the beast," the squirming youth shrieked. "The book
said so . . ."

"Wait." Serge's injunction was even-toned, calm as ever.
"We must make sure. He cannot get away, and . . ."

"It wasn't he." Sudden recollection prompted Elise's denial
"I felt the killer pass. He was shaggy, repulsive."

Was she sure? Faint, almost intangible, that same odor of
putrescence hung about her even in the driving rain. But another lightning flash showed her Hugh's drenched raincoat,
and it was of smooth rubber. There was a blue bruise on his
forehead, under his wet-plastered red hair.

"You felt him!" Serge's voice. "Elise! It might have been
you instead of May!" A strange note in it. Was it of fear? Or
threat?

Rayne groaned, checking the fevered speculations in
Elise's brain. He quivered, thrust big-thewed arms against the
ground, shoving himself up to a sitting posture. "What . . .?"
he mumbled thickly. "What's going on . . .?"

"What's your story?" Wally Falk demanded, somewhere
above Elise. His tone was sharply authoritative, as she had
heard it once in court. He was cross-examining Hugh, making him talk while he was still half-stunned, and incapable of
fashioning a plausible lie. "What happened to you?"

"I—I don't know exactly." Rayne pressed a hand to his
forehead. "Someone hit me . . . jumped me out of the dark.
The house lights had just gone out . . . I couldn't see who it
was . . ."

"How did you get here? The bridge is gone."

"Worried about you folks. 'Phone line out. Stole a boat . . .
Guy's fist was like a club. My head's still ringing . . ."

Relieved breath hissed from between Elise's teeth. It was
like Hugh to have risked his life if he thought his friends
needed help. An electric flare washed the macabre scene with
blue light, and she saw there was no blood on his hands or his
clothing. The storm could not have washed it entirely
away . . . But a furtive doubt lingered.

Wally Falk voiced it. "How on earth did you mange to keep a boat afloat in that freshet?"

"I—I . . . It was hell. I . . ."

"Who's there?" Dick, spinning, shrieked the challenge. "Who . . .?"

"Steady, Tyler." Gornoff murmured. "Steady. There's nothing . . ."

"Someone's in the brush. Watching us. I heard . . . Listen."

The blackness was grotesque, ominous with gigantic forms felt rather than seen. Were they only the trees? Only . . . Someone, something, breathed, heavily, close by.

The men half-crouched, tensing to meet an attack, cowering in a grisly fear. Elise tried to turn, to dash back to the shelter of the house, but her limbs were water-weak, would not obey her. Serge left the group, walking stiff-legged into the terrible darkness.

"Gornoff," Rayne exclaimed, surging to his feet, "you . . ."

A groan came out of the midnight murk into which Serge had gone. "Pavel!" he exclaimed. "It's Pavel . . ."

That released the others from the terror that held them rigid. But as they got to where Serge Gornoff was standing above his servant they huddled together again, huddled as sheep do scenting the prowling wolf near their byre.

"Pavel!" Gornoff said again, sharply, and the Russian sank to his knees beside the prone figure of his servant. Nikita, Elise thought, must have lit a lamp in the house, for yellow light sifted now through the trees. She saw that Pavel clutched a gnarled, thick club in one ham-like fist.

"Pana," he husked. "Zje . . ."

"Talk English," Serge snapped. "They all want to know."

"Lights go out, master. I look kitchen window, see someone, something—how you call?—gray, run away from house. I run after, hit with club. Hit hard, he no hit back. But everything go black . . . Then you say my name."

"Was it this man you hit with your club?" Wally thrust Hugh Rayne forward. "Was this he?"

Pavel peered at Hugh, hesitation, doubt in his uncouth, broad-sculptured countenance. Then, "No. Other big. Big. Like . . . man-monkey."

"That's what the fellow jumped me seemed like. A white ape, man-size." Did Rayne snatch at the suggestion too eagerly? "Smelled like one too. I remember that now. It was the smell I noticed first, just before he hit me."

Elise's spine prickled. The thing that had attacked May had carried a fetid odor with it, and bristly fur had scraped her as it passed. Was there truth in the old, grisly legends about Phantom Island . . .? She thought of something.

"Serge! The girls are alone in the house. Shouldn't we . . .?"

"Get back to them!" Falk interjected. "Good Lord! We're fools, leaving them alone . . ."

They were running across the clearing. Someone boosted Elise through the open window. Her wide-eyed glance searched the desecrated room for her sister, found her.

Naomi's face was ghastly, her dress blood-smeared. "Elly!" she gasped. "Do something for May. Do something . . ." It was May's blood that was on the blonde girl. She was all right, unhurt. May was on the couch, they must have lifted her there. Her hand was shoved with fierceness of unendurable torture against raw, glistening flesh. Ida Falk was dabbing her with an ineffectual handkerchief, a wisp of fabric dyed carmine . . .

"Where's Nikita?" Serge demanded. "Where's that woman?"

"I—I don't know." Naomi's pupils were dilated, so that the blue of her eyes had given place to black in which hysteria flared. "There was a scraping noise from inside, and she went into the hall. She hasn't come back."

"Bozhe moi!" Gornoff exclaimed and lurched out through the curtains, Pavel close behind him. That room again, Elise thought, inconsequently. Always that damnable room.

"What—who did that to her?" asked Hugh Rayne in a shocked voice. All this was happening in seconds, was overlapping. "Who did . . .?"

"You ask that!" Dick shrieked, whirling to the red-headed man, springing at him, gore-gloved hands clawing. "You . . ." Rayne lifted startled arms to protect himself. Elise threw herself between them.

Wally grabbed Tyler, pinning the frantic lad's arms to his sides. "Stop it, Dick," Elise cried, her voice choked with grief and terror. "You're keeping us from helping May. May needs our help, and we can't give it to her if you act like this."

"May!" Dick moaned. He stumbled blindly toward the couch.

Serge Gornoff came through the portieres, gaunt, unsmiling. The lamplight glinted on something silvery in his hand. Elise saw that it was a hypodermic syringe. Serge went to the couch. Just as Dick reached it the gleaming needle sank into May Bailey's lacerated arm. There was something ghoulish in the way Gornoff stabbed the torn flesh, something that prickled Elise's spine with a queasy chill. But the dreadful moaning stopped.

"We cannot telephone for a doctor," Serge said, "and if we could it would be impossible for one to reach us. But fortunately I have some smattering of medicine . . . Elise—if you will wash out these wounds with hot water and bandage them . . ."

"Yes, Serge." It was a relief to have something to do. A relief not to have to think . . .

"I've got this window locked," said Wally, turning away from it. "How about the others, and the door? There's a chance the—whatever it was—will come back."

"An idea. If it will avail anything." Serge's brooding glance rested briefly, significantly, on Hugh, turned back to Wally Falk. "You and Pavel make the rounds down here, Mr. Falk. I shall go upstairs, with Mr. Rayne. I have a gun, the only one in the house."

"We'd better leave that here with the girls, hadn't we?" Rayne suggested. "I don't know yet what it's all about, but if there's any danger . . ."

"No." Gornoff answered flatly. "The danger will not be here." If you are not, he might as well have gone on to say, thought Elise. He still suspected Hugh . . . Or was he trying to build up suspicion of him in the minds of the others? Suspicion that had its beginnings in that eerie sentence in the book—the book that only Serge Gornoff could read?

He picked up one of the candles, Wally the other. As the three men trampled out through the portieres, Elise glimpsed Pavel in the hall. He was standing in front of the place where the secret room was concealed by its sliding panel. Had he just come out of it? . . . The curtain swished back into place.

A shiver ran through the girl's slender body, as she realized that there was left in this room only three frail, helpless women, and a moaning youth whom grief and horror had made worse than helpless.

The chimney of the lamp was already blackened by soot, so that its light was dim, and the great chamber again a place of eerie, threatening shadows.

Ida snatched at her arm. "Elise," she chattered through blue lips, "I'm scared, in . . ."

"There's nothing to be frightened of any more," said Elise. She had found some new well of courage from which to draw. "We've got to take care of May. I'll go and get some hot water from the kitchen. Nikita always has a kettle on, for her interminable tea."

"I'll go," Naomi jerked out. "I know where it is." Before her sister could object, the girl's slender form slipped through the archway drapes. Elise started to follow.

"Don't leave me alone here," Ida whispered fearfully.

Elise swung around, read in the wide hazel eyes confronting her the tale of nerves jangled to the breaking point, ready to abdicate to shrieking madness.

"All right," she said, quietly, trying to calm the other by her own forced calmness. "I won't. Help me get the clothes off May so we'll be ready when Naomi gets back."

"Yes," Ida whimpered. "We've got to . . ." The effort she was putting forth to control herself showed in the throb of the pulse in her corded throat, in the way her small fists were clenched, nails digging into her palms.

"Dick." Elise put a gentle hand on the sobbing man's shoulder. "Go over there and sit down. You're in the way."

He obeyed, moving jerkily, like an automaton. Elise bent to the couch . . .

Running footsteps pounded. Upstairs. Through the muffled sound of fists pounding on wood, of heavy soles kicking at a door. Wally's voice roared:

"Hugh! Gornoff!" And then it broke into shrillness. "They're in there. They must be in there. What's happened to them?" Shrill and jittery. "Gornoff!"

Chapter 4

VANISHED!

Wally Falk's thin cry was a flailing whiplash, striking terror to Elise's heart. Serge! Something had happened to Serge! In that searing instant her doubts, her fear of him were gone, and her love was reborn in a terrible fear for him. She whirled, and ran up the dark obscurity of the broad staircase outside.

A splintering crash met her on the landing above. Lightning glimmer was blotched by two hulking forms lurching through a door they had battered down. Elise threw herself after them, past the ripped casing. An acrid tang was sharp in her nostrils.

The smell cut her lungs with tiny slicing knives, vertigo swirled in her head. She gasped, pulling in air, cold and wet and refreshing. Her vision cleared and she was aware of Wally Falk at a window, of curtains bellying in with the draught that had cleared away the choking fumes.

"Baronn," Pavel groaned, bending over something on the floor. "Baronn . . ."

There was light in the bedroom, dancing light from a candle to which Falk had touched a match flame. Serge was sprawled on the floor, and Hugh Rayne. Their faces were dough-yellow in the flickering candle-light . . .

"We were through downstairs, came up here to look for them," Wally whispered, his aplomb shattered at last. "They weren't in any of the other rooms, and the door to this one was locked.

"Are they—are they . . .?" Rayne rolled, staggered to his feet and she did not need to finish her question. Serge pulled in a single, gasping breath, sat up. The revivifying air had worked swiftly.

"What happened, Serge? What happened?"

They seemed unhurt. Only dazed, bemused . . .

"Rayne went into this room first, and I was close behind him. He stumbled against me. My candle went out. I smelled something—and that was all I knew till this moment."

"Gas," Falk supplied. "Some kind of gas. I got a whiff of it as the door gave way, felt it getting me. That's why I jumped to fling this window open."

"That's it," Rayne said thickly. "That's what knocked us out. But I thought I saw someone in here before I caved."

"Door locked," Pavel put in. "No key."

"Someone asphyxiated us and locked us in," Gornoff mused, maintaining a calm, strange, uncanny under the circumstances. "But he did not harm us. Why?"

"Maybe the—whoever it was that attacked May—was hiding up here while we were looking for him outside," Falk suggested. "Maybe he's still in the house."

"He is still in the house." Gornoff's eyes rested on Rayne, voicelessly accusing him once more. "There is no doubt of that."

"We went through all the rooms downstairs, and all up here but this one." Falk had collected himself again, but under his left eye a little muscle twitched and would not be still. "No one passed us on the stairs."

"There is another set of stairs, in the rear," Gornoff said. He bent and picked up something from the floor. "He could have avoided you that way."

"I can't understand how he got so strong a concentration of gas in here," Falk pondered, "without making it airtight, first."

"This is how," said Gornoff, straightening. He held out a palm on which some sharp slivers glinted. "He broke a globe or ampoule of thin glass just as we came in, probably smashed it against the jamb. And . . ."

"Elise! Elise!" Ida was calling from below. "What's happening up there? What . . .?'

"It's all right, Ida," Wally called, striding through the door. "No one's hurt."

"Then why don't you come down? Why is everybody leaving me alone down here?"

"Alone!" Elise was suddenly cold. She swung around. "Isn't Naomi there? Didn't she come back . . .?"

"Naomi? No. Isn't she up there?"

"Up here . . .?" Comprehension exploded in Elise's skull. "No . . ." Naomi had not returned from the kitchen and the backstairs led right down into it!

Elise ran through the dark passage outside, threw herself down the lightless well at its other end. "Naomi!" The cry tore her throat. "Naomi!"

No answer! The kitchen, lit only by red glow from the range, was starkly, appallingly empty, and there was no one in the dining room she could see through the open door.

Had Naomi opened that door? Had she gotten that far? There were no signs of a struggle anywhere . . .

"The door's locked from the inside," Wally Falk said. "The window hasn't been opened." Elise hadn't been aware they had followed her, but the men were here, were scattering through the ground floor rooms. Rayne called in from the dining room that the windows there, too, were tightly barred.

"She is in the house, then," Gornoff growled. "She must still be somewhere in the house."

"Find her. Do something to find my baby sister," Elise choked, sobbing. There was no strength any longer in her limbs. There was no reason in her mind. There was only the vision in her eyes of Naomi as she might now be—a bedraggled, mangled ruin of a body such as lay out there on the couch. "Find her, if you love me."

"Falk!" Gornoff snapped. "Come back upstairs with me. Pavel, you take Rayne down into the cellar."

They were gone. Elise could hear trampling feet upstairs, could hear dull noises made by the searchers below. They were hunting the house for Naomi . . .

They were searching the house—but they weren't looking for Naomi where she must be. Where Elise knew now she must be.

Serge Gornoff had told them where to search. But he hadn't told them of the secret room in the long hall on this very floor.

Suddenly something snapped in Elise's brain, and the girl laughed madly. Serge was fooling them all . . .

"Elise!" Her wild laughter, that had brought Serge back down the stairs to her, choked off. "Why are you laughing like that?"

"I was laughing at what a fool I have been," screamed Elise, "loving you, trusting you—like a fool!" She leaped at him, her curled fingers clawing for his eyes. "Give me back my sister. Give her back . . ."

His hands caught her wrist, and they were manacles of steel holding her in an inescapable grip. "I am trying to find her for you," he said, still with that curious, frightening quiet of his—that calm which nothing seemed to break. "I am searching for her."

"You lie," Elise shrieked. "You lie. She's in the forbidden room. You know she's in there. That's why you didn't say anything about it. That's why . . ."

She checked, terrified even in her rage. She had broken through his unnatural calm at last. His face was suddenly colorless. It was like marble, its expression stiffly menacing and demoniac wrath burned deep in his eyes. The basilisk glare held her, paralyzed. Even if her life had depended on it, she could not have moved.

Words seethed from his stiff, white lips. "So it was for that, you asked your lover here. To spy upon my secret. You have failed twice, and you will not succeed the third time."

"What . . .?" the accusation shocked her into speech. "What do you mean?"

But she knew . . .

"He tried to scare everyone out of the house with his attack on the girl. That failing, he suffocated me with his gas, slipped down here to force the door. Your sister interrupted him. He disposed of her somehow, heard Pavel and Falk start upstairs, got back up there in time to lock the room and pretend to have met the same fate as I. Now you . . ."

"Stop!" Elise screamed at her husband, her love for him metamorphosed to virulent hatred. "That is very plausible—but it doesn't fool me. It was you who played that trick on him. You hate all my friends because you have no friends. You hate Hugh because of mad, uncalled-for jealousy. When you consented to my having visitors here you made your plans. Your plans for murder, with suspicion pointing at him. That's why you were disappointed when you thought he was not coming. That's why you brought in the book when Pavel told you, that because he was unselfish and brave, Hugh had managed to reach the island. It's you . . ."

"You—you wench . . ." Gornoff's right hand let go its hold on his wife's wrist, and rose to strike her in white passion . . .

A thunderous thud that shook the house with its impact stopped that blow.

"Bozhe moi!" Gornoff gasped, whirling to face the hall door from the kitchen.

A scream sliced through the house, piercing, agonized. "Wally!"

It cut off. Gornoff darted out into the hall from which that thud, and the scream, had come. Elise got to the doorway, and halted. At the foot of the broad front stairs Ida stood as rigid as a statue, the lamp from the living room held high in her paralyzed hand. Its light sifted down on the thing at her feet, on the thing at which she stared, open-mouthed, her face frozen by ineffable horror after that first ear-piercing scream.

As Gornoff reached it, Elise saw what that thing was. A bundle of clothes, collapsed like a pricked balloon. Pulp oozing from it. Quivering, smashed pulp that had been a man once. No fall could have done that to him. He had been hurled down from above, with incredible force!

Chapter 5

SATAN'S EMISSARY

Wally Falk lay smashed against the floor as a rotten apple might be smashed wantonly against a wall. His pulped body had burst through his clothing. But unholy joy throbbed in Elise Gornoff's breast.

Serge hadn't done that. Serge had been in the kitchen with her and he hadn't done that thing!

Instantly the fierce elation was quenched by a surge of quivering self-disgust that this should be her first reaction, and then a new terror probed her brain. If not Serge, who? Wally had been alone up there! The others, Pavel and Hugh Rayne, were in the cellar . . .

Were they? Esther was strong enough, powerful enough to have lifted the lawyer and flung him down . . . Had one overcome the other, slipped upstairs to attack Wally?

Elise Gornoff prayed that this was so. The alternative was . . . unthinkable.

A door burst open, under the slant of the stairs, and Pavel lurched out of it. Pavel—and Hugh, behind him. Both dust-covered, smear-faced with the dust and soot of the basement. They caught sight of Gornoff bending to the grisly mass, rushed toward him . . .

Elise caught hold of the jamb to keep from falling. None of the three could possibly have been above. Someone—or some thing—else prowled the house. Some fiend incarnate, unseen, perhaps unseeable, had mangled May Bailey, murdered Wally—and carried Naomi off to its grisly lair!

"Naomi!" the shuddering girl whimpered. "Naomi."

What macabre doom had befallen her? Where was the laughing-eyed, endearing sister, whose chubby hand she had held in her own, teaching her her first toddling steps?

"I can't stand it," Ida wailed; her voice knife-edged with sheer madness. She whirled, dashed through the portieres.

"She's gone mad," someone gasped. "She'll kill herself." They were gone, hurtling through the portieres after the hysterical girl. Elise was alone in the dark hall, alone with that horror . . .

Alone and unwatched in the hall where the panel was behind which lurked that secret room. Out of the swirl of terror encompassing her, the girl remembered her earlier thought. Naomi might be in there. She might . . .

This was her chance, her only chance. She needed no light to find the spot, to grope for the shrewdly simulated knots in the graining that were the open sesame, knowledge of which she had nursed in her bosom, not daring to use. She thumbed them. That too familiar scrape of wood on wood grated at her feet, and she felt the apparently solid fabric slide aside.

The noisome odor of putrescence swept toward Elisa from out of the dark void that was opening in front of her. Her nerves tensed.

Suddenly a scratching, mewling fury pounced out upon her. Slicing claws ripped her face. Bony fingers knotted on her throat. A form battered against her, flinging her back—a skeleton clothed in swirling, sleazy fabric. She was on the floor of the hall. She was whirling over and over in a snarling, primordial battle with a harridan who bit and scratched and yowled. She was fighting back; biting, gouging, clawing; civilization stripped from her; fear blasted out of her. She had become a primitive woman, battling for her life . . .

Desperation and rage against the evil mysteries in this place, coupled with her youth and natural strength, soon gave Elise the advantage over her grisly antagonist. She clenched a scrawny, dry-skinned throat with her hands. Tightened her grip.

A clutch fastened on her shoulders, dragging her up and away from her victim. The throat she throttled came up with her; then fingers tore her grip away. Elise's vision cleared. She saw candlelight dancing on Nikita's prostrate, gasping form, realized that it was Gornoff who had separated them. That Pavel and Rayne were gaping at her. Saw Dick Tyler's white face, to which some semblance of intelligence had returned.

"What on earth?" Hugh groaned. "What now?"

"I come from pantry," Nikita gasped. "Panya try to kill me."

"You lie!" Elise flared. "You jumped out at me from the secret room. You've got Naomi in there and . . ."

"What room, my dear?" Gornoff's countenance was ashen, bleak as the visage of a soul condemned to eternal torment. "What room do you mean?" His low voice was still steady, still controlled, but there was a quiver in it now, as though he were holding on to himself only by the exertion of an indomitable will.

"You know what room. That one." Elise tore herself from his grasp, whirled about to point toward it. "The one you never let me enter. That's where Naomi . . ." She gasped. The wall was solid-seeming as though there never had been an opening there! "You've closed it!"

"I closed nothing, my dear. I do not know what you are talking about."

"You don't know . . . I'll show you, then. I'll show you." She flung herself at the panel, thumbed the swirls in the graining that would open it.

Nothing happened. Nothing at all.

"You've locked it," she screamed. Her fingers fumbled at the borders of the panel, she was trying to dig with her nails into interstices that didn't exist. She pounded madly on unyielding wood.

"Naomi! Naomi!" she shrieked. "Let me in to her! Let me in to my sister."

Then she couldn't pound any more because Dick and Pavel were holding her arms, were pulling her away from the wall.

"God!" Hugh Rayne grunted, drawing a shaking hand across his forehead. "She's . . ."

"Hysterical." That was what Serge said, but he meant—mad. "No wonder, with all that has happened."

"I—I will be all right, now," she muttered.

A terrible weariness welled up within the girl, the languor of defeat and despair. May, Naomi, Ida. The gruesome night had taken them all. She was the only woman left within this infernal house. Nikita, scrambling to her feet, was not a woman. She was a sexless avatar of weird hate, a witch-woman who had evoked some monstrous entity that ravaged and slew, and made of the storm-beleaguered house a shuddering enclave of hideous evil.

"I'm all right now," Elise said again, repeating the words in the voice of a dazed child. "Serge. Hugh. Dick. I shall be all right, if only you will find Naomi. If only you will find my little sister for me."

There were tears in her eyes as she looked from one to the other of them, tears that burned like acid. "Please find her. Please." And in her breast there was leaden despair. Could they help her? Would they? Dick Tyler was a white-faced, quivering non-entity, his grief and his fear making him less than a man. Pavel was—Nikita's mate. The others—Serge—Hugh—the finger of suspicion had pointed to each in turn. "Find my baby sister. If you love me . . ."

The tiny green candle-flames of hell flickered again in Gornoff's brooding orbs. His lips whitened. But it was Rayne who spoke first. "We can't leave her alone," he groaned. "She's likely to . . ."

"I shall take care of that," Gornoff interjected, and his hand came out of his pocket. It held the hypodermic syringe with which he had given May Bailey relief, the plunger only half-down. Before Elise could jerk away, before she could shriek her protest, he had bared her arm and plunged the gleaming needle into it.

The steel slid sickeningly in, and the syringe plunger squeezed down. A warm tingle spread up Elise's arm from the wound, tracing the punctured artery. Nausea twisted at the pit of her stomach, twisted in her brain. The hall blurred . . .

An unintelligible voice muttered something. She was being lifted, she was being carried somewhere. Oblivion blotted consciousness . . .

Nausea twisted at the pit of her stomach. The blackness in which she lay was charged with some deadly threat, with shadow shapes that took forms of unearthly menace, and dissolved, and reformed again to swoop down upon her . . .

Somewhere in the terrible gloom a pinpoint of light pulsed—steadied. It was the soot-dimmed wick of a kerosene lamp, and the vague light it gave did little to dissipate the gloom of the raftered living room of the old house on Phantom Island. Slowly the understanding came to Elise that she was slumped in a high-backed, high-armed chair, carried there no doubt after the narcotic had taken her senses from her.

She was faced anglingly toward the front of the room, perhaps to avert her gaze from that which lay on the couch and babbled. But whoever had placed her so had forgotten the oval mirror on the wall. Darkly in that mirror she could see what was behind her.

She could see the body of May Bailey on the couch. She could see Dick Tyler, a statue of pallid fear standing against the dark folds of the archway portieres, his white fingers clutching a weapon of some sort, half-lifting it as though every muscle, every sinew of his quivering frame were ready to lash out at an unseen antagonist. There were beads of cold sweat on the youth's pallid forehead, and there was no color, no color at all, in his face.

Otherwise the murk-walled room was vacant. Of Ida Falk there was only a wet stain on the window curtains to show what had become of her.

Elise tried to speak to Dick, but it was as though her vocal chords had become paralyzed. No sound came from her lips! They had not even opened. She was incapable of speech— but she had to get his attention somehow. She had to know what was going on. If she got up out of the chair, showed him that she was awake . . .

She couldn't. She had no control of a single muscle. The opiate, whatever it was Serge had injected into her veins, held her in a weird catalepsy, in which she was fully conscious but incapable, utterly incapable of movement. Her brain was alive; fiercely, poignantly alive; but her body was dead.

It was then that madness swooped down on Elise Gornoff, like a black, enveloping cloud. She could feel her reason slipping away from her under the impact of the horror with which she was surrounded and submerged in.

She knew she must not give way to it. If she went mad Naomi would be alone, utterly alone and without hope, in this house of dreadful doom.

But Naomi perhaps was dead. God grant that she was dead. Even terribly, like Wally Falk. God grant that she was not lying somewhere, torn, shredded, mangled, like May Bailey . . .

Or that a worse fate had not overtaken her.

She must think of a way out—for herself and for Naomi. She could at least force herself to think, to trace out the truth in the chaotic delirium of the night's happenings. Then, when and if the effects of Gornoff's dose wore off, she might know what there was for her to do. It would be by thought, and thought alone, that she would be able to fight off the grisly madness that threatened her.

Think . . . Who of those in the house might be responsible for what was occurring there?

Not any of the girls. Not Dick. Not Wally Falk.

Nikita was somehow involved in it. But Nikita alone could not have done the things that had been done. She had neither the strength not the opportunity.

Pavel? He might have attacked May, stunned Hugh Rayne. But he was in the cellar with Hugh when Wally . . . Those two had been in the cellar then, and Serge had been in the kitchen with her . . .

Inevitably, then, there was someone else in the house. Some one or something else. Was it some thing of demoniac terror, materialized from the storm and the ancient legends of Phantom Island, from the ancient, weird past of the island that had kept it uninhabited . . .?

The secret room was bound up in the mystery, and the brooding, almost tangible fear that had tormented Serge, that she had sensed was dogging him from the first day she had met him. It had been that sense of torment, of inescapable dread that had drawn her to him. Something in that room that he had hidden from her, hugging his dread secret to himself as the Spartan boy hugged the wolf that gnawed at his vitals.

What did she know of that room? Only that something fearful went on in there. Only that he had brought the syringe, and the liquid it contained, from there. He had brought the book from there . . .

The book! Wait . . . What was it he had said about the book? "There was only one thing missing from Rasputin's house, where so many men and women had lost their souls. This book." How had it come into Serge's possession? Was he one of those men who had invaded that lair of iniquity, bent on purging Russia of him who was consummating her downfall? They had been nobles, the story went, princes and barons . . .

"He was not mad. He was a monk, but he did not serve God." Serge had said that. And he had said, "They killed him—his body at least—" Only his body, he had meant! Rasputin, the dark essence of evil that had consummated the pain of a nation, had not been killed. Could not be killed . . .

Those who were known to have been members of that midnight band of patriots, were known also to have died, horribly . . . Elise knew at last—knew as surely as though he had told her—what it was from which Serge Gornoff had fled his Russia. What terror it was he had fled from and which had pursued him across half a world.

And she knew what it was he had been doing in that hidden room. Frantically, desperately, with feverish hope and icy despair, he had been conning that book of Satan's secrets for some formula to use against the vengeance of Satan's servitor. Against the time when the monk, who was not mad and who did not serve God, should find him out at last.

What an agony of hellish fear his life must have been! No wonder he had turned pale when Pavel had come in to tell him that someone inexplicably had attained the island, despite the flood and the storm. No wonder something transcending terror had gripped him when that very book had informed him that that man bore the number of the—beast!

In that instant blackness had smashed down and the terror had begun. They had found Hugh Rayne outside the window. Stunned. Or pretending?

But Elise had known Hugh all her life. He could not be . . .

What if Hugh Rayne had been drowned in the flood? What if that which had come to the house out of the night and the storm were Hugh Rayne's body indeed, but animated by some other spirit? Some grisly temporary tenant of that body, which, for its own dark purposes had . . .

Elise never finished the thought. A flicker in the mirror stopped it, a slither of cautious stealthy movement. In the splotched glass, the portieres were stealthily moving behind Dick Tyler. Slowly, with infinite stealth, they drew minutely apart—and a hand slid soundlessly through the aperture. Or was it a hand? The silvery fingers were curled, claw-like, and they ended in long, sharp talons that were brown and granular with dried blood. The wrist, the arm behind, were shaggy, bristling with hair of a gleaming, startling whiteness.

A scream formed in Elise Gornoff's breast—but it found no utterance. Held rigid and voiceless, she could not warn the youth. She could not . . .

The claw struck, swift and silent as a snake. It fastened on Dick's throat. The nails dug into quivering flesh. Little scarlet jets spurted from the wounds they made. Little fountains of scarlet death . . .

Dick hung, a limp doll out of which the scarlet sawdust had run, beneath the silver-grey hand. The curtains bellied inward to the pressure of an unseen form. The claw opened and the flaccid body dropped from it, straight down, no stiffening to it at all. The drapes moved apart.

The killer slid into view.

Chapter 6

Naomi's Fate

The thing that swayed in the doorway was an apparition out of the depths of such a hell as man in his most macabre imaginings could not have devised. It was a silver, wraithlike obscenity against the somber background of the drapes, a huge hulk clad in a black monk's robe that hung open to reveal a pelt of bleached, shaggy bristles, the precise shade of those blind things that wriggle under wet rocks in the dank depths of a light-less forest. Its furred legs were columnar, its arms thick-thewed and powerful as those of a gorilla. It had no neck—and it was faceless.

There was only hair where the thing's face should have been—curled, colorless hair that made of its head a shaggy monstrosity. And yet, in some manner, the creature must have been able to see. For that featureless head moved, while it swayed momentarily in the archway, as though it were scanning the room. Its claws, the one scarlet with new blood, the other brown with old, opened and closed beside its ponderous thighs, opened and closed as though still avid for the feel of quaking flesh within their grasp, as though hungry for the feel of screaming life ebbing from beneath their terrible grip.

Elise Gornoff was unable to move. But she cowered within the chair, cringing from the horror of that which was in the room with her, while blind terror ran riot in her veins.

A sound came from out of the depths of the thing's throat—a sound that was a hollow, deep-chested chuckle, as his unseen gaze found and rested on the shrinking, pitiable girl on the couch. A lascivious chuckle of glee at the sight of his handiwork.

He liked what he had done! Red fury exploded in Elise's brain. Her fingers curled in a small fist . . .

Her fingers had curled! They had moved! The dread paralysis was fading. Too late! A sob gurgled, far back in her throat . . .

The pale monster heard it! He launched into movement, into padding, swift movement. He reached the chair whose high back had hidden her, might have kept her safe had it not been for that single, uncontrollable sob. He reached the chair, and swung about in front of it. And again he laughed. That laugh was a hideous, hissing whisper, more fearful than any growl. An arm lashed out, its hand clutching . . .

Elise jerked backward, with the newly found small strength that had returned to her, and the talon that had aimed to rip her throat caught in the neckline of her frock instead. It ripped the fabric, tearing it away from the girl's gleaming skin, exposing the swelling curves of one dimpled breast . . .

The white-furred monk was suddenly motionless. Elise felt his inscrutable gaze on her, devouring her, sliding over her body, that of it which was exposed and that which seductively was still half-concealed. Clearly as though he had spoken she knew the thoughts in its brain.

And then the beast lashed out again. One hot palm clamped over her lips to stifle a beginning scream. The other arm slid around her waist, pulled her against the bristling, repulsive body. The gagging hand slid away and a lipless, hairy face nuzzled her lips.

Somewhere, far off, there was the sound of thumping footfalls. Were Serge and Rayne coming, in time to save her? Would they get here in time?

The girl's small fists beat frantically on the monstrous, noisome chest against which she was hugged. Waves of repulsion shuddered through her. Overpowering even her terror was the sense of defilement with which the thing's touch sickened her.

His body was no longer pressed tight to hers. She had won. The fury of her defense had driven him away from her, and gained for her the few moments time needed for rescuers to reach the living room. The sound of their slow footfalls were nearer. They were in the hall . . .

The gagging hand slapped across her mouth again.

The Monk chuckled. He slung her effortlessly up from the floor, swung around, and in a single lightning-like surge of movement was out through the window, was dropping lightly to the ground. Elise dangled from his arms like a broken puppet, knowing it was useless to attempt to call out, useless to attempt to straggle. The white thing was carrying her off to his lair in the woods . . .

But Elise's captor was not headed for the woods. He was loping around the house, keeping close to the foundations. He went around a corner, and abruptly he was climbing. Straight up the rugged stone wall he climbed, over a decorative ledge . . .

The ledge was not wholly ornamental. It protruded from the wall just sufficiently to hide from below an aperture in the stone, a window Elise had not known was there. Her captor thrust her through that window, held her suspended while he squirmed in after her. They dropped into a dim glimmer of light.

This was a room, narrow but long. A lamp on a table gave it light. There was a padlocked cupboard, a chair. The further end was closed off by a ceiling-high partition of steel bars.

And behind that cell-like wall Elise could see in that one fearful glance a bed. A tousled bed, and on it—was it joy or consternation that burst in a white glare of fire within her brain—on that bed lay Naomi, stark naked.

Elise twisted about, realizing for the first time that the beast no longer held her. He was crouched against the wall opposite that through which they had entered. He seemed to be listening.

The scarred, unfinished wood of that wall told the girl what it was. The inner side of the panel in the hall! She was in the secret room, at last . . .

A bundle of rags at the thing's feet moved. A bony hand flung out from it in a spasmodic, involuntary movement. A

wisp of fabric fluttered away from a cadaverous face—
Nikita's face!

Something clinked on the floor, falling out of the old
woman's clothing. A key! The clink jerked the white monk
around. He bent swiftly, snatched up the key. He swayed for
a moment, his faceless visage turning, now to the panel, now
to Elise, now to the bars that intervened between him and the
nude, unconscious form of the girl for whom Elise had
searched so long. Back and forth, back and forth, as though
the possession of the key he clutched in his bloodstained
claw enforced upon him the necessity for some decision with
which his mind could not cope.

Elise knew what the dilemma was with which the white-
haired thing struggled.

She was here, ready to his hand, to his lust. The other was
behind the bars, to get at her he must go there, must fit the
key into its lock. But it was the other, Naomi, who had first
inflamed him.

He seemed suddenly to come to a decision. He loped, with
that uncannily soundless shuffle of his, down the length of
the room. His hand fumbled at the lock in the cell door, and
metal clinked against metal as he struggled to fit it in.

Elise's desperate glance darted about the chamber, searching for a weapon. There was none. And if there had been,
with her feeble strength, what good would it have done?

But she had a weapon. Woman's strength. Her body.

"Look," Elise screamed. "Look at me." With a single frantic tug of her shaking hands she tore from herself what little
clothing there was left to cover her. "Look."

The beast twisted about, growling.

She stood there, a white, flowerlike glow in the dimness,
her arms outstretched to him, every inch, every luscious inch
of her perfect body a separate seduction. The very nausea that
pulsed within her, the very revulsion which drove the blood
from the surfaces of her sculptured figure, to leave it pallid
and gleaming, made her ineffably, ineluctably desirable.

"Come to me," she whispered. "Come."

And he was coming. Slowly, as if to tantalize with anticipation his boiling blood, as if to savor to the last poignant drop the lust that drove him, the white beast came.

Five feet remained between them, four. His breath reached Elise, the leprous stench of his body, the putrescent odor of a sepulcher. Three feet . . . Two. "God forgive me. God . . ."

"Panya!" Nikita's screech was a cry from hell itself! The old woman was somehow on her feet, was lurching between them. "No. No!" There was a whip in her hand. It lashed out.

A roar of rage, bestial, overwhelming, blasted from the beast. He leaped. His claws fastened on the screaming old woman. She whirled aloft. Smashed sickeningly against the stone wall under the window—became a pulped, red horror . . .

Elise was in the monk's arms. His bristles rasped her skin. His harsh palms stroked her flanks . . .

The world exploded in a splintering crash, in a chaos of shouting voices, of smacking blows. Elise was flung out of the maelstrom, hurled against the wall, slid unnoticed to the ground. Somewhere near her a woman screamed, shrilly, unendingly. Pavel's face appeared out of the mad tumult that whirled in the center of the room. Hugh's. They were obliterated by the silvery hair of the Devil's Monk.

Suddenly Serge Gornoff reeled out of the whirlwind, his chest bare, gory, his countenance a writhing mask of satanic fury. He bent, snatched up a long, ragged splinter of wood from the shattered panel, leaped in at the combatants, leaped out again.

The wood in his hand dripped blood that spattered on the stone floor of the secret room. There was sudden silence in the chamber, a silence that hurt. The swaying mass split. Pavel and Hugh staggered back from it. The white monk lay, a shuddering, writhing, incredible form, on the floor. His robe was torn from him and his chest was no longer white, but a mass of matted, gory hair.

"Nikolai! Nikolai!" Serge Gornoff was on his knees beside the dead monster. He was lifting the shaggy head in straining arms. "Nikolai." The name was a heartbroken cry wrenched out of a strong man's soul by unutterable grief. "I had to—do it."

Somehow, in that moment, the monk's head was no longer faceless. Elise saw that the eyes, the features, had been obscured by a wiry, overgrown beard, by hair that had grown straggly and wild to fall down over his forehead and meet that beard.

"Elly. Elly." Naomi's voice. "Get me out of here."

The key was still in the lock. It was Elise who first got to the door, who turned the key. Naomi, quivering, shuddering as though never again she would be free of hysterics, was in her sister's arms.

"Elly. It was awful. He caught me in the kitchen and carried me into this room. The old woman saved me. She was in here and she made him let me go. She locked me in here. Then I heard you calling me, and that other door started to open, and she jumped out. He tried to get at me then, and he couldn't. But he was so maddened by his efforts that he knocked her out and I thought he would get the key from her. Some noise outside distracted him, he listened at the panel, and then went out.

"A little while later I saw him push you in at the window. I fainted then . . . Who is he, Elly? What is he?"

"Yes, Gornoff. It's about time you explained that to us," Hugh Rayne rasped, his face white, strained.

Serge looked up, his countenance was like a bed of burned out ashes from which the fire had died. "My brother," he said simply. "Baron Nikolai Gornoff. The man who fired the shot that killed Rasputin."

"But—but I don't understand . . ."

"Pavel drove the car in which Nikolai fled from the scene of his crime. He brought Nikolai to me, white-haired, a raving maniac. The book—I showed you outside—was clutched in his arms.

"I hid him in our castle till the Bolshevist uprising forced me to flee. I brought him here then, with Pavel and Nikita,

smuggled him into the country as the alien Chinese are
smuggled. He became violent, but I had to keep him hidden.
If I had revealed his presence, then we should both have been
deported to Russia, and you know what fate we should have
encountered. The only one he would let enter his cell was
Nikita, but he wouldn't allow her to cut his hair. He had the
idea that Rasputin's soul had entered his body, that he must
take revenge on everyone else for that assassination of which
he himself was guilty.

"I tried every way I could learn to cure him. One way was
treatment with a certain asphyxiating gas. It must have been
an ampoule of that which he used to knock the two of us out.
When May Bailey was attacked I knew that somehow Nikolai had gotten loose. Even then, even in spite of all the terrible things he did, I tried to keep the secret. I must have
been—a little mad myself by then.

"But I can't understand how he got free."

"Nikita." It was Pavel who spoke. "Nikita. The panya, the
mistress, struck her. She do it—for get even."

"But is was she who saved me at the last," Elise broke in.
"Pavel—I don't understand."

"She not save you," the Russian said slowly, painfully.
"She save the—how you say—honor of the House of
Gornoff."

~ ~ ~ ~ ~

Extract from the Flood Edition of the Waterville Evening
Star, printed on the presses of the Haynesburg *Daily Clarion*:

It was learned this morning that a party of four who were
to be the week-end guests of Mr. and Mrs. Serge Gornoff
at their home on Phantom Island were caught by the flood
on the bridge to that island and swept away. They were Mr.
and Mrs. Walter Falk, May Bailey and Richard Tyler, all of
this city. Their bodies were recovered, so smashed by the
debris carried down on the face of the freshet that they
were identified only with difficulty.

Miss Naomi Wilson, sister of Mrs. Gornoff, was miraculously able to reach shore, and was rescued from a tree to which she was clinging by Mr. Hugh Rayne, of Waterville, who was to have been one of the party but was delayed on business and managed to reach the island only with great difficulty later in the evening. A relieving touch is given to the tragedy by the announcement of the engagement of the two young people to be married.

After the solemnization of the ceremony, which will be private, the Gornoffs and the Raynes plan to take up their abode on the mainland.

Far better, that pitifully tragic lie which blamed the flood—than that the whole ghastly truth be published for the world to read . . .

SOFT BLOWS THE BREEZE FROM HELL!

Chapter 1

MESSENGER OF HORROR

It was ball-shaped and about the size of a five-year-old's fist. Its color was the yellow-tainted white of a corpse dead a day. It was so weightless that although the lightest of breezes breathed down Stalton's elm-lined Blossom Street it fled before the zephyr, curiously swift, curiously without sound.

In the dusk's dim grey hush the thing was at first noticed by no one, so that for minutes no one thought its presence strange, though the hamlet lay in the midst of rolling fields, and the nearest spot sunless and dank enough for the fungus to grow was Roget's Wood, a full five miles away.

It darted along the narrow, sod-bordered walk, leaping the grass-shoots between the worn flagstones, flitting beneath the feet of the strollers in the dreamy twilight.

None had any hint of how soon all laughter would be stifled in Stalton, of how soon eyes now sparkling with gaiety would be dark and brooding with dread.

It was Hilda Mead who first saw the round thing as it scudded past her along a picket fence pale in the evening's greyness. "Look!" she exclaimed, snatching her slim hand from Hal Curtin's warm clasp to point at it. "Look, darling! What *is* that?"

"What?" her stalwart lover asked, his gaze reluctant to drag itself from her olive, elfin face, from the sweet promise of her velvet lips. "What is what, dear?"

"That . . . Oh, I don't like it, Hal." A tiny shudder went through her small-boned, round little body. "I don't like the way it's running along as though it were alive with a queer kind of life, and *knows* where it's going."

"Silly," the young man exclaimed, his teeth flashing in a fond smile as he peered after that at which Hilda pointed. "It's nothing but a puffball. It's a common fungus, and—"

"And I still don't like it," the girl interrupted, pouting prettily at Curtin. "I'm afraid of it."

"Afraid!" Instinctively wise in the ways of love, Hal Curtin had sense enough not to laugh, had sense enough to draw Hilda within the strong curve of his arm, to hold her close against his body's slender strength and say, deep-voiced: "You need never be afraid of anything while I'm alive to protect you."

The puffball veered sharply from its course, almost as if possessed of the weird sentience Hilda had ascribed to it. It leaped at a dim-seen gate, struck a piling and vanished in the spurt of spore-smoke that gives its kind their name.

In the next moment the cottage beyond that gate seemed blotted out by a dark pall; its outlines merged with the night, the yellow rectangles of its windows gone . . .

Something's happened to the lights, Hal Curtin thought . . .

In the blackened house someone laughed. The laugh was edged with shrillness and utterly humorless, and threaded by a mad sort of agony. More appalling than any scream, it held Blossom Street in thrall to a sudden, icy paralysis so that there was no movement under the elms but only blanching faces and the gasp of caught breaths.

Then there was light again in those windows, a burst of lurid light that lay in whirling sheets against the panes and smashed through them with a great shattering of glass, and spouted out of the gaping holes thus made in huge roaring tongues of flame. There was light in the street and on the ivy-clad small homes in the gardens, the terrifying orange-red light of fire. There were shadows; the gigantic black shadows of the trees wavering as the flames wavered; the shadows of humans, arms flung overhead—shouting shadows, screaming shadows pelting toward the blaze.

Shouts and screams and the roar of the flames, and always through the roar that terrible laugh . . .

"God!" Hal Curtin gasped, Hilda tight within his arm. "They haven't the ghost of a chance!" Those who had been strolling on Blossom Street were past them, those coming from farther off had not yet reached them, and for breathless seconds the lovers were isolated. "They're done for . . ."

"Look!" the girl throbbed. "Look!" Her free hand flung out to the ridgepole of the blazing house. "There . . ."

Against sky-glare was blackly silhouetted a thing man-form yet grotesquely not a man. On the narrow crest of the slanted roof that was not yet alight, it capered in a queerly simian frenzy and it was from that capering monstrosity that the brain-curdling laugh came.

From the dark human mass surging against the fence of the doomed house, surging away from the blasting heat of that furnace, a shout went up. Curtin could not know whether it was evoked by sight of the thing on the roof or by the explosion of flame through the black roof-slant. The house was a vast torch now, a pillar of seething orange and crimson and strange greens supporting on its apex the affrighted vault of the sky, within which nothing could live.

Nothing . . . Hal tore himself away from Hilda's clinging hands, a strange cry in his throat! He vaulted the pickets beside them, his leap a lithe and effortless bound, was hurtling away from her.

His feet thudded into soft garden loam and in his nostrils was the sweet fragrance of honeysuckle. His toes flung the crunch of path-cinders behind him. He whipped past the red-bathed porch of a small home, past its end wall whose dark ivy strove to shield it from the lurid glare. He was beyond it, on the soft turf of its kitchen yard, angling toward the roar whence that glare came and had plunged into the shadow of the next house, stygian by contrast.

Blinded, Curtin battered into a back hedge he did not see, was ripped by its stems, its stiff leaves, as he burst through it into blackness. Tall grass whipped his legs and he knew he was in the vacant lots that lie between Stalton and the fields. He halted for a moment to get his bearings, projected almost useless sight, taut hearing, into the gloom that was the deeper because overlaid by the rubid heavens.

Somewhere within that murk was furtive movement . . . There! Almost straight ahead was a darkening of the black. Hal launched himself at the vague forms, wrath wrenching a shout from his lips.

The forms were plainer . . . his ankle was caught by some ground-creeper, pulled from under him. He lurched forward into a blow that exploded white light within his skull . . .

Hilda Mead squatted in the tall grass, reckless of her filmy white frock. "Hal!" she whimpered. "Hal. I thought I'd never find you." Her hands tugged at the recumbent form, tugged its head on to her knees. "Hal!" Her fingers found wetness on that head, viscid wetness matting the hair, staining her fingers.

"Ouch!" Curtin winced, jerking his head from the fierce pain of that touch. "Don't . . ." then, "Hilda. You . . ."

"Hal! What was it? What were you chasing? What—who did this to you?"

"I saw . . ." he checked himself. "Hilda! Don't ask me what I saw. Don't let me tell you."

"Hal, you're still dazed. You're talking wildly."

"No." Curtin pushed hands against the ground, pushed himself to a sitting posture. "No. I'm not dazed. I . . . Hilda, you must not know. It would be dangerous for you to know." Something in his tone told the girl there was utter truth in the words that otherwise were so mad. "And listen. Tell no one it was I . . . How I got this cut on my head. Say that I started to run to the fire, tripped, banged my skull. Perhaps—perhaps I was not seen clearly, was not recognized." It was fear that sounded in Hal's voice, and Hilda had not dreamed that he could ever be afraid. "Do you understand?"

"No," she said. "I don't understand. But I'll do as you say."

A crash pulled their eyes to where the fire had blazed. Sparks fountained above the dull red glow that was all that was left of the blaze. High into the sky they went, till they were golden stars dancing in the heavens, and then they were drifting down again upon Stalton. Hilda Mead had a queer fancy that they were tiny lanterns guiding a horde of imps to their landing place.

Chapter 2

DISASTER!

It was not till long after dawn that the ruins of the house on Blossom Street had cooled sufficiently to permit inspection, and the full extent of the horror made certain.

The searchers found the skeletons then, in the jumble of charred timbers that once had been a home, enough of the incinerated bones to identify whose they were when the holocaust seared life from them. There were five of them, five heaps of whitened ashes.

"That's the full count," the haggard-faced Fire Chief said when he had received the last report from one of his men. "Not one escaped."

"How could they," John Wayne, village president, responded, "the way that fire burst out?" He was tall and gnarled and sturdy as an oak. His hatless white hair was smudged by the embers that had drifted into it while the blaze still burned, for he had been early on the scene. "They tell me it was everywhere at once, upstairs and down." His grizzled, kindly countenance was grey with his distress. "Everywhere."

"That's what's got me," Chief Rail muttered. "It was a wooden house sure enough, but it was well built and should have resisted the flames if I know anything at all. I'd understand it if they'd been cut off in a single room, but from the position of the bodies and the things around them, the maid was in the kitchen washing dishes. Bob Dutton and the boy were in the living room, Mary upstairs in the nursery."

"And the baby?"

"The baby was in its crib," Rail said softly. "Mary—the way she lies tells us—threw herself over it to save it. Even with the flames around her, as they must have been, the mother did that."

A murmur went through the group of mourning neighbors that, silent save for a shifting of uneasy feet and an occasional muffled sob, had been listening to the report. In the depths of Hal Curtin's brown eyes a smolder of wrath deepened and the line of his blunt jaw hardened to a knotted ridge.

He moved closer to Wayne and Rail, addressed the latter. "Chief," he asked, low-toned, "are you sure that was all who were in the house?"

The tired man turned to him. "We've raked the ashes clean and that's all we've found."

"That isn't what I mean. I thought there might—that someone might have escaped. I know the family's all accounted for, but there might have been some visitor . . ."

"There wasn't none," a pillow-bosomed woman, Lena Corbitt, put in. "I was just in there to ask Mary for a dress pattern I knew she had, and there wasn't anyone but Bob and little Bob and her around. And there couldn't have been anybody come in because I was scarcely back to my own gate, two doors away, when the thing happened."

"In the kitchen maybe? Someone calling on the maid?"

"No. I went to the door to ask Jennie for a glass of water and I saw the whole room. There wasn't anybody!"

That was that, then. The capering figure on the roof was unexplained. The figure that had laughed not in glee but in agony. No one had mentioned it, hence no one but he and Hilda had seen it; but that was reasonable. The spectators' gaze had been riveted on the flame-filled windows.

"Why did you ask that?" Rail inquired. "What's on your mind, Hal?"

Curtin shrugged. "Nothing." Now why had he lied? He had intended to tell them of what he'd seen. "Just a hunch I had." He glanced at the watch on his wrist. "It's late. I've got to be getting to work much as I don't feel like it."

The knot of watchers broke up as he walked away, reminded of waiting offices and workrooms, of housework to be done and children to be sent off to school. But those children were kissed more lingeringly that morning, more reluctantly dispatched. Infants too young for school were held tightly to their mothers' breasts.

"Hal!" Hilda's dear voice called his name. She was at the gate of her home, halfway down the block, fresh and sweet in a filmy negligee, her eyes still dewy with sleep.

"Hal! I saw you . . . Is your head all right?" She touched the plastered bandage that made a white patch in his shock of chestnut hair. "I had to run out and ask."

"Quite all right, darling." His brown, strong hand closed on her fingers, took them to his lips. "I haven't even a headache left."

"Hal, I was awake for a long time. I was thinking . . . could that thing we saw have had anything to do with—what happened? That puff ball?"

"Good Lord, what a queer idea!" Curtin was queerly uneasy. "How on earth could it?" He had an obscure sensation as of eyes upon him, watching, evil eyes. He half turned to the street with careful carelessness calculated not to alarm his sweetheart.

"It couldn't, of course," he heard her. "Of course it couldn't."

Nobody was watching him. There was no one who had any reason to watch him. They were all familiar, all friendly, warmhearted people who had been his neighbors and friends.

"That's more sensible." He leaned over the gate, kissed Hilda full on her sweet, warm mouth. " 'Bye, love. I've got to go and tend to business."

She held him a moment longer. "Hal," she breathed, "I want to ask you something."

"Yes?"

"Did you mean what you said last night? That you'll protect me from anything?"

"All my life. From the devil and all his imps." His voice was deep, as if he suddenly had some prescience of how soon he was to be called upon to fulfill almost literally that promise.

The second puffball was seen by many of the townspeople. It appeared in Main Street at three-fifteen that afternoon, when traffic there was at its height. It bounded straight down the center of the street, and it was the way that it avoided the rolling wheels of the autos, the trampling hooves of the farmers' horses that drew amused eyes, pointing fingers, to it.

The wind was stronger than it had been on the previous evening and the bit of fungus was much like a tiny, pallid animal scudding legless and armless before it. It was shooting across the intersection of Apple Street when Hal Curtin, driving back to his law office from the Town Hall, spied it.

Unaccountably his skin crawled with sudden apprehension. Almost without volition he skidded his roadster into Main Street and darted after the swiftly rolling thing like a terrier after a rat.

The instant before his mind had still been filled with the scene in the village's Council Room. John Wayne had presided with unaccustomed solemnity, the morning's tragedy brooding in his eyes. Curtin himself, butcher Rudolph Schalk, portly, ruddy-cheeked; gaunt and acidulous Doctor Adam Ranier, and Stephen Brinn, pompous with the dignity of his bank, had sat slouched deep in their chairs, attentive but wordless. But there had been debate verging on acrimony at that meeting.

The protagonists had been fussy little Mark Yarrow the druggist, and realtor Reddon Gast; the issue, approval by the Council of a great trunk highway proposed to run through Stalton's very center.

Gast was violently in favor, Yarrow opposed. Brinn and Ranier were lined up with the realtor, Schalk and Curtin with Yarrow. That left Wayne with the deciding vote, and there was no doubt of how that vote would be cast.

Stalton was the old man's very life: its tree-lined streets, its neat, white homes, its peaceful atmosphere of neighborliness created almost by his very hands. When first he'd come here the town had been a rambling, dingy hamlet, a trading center for the farmers roundabout, and nothing more. By his influence, by his unremitting toil, it had become what it was. A trunk route through it would bring turmoil and confusion, a mushroom growth of gas stations and hotdog stands and roadhouses, a stench of exhaust fumes by day and a clamor of honking horns by night.

Yet such was the fairness, the passion for justice of the man that, because Gast and his party saw prosperity for Stalton in the change, he had agreed to reserve the vote given him only in case of a tie, till they had had every opportunity to win over one of those who thought as he.

Wayne had gone further. He had offered to resign from his presidency and call a special election in which he would run against anyone Gast chose. This, however, the realtor had refused, knowing well enough that, no matter what the question, John Wayne would be re-elected by an overwhelming margin, so dearly loved was he by the people of Stalton.

Gast preferred, however, to attempt to win to his side one of those who was not too strongly opposed to the idea. If he succeeded, his paltry land holdings would become a veritable gold mine.

Wealth, then, had been the gauge for which Reddon Gast had battled, his alpaca coat hanging in loose folds on his huge, rawboned frame, his countenance granite-hard and expressionless except for the faint sneer of his lifted lip at Mark Yarrow, his predatory eyes contemptuous of the little man whose Vandyke had bristled and voice grown shrill and stuttering.

Hal Curtin had watched the dispute with a curious intentness he was careful to mask, with a curious excitement manifested only by the throb of a pulse in his temple. If he could only be sure of what he had seen last night, just before that terrific blow had smashed him into oblivion . . .

There had been no decision. Gast, sensing that he had made no progress, had demanded another week's consideration. Curtin had left the Town Hall with that pump of blood still in

his temple, had driven mechanically east with a strange, unbelievable speculation throbbing in his skull. Then he saw
that small puffball scuttering up Main Street, and Hilda's
queer remark of the morning flashed out of memory.

It kept just ahead of his car's hood, a bounding, irregular
sphere all but animate. He recalled Hilda's words: " . . . alive
with a queer kind of life. It *knows* where it's going." Something grated along the side of his roadster, caught a fender, let
go . . .

The puffball leaped sidewise, darted toward the sidewalk,
darted across it and straight into the lobby of a movie theatre
whose canopy was overhung with flamboyant signs proclaiming: Kiddies Matinee—Mickie Mouse—Rustlers of
Sunset Range, Episode 8—Kiddies' Matinee.

Hal jammed his brakes, hurled out of his car, hurtled into
the lobby. A swirl of gray smoke, spore-puff of the fungus,
lay against the white base of the door into the auditorium.

Curtin's palm slapped the door—fingers grabbed his arm
and a voice rasped, "Ticket, mister."

Blackness billowed through the aperture between door-
edge and jamb, as if an inky fog that filled the interior were
finding exit. "Where's your . . .?" *The door was blasted outward by a thunderous crash!* Screams came with the thunder
and the black fog was suddenly solid with plaster dust. These
were children screaming, children in terror, children in
pain . . .

A laugh threaded the chorus of agony! It was the same
chattering, mad laugh he had heard not many hours before,
the laugh whose sound had never quite died out of Hal Curtin's brain . . .

The doorman's clutch was a desperate, insensate grip on his
arm. He ripped loose from it, battered the door out of his
way, plunged through it into an impenetrable darkness, dust-
filled and filled with shrill cries, with whimpers, with other
sounds indescribable—

And with that damned laugh!

Curtin jerked to a halt, bewildered by that sightless void.
Abruptly the black fog seemed to dissipate. A glow spread

through it and he could make out jumbled timbers, small forms inextricably entangled with them; small forms struggling, jerking feebly, and not moving at all.

Realization of what had happened beat in on Hal. The balcony had fallen with its load of children on the children below . . . Not all the balcony . . .

The projection booth was still erect on its stilts, light streaming from its square window, white light which caught the swirling dust and cast a murky glow by which he saw the broken little bodies. Horrified, he saw a tiny hand reach out from between two shattered beams, its wee fingers gloved with blood, twitching . . .

The laugh beat at his brain, the laugh so weirdly evil with insane pain. Where did it come from? Who could be laughing in this hell?

Men and shouts poured through the door behind Curtin, battered him, and caught him up in their swirl. Men were clawing at the chaos; cursing, sobbing, frantic with horror and with grief. A voice, scarcely human, jabbered, "Lila. Where's my Lila. She's in here."

The dust swirl, heavy, was settling, the cloud thinning. The light from the projection booth was gathering into a sharp-edged beam boring through the terrible darkness. Its end was a great white square on the further wall. This was the screen that should be displaying an antic rodent. On it, black, shaggy and grotesque, capered the gigantic shadow of that which laughed!

Chapter 3

THE THIRD PUFFBALL

Hal Curtin was abruptly aware that somehow he had struggled far down toward that screen, dragged there perhaps by his stunned, unthinking search for the source of the laugh. He must have clambered over the worst of the wreckage for there was little here. The seats were empty, open exit doors showing where those who had occupied these seats, and still were able to move, had gone.

Behind him was the terrible clamor of disaster and rescue. Ahead of him that shadow on the screen and, on the stage-like narrow platform just before the screen, the—thing—that cast it.

It danced its evil rigadoon, laughing—Curtin vented an incoherent shout—threw himself down the aisle. His weaponless fingers were clawed, his throat swollen with the terrible anger that possessed him. Beneath his tongue was the salt-sweet taste of blood. He passed the final seat-row, glanced up at the high rise of the stage-front close before him, jumped for its summit.

His hands caught the platform edge, clung. The momentum of his leap carried his torso high enough so that he could straighten his arms, get a toe-hold, lift and come erect on the little stage.

He was alone on it! The laughter had vanished.

Dazzled by the reflection from the screen's silver surface, Curtin started to turn—the flooring went from beneath his feet. *He dropped plummet-like into darkness!*

There is no consciousness of time in a sudden fall, only marrow-freezing terror.

A split-second or many minutes might have elapsed before Hal crashed on solid support.

Jarred, half-dazed, he contrived to flail gritty hands, already fisted, to fight whatever it was that had trapped him. He was on his feet . . . surprisingly . . .

A black shape loomed in the blackness! Before Curtin could move there was a click, yellow light . . .

Reddon Gast, his hand on a switch panted. "What is it? What's happened in the theatre? I heard a crash from my office . . . ran out the back way, through the alley and in here . . ." Metal armored cables twisted reptilian in the confined space, undulated upward to black, conelike objects, over Gast's head. "What's happened, Hal? You look . . ." Hal realized they were loud-speakers, behind the screen. This was the chamber beneath it where they were adjusted. That fall of Hal's had brought him only level with the theatre floor.

"Happened?" he gasped. "Enough. But—did you see any-one coming out of here? A man—like a huge ape?"

"Ape!" The realtor stared at him, his eyes widening, as though with doubt of the other's sanity. "No. Of course not. No one passed me. *What's that?"* A woman's wail, pent with excruciating suffering, came through the overhead aperture through which Hal had fallen. "What's going on in there?"

"The balcony fell." The answer came absently, without in-tonation. "Hundreds of children killed."

"Great Jupiter!" Gast lurched past Curtin, was heaving up a vertical iron ladder that came down from the trapdoor through which the lawyer had fallen . . .

The rest of that afternoon was a blur to Curtin, Afterward he had a dim memory of helping to lift great beams, of carry-ing limp and moaning small forms tenderly in his arms, of laying lifeless bodies in a lengthening, terrible row.

He was not quite clear-minded again till he found himself in the kitchen of Hilda's home on Blossom Street, weariness a dull ache in his muscles and his bones, his brain a boil of dark and dreadful thoughts, black as the night pressing against the unshaded windows.

"Eat this salad, darling," Hilda was saying. "Look, I made it for you just the way you like; only white meat, nice, crisp lettuce and plenty of mayonnaise. And here's iced tea. You must eat or you'll be sick."

He looked up at her from his chair at the kitchen table. "You made it," he said dully. "Where's Ethel?"

The girl smiled through the glimmer of tears in her eyes. "I told you," she answered with tender patience, "that Ethel went to the hospital where her little brother is, and that dad and mother are out seeing what they can do to help the Widow Simpson, whose son and daughter both were killed this afternoon."

"Yes," her lover muttered. "Yes. I remember." Because Hilda seemed to want it so much he reached for the dainty plate she had prepared. His sleeve brushed a crumpled newspaper on the table.

The lurid headlines leaped from the page at him:

Forty Killed, Scores Hurt in Theatre Crash
Balcony Collapse Blamed on Lax Inspection

Gast Accuses President Wayne of Weakness
Links Failure to Find Cause of Blossom St. Fire
and Demands Thorough Investigation!!

"Gast accuses!" Curtin exclaimed, jumping to his feet. *"Gast* demands!" He stared wild-eyed at the startled girl. "But it was Gast who was in the sound room, Gast who said he saw no one come out of it. I've got it, Hilda. By God, I've got it and I'm going to stop it." He whirled, was running through the dining room, was through the hall and out on the porch. He was in his roadster, parked outside, and was pounding his heel on the starter.

The car jumped away from the curb, roared off, roared past the blackened ruins of the house where five had been seared to death, past houses still standing that were blackened with heart-rending grief or with an anguish of doubt more poignant than mourning. Last night, Hal Curtin thought, little children were laughing inside those houses . . .

Laughing! Twice he had heard another kind of laugh—how did that fit into the dark pattern that had formed in his mind?

He twisted his wheel, changing his course. To fill out that pattern there was a bit of information he must obtain, and Mark Yarrow would have it for him. The little druggist was the village gossip . . .

The loungers in the pharmacy were pallid tonight, their faces sultry with recollection of the scenes they had witnessed not long since. There was little talk from their tight-lipped mouths, but what there was, was of John Wayne and how he had failed them.

"I've got a hunch there's plenty more due to happen," someone said. "The way the town's gone to rack and ruin lately. I got a feeling in my bones this ain't the last."

"Cut it, Bill," another protested. "Ain't we got enough to think about?" But the first speaker had voiced the sense of impending doom, the prescience of further disaster that brooded over all Stalton.

Ancestral fears were revived tonight in the mourning town, inchoate as these might have been in the souls of their ancestors. The gods were wroth with them, and prepared their destruction. The gods must be appeased by a human sacrifice, and that sacrifice was ready to their hand.

"I say we all ought to go up to John Wayne's and . . ."

The sentence was interrupted by the entrance of Hal Curtin. Disheveled, his eyes burned-out coals in a yeasty mask, he strode stiff-legged through them. He shouldered them aside from his path, and none took offense because it was so evident he did not know he had done so. He went straight back through the store, past the end of the counter that closed off its public space, through the swinging door in the partition behind it.

Mark Yarrow, dapper in a white half-smock, looked up from the pills he was rolling to see the apparition stride into his prescription room. Before his indignation at the intrusion could find more expression than a pursing of his lips, a hand had clutched his collar and thick words were choking off his own utterance.

"Mark," Curtin demanded. "Tell me. Has Reddon Gast any connection with the county madhouse?"

He gasped, "Yes. He's on the Board and he leased the place to the county. That's one of his little grafts. Why . . .?"

He was left with the question unfinished, his mouth gaping like a pouter fish's. Hal Curtin had wheeled away and was gone.

"Gawd," he heard an exclamation from outside. "What's eating you . . ." and then the hammer of heels across the floor out there was ended, to be succeeded an instant later by the *thrrrrr* of an auto starter and the clash of gears viciously meshed.

The night seemed darker to Hal Curtin, and more foreboding, as he catapulted through the village, retracing his course. A block from Hilda's he braked again, sat for a minute with clenched hands, with lips biting hard on one another. He must get control of himself, must speak coherently, convincingly. That which he was about to say would be difficult enough to get across without the impediment of its being said by one who looked as if he were on the brink of madness.

Mark Yarrow's expression had told him what he looked like.

There was a comb somewhere in his pocket. He fumbled for it, used it. He adjusted his tie, straightened his coat. These small actions helped to reduce the fever in his blood, the pound in his temples. Now he could trust himself.

He got out of the roadster, walked quite slowly up the path that led through a garden to the Colonial entrance of a small but somehow stately white house. He read the name in letters of wrought iron set in the weathered boards of the door:

John Wayne

His hand did not tremble as he lifted the knocker and rapped once with it.

The door opened more quickly than he had expected. It was Wayne himself who opened it. The sight of his countenance, ashen, haggard, the visage of an almost senile ancient now, and not that of gracious age, undid all Hal Curtin had accomplished with himself.

"Mr. Wayne," he blurted. "I've come to tell you . . . I know who's behind what's happening in town. I've seen . . ."

Something flared into Wayne's sunken eyes, something that silenced Curtin more surely than the old man's, "Wait a minute, Hal! Come in . . ."

And then there was another voice, from behind Wayne. "Looks like I'd better cut my good-night short, John. Well,

we understand each other, don't we? The old man turned . . .
to Reddon Gast!

"Yes," he said. "Yes, Reddon. I understand. Thank you for
coming." They were shaking hands. Gast was passing Curtin
with a curt nod. Did Hal imagine it or was there dark flame in
the pouch-underlaid eyes that caught his own briefly, flame
of a hellish hate?

"What was he doing here?" Curtin croaked. "What did he
want?"

Wayne smiled wearily. "He came to apologize for what he
said to the *Gazette*'s reporter. He was excited, didn't mean it.
He does not honestly blame me for—the fire and the accident, and he's going to make a statement tomorrow retracting
what he said today."

"After the damage is done," Curtin commented, bitterly.
"After he's set Stalton against you as he planned from the
beginning. You're through now. They'll demand your resig-
nation, and some creature of his will be elected. Which is exactly why he's done what he has. He wants that highway and
the fortune it means for him, and he's stopped at nothing to
get it. Not even at murder."

John Wayne took a step backward into the open doorway,
one almost transparent hand lifting as if to ward off an attack.

"What?" the old man whispered. "What do you mean?"

"Just that. Gast is responsible for the fire on Blossom
Street, for the collapse of the theatre balcony. And if those
are not enough, he's ready to perpetrate another outrage. All
this to discredit you, to get you out of the way."

"You're—you're upset, my boy. What you say is—
impossible. Those were accidents."

"The hell they were accidents. Look!" The words were
tumbling out of Curtin's mouth now, the words that had been
pounding in his skull. "If that house were filled with lyco-
podium, a haze of fine powder, no one would have noticed. If
a match were struck, it would have blazed up all at once, the
way it did. A very little dynamite, placed under the supporting pillars of the theatre balcony, would have brought it

down. Gast had access to dynamite. He's blasting foundations for that office building on Apple Street and he could have . . ."

"What are you saying? I've known Reddon for years. Gast couldn't . . ."

"No. Not Gast with his own hands. But Gast in the person of some madman he released from the asylum. I've seen him, I'd know him anywhere. I saw him in the theatre and he got away. I saw him before that, on the roof of the burning house, saw him leap for the telephone wires just before the final burst of flame came, and drop to the ground. I almost caught him that time, would have if there hadn't been someone with him who clouted me . . ."

"Hal!" Wayne interrupted. "That's it! You were hurt more badly than you thought when you fell that night, and your experience today finished the job. Go home. Get some sleep. Tomorrow you'll be rid of these wild ideas."

"I can prove it to you. I can, I'm almost certain, show you the madman. I've got an idea where he's hiding. Those puffballs that have been appearing just before each thing happens, can come only from Roget's Wood. He brings them—that's where his lair is. We'll organize a posse and go there and capture him, and that will prove my ideas aren't as wild as you think."

"Yes. Yes I know. They seem so logical now, but after you've slept you'll see how fantastic they are. Look, I'll go get my hat and take you home. Wait here." The door shut between them, as if the old man were frightened of his visitor and wished a solid barrier for protection.

"God!" Curtin groaned, his hands fisting at his sides. "God help me. God help Stalton . . ." He turned to go back to his roadster, some idea of running back to Yarrow's, of telling his tale to the men there, beginning to form in his desperation . . .

On the sidewalk, bounding along with a noiseless swiftness now terrible to him, was a puffball. It shot by, went on up the street.

Something more was about to happen! Some new horror was coming to one of the houses on Blossom Street! *Hilda Mead's house was in the direction the puffball fled. Was that the house that was marked for doom?*

Chapter 4

THE DARK CLOAKS DEATH

Hal Curtin was running, but it seemed to him he made no progress at all along that quiet street, that as in a nightmare the faster he ran the more firmly was he rooted to the spot where he was.

And always fifty feet before him bounded the pallid bit of fluff he could not overtake, though overtaking it meant so terribly much.

Abruptly it veered, as he'd seen two exactly like it veer. It *was* Hilda's gate, open as he himself had left it, through which the thing darted. It was Hilda's garden pathway up which it scuttered, Hilda's porch steps it struck to puff out of existence in a gray swirl of spore dust.

As he flung himself up the path icy terror jelled Hal Curtin's veins. But nothing happened. The structure that housed the girl he loved did not burst into flame, did not collapse, did not, as he half-expected, vanish as the puffball had in a swirl of grey smoke.

He gasped with relief as he leaped the porch steps, seized the doorknob, jerked the portal open and flung through into the foyer that had known the kisses and the whisperings of so many lingering good-nights . . . And gasped again with terror, finding himself in black darkness, even the street-lamp light close behind blotted out!

This was not merely the absence of light. This was blackness that swallowed sight, which swallowed reality itself and left nothing but terror. This was the black fog that had filled the house up the road just before the lurid flames had made it a roaring furnace, the fog that had swirled out of the theatre auditorium just before its balcony had crashed! Now it was here, and somewhere within it was . . .

"Hilda!" Her name burst from Hal Curtin's clamped throat. "Hilda!"

There was no answer!

"Hilda!"

His cry was quenched by vacant silence, by the muffled hush of doom . . . Was there, somewhere ahead, the faint shadow of a laugh, of a chattering, mad laugh . . .? Ahead . . . from the kitchen where he had left Hilda . . . there was a glow, vague, vertical and narrow. It was light, blessed light, seeping past the edge of the kitchen door.

Curtin's footfalls made hollow, empty echoes in the empty house. He flung into the kitchen—the *lighted* kitchen . . . halted . . .

No Hilda. Not even her body, as he had feared, dead in some awful way. No sign of her at all. But the table at which he'd sat was overturned. A chair was smashed by a struggle, a fragment of her flowered dress caught in its splinters—and the back-door swung open to the mystery of the night.

That was all, the table, the chair, the door . . . not quite all. There was something chalked on the scrubbed white tile of the floor, letters scrawled crudely in crimson chalk and obscured by the breakfast cloth that had slid from the table.

Hal Curtin twitched the gay cloth away. He read the message:

Curtin
  You keep your dam mouth shut if you want to see her again

He stood there, looking at it, the tablecloth trailing from his clenched hand, his mouth working. He had brought this upon her. He . . . His "dam mouth" blurting a warning to Reddon Gast, not waiting to ascertain that he was alone with Wayne. Giving Gast time to hasten here and . . .

How had Gast dared? If he'd been seen entering or found here when Hilda's parents returned . . .

It was not Gast who'd entered here. Not Gast. A clearing of Curtin's vision had revealed to him something more caught in the splintered end of that chair rung than the bit torn from Hilda's dress. Not very much. Just a wisp of black hair, of short hairs black and coarse and kinked.

It was not Reddon Gast who held Hilda Mead prisoner, but Gast's Jock, his mad creature who had capered in the midst of horror laughing a weird and insane laugh!

That was worse, far worse. A madman knows no set design, no fixed purpose. He is swayed by sudden impulses, by the surge of mindless frenzies, *of insane lusts* . . .

"I will protect you always," Curtin's own oath sounded in his ears. "Against Satan and all his imps."

Protect her! She was in the hands of a mad thing. His Hilda, her rounded, warm body, her soft curves, prisoner to a thing half-human perhaps, perhaps all beast, subject to his whims, his will.

Find her! Save her! Save her before it was too late from—Curtin's mind shuddered away from thought of the peril his loved one was in. Find her! But where? How?

Gast knew. He whirled, about to dash out to Gast, to choke the truth from him, to tear him limb from limb if he would not give it. It would take time, valuable time. Hilda's captor could not have gotten far as yet, by the time he had dragged the truth from Reddon Gast they would be God knew how far away. God knew what would have occurred before he could reach them. But he had no choice . . .

Wait! Once more the tortured man recalled his own words, more recently spoken. "Those puffballs—Roget's Wood—That's where his lair is—I'll take you there."

Roget's Wood! Five miles across the fields. But they were gone only ten minutes, fifteen at the most. That was all it was since Gast had left Wayne's. If he went after them at once—no time to get help, no time to get a weapon—he might overtake them, might reach the madman's lair, at least, before . . .

Hal Curtin whirled again, went sprinting out of the kitchen door, out into the lonely night.

Hal Curtin never knew how long it took him to run those five lightless miles over rough fields, up hills that became mountains in the dark, splashing through streams, sliding gasping, torn by his own breathing, torn by thorns of berry bushes, by barbed wire unseen till he was upon it . . . But he raced through, a featureless chiaroscuro of shadows, feeling his hurts not at all, feeling not at all that the clothes were torn from him, that he was lacerated and bleeding, that an iron band was about his chest and the hammers of hell beating upon his skull.

Chapter 5

THE HOUSE OF HORROR

Somewhere in that nightmare flight there was the thrumming of a far-off auto. Somewhere in that Gethsemane there were twin beams of distant headlights scything the darkness . . . and then there was the loom of black woods ahead of him, and he was in their earth-odorous dankness, and he was slowing to a halt.

Careful now. He must be careful. If the madman heard him, got warning of his approach, Hilda would be . . . Hal was weaponless, he had only his arms, and his fists to use against the Lord alone knew what insane strength. The advantage of surprise must be his.

Surprise. But how? There was impenetrable darkness here. There was only the shrill piping of cicadas and the scutterings of the woods' night-kind . . . *There was a glimmer of light, far within the tree-deepened blackness.*

Cautiously, with an instinctive woodsmanship called out of racial memory by his great need, with a taut check on his urge to run, shouting, to the source of that light, Hal Curtin crept up on it. He reached it at long last, at last was crouched at the edge of a tiny clearing, was gazing with aching eyes at a tumbledown cabin of crumbling logs, some shelter left by ancient lumbermen, through whose gaping chinks came the gleam that had brought him here.

Only an instant Curtin crouched there, then he stole across the narrow space between and flattened himself against the moss-slimy wall.

He peered through a crack into the shack's interior. He could see only a small portion of it, but that was enough.

A candle guttered within the hovel. By its wavering, weird luminance he saw Hilda.

Two roughly hewn beams had sometime fallen from the decrepit cabin's roof. They slanted now from roof to earthen floor. The girl lay on one of these, lashed to it hand and foot, half-covered by the rags to which her neat, crisp frock, her dainty undergarments had been reduced.

She was as yet unharmed. Physically at least. All concealment had been torn from one rounded breast. Her arms, her olive, rounded thighs, strained at the lashings that cut into their soft, warm flesh. In her fear-widened eyes there was ineffable terror.

Grotesque and horrible as the creature had appeared when capering on a blazing roof, when laughing from the stage of a smashed theatre, he was now utterly appalling.

Clad only in ragged trousers, his body was the scarred wreck of a frame once clean-cut and stalwart. It was malformed with a rottenness not so much of its tissues as of the soul within it, and shaggy with hair black and kinked and matted as a wild beast's fur. His straddled, columnar legs, his big-thewed arms bulged with swollen muscles. His unshaved, black-bristled countenance was high-browed, its features finely chiseled, but it was empty of all intelligence, of all emotion save the vapid, long-toothed grin of a mindless idiot, while its skin twitched with tiny spasms as though beneath it vermin scuttered and pinched it with their microscopic jaws.

He towered above the bound, half-naked girl, his lips drooling, his soulless eyes repeating their imbecile grin. It was as if he were calling upon her to witness the cleverness of that which he was about.

With a curious deftness one of his great paws juggled three of the puff balls that had accumulated so much of terrible meaning for Hal Curtin, catching and tossing the fragile globules so that they did not burst but danced like down in the wavering light. In and out and about the flickering balls he flashed the braided metal lash of a small whip in gleaming intricate maneuvers.

The madman missed one of the puff-balls. It dropped on Hilda, touched her just where the ragged edge of her torn slip lay against her abdomen's throbbing skin. Her captor snatched at it. His spatulate fingers, clumsy now, caught in the pink fabric. There was a ripping sound . . .

The ball struck the floor, burst. Not spore dust but a black cloud spurted from it, billowed upward to meet the other two that still were floating down . . .

The madman's frenzied fingers were ripping the last vestige of clothing from Hilda. She screamed . . .

Her scream came to Curtin out of blackness that enveloped her, that was filling the cabin, the blackness that had been spewed from the burst puff ball, from the two others. He thrust himself away from the wall, whirled to hurl himself along it to search for a door—there must be a door somewhere by which he could get inside, get to Hilda, fight for her . . .

There was no longer any light. The candle must have gone out. No, not out. Its light quenched by the black fog of the puffballs, by the material blackness that was pouring out through the chinks between the logs, clouds darker than the forest darkness, darker than evil. There was no light, so Curtin had to guide himself by a hand against the log wall, while from behind the wall came the screams of the girl he loved, and the bestial snufflings of the man-beast who . . .

He came to a corner, whirled around it; saw a billow of the stygian vapor pouring out of the door he sought. He vented something between a groan and a shout, plunged through it . . .

Into sightlessness that was alive with sound, Hilda's shrieks, fainter now, the sound of rending cloth, snuffling, and horrible snarls.

"Stop it!" the yell tore Hal's throat. "God blast you," he yelled, "stop it!", hurtling toward those sounds, blinded by the eye-blinding black. "Stop . . ." A heavy blow smashed the back of his head, smashed into his skull. He spun down and down into oblivion . . .

Hal Curtin's head ballooned with pain that expanded within it, as though to burst it. Because of the pain he could not move though he tried to lift his hand to his head, to still that throbbing torture.

It wasn't because of the pain that he could not lift his hand! As returning consciousness became surer he was aware of tightness about his wrists. He was bound, wrists and ankles, to a heavy beam.

He opened his eyes. A wall slanted toward him at a mad angle, an earthen floor slanted up toward him. The guttering light through which he saw them held a curious quality of darkness, as though it were strained through a black mist. This was unreal, dreamlike.

Someone moaned, beside him. Curtin's head rolled to the sound . . . It was Hilda who moaned! Hilda naked, a grey pallor underlying her skin that was crisscrossed with red and angry weals. Her eyes were closed. She was lashed to a beam that slanted downward from above. Curtin realized that he too was lashed to a beam similarly slanted, that it was he and not the wall, the floor, that lay at this unaccustomed angle.

"Hilda!" He managed only a whisper. She did not move.

There were ropes around her ankles, her wrists. But there was also a rope about her neck. This did not go around the beam on which she lay. It went straight up. It went over a hook in the broken ceiling and came down again. Its other end was fastened to the beam to which Hal Curtin himself was bound, and it was just short of tautness. Beneath Hilda's ear the looped rope was tied with a hangman's slipknot.

"Hilda!"

She did not hear him. Could she hear him? Was she . . .?

"She has fainted," someone said, the voice oddly familiar. "But she will come out of it in a moment." Curtin jumped, hearing it. The timber supporting him rocked. Its upper end started to slip from the cross-beam holding it . . .

It was slipping off that cross-beam! A quarter inch more and it would come down—*jerking tight the rope fastened to it, jerking tight the noose around Hilda's neck. Strangling her!*

It didn't. Not this time. Something steadied it, stopped that fearful rocking. A hand, Curtin saw as his head rolled, a great callused paw with black, kinky hair on the backs of its fingers. He saw the owner of that hand, the madman!

That fatuous, leering grin was still on the creature's face. In his other hand was still the metal lash with which he had toyed with the puffballs that had spewed the blackness.

The same voice spoke again, from behind Curtin, where he could not see the speaker. "The next time Jock will let the timber come down," it said, "and you know what that will do. It may interest you to know also that the cords with which you are tied may be broken with not too great effort. You can free yourself, but not quickly enough to stop the beam from falling."

There it was. Hal Curtin was imprisoned not by lashings that he might break, but by the knowledge that his escape meant—Hilda's death.

"You fiend!" he grunted. "Who are you?" He had heard that voice before, many times. Was it because of his physical and mental agony that he could not identify it? It was—no, it could not be Reddon Gast's. Whose then? "Come around here where I can see you." The madman Jock was drawing his whip between his fingers, lovingly. What did he mean to do with it? What in the name of Satan was he going to do with that braided metal thong?

"So that you can see me?" the Voice mused. "Well, it hardly matters now whether you see me or not, you will tell no one who I am. And your reaction will amuse us, perhaps, while we wait for your—sweetheart—to waken."

There was a shuffle of feet on the hard-packed earthen floor. There was a flicker of Jock's eyes to the sound, the look of a fawning dog coming into them. And then a man moved into the range of Hal Curtin's vision.

He was tall and gnarled. His hair was a lustrous white mane crowning a face seamed by deep lines, sunken-cheeked, with eyes that now gleamed wildly.

"Wayne!" burst from Hal Curtin's lips.

Wayne gave a humorless smile. "Clever of you to recognize me. As clever as your guessing how that fire was started, and how the theatre balcony was brought down, and that this was Jock's lair. You are a very clever man, Hal Curtin. I wonder if you have reasoned out the connection of the puffballs with all that has happened."

Curtin's brow knitted. Perhaps by humoring his captor he would gain enough time to work out some escape for Hilda, from this imprisonment, from the threat of the lash Jock fondled. "They're not quite—natural. The blackness. Some variation in them has increased their spore-puff to a vast cloud of blackness. Perhaps the puffballs were treated chemically, carefully grown, crossed with unknown varieties. This cloud cloaked Jock when he was setting the fire, when he was mining the theatre balcony."

"Not Jock," Wayne grinned. "Not Jock. He was to be the scapegoat, the whipping boy, taking the blame if some human agency were uncovered in connection with the disasters. The spore-cloud cloaked me, Hal Curtin. It was I who . . ."

"You!" the bound man gasped, the unbelievable truth against which his mind had rebelled was now stark and inescapable. "You are the one . . ."

"Yes." Wayne's features were no longer kindly. They were dark and contorted with evil triumph, and evil leered from beneath his shaggy brow. "I set the fire, I mined the balcony . . ." He laughed, and there was the same fierce pain in his laugh as in Jock's.

"You," Curtin groaned. "But why . . .?"

"Why?" Tiny light worms crawled in Wayne's slitted eyes. "You can ask that, when . . . But I forgot. You were not born when Stalton damned my brother to horror."

"Your brother?"

The old man's tortured look went to Jock, who was leaning forward now, his avid tongue licking his lips, his burning look fastened on Hilda's nude beauty.

"They were too penurious to pave the streets," Wayne grated. "Jock, a fine young lad, slipped in the mud as he played, sprawled into the gutter. The hoof of a passing horse just flicked his skull—and made him what you see.

"It was murder, the assassination of a soul, but they called it an accident, and I believed them. Dreamer that I was, I dedicated my life to making certain no such accident should occur again, to making Stalton a safe place for its children, for their lives, and a beautiful place for their play. Stalton thanked me with its lips but always behind their eyes, behind the eyes of Gast and Yarrow and the others who knew, I could see the taunting mockery, the reminder of my brother, an animal imprisoned within the asylum's grey walls.

"He was the only human I ever loved; I was lonely, and they had made me so. I grieved, and it was because of what they had done that I grieved. But I forgave them, because I thought they knew not what they had done. I forgave them— till once more, because of greed, they were determined to enrich themselves at the price of the soul of that which I loved, of this town I had created—my all. If I allowed that road to be put through it would have taken the town from me.

"I knew then what I had to do. *They* should not kill Stalton, I would, and swiftly. Stalton's soul was its children; its children should die ... Stalton had taken the soul of my brother—I would take the limbs and lives of its children."

Jock grunted. His shaggy, muscled arm thrust out, jabbing a thumb at Hilda. She stirred, and her eyes opened ...

"Hal!" she exclaimed, joy flaring into her tear-streaked countenance. "Hal ...! You've come for ..." and then all the joy was gone; terror, anguish were replacing it. "But you're tied up too. He's got you ...!"

"I've got him," Wayne broke in. "As I planned. I've got him to punish him for interfering with me in the way that will hurt him most, and Jock will take the blame for that as he would have done for all else if he had been caught. Jock! Go ahead."

The madman whimpered, like a grateful dog, sprang forward. The whip in his hand lifted. The metal lash whistled up, whistled down . . .

Struck Hilda's flesh! A fiery circle sprang out upon it, a bleeding cincture belting her palpitating breast. She screamed . . .

Hal screamed too, screamed mad blasphemy as that biting whip flashed up, flashed down again on the naked flesh of the girl he loved. Screamed wild oaths at the madman, at the white-haired man who stood, impassive, eyes glittering, and lips tight and white. Hal yelled his protests, but he did not dare to move, did not dare to stir so much as a finger lest he rock the beam upon which he lay and bring it thundering down to strangle the life out of her.

Whirr, *smack!* Whirr, *smack!* The madman was laughing now, was laughing and capering as he had laughed and capered before. He was dancing about his victim, her flesh netted with weals now, with spurting wheels, her round soft body clothed with scarlet from her wounds . . . He laughed . . .

And Hilda moaned; "Kill me, Hal! Kill me! I want to die."

There it was! That was the way he could save her from this agony. Death—the only gift for her lover to give her. His muscles knotted, ready for the leap . . .

And still he waited while that whistling lash cut, and cut again, winding itself about an olive, quivering thigh, slashing across a taut abdomen. While a beast-man capered . . .

Then Hal Curtin leaped, tearing loose from the cords that lashed him. The beam leaped with him, crashed down . . .

On the head, the shoulders, of the madman, crushing Jock's skull and pulping his addled brain! It was held for a moment, as Hal had planned it, by the great shaggy form that had danced beneath its slant, held there long enough for Hal to tear free the noose from his sweetheart's neck—and then it crashed, with the bulk of the creature it had slain, to the ground.

But Curtin had whirled, had thrown himself, ravening and mad himself in that moment, at the white-haired Wayne. Curtin's fists, sledge-hammers of vengeance, catapulted—smash—smash—into the hollow-cheeked countenance of the madman's brother.

Smash! There was the crack of snapped bone. Those furious blows had broken John Wayne's jaw—had broken John Wayne's spine . . .

Long after, Hilda Curtin would wake from a dream of never-to-be-forgotten terror, and Hal would wake with her.

She would turn to him, and he would take her in his arms and hold her close to him, knowing as lovers always know, why she was trembling so. And after awhile the trembling would cease, and Hilda would whisper, "Hold me, Hal. Hold me close, close, so I'll know you're here, so I'll know that always, always, you will protect me against . . ."

"Satan and all his imps," Hal would whisper. "Forever, my dear."

And he would hold her close . . .

THE LITTLE WALKING CORPSES

Chapter 1

FEAR COMES TO STANEVILLE

Fear was a living presence in the streets of Staneville. It was visible in the pallor that underlay the weather-beaten countenances of the small town's inhabitants, in the furtive glances with which their eyes, bloodshot by sleeplessness, searched every chance-met face with suspicion and challenge.

Worst of all, it was manifest in the flare of their nostrils as eternally they tested for an alien taint a breeze otherwise fragrant with the crisp autumn tang of the forest that coated Buzzard Mountain.

The odor of death was what they sought and found; the stench of a corpse from whose bones the flesh sloughed, moldering.

On Thursday the smell was faint as the smoke-haze from some brush fire the wardens fought where the Range dipped below the northern horizon. Between Monday and Tuesday last, it had been a fetid reek flooding a moonless midnight in which the shrill of the cicadas was stilled, and the countless small noises that make up the country's nocturnal hush were utterly absent.

No one in Staneville had not been waked by that sudden cessation of all sound. None there was who had not lain for interminable minutes stifled as by a noisome, intangible palm folded over nose and mouth while the darkness, pressing against the houses, throbbed with the beat of vast, unseeable wings.

Rousing to a breathless, sultry dawn, none at first knew his nocturnal experience to be other than a peculiarly vivid nightmare. Then the shadow of a charnal stench drifted into opened windows of the houses on the Slope, into the drab shanties of Frog Hollow, and faces turned questioningly to one another.

In dark pupils the knowledge grew that what had passed in the night had not been a dream, but before paling lips could form the words trembling upon them a scream shrilled through the hamlet.

Knifelike where the woods stretch the tentacles of their underbrush toward the last white dwellings of the well-to-do; distance-dulled yet still startling in the lowly slum west of Main Street; it pulled all Staneville into the open, and streams of half-dressed humanity frothed up the steep eastward ascent to Oxford Lane.

Pouring into the Lane they saw the woman on the trim lawn before her cottage, her countenance contorted, her dark hair a tumbled storm on nude shoulders, her arms outflung and imploring.

Sun-blaze striking through a gossamer nightgown stripped her taut body of all concealment, its broad hips and full-formed breasts, its rounded, sturdy thighs; but no one saw her as a naked woman, only as a frantic and terrified mother. For now that they were near, the scream formed into an intelligible shrill call.

"Dickie! Where are you Dickie? *Dick!*"

"It's Jane Horn," the word passed back to those who could not yet see nor hear. "She's screaming for her little Dickie."

Icy fingers closed on every heart at the mention of misfortune to the freckle-faced, tow-headed ten-year-old, whose cheery whistle and twinkling eyes everyone in the village knew.

Cole Simpson was already at the gate, his gaunt fingers on its latch, having beaten them there because his was the next house to the Horn's. He twisted to the fore-runners and flung at them a barked command.

"Stay back! I'll take care of this."

He went through onto the lawn, his slippers flapping on the dew-wet grass, his tall, spare figure clothed only in trousers and long-sleeved undershirt, his iron-grey hair unkempt. Behind him the first of the crowd stopped short, thrusting back against others who halted in turn. A hush spread swiftly among them and although the woman's cries had died to a sobbing whimper it was distinctly heard by even the farthest removed.

Distinctly heard too was Simpson's voice, strangely gentle, not dry and harsh as was its wont. "What is it, Jane?" The woman's head turned to him but there was no recognition in her eyes.

"Jane!" Simpson snapped sharply, grasping her elbow. "What's the matter?"

"Dick," the name ripped from her. "Gone!" With that she seemed to break up, the tenseness leaving her, her legs folding so that save for the dart of the man's arm about her waist, she would have crumpled to the ground.

"Listen," he said, his narrow, hallow-cheeked face more like grey granite than ever, "listen to me. You must hold yourself together. You must tell us exactly what has happened so that we can help you, so that we can find Dick for you. Tell us what you know."

Somewhere in the crowd a voice whispered, "That smell! It's stronger here . . ."

"Know?" Jane Horn was saying, looking at Simpson now, seeing him. "All I know is that I went to his room to wake him up and he wasn't there. Not there—nor anywhere."

"Maybe he sneaked out to go swimming before school, or for some other kid's nonsense."

"In his nightshirt? Barefoot? His shoes are there, all his clothes. And he wouldn't do that without telling me. Not my Dickie. Not while his father is away."

"Even your Dick might. He's a boy, after all, and thoughtless. Go into the house, my dear, and get something on Meanwhile I'll look around. There will be footprints. The ground is soft and I've kept the people from trampling your lawn. Don't worry, we'll find him."

"Footprints! That's it. Look for them. We'll look for footprints under his window." The mother pulled free from Simpson, darted toward the side of the house, her uncovered feet splashing the dew.

There were no footprints in the loam where she bent, peering at the ground. There were no footprints anywhere on the lawn. There was nothing to tell where Dick had gone, or what had happened to him.

By the time this had been ascertained the police arrived: the trio of peace officers that was all Staneville could boast. Balloon-paunched, dull eyes fat-drowned, Chief John Mault wheezingly posted his two lank constables to bar out the buzzing throng by a show of authority less effective than Cole Simpson's simple command, and waddled through the gate to join Cole in his search.

While pendulous jowls concealed Mault's collarless state, no amount of fussy self-importance could hide his fat-brained futility, yet it was he who discovered the only trace of the vanished lad. It was a book, *Ken Thomas: Junior G-Man,* that he picked up out of the rank weeds where the Horn property ended at the rear of the house and the ground lifted sharply to the forest edge.

He turned it over in his pudgy hands, an abrupt stillness cloaking him. Staring at it over his shoulder, Jane Horn vented a tiny scream.

"It's Dick's!" she exclaimed. "Lou sent it to him from Buffalo. It came last night and Dick took it to bed with him. He fell asleep holding it so tightly I couldn't take it away. Give it to me."

She reached for it. Mault evaded her grasp. "No," he sighed. "No, I've ... I've got to keep it." The pink of his plump cheeks had faded to a sickly green.

"What is it?" Simpson demanded, coming up. "Fingerprints?"

"No," the police officer replied, his voice low and toneless as though it were being squeezed out of a clamped larynx. "They'd be washed away by the dew. But ... but ..." His one hand jerked away from the book. There was a dark brown smear on it, of some viscid, sticky gum. The hand lifted to Simpson's nose.

"Smell," Mault husked.

There was no need to bring that stain so close to the man's nostrils. The stuff that Mault's hand had rubbed from Dickie's book had the unmistakable stench of rotting flesh!

Jane Horn smelled it and her mother's instinct, swifter than any man's thoughts, seized its meaning. "The Thing took him," she shrieked. "The Thing in the night." Then she was a crumpled and pitiful heap in the grass.

They heard that scream, the people buzzing in the road, and blanched, recalling the black quarter-hour they had forgotten, recalling how close the beat of vast, unseen wings had throbbed to the walls behind which their own children were.

That was when the Fear was born in Staneville, the Fear Staneville had not for one moment forgotten because never for one moment of the dreadful days or the sleepless nights since had the air been untainted by the smell of the unknown Thing in the night.

Chapter 2

DEATH IN THE GRAVEYARD

Rosalie Carter fought to drive the brooding fear from her classroom, piling on her nineteen charges more work than their little minds and their little hands could cope with. Smiling with her lips, though in her brown eyes there was no smile, she drove them, cruelly kind, while all the time she was poignantly conscious of the empty seat at the back of the room, of the armed men guarding the schoolhouse on Oak Street.

Last Tuesday there had been no school. The mothers had kept their children behind locked doors and barred windows while the fathers, and the young men of the village, had combed every cellar, every yard, and had quartered Buzzard Mountain and the tilled lowland west of Staneville, with no result.

Ostensibly it had been Chief Mault who directed the search, but it was Cole Simpson who had taken a map of the township, penciled numbered squares upon it and assigned each small plot to a group of three. It was Simpson who, drawn, haggard, had checked the last number against a fruitless report just as Wednesday's dawn was greying the sky.

"Nothing," he had said, tonelessly. "No trace of Dick. No trace of whoever took him. No trace, even, of the dead thing we keep smelling."

That had been in this very building. Because Simpson was principal of the Consolidated School it had been used as headquarters for the searchers. Rosalie, brewing coffee through the night for the hunters, had watched the hope drain slowly out of them and the fear grow steadily in their tired eyes. She had heard what Simpson had said at the last, had seen him throw his hands wide in token of despair.

She had come to his support when he had insisted it would be better for the children of Staneville if they resumed their normal routine rather than remain shut in with terror. Despite the alarm of the parents, there was no real evidence that the menace of the Thing was directed against them or, except for the brooding, ominous odor, that it would return at all. At all events the youngsters would be safer carried to and from their homes in convoyed buses, more easily guarded when assembled in a group.

Thus they had argued; but it was not reason, it was the force of Cole Simpson's personality, the respect for him almost amounting to awe that the parents had not lost since they had been tiny tads under his tutelage, that had prevailed.

These recollections ran through Rosalie Carter's mind while a pigtailed miss swayed from one scuffed shoe to another, dumbly twisting the hem of a flowered dress too short for her.

"Come, come, Joan," the teacher's clear, young voice chided. "You ought to know all about how the wasps lay their eggs. This is only Thursday and we heard such a grand report about them on Monday. Who was it brought in that nice composition . . .?" She gulped, went spinning to the window to hide the appalled dismay in her face! That had been Dick Horn's last recitation to her, his last recitation anywhere!

Her figure was slight against the bright window, graceful, with the lilting rhythm of youth and the out-of-doors. One tanned arm was visible, its firm roundness hardening as its fingers dug into the sill. A straight back shadowed under crisp, white organdie shook with a repressed sob.

"I know, teacher, I remember," an eager pipe brought Rosalie around again. "Let me tell." A spectacled youngster, half out of his seat waved an excited hand.

"All right, Charles." The girl, her winsome small countenance hardly more mature than those of the tots she taught, was for once grateful for the impetuousness of the class pest. "Go ahead."

Joan Hardie dropped into her seat as the lad stumbled into the aisle. "The wasp is the bandit of the insect world," he began in a singsong monotone whose intelligibility was somewhat impaired by the absence of two front teeth. "It stings other insects but it doesn't kill them. It makes them . . . in . . . in-sen . . ."

"Insensible, Charles," Rosalie supplied. "That means puts them to sleep so that they don't move and seem dead, though they are really alive. The word's insensible."

"Yes'm. Insensible. Then the wasp drags them to its burrow where it lays an egg on them. Then it closes up the burrow so that its enemies can't find it and . . ."

The boy's mouth was still open but speech was no longer coming from it. His eyes were enormously magnified behind their lenses, bulging and abruptly black. The class was a mass of pallid, staring faces, wavering queerly—and the stench of a rotting cadaver was as thick as an unfelt fluid in the blurring room!

Rosalie's dry throat gave a soundless rasp. A greyness obscured her sight, deepened swiftly into black . . .

Rosalie was on the floor, awkwardly jammed between iron legs of a desk and a ventilator grating in the wall. The smell had faded almost to its former vagueness. Above her there was the sound of startled movement and the beginning of scared whimperings. She shoved a desperate hand against wood gritty with chalk dust, twisted, somehow managed to regain her feet.

"It's all right, children," she called out. "There's nothing to be frightened of."

She was sick with nausea, her vision scarcely clear yet, within her brain the beat, beat of vast and dreadful wings, but she must reassure them, must ward off from them the panic that was throttling her. "Everything's all right."

The class swam out of the blur, the youngsters straightening from the desks over which they had slumped. Charley Collins was scrambling erect. Nothing was changed, nothing at all.

Get them back into routine! She must get them back.

"Go on, Charles. What happens after the wasp closes up its burrow?"

The boy wasn't looking at her. Then he was, and he was trying to tell her something but his twitching lips made no words. He pointed a grimy forefinger . . . at a vacant place.

It wasn't the seat Dick Horn used to occupy. It was in the front, near the door. It was where Joan Hardie ought to be, but she wasn't there. She wasn't anywhere in the room.

At Staneville's northeast corner, Oxford Lane curves west and becomes Oak Street. Along the outer edge of this curve is a low wall of lichen-covered stone blocks, and from this a graveyard runs back, gently rising till it ends against a vertical crag outthrust from the forested steep of Buzzard Mountain.

With uncommon foresight the earliest burials were made at the base of this dark and forbidding cliff, and the village of the dead grew outward toward what was in its beginning merely a road climbing to the spring, high in the mountain, whose icy flow was at that time sufficient for the infant hamlet's needs. As a result, the portion of the cemetery bordering the Lane is an expanse of velvet greensward upon which row after row of carefully tended tombstones give a decorative dignity to the graves.

Far back, however, in the shadow of the terminal precipice, neglect has allowed Time and Nature to run their course. Vines, torn by winter storms from the rocky façade, tangle with lush weeds and rank brush to form a gloomy thicket. Here oblong depressions grow slowly deeper as the dank loam settles into hollows once filled by caskets now inextricably mingled with their ancient occupants. Here green-slimed stone slabs, gnawed by decay, lean crazily askew, their inscriptions moss-filled and illegible.

Into this miniature jungle, the Thursday of that dreadful week, Jethro Anther forced his grumbling way. Brambles tore at the dirt-stained, tough fabric of his overalls. He protected his face from the lash of resentful withes with a pair of hedge-clipping shears gripped tightly in one gnarled hand, and dragged a long-handled spade after him with the other.

"Fool idea," Anther mumbled with toothless gums, "Fixin' up a grave nobody's thought of long as I been diggin' 'em here, an' that's more'n thirty year."

Completely bald, his skin leathery, hatched by fine lines and the color of sunbaked clay, there was a more than fancied resemblance between the gravedigger and his clients. Of all Staneville's inhabitants he was the least affected by what was going on. The smell of death was the odor of his livelihood. He was too old for curiosity, too old for fear.

"But mebbe I ought ter be glad Cal Thomas seed his great-gran'ther's name on thet stone, pokin' around in here Tuesday," he continued, "an' give orders ter have it made decent." He gave vent to a cackling laugh. The thicket seemed to absorb the sound, and Anther came through into a clearing, although the shadow of foliage and of the mountain was no less deep.

He halted at the edge of one of the rectangular depressions. Its stone lay on the ground at its head, fallen backward. Moss was freshly scraped away to reveal faint letters; B-REB-N-S-HO—S.

"Barebones Thomas," Anther cackled, "Mebbe thet wuz yer name when they put ye in, but there ain't even bones left o' ye now, let alone flesh ter cover 'em. Well, I better be gettin' started manicurin' yer garden."

He dropped the shears on the ground to one side, leaned the spade against his knee while he spat into his callused palms, then gripped its handle. The heart-shaped blade went easily into the ground.

Jethro Anther lifted an unexpectedly large first shovelful, grunted. "Huh!" he exclaimed. "If I didn't know better I'd say some 'un's been an' dug this up not more'n a week ago. An' . . . an'," he sniffed. "Say, thet's funny. This dirt still smells . . ."

He checked abruptly, his wiry body rigid. There was the sound of movement behind him. A rustle of leaves, a slither. Anther started to turn . . .

A shriek sliced the stillness of the graveyard, a single gibbering shriek . . . The silence of death's sleep closed down.

Chapter 3

THE SHAPE IN THE DUSK

"Joan has gone out without permission," Rosalie Carter said, surprised at her own calmness. "She knows she should not have done that." She went along the front of the desk rows. She was opening the door, was leaning out.

The long corridor was dim. From behind shut doors came the drone of the other classes. She could hear Mr. Waite's thin voice declaiming with querulous emphasis: *"amo, amas, amat,"* . . . the muffled laughter of the kindergartners. There was no small, pigtailed figure in the hall. There was no patter of small, scuffed shoes.

Rosalie Carter felt eyes on her back; watching, expectant eyes. If she called out she would alarm the whole school. But she dared not leave her eighteen youngsters alone, dared not send one of them to Mr. Simpson's office upstairs.

She shut the door quietly, turned to meet the eyes that were upon her, eyes in which deepening fear mingled with childish trust.

"I'll have a talk with her when she gets back," she smiled. "A very serious talk. In the meantime get your notebooks and your spellers and copy the list of words on page twenty-seven." She strolled unconcernedly back across the room through an obedient rustle. "Five times ... I want you to know them well." She reached the window, stood against it, peering out.

Her hands, in front of her and hidden from the children, gripped the sill tightly and were trembling uncontrollably. In the moment of thought Rosalie had gained for herself she had abruptly realized that time had elapsed between the surge of that odor and her struggle to rise from a floor to which she did not recall falling. She had lost consciousness for a period the length of which there was no way of estimating. The Collins boy too had fallen to the floor. Every child in the room had known oblivion ...

Every child! Joan also. Joan had not left the room. She had been *taken* from it!

Rosalie's body was hollow within, and the hollow was filled with a quivering jelly of dread.

A footfall thudded through the glass. Jim Tarr was coming past on his patrol, a rifle gripped in strong, capable fingers, his frame big-boned, lithe, the ripple of silky muscles somehow evident beneath the rough tweeds cloaking them. His head turned to her window, as Rosalie knew it would, and a comradely grin illuminated his blunt-jawed, broadly sculptured face.

Her arm lifted in what to any watching from behind would look like her usual wave of greeting. But the fingers of its hand beckoned imperatively, then went to her lips with a signal for discretion.

Jim's grin vanished. He nodded quick understanding, his blue eyes narrowing with concern. He wheeled, broke into a ground-covering lope. Rosalie saw the dark auburn of his hatless head vanish beyond the corner around which was the school's entrance.

Warming with the knowledge that she had secured aid, that it was Jim who was coming to help her, the teacher turned back to her class. For a short space the silence was broken only by the scrape of busy pencils. Then knuckles rapped briefly against the door. Breath hissed almost inaudibly from between the girl's cold lips as she turned the knob and opened it.

"Pardon me, Miss Carter," Jim said, his tone low but pitched just right to reach into the room. "I've just made a bet with one of the boys about how to spell a word and if you've got time we'd like to have you settle the question."

"Glad to, Mr. Tarr," Rosalie smiled, "but we mustn't disturb the class." She slipped through between the edge of the door and its jamb, keeping the portal half-open.

"What's up?" Tarr breathed. "You looked . . . jittery."

He wasn't alone. Cole Simpson was there beside him, grave, anxious. "Jittery?" Rosalie murmured. "I'm terrified . . ." and then she was telling them what had occurred, her eyes not on them but watching through the slitted opening the room where there were now two vacant places. "Joan's gone," she finished. "I'm sure she's gone just like Dickie Horn."

There was a throbbing moment in which the men's faces visibly greyed.

"She must be somewhere in the building," Jim husked. "Every side of it, every window and door is being watched by armed men and even a rat couldn't get out without someone seeing it."

"I'll have every inch of the school gone over at once," the principal put in. "Can you keep on with your class?"

Rosalie's lips were icy but there was no lack of courage in her voice. "Of course."

"Then do so. Don't worry. We'll find Joan. We'll find her if we have to take the structure apart brick by brick."

"No," Rosalie Carter said. "No. You will not find her."

Nor did they, though under Simpson's direction not even a fly's resting place was left unsearched. They had to invade the classrooms at the last, had to let the pupils know what was going on, had to question every one of them, every teacher, and send the children home in busses bristling on the outside with weapons and shuddering inside with white-lipped terror. But they did not find Joan Hardie.

Not then.

Jim Tarr had ridden the doorstep of the school bus that made the outer circuit of the town. It was returning now through the early dusk the shadow of Buzzard Mountain brings to Staneville, and he was seated alongside Walt Smeed, its driver, but his forefinger still hovered near the trigger of the rifle in his lap and his anxious look still probed the dimness gathering in Oxford Lane.

"Lou Horn got back this mornin'," Walt remarked nodding at the pale bulk of the house from which the Thing had taken its first victim. "They say he's near crazy with grief."

"I don't wonder," Tarr responded. "It would be a hell of a sight better for him and for Dickie's mother, to know what's happening to the kid than to be like this, imagining almost anything."

"Yeah," Smeed agreed. "Yeah. You're right. Even if he was a layin' in the graveyard here." He slowed for the bend just ahead.

"STOP!" Jim yelled, clawing the door handle. "Stop!" He was out of the bus, was vaulting the cemetery wall. Walt, slammed on his emergency, snatched a forty-five out of a holster hanging from the wheel, lurched to the ground, scrambled over the fence. Thudding feet gave him his direction. He saw Tarr, a spectral apparition dodging among tombstones in the spectral greyness, plunged after him.

Jim slowed, stopped as Smeed came up to him. "What is it?" the latter gasped.

Tarr peered into the colorless murk that was almost more concealing than darkness. Smeed stiffened, fiercely aware of the cadaveral odor, omnipresent for so long but weirdly appropriate here. There was no comfort in the hardness of the revolver butt grinding into his palm, but a strange sense that what menaced Staneville was immune to bullets, to any human weapon.

"What did you take out after?" he demanded again, speech an effort.

"I don't know," Tarr whispered, as though he could be overheard. "I saw—thought I saw—someone moving in here. Or some *thing*. It didn't seem to be shaped like anything human, no more than those . . ." he jerked a hand to the huddled, shapeless bulks about them that might be headstones or—beasts—crouched, motionless, waiting for a chance to spring upon them. "I saw it for just an instant and then—it was gone."

"Hell," Smeed grunted, with no assurance. "It wasn't nothing. Come on back to the bus."

Jim stared at the gloomy mass of the thicket against the cliff. "I wonder . . . I'd like to poke around in there. I've got a hunch . . ."

"You go in there, buddy, and you go alone. You're nuts anyways. The boys went through that mess with a fine tooth comb last Tuesday and Wednesday and scratches were all they got for their pains. Are you coming?"

"All right," Tarr yielded, still reluctant. "I'm coming."

They went toward where they thought the Lane was. It took so long to reach the wall that Walt began to think they were twisted around, but they hit it after awhile. They climbed over. Smeed slid in under the big steering wheel, switched on headlights ceiling lights, released the brake.

"Hey!" Tarr exclaimed, behind. "There's one of the kids still . . . No. Good God! Walt! Look . . ."

Smeed turned. Tarr was halfway down the aisle, his hand on a boy's shoulder. The boy was toppling forward in the seat, strangely stiff. The boy's lids were open but there were no eyes between them, only balls dully white. There was a spray of freckles across the small, still face and it was the face of Dickie Horn.

A night shirt had slipped half-off Dick's bony little chest and Jim's fingers, keeping him from falling, lay in the corner between shoulder and neck, their bronze darker by contrast with the sickly grey-whiteness of the skin there.

"Dead," Walt said. The one word, a statement, not a question, was all he could manage. Somehow he couldn't move, couldn't get up, but he knew there was something queer about Tarr, about the way he stood, rigid, about the way he stared at the small boy.

"No," Jim Tarr said. "Not dead. Maybe he'd be better off if he was."

Chapter 4

DISCOVERY

Jim Tarr's mouth was a tight, colorless line but his nostrils were flaring. Walter Smeed got it too, the smell of dead rot in the bus, stronger here than it had been in the graveyard. The odor of fear. He gulped.

"What . . . what do you mean?"

Jim's head lifted, turned to him, its face a deep-lined, still mask. "I felt a throb, here in the artery. Another, just now.. His heart's beating, very slow, but beating. And the skin's cold, icy, but soft. He isn't dead, Walt. But . . ."

"But what?"

"I don't know." It was a groan. "We've got to get him to a doctor. The hospital. Get going, Walt. For God's sake *get* going."

The rasping burr of the starter, the roar, the bus's racketing lurch into motion and its rushing thunder as it hurtled down the long descent of Oak Street brought some sense of reality back to Smeed. It was fully dark now, but the night was filled with the yellow oblongs of lighted, blind-drawn windows, with windows tight shut, nailed shut, with houses whose doors were locked and double-locked against terror.

"What you saw," Walt threw back to Jim. "It slipped around us and put the kid in the bus while we were looking for it. If we'd been smart enough we might have caught it."

"We might have caught it," Tarr husked. "But we didn't. If any more children go . . ."

It was not until the dusk had deepened almost into darkness than anyone thought to switch on the light. Rob Wood, the school janitor, did it then.

Rosalie Carter, pallor lending her a fragile, almost ethereal quality, blinked. Then, from her habitual post at the window, she could see again the room where she had taught for months, unfamiliar now because its occupants were adults and not the youngsters who had trusted her and whom she had failed.

Cole Simpson sat at the big desk up front, her desk, and beside him was seated John Mault; the grey, poised slenderness of the one an almost painful contrast to the other's gross bulk. Standing to Simpson's left were the school's two handymen: stooped, shabby, stockily built Wood, competent and powerful in his suit of blue dungarees, despite the years evident in the grey bristle blurring the square line of his jaw.

The other teachers were squeezed into the children's seats, a half-dozen angular spinstresses and two men. Julius Waite, the Latin instructor was as sere as his subject; wizened, his countenance sallow and wrinkled as a dried apple; Doctor Holzer, teacher of science, white-bearded, ruddy-cheeked; even brooding fear failing to iron out the good-humored wrinkles at the corners of his small, twinkling eyes.

Grim, quivering with leashed wrath, two young men stood at the door, rifles horizontally across their chests, fingers curled on the triggers.

Mr. Simpson sighed, and began to speak. "One of you," he said in his low, harsh voice, "knows where Joan Hardie is. It is impossible, with the school watched as closely as it was, that she had been taken from it. No one but those here and the children were in the building. No one except the children has been permitted to leave it. Therefore she is somewhere within its four walls and one of you knows where."

"That's logic," Mault put in. "Nobody can't argue with that."

"I can." Surprisingly, it was Mr. Waite whose querulous tone interrupted. "I agree that the child was not seen leaving the school. But she *is not* in it. We have searched every nook and cranny of it."

Simpson's expressionless visage moved slightly to bear upon him. "What do you suggest, then?"

The Latin teacher shrugged. " *'Facile est descensus Averni!'*, 'The descent to Hell is easy', but no easier than to pose objections to a faulty solution of this mystery that confronts us."

"Nevertheless," the principal insisted, "you have something in mind or you would not have spoken. What is it?"

Mr. Waite looks like a scared brown hare, Rosalie thought, twisting a handkerchief in her fingers. He's simply terrified of answering, but Mr. Simpson will make him.

"What is it, Julius Waite?"

Waite's fleshless lip quivered. "As Miss Bunker will bear me out, Joan Hardie is neither outside nor inside of this building. Hence she must have . . ."

"Vanished into thin air," Dr. Holzer snorted. "Bunk! I've worked with you and Cole a quarter of a century but this is the first time I've discovered any of us is feeble-minded. I . . ."

"Just a minute, August," Simpson intervened. "Please let me handle this. Julius, we may in the end be forced to accept your views, but we are not yet ready to admit there is anything of the supernatural about what has happened. We will adhere to the probabilities. I want to know where each one of you was at two-twenty today, which was when I came out of my office and met young Tarr responding to Miss Carter's summons. Suppose you tell us first."

"I was in front of my class, teaching the blockheads the conjugation of *amo.* I . . ."

"That will do. How about you, Miss Bunker?"

The response of the parrot-faced English instructress was similar, as was that of the rest except for Dr. Holzer. He alone had not been in full view of a score of pupils at the crucial moment.

"I was in my office," he explained, "but the only door to it is into the laboratory and there were a dozen students there dissecting frogs. Its window is right over the lawn Tarr was patrolling and even if I were still agile enough to climb down from the second story and back again I would surely have been seen. However, you may search the room if you wish."

"We've already done that," Mault said grimly. "And found nothing. Well, Simpson, it looks like . . ."

Sound rattled the window panes, cutting him off; the roar of a racing motor, the blare of a frenzied horn from outside. Rosalie whipped around, peering through the glass, was jostled by others jumping to look out. A huge vehicle lurched past, its row of windows lighted.

"It's one of the school buses," someone exclaimed. "It's shooting into the hospital driveway. Something new must have happened."

The rush was away from Rosalie now, to the door, but it piled up there against the stalwart guards. "Stop!" Mault called, "You're not going out. None of you is going out till we find out who's tied up with this thing."

There was a sudden chatter of outraged protest, stilled by Simpson's calm, "Take your seats, ladies and gentlemen. Please take your seats." Rosalie noticed that she had dropped her handkerchief in the excitement, bent to pick it up.

When she straightened her pupils were dilated, her face taut, her slim frame trembling.

"We are still of the opinion that one of you is concealing something," Cole Simpson was saying, "and until that one confesses you are all under arrest. You will be held here under guard, all night, all week if necessary. There will be armed men posted outside the doors and armed men under the windows and their instructions will be to shoot to kill anyone who tries to leave."

"What about you, Simpson," Julius Waite demanded. "Seems to me you're in this as much as the rest of us. Even more. The first child disappeared from the house next to yours, and . . ."

"Chief Mault will be in my office with me," came the steady reply. "He cannot be suspected."

"Mr. Simpson," Rosalie found her tongue at last. "I've found out something."

"Hold it. If you've discovered something it would be better that the culprit, if he is in this room as we suspect, should not hear you. Suppose you come to my office, with me and Chief Mault, and tell us about it there."

Rosalie nodded agreement. "Meantime," Simpson continued, turning to the others, "the guards are already posted. Remember their instructions."

Rosalie Carter went down the first floor corridor between the slender old educator and the wheezing, puffing police Chief. There were too many in the hall for her to speak; too many hard-eyed, set-jawed men with guns of all description, watching her curiously. Simpson unlocked a door, clicked a switch button. The familiar furniture seemed to take on a new aspect, seen thus by artificial light. This was the outer office and Simpson led the other two toward the door to his private sanctum. He was moving very slowly, very wearily. He had to hold on to the jamb while he fumbled his key into the lock of that inner door.

"I better 'phone the hospital," Mault wheezed, "and find out about that bus. You two go on in, I'll be right with you."

The door opened. Simpson found the switch, filled the small room with light. The door closed behind Rosalie. She heard the spring lock click. The principal staggered, turned a face toward her that was green-filmed, pallid.

"I—I'm not as strong as I thought." He made a pathetic effort to smile, and suddenly Rosalie was sorry for him. "These three days . . . I have had no sleep."

He gained his desk, stumbled into the chair. His hands were hidden by the glass-topped walnut. "The school—my dream of the years, one great school instead of the little one room shanties scattered around—slipping away after I had attained it. If this keeps up . . . already the farmers are refusing to send their youngsters into Staneville, refusing to pay their assessments . . . the builders threatening to foreclose their mortgage . . . But what was it you found?"

"This." Rosalie held her handkerchief out to him. "I dropped it, rubbed it against the ventilator grating when I picked it up, and . . .

The wisp of linen was blotched by a dark brown smear. There was no need to bring it closer to Simpson. The odor of a corpse, the odor of the fear that had been throttling Stane-ville so long, was very strong in the room—as if a corpse were present.

There was something queer in the old man's eyes. "You think . . .?" His arm moved, as though his unseen hands were doing something under the desk-top.

"It was on the grating. The hole's large enough for a man to get through, and the network lifts out easily. It's some gas that makes you unconscious. That's the way Joan was taken!"

That smell! It was strangely more powerful! It was choking her, was stoppering speech. Rosalie swayed, clutched for support.

Through a darkening swirl she could make out Cole Simpson's face, contorted, his eyes growing till the face was all eyes, hating eyes . . . Simpson!

She was going down, down, down into bottomless dark. Hands caught her, lifted her . . .

The bus roared into the hospital courtyard, racked to a halt. Men in white sprang out of a doorway over which a brilliant lamp globe was lettered, ADMITTING ROOM—started running across the asphalt toward the ambulance.

"Take care of it, Walt," Jim Tarr snapped. "I'm off." He was in the vehicle door, was dropping to the ground.

"Hey!" Smeed blurted. "Where are you going?"

"Back to the graveyard," Jim snapped. "Back to find out what's hiding in the jumble beneath the cliff." Then he was gone, dodging the approaching orderlies; gone into the darkness that lay on Staneville like a funereal shroud.

Chapter 5

STING OF THE HUGE BLACK WASP

Rosalie Carter came up out of a sick nothingness to dazed awareness of motion, to dull realization that she was cradled in arms that felt her weight not at all, that she was being carried to some unknown place. There was the beat of vast, unseen wings about her, the flow past her cheek of air dank and damply chill. There was that smell in her nostrils, the stench of corrupt flesh waking memory, waking fear to claw her . . .

Over and over she kept sinking into oblivion, over and over, but each time the fear was greater, the dread grown, till almost the girl was praying, inchoately, that there should be no next time.

Sometimes there would be the horror of that moment of discovery that Cole Simpson, venerated and venerable, was the perpetrator of that which had come to Staneville. Sometimes there would be only the terror of what lay ahead, at the end of this strange, dark journey. But always there would be that throb, throb, throb and always the reek of a charnel house.

Time blurred and had no meaning. It might be minutes or hours since the beginning of this too real nightmare. Rosalie did not know and did not care.

At length, however, she came to a space of awakening and though the beat of something enormous but unseen met her, and the sepulchral stench, she was no longer moving, no longer held in muscular arms. There was hardness under her, a painful hardness, and there was a rustling sound about her.

She forced her lids apart.

A glow, greenish, unearthly, lay against Rosalie's aching eyes. Inconsequentially, she recalled a rotted stump once seen in the lightless woods, a luminous ghost shape. This glow was exactly like that shining inner phosphorescence of decay.

It seeped down out of a ceiling above her, so low that it seemed to press ponderously upon her, so irregular in surface that it seemed to have no shape, that it seemed momentarily about to cave in and crush her. Dark, slender threads crawled over it, immobile at the instant but surely about to wake to loathsome life.

The rustling sound rolled Rosalie's head to it, to a swirl of blackness moving toward her, apparently out of a wall eerily glowing and formless as the roof!

The Thing was man shape, yet in some curious manner not human. It was faceless in rustling, stygian draperies and the limbs growing out of it were like great black wings, but the sound they made, reaching for her, was a flutter and not the throb, throb that still beat against her ears.

Terror, imminent and awful, struck icily to the very core of the girl's being, stripping her of will, of strength, so that she was held in a nightmare paralysis. The motion of the Thing took it out of the line of her sight and she saw past it.

An abortive scream rasped the tight cords of her throat.

A black hole gaped in the wall, entrance to some tunnel. Before it, stark nude and incredibly rigid on a green-slimed pallet that had the very size and shape of a gravestone, Joan Hardie lay. One pigtail coiled in a lax position across the pitiful, small neck and tiny white fingers were outspread as if to fend off horror.

"No," the Thing had a voice, muffled, hollow. "She is not dead, my dear." And a chuckle came, slow, hateful. "Not dead, but she will remain like that for years. Forever, if I wish it so."

Yes, the apparition had a voice. Though changed by the fabric through which it came there was still something familiar in its timbre. Of course! Rosalie remembered. This was Cole Simpson. It was Cole Simpson who had tricked her into being alone with him, had gassed her to insensibility and carried her off.

"Look at her. You will be like that in a moment—and for-ever." He was right above her now, was bending to her, those grotesque arms of his descending to her, like wings of black horror closing down. "You know too much—but you will be silent about what you know, forever." He was going to kill her, this man whom all Staneville revered, this man she, her-self, had so venerated. "Not dead, but silent, unless I choose to wake you." A hand, cold, clammy, closed on her bare arm.

"Wait!" Astounding that Rosalie could speak even with this harsh croak. "Wait." Somehow she must deter him, must stave him off. Perhaps Mault had battered down that locked door, found them gone, found the way they had gone. "What are you going to do to me?" There must be rescue for her. There must be! "What do you mean, not dead but silent for-ever?"

Again that slow chuckle, but the black form was stayed. "In-sensible, my dear." Where had she heard that word before? "Unable to move, to speak, to see. Needing no food nor drink. Not dying even though centuries pass, because there is no waste of tissue, the functions being suspended. It can be done. I am the first man to have accomplished it, though aeons ago the way was discovered by the wasps."

The wasps! That was it! Strange that it should have been Dickie Horn who had told how the wasps stung their victims, dragged them to their burrows and left them alive for ten times their span of normal life, in order that the hatched grubs might have fresh food. Strange that thus he should have predicted his own fate.

Recollection struck at Rosalie of a digger-wasp burrow she had unearthed one spring, of the living-dead cicada bodies within and how they were acrawl with the little white grubs; eating, eating. That was what was in store for her! Here, in this dark cavern, the blind pallid crawlers of under-earth would find in her inanimate body fresh food for their hunger and . . .

The claw on her arm tightened, and in the other, thrust abruptly out of the black drapery, was the bright glean of a glass tube, the sharp gleam of a long, keen needle . . .

"This will do it," her captor husked. "The venom of a thousand wasps in this hypodermic syringe. It will . . ."

From the tunnel's Nubian maw there was the faint thud of distant feet. *Of approaching rescue.* He had not noticed it, she must keep him from noticing it. "I know why you are doing it to me, but why did you do it to the children? You have always loved them, why are you making them suffer?"

"So that others, millions of others, should not suffer." It worked! The slow thrust of that terrible needle was halted. "The world stirs to war, and with the next war will come clouds of lethal gas descending on the cities, enveloping them for years, perhaps. No way to escape it, no way to bar it out and still have air to breathe, food to eat, water to drink. But I will show them the way. A dose of the living death in this vial, then they can be closed up in chambers hermetically sealed against the gas. When it is gone the chambers will be opened and they will be taken from them and brought back to life, the children and the women who but for me would be long dead. A million against a few, but I had to devise a method to obtain the few I needed for experiment, a way to hide them . . ."

The oncoming feet were nearer, but still far. Too far. "Then there *is* a way," Rosalie said, "to bring your victims back to life."

"My subjects," he corrected. "There must be. There has to be." Was that a sigh that came out of the faceless mask? "But my knowledge was not sufficient to find it." Then a chuckle. "That is why I gave them back my first subject so that those who do have the knowledge might work on him, might find that way for me. Clever, wasn't it?"

"Clever," she praised, fighting for the little time she needed now. "As clever as the way you sent the gas through the ventilators into my classroom, making me and the children unconscious while you stole Joan from among us. Clever as the gas itself, from which people wake without knowing they have been asleep. What is that gas?"

"My own invention. An organic compound, distilled from the half-putrefied bodies of animals. I . . ."

He checked, whirled to the pound of feet in the tunnel mouth. Out of it lurched a bulky form. In the grisly light Rosalie glimpsed a curious contraption clamped over the man's nose and mouth, but she knew he was Rob Wood, the janitor.

"Rob!" she yelled. "Thank God you've come." She flailed hands against the gravestone beneath her, pushing herself up to aid him in the coming struggle.

"Hurry it, Chief," Wood panted. "They're comin' awake in the schoolhouse. We got ter get back quick afore they find out we're missin' . . . *Look out!* She's gettin' away!"

He jumped on Rosalie, half-risen. His spatulate fingers caught her frock at the throat, it tore away with a ripping sound. The dank air of the subterranean hollow was chill against her bared breasts, and against them his callused palms thrust cruelly, shoving her down upon the stone, holding her down, helpless, immovable.

Above her the other's black shapelessness swooped down, and the terrible needle darted for her. A scream broke from Rosalie Carter's throat, shrill, agonized.

Chapter 6

WITHIN THE PRECIPICE

From the schoolhouse on Oak Street the reek of a hundred moldering corpses was gradually fading. Among the still bodies slumped in the hallways, in the seats of the two classrooms that had been guarded as prison cells, one stirred a little, then another.

The thicket where the graveyard lay against its terminal cliff battled Jim Tarr as though it were endowed with a malevolent life. His flashlight beam bored a tight hole in the tarbarrel murk, but from the darkness on either side the bushes lashed him, thorns tore at him. He panted, struggling through it, struggling on.

What was it he thought he was going to find here?

His face, his hands, were torn and bleeding. The weariness of sleepless nights, of brooding fear, weighted his limbs so that they were numbed, leaden. Every deeper shadow, every half-seen shape blacker against the black threatened him with a menace the more dreadful because its nature was unknown. But he bored deeper into the tangle, a convulsive grip flattening his fingers on flashlight cylinder and rifle butt, his blunt jaw grimly outthrust, his eyes narrowed and smouldering.

Behind those eyes was the vision of a small form rigid in a death that was not death. Behind those eyes was the recollection of a grey shape drifting in greyness out of this thicket, drifting, he could almost swear, into it again. And in Jim's nostrils was the stench of death's putrescence, deepening as though he neared its source.

A slanting tombstone jutted out of the greenery in front of him. He veered to pass it. Something clutched his ankle—a vine loop—tripped him. He sprawled forward, throwing the rifle over his head, thumped hard, breath gusting from between his lips. The flashlight jolted from his hand, rolled beyond grasp.

Its beam scythed the blackness, fell across a ghastly visage peering through a flutter of leaves. A toothless skull half obliterated by a dark stain. Not a skull, a mummy-head, parchment skin shrunken into the hollows, and the stain dried and clotted blood.

Tarr's fists pounded the earth. He was fighting to rise, to flee. Ancestral panic prickled the hairs at the back of his neck, surged darkly in his veins. Black lips in that mummy face twitched. Sound mumbled from them.

That jerked Jim forward, to the hitherto unseen body lying crumpled in the depression of a sunken grave. "Another," he gasped. "Good God! It's Jethro Anther. What happened, man? What is it?"

"Socked me," the blackening gums mumbled. "Bruk me skull." It was only the merest shadow of a voice, as though by some hideous necromancy of hate it projected from beyond death a message of vengeance. "Rob Wood. Thought I was dead, but I saw . . ." The voice died, but there was a scrabble in the dark beside his contorted form, a movement of his twisted shoulder that told Tarr it was his hand that scrabbled, and an imperative jerk downward of the fleshless chin.

Jim snatched for his hand-torch, within reach, darted its light to where that scrabble came from. He saw . . .

Dark dirt upturned out of the ancient grave. Jutting from it a metal cylinder topped by a metal wheel, a gas tank beyond doubt!

Anther's fingers, like horny bird's claws, made a turning movement. Understanding the speechless command, Tarr reached to the valve wheel, twisted a bit. The gas hissed out, and the reek of rotted cadavers was rank in Jim Tarr's nostrils!

"What the . . .!" he exclaimed, twisting the valve closed. "It came from here. Leaking . . ."

A scream cut him off, a woman's scream, oddly muffled but still high and shrill and agonized.

Jim jumped to his feet, rifle in one hand, flashlight in the other. His frantic beam swept the thicket, impinged on the frowning rock-face. Nothing. Nothing but darkness. Nothing but netted, baffling bushes and the black, solid crag.

In a hospital room light beat down, white and merciless on a bed where a small, still figure lay; beat mercilessly down on storm-dark hair framing the anguish ravaged face of a mother who had lived through agony only to find greater agony.

"Give him back to me," Jane Horn cried. "Give my Dickie back to me."

There was speculation, doubt, in the eyes of the man in white who tugged at a clipped Vandyke. "We might try an injection of adrenaline in the heart tissue," he mused. "It might bring him out of it. Or . . ."

"Or what?"

"Or it might kill him."

"Even that would be better than this. Try it, doctor. Try it."

"God!" Jim Tarr groaned, staring helplessly at the defiant blackness, the scream still ringing in his ears. "Where . . .?"

"There." The croak came from his feet. Jethro Anther was miraculously half-raised from the ground, miraculously his quivering arm was extending. "Through there." He was pointing at the precipice. "It opens." The hand dropped, never to point again.

Jim flung himself at the crag. His fingers caught a knob. The face itself on the rock was moving, was grating inward. There was a gaping hole at his feet, visible by a strange, eerie luminescence.

Tarr jumped down into that hole, reckless of what might meet him, whirled to a sharp exclamation. He saw tawny hair, a hand clamped over Rosalie Carter's face. He saw a black, stooped shape, fingers spreading the skin over Rosalie's jugular vein, a hypodermic needle sliding sickingly into the white skin. And in the same instant, he leaped.

His flailing gun-butt crunched black-swathed skull-bone, flung the robe-wearer sprawling against the farther wall. His rifle's steel-clad heel jolted Rob Wood's chin, split it, so that as the grizzled janitor fell, scarlet blood gushing from the crushed jaw. And then Jim was kneeling to Rosalie, was gathering her in his arms. As quickly as that it was all over.

"Jim," the girl sobbed, "Oh Jim!" Suddenly she was thrusting at him, thrusting him away, from her.

She was laughing. Most awfully she was laughing the thin, high laugh of hysteria while the tears rolled down her cheeks. She was pointing past him.

"Not Simpson," she jabbered. "Look, Jim, it's not Simpson."

Tarr turned. Somehow in his fall the robes had been torn away from the head of the man in black. Through the torn fabric jutted the white-bearded, ruddy-cheeked countenance of August Holzer!

Rosalie Carter's laugh cut off. She slumped against Jim, a dead weight in his enfolding arms.

The walls were painted a cool green, and every corner was rounded, so that Rosalie knew it must be a hospital room. It was sunlight that had awakened her, and the sound of a shade rattling up to let the sunlight in.

The nurse turned to her. "I see you are awake, my dear, and feeling better. These just came and I brought them in."

These were flowers—a great, gorgeous bouquet glorifying the agate pitcher serving them as a vase.

"Oh, lovely," Rosalie exclaimed.

"Aren't they?" the nurse smiled. "And the gentleman who brought them is waiting outside to see you. A Mr. Tarr."

After awhile Jim Tarr was in the room, perched on the edge of a chair, his blue eyes glowing. "I've got good news for you, Miss Carter," he was saying. "Dickie Horn is all right again, and Joan Hardie will soon be."

"Oh wonderful! But what of Dr. Holzer?"

"Dead. Wood's going to live, till he burns in the chair."

"Jim, I don't understand why Holzer went after the children. He told me his idea, but I don't know. I can't decide whether it was madness or genius that impelled him to his acts." She repeated what she had learned in the lair of fear. "I can't quite judge whether he was right when he said it was just that a few suffer to save millions from suffering, but it seems to me adults would have been better subjects for his experiment than children."

"Maybe. But there was something else behind what he did than a way to save people from being killed by gas. You see, there was a scheme on foot for breaking up the school district before the building of the Consolidated School was decided on. If that had been done Simpson would have been put in charge of one of the districts and Holzer of the other, but the Consolidation stopped it. By terrifying the farmers into withdrawing from the merger he hoped to regain that position and no longer remain Simpson's underling. That's the way it's been figured out, anyway, by Julius Waite and Simpson, but we'll never know."

"No," Rosalie sighed, "we'll never know whether he was a philanthropist or a madman, a genius or a greedy, avaricious monster."

"There's no doubt about Rob Wood. Holzer had caught him accepting bribes, falsifying his records and so on. He held that knowledge over Wood's head and made him help him, promising him a fortune if his schemes were successful. It was Holzer who sprayed the gas through the Horns' window, and later filled the school's ventilating system with it from the duct in his private office. But it was Wood who actually carried the kids off. They had the cylinders buried in a grave, and Wood also went back and forth through the tunnel. That's why he killed Anther, who was digging into that very grave."

"The tunnel?"

"Oh, I forgot that you didn't know. It's the old water tunnel that used to run down from the spring on Buzzard Mountain before the new pumping system was installed. They used it to get from the school to their hidden roost in the cliff. The new aqueduct joins the old just past the hospital here, and the sound came through."

"Jim!"

"Yes?"

"Jim, I haven't thanked you yet for saving me, for taking care of me."

"Hell, you don't have to thank me for that. Matter of fact, I'd like . . ." The chap broke off, red suffusing his big-boned face.

"You'd like?" Rosalie prompted softly. "What is it you would like, Jim?"

Jim Tarr smiled. "Well . . . Might as well say it . . . I'd like . . . to take care of you . . . for . . . for . . ."

"For always, Jim?" Rosalie murmured. "Perhaps I would like that too. Why don't you ask me?"

Minutes later the nurse opened the door, her knocking having met with no response. She closed it again, very softly.

"Doctor or no doctor," she whispered to herself, "that's better medicine for that girl than all the drugs in the storeroom."

RAMBLE HOUSE's

HARRY STEPHEN KEELER WEBWORK MYSTERIES

(RH) indicates the title is available ONLY in the RAMBLE HOUSE edition

The Ace of Spades Murder
The Affair of the Bottled Deuce (RH)
The Amazing Web
The Barking Clock
Behind That Mask
The Book with the Orange Leaves
The Bottle with the Green Wax Seal
The Box from Japan
The Case of the Canny Killer
The Case of the Crazy Corpse (RH)
The Case of the Flying Hands (RH)
The Case of the Ivory Arrow
The Case of the Jeweled Ragpicker
The Case of the Lavender Gripsack
The Case of the Mysterious Moll
The Case of the 16 Beans
The Case of the Transparent Nude (RH)
The Case of the Transposed Legs
The Case of the Two-Headed Idiot (RH)
The Case of the Two Strange Ladies
The Circus Stealers (RH)
Cleopatra's Tears
A Copy of Beowulf (RH)
The Crimson Cube (RH)
The Face of the Man From Saturn
Find the Clock
The Five Silver Buddhas
The 4th King
The Gallows Waits, My Lord! (RH)
The Green Jade Hand
Finger! Finger!
Hangman's Nights (RH)
I, Chameleon (RH)
I Killed Lincoln at 10:13! (RH)
The Iron Ring
The Man Who Changed His Skin (RH)
The Man with the Crimson Box
The Man with the Magic Eardrums
The Man with the Wooden Spectacles
The Marceau Case
The Matilda Hunter Murder

The Monocled Monster
The Murder of London Lew
The Murdered Mathematician
The Mysterious Card (RH)
The Mysterious Ivory Ball of Wong Shing Li (RH)
The Mystery of the Fiddling Cracksman
The Peacock Fan
The Photo of Lady X (RH)
The Portrait of Jirjohn Cobb
Report on Vanessa Hewstone (RH)
Riddle of the Travelling Skull
Riddle of the Wooden Parrakeet (RH)
The Scarlet Mummy (RH)
The Search for X-Y-Z
The Sharkskin Book
Sing Sing Nights
The Six From Nowhere (RH)
The Skull of the Waltzing Clown
The Spectacles of Mr. Cagliostro
Stand By—London Calling!
The Steeltown Strangler
The Stolen Gravestone (RH)
Strange Journey (RH)
The Strange Will
The Straw Hat Murders (RH)
The Street of 1000 Eyes (RH)
Thieves' Nights
Three Novellos (RH)
The Tiger Snake
The Trap (RH)
Vagabond Nights (Defrauded Yeggman)
Vagabond Nights 2 (10 Hours)
The Vanishing Gold Truck
The Voice of the Seven Sparrows
The Washington Square Enigma
When Thief Meets Thief
The White Circle (RH)
The Wonderful Scheme of Mr. Christopher Thorne
X. Jones—of Scotland Yard
Y. Cheung, Business Detective

Keeler Related Works

A To Izzard: A Harry Stephen Keeler Companion by Fender Tucker — Articles and stories about Harry, by Harry, and in his style. Included is a compleat bibliography.

Wild About Harry: Reviews of Keeler Novels — Edited by Richard Polt & Fender Tucker — 22 reviews of works by Harry Stephen Keeler from *Keeler News.* A perfect introduction to the author.

The Keeler Keyhole Collection: Annotated newsletter rants from Harry Stephen Keeler, edited by Francis M. Nevins. Over 400 pages of incredibly personal Keeleriana.

Fakealoo — Pastiches of the style of Harry Stephen Keeler by selected demented members of the HSK Society. Updated every year with the new winner.

Strands of the Web: Short Stories of Harry Stephen Keeler — 29 stories, just about all that Keeler wrote, are edited and introduced by Fred Cleaver.

RAMBLE HOUSE's LOON SANCTUARY

A Clear Path to Cross — Sharon Knowles short mystery stories by Ed Lynskey.

A Corpse Walks in Brooklyn and Other Stories — Volume 5 in the Day Keene in the Detective Pulps series.

A Jimmy Starr Omnibus — Three 40s novels by Jimmy Starr.

A Niche in Time and Other Stories — Classic SF by William F. Temple

A Roland Daniel Double: The Signal and The Return of Wu Fang — Classic thrillers from the 30s.

A Shot Rang Out — Three decades of reviews and articles by today's Anthony Boucher, Jon Breen. An essential book for any mystery lover's library.

A Smell of Smoke — A 1951 English countryside thriller by Miles Burton.

A Snark Selection — Lewis Carroll's *The Hunting of the Snark* with two Snarkian chapters by Harry Stephen Keeler — Illustrated by Gavin L. O'Keefe.

A Young Man's Heart — A forgotten early classic by Cornell Woolrich.

Alexander Laing Novels — *The Motives of Nicholas Holtz* and *Dr. Scarlett*, stories of medical mayhem and intrigue from the 30s.

An Angel in the Street — Modern hardboiled noir by Peter Genovese.

Automaton — Brilliant treatise on robotics: 1928-style! By H. Stafford Hatfield.

Away From the Here and Now — Clare Winger Harris stories, collected by Richard A. Lupoff.

Beast or Man? — A 1930 novel of racism and horror by Sean M'Guire. Introduced by John Pelan.

Black Beadle — A 1939 thriller by E.C.R. Lorac.

Black Hogan Strikes Again — Australia's Peter Renwick pens a tale of the 30s outback.

Black River Falls — Suspense from the master, Ed Gorman.

Blondy's Boy Friend — A snappy 1930 story by Philip Wylie, writing as Leatrice Homesley.

Blood in a Snap — The *Finnegan's Wake* of the 21st century, by Jim Weiler.

Blood Moon — The first of the Robert Payne series by Ed Gorman.

Bogart '48 — Hollywood action with Bogie by John Stanley and Kenn Davis

Calling Lou Largo! — Two Lou Largo novels by William Ard.

Cornucopia of Crime — Francis M. Nevins assembled this huge collection of his writings about crime literature and the people who write it. Essential for any serious mystery library.

Corpse Without Flesh — Strange novel of forensics by George Bruce

Crimson Clown Novels — By Johnston McCulley, author of the Zorro novels, *The Crimson Clown* and *The Crimson Clown Again*.

Dago Red — 22 tales of dark suspense by Bill Pronzini.

Dark Sanctuary — Weird Menace story by H. B. Gregory

David Hume Novels — *Corpses Never Argue, Cemetery First Stop, Make Way for the Mourners, Eternity Here I Come*. 1930s British hardboiled fiction with an attitude.

Dead Man Talks Too Much — Hollywood boozer by Weed Dickenson.

Death Leaves No Card — One of the most unusual murdered-in-the-tub mysteries you'll ever read. By Miles Burton.

Death March of the Dancing Dolls and Other Stories — Volume Three in the Day Keene in the Detective Pulps series. Introduced by Bill Crider.

Deep Space and other Stories — A collection of SF gems by Richard A. Lupoff.

Detective Duff Unravels It — Episodic mysteries by Harvey O'Higgins.

Diabolic Candelabra — Classic 30s mystery by E.R. Punshon

Dictator's Way — Another D.S. Bobby Owen mystery from E.R. Punshon

Dime Novels: Ramble House's 10-Cent Books — *Knife in the Dark* by Robert Leslie Bellem, *Hot Lead* and *Song of Death* by Ed Earl Repp, *A Hashish House in New York* by H.H. Kane, and five more.

Doctor Arnoldi — Tiffany Thayer's story of the death of death.

Don Diablo: Book of a Lost Film — Two-volume treatment of a western by Paul Landres, with diagrams. Intro by Francis M. Nevins.

Dope and Swastikas — Two strange novels from 1922 by Edmund Snell

Dope Tales #1 — Two dope-riddled classics; *Dope Runners* by Gerald Grantham and *Death Takes the Joystick* by Phillip Condé.

Dope Tales #2 — Two more narco-classics; *The Invisible Hand* by Rex Dark and *The Smokers of Hashish* by Norman Berrow.

Dope Tales #3 — Two enchanting novels of opium by the master, Sax Rohmer. *Dope* and *The Yellow Claw.*

Double Hot — Two 60s softcore sex novels by Morris Hershman.

Double Sex — Yet two more panting thrillers from Morris Hershman.

Dr. Odin — Douglas Newton's 1933 racial potboiler comes back to life.

Evangelical Cockroach — Jack Woodford writes about writing.

Evidence in Blue — 1938 mystery by E. Charles Vivian.

Fatal Accident — Murder by automobile, a 1936 mystery by Cecil M. Wills.

Fighting Mad — Todd Robbins' 1922 novel about boxing and life

Finger-prints Never Lie — A 1939 classic detective novel by John G. Brandon.

Freaks and Fantasies — Eerie tales by Tod Robbins, collaborator of Tod Browning on the film FREAKS.

Gadsby — A lipogram (a novel without the letter E). Ernest Vincent Wright's last work, published in 1939 right before his death.

Gelett Burgess Novels — *The Master of Mysteries, The White Cat, Two O'Clock Courage, Ladies in Boxes, Find the Woman, The Heart Line, The Picaroons* and *Lady Mechante.* Recently added is A Gelett Burgess Sampler, edited by Alfred Jan. All are introduced by Richard A. Lupoff.

Geronimo — S. M. Barrett's 1905 autobiography of a noble American.

Hake Talbot Novels — *Rim of the Pit, The Hangman's Handyman.* Classic locked room mysteries, with mapback covers by Gavin O'Keefe.

Hands Out of Hell and Other Stories — John H. Knox's eerie hallucinations

Hell is a City — William Ard's masterpiece.

Hollywood Dreams — A novel of Tinsel Town and the Depression by Richard O'Brien.

Hostesses in Hell and Other Stories — Russell Gray's most graphic stories

House of the Restless Dead — Strange and ominous tales by Hugh B. Cave

I Stole $16,000,000 — A true story by cracksman Herbert E. Wilson.

Inclination to Murder — 1966 thriller by New Zealand's Harriet Hunter.

Invaders from the Dark — Classic werewolf tale from Greye La Spina.

J. Poindexter, Colored — Classic satirical black novel by Irvin S. Cobb.

Jack Mann Novels — Strange murder in the English countryside. *Gees' First Case, Nightmare Farm, Grey Shapes, The Ninth Life, The Glass Too Many, Her Ways Are Death, The Kleinert Case* and *Maker of Shadows.*

Jake Hardy — A lusty western tale from Wesley Tallant.

Jim Harmon Double Novels — *Vixen Hollow/Celluloid Scandal, The Man Who Made Maniacs/Silent Siren, Ape Rape/Wanton Witch, Sex Burns Like Fire/Twist Session, Sudden Lust/Passion Strip, Sin Unlimited/Harlot Master, Twilight Girls/Sex Institution.* Written in the early 60s and never reprinted until now.

Joel Townsley Rogers Novels and Short Stories — By the author of *The Red Right Hand: Once In a Red Moon, Lady With the Dice, The Stopped Clock, Never Leave My Bed.* Also two short story collections: *Night of Horror* and *Killing Time.*

John Carstairs, Space Detective — Arboreal Sci-fi by Frank Belknap Long

Joseph Shallit Novels — *The Case of the Billion Dollar Body, Lady Don't Die on My Doorstep, Kiss the Killer, Yell Bloody Murder, Take Your Last Look.* One of America's best 50's authors and a favorite of author Bill Pronzini.

Keller Memento — 45 short stories of the amazing and weird by Dr. David Keller.

Killer's Caress — Cary Moran's 1936 hardboiled thriller.

Lady of the Yellow Death and Other Stories — More stories by Wyatt Blassingame.

League of the Grateful Dead and Other Stories — Volume One in the Day Keene in the Detective Pulps series.

Library of Death — Ghastly tale by Ronald S. L. Harding, introduced by John Pelan

Malcolm Jameson Novels and Short Stories — *Astonishing! Astounding!, Tarnished Bomb, The Alien Envoy and Other Stories* and *The Chariots of San Fernando and Other Stories.* All introduced and edited by John Pelan or Richard A. Lupoff.

Man Out of Hell and Other Stories — Volume II of the John H. Knox weird pulps collection.

Marblehead: A Novel of H.P. Lovecraft — A long-lost masterpiece from Richard A. Lupoff. This is the "director's cut", the long version that has never been published before.

Mark of the Laughing Death and Other Stories — Shockers from the pulps by Francis James, introduced by John Pelan.

Master of Souls — Mark Hansom's 1937 shocker is introduced by weirdologist John Pelan.

Max Afford Novels — *Owl of Darkness, Death's Mannikins, Blood on His Hands, The Dead Are Blind, The Sheep and the Wolves, Sinners in Paradise* and *Two Locked Room Mysteries and a Ripping Yarn* by one of Australia's finest mystery novelists.

Money Brawl — Two books about the writing business by Jack Woodford and H. Bedford-Jones. Introduced by Richard A. Lupoff.

More Secret Adventures of Sherlock Holmes — Gary Lovisi's second collection of tales about the unknown sides of the great detective.

Muddled Mind: Complete Works of Ed Wood, Jr. — David Hayes and Hayden Davis deconstruct the life and works of the mad, but canny, genius.

Murder among the Nudists — A mystery from 1934 by Peter Hunt, featuring a naked Detective-Inspector going undercover in a nudist colony.

Murder in Black and White — 1931 classic tennis whodunit by Evelyn Elder.

Murder in Shawnee — Two novels of the Alleghenies by John Douglas: *Shawnee Alley Fire* and *Haunts*.

Murder in Silk — A 1937 Yellow Peril novel of the silk trade by Ralph Trevor.

My Deadly Angel — 1955 Cold War drama by John Chelton.

My First Time: The One Experience You Never Forget — Michael Birchwood — 64 true first-person narratives of how they lost it.

Mysterious Martin, the Master of Murder — Two versions of a strange 1912 novel by Tod Robbins about a man who writes books that can kill.

Norman Berrow Novels — *The Bishop's Sword, Ghost House, Don't Go Out After Dark, Claws of the Cougar, The Smokers of Hashish, The Secret Dancer, Don't Jump Mr. Boland!, The Footprints of Satan, Fingers for Ransom, The Three Tiers of Fantasy, The Spaniard's Thumb, The Eleventh Plague, Words Have Wings, One Thrilling Night, The Lady's in Danger, It Howls at Night, The Terror in the Fog, Oil Under the Window, Murder in the Melody, The Singing Room.* This is the complete Norman Berrow library of locked-room mysteries, several of which are masterpieces.

Old Faithful and Other Stories — SF classic tales by Raymond Z. Gallun

Old Times' Sake — Short stories by James Reasoner from Mike Shayne Magazine.

One Dreadful Night — A classic mystery by Ronald S. L. Harding

Pair O' Jacks — A mystery novel and a diatribe about publishing by Jack Woodford

Perfect .38 — Two early Timothy Dane novels by William Ard. More to come.

Prince Pax — Devilish intrigue by George Sylvester Viereck and Philip Eldridge

Prose Bowl — Futuristic satire of a world where hack writing has replaced football as our national obsession, by Bill Pronzini and Barry N. Malzberg.

Red Light — The history of legal prostitution in Shreveport Louisiana by Eric Brock. Includes wonderful photos of the houses and the ladies.

Researching American-Made Toy Soldiers — A 276-page collection of a lifetime of articles by toy soldier expert Richard O'Brien.

Reunion in Hell — Volume One of the John H. Knox series of weird stories from the pulps. Introduced by horror expert John Pelan.

Ripped from the Headlines! — The Jack the Ripper story as told in the newspaper articles in the *New York* and *London Times*.

Rough Cut & New, Improved Murder — Ed Gorman's first two novels.

R.R. Ryan Novels — Freak Museum and The Subjugated Beast, two horror classics.

Ruby of a Thousand Dreams — The villain Wu Fang returns in this Roland Daniel novel.

Ruled By Radio — 1925 futuristic novel by Robert L. Hadfield & Frank E. Farncombe.

Rupert Penny Novels — *Policeman's Holiday, Policeman's Evidence, Lucky Policeman, Policeman in Armour, Sealed Room Murder, Sweet Poison, The Talkative Policeman, She had to Have Gas* and *Cut and Run* (by Martin Tanner.) Rupert Penny is the pseudonym of Australian Charles Thornett, a master of the locked room, impossible crime plot.

Sacred Locomotive Flies — Richard A. Lupoff's psychedelic SF story.

Sam — Early gay novel by Lonnie Coleman.

Sand's Game — Spectacular hard-boiled noir from Ennis Willie, edited by Lynn Myers and Stephen Mertz, with contributions from Max Allan Collins, Bill Crider, Wayne Dundee, Bill Pronzini, Gary Lovisi and James Reasoner.

Sand's War — More violent fiction from the typewriter of Ennis Willie

Satan's Den Exposed — True crime in Truth or Consequences New Mexico — Award-winning journalism by the *Desert Journal*.

Satans of Saturn — Novellas from the pulps by Otis Adelbert Kline and E. H. Price

Satan's Sin House and Other Stories — Horrific gore by Wayne Rogers

Secrets of a Teenage Superhero — Graphic lit by Jonathan Sweet

Sex Slave — Potboiler of lust in the days of Cleopatra by Dion Leclerq, 1966.

Sideslip — 1968 SF masterpiece by Ted White and Dave Van Arnam.

Slammer Days — Two full-length prison memoirs: *Men into Beasts* (1952) by George Sylvester Viereck and *Home Away From Home* (1962) by Jack Woodford.

Slippery Staircase — 1930s whodunit from E.C.R. Lorac

Sorcerer's Chessmen — John Pelan introduces this 1939 classic by Mark Hansom.

Star Griffin — Michael Kurland's 1987 masterpiece of SF drollery is back.

Stakeout on Millennium Drive — Award-winning Indianapolis Noir by Ian Woollen.

Strands of the Web: Short Stories of Harry Stephen Keeler — Edited and Introduced by Fred Cleaver.

Summer Camp for Corpses and Other Stories — Weird Menace tales from Arthur Leo Zagat; introduced by John Pelan.

Suzy — A collection of comic strips by Richard O'Brien and Bob Vojtko from 1970.

Tales of the Macabre and Ordinary — Modern twisted horror by Chris Mikul, author of the *Bizarrism* series.

Tales of Terror and Torment #1 — John Pelan selects and introduces this sampler of weird menace tales from the pulps.

Tenebrae — Ernest G. Henham's 1898 horror tale brought back.

The Amorous Intrigues & Adventures of Aaron Burr — by Anonymous. Hot historical action about the man who almost became Emperor of Mexico.

The Anthony Boucher Chronicles — edited by Francis M. Nevins. Book reviews by Anthony Boucher written for the *San Francisco Chronicle*, 1942 – 1947. Essential and fascinating reading by the best book reviewer there ever was.

The Barclay Catalogs — Two essential books about toy soldier collecting by Richard O'Brien

The Basil Wells Omnibus — A collection of Wells' stories by Richard A. Lupoff

The Beautiful Dead and Other Stories — Dreadful tales from Donald Dale

The Best of 10-Story Book — edited by Chris Mikul, over 35 stories from the literary magazine Harry Stephen Keeler edited.

The Black Dark Murders — Vintage 50s college murder yarn by Milt Ozaki, writing as Robert O. Saber.

The Book of Time — The classic novel by H.G. Wells is joined by sequels by Wells himself and three stories by Richard A. Lupoff. Illustrated by Gavin L. O'Keefe.

The Case in the Clinic — One of E.C.R. Lorac's finest.

The Strange Case of the Antlered Man — A mystery of superstition by Edwy Searles Brooks.

The Case of the Bearded Bride — #4 in the Day Keene in the Detective Pulps series

The Case of the Little Green Men — Mack Reynolds wrote this love song to sci-fi fans back in 1951 and it's now back in print.

The Case of the Withered Hand — 1936 potboiler by John G. Brandon.

The Charlie Chaplin Murder Mystery — A 2004 tribute by noted film scholar, Wes D. Gehring.

The Chinese Jar Mystery — Murder in the manor by John Stephen Strange, 1934.

The Cloudbuilders and Other Stories — SF tales from Colin Kapp.

The Compleat Calhoon — All of Fender Tucker's works: Includes *Totah Six-Pack*, *Weed, Women and Song* and *Tales from the Tower*, plus a CD of all of his songs.

The Compleat Ova Hamlet — Parodies of SF authors by Richard A. Lupoff. This is a brand new edition with more stories and more illustrations by Trina Robbins.

The Contested Earth and Other SF Stories — A never-before published space opera and seven short stories by Jim Harmon.

The Crimson Query — A 1929 thriller from Arlton Eadie. A perfect way to get introduced.

The Curse of Cantire — Classic 1939 novel of a family curse by Walter S. Masterman.

The Devil and the C.I.D. — Odd diabolic mystery by E.C.R. Lorac

The Devil Drives — An odd prison and lost treasure novel from 1932 by Virgil Markham.

The Devil of Pei-Ling — Herbert Asbury's 1929 tale of the occult.

The Devil's Mistress — A 1915 Scottish gothic tale by J. W. Brodie-Innes, a member of Aleister Crowley's Golden Dawn.

The Devil's Nightclub and Other Stories — John Pelan introduces some gruesome tales by Nat Schachner.

The Disentanglers — Episodic intrigue at the turn of last century by Andrew Lang

The Dog Poker Code — A spoof of *The Da Vinci Code* by D.B. Smithee.

The Dumpling — Political murder from 1907 by Coulson Kernahan.

The End of It All and Other Stories — Ed Gorman selected his favorite short stories for this huge collection.

The Fangs of Suet Pudding — A 1944 novel of the German invasion by Adams Farr

The Finger of Destiny and Other Stories — Edmund Snell's superb collection of weird stories of Borneo.

The Ghost of Gaston Revere — From 1935, a novel of life and beyond by Mark Hansom, introduced by John Pelan.

The Girl in the Dark — A thriller from Roland Daniel

The Gold Star Line — Seaboard adventure from L.T. Reade and Robert Eustace.

The Golden Dagger — 1951 Scotland Yard yarn by E. R. Punshon.

The Great Orme Terror — Horror stories by Garnett Radcliffe from the pulps

The Hairbreadth Escapes of Major Mendax — Francis Blake Crofton's 1889 boys' book.

The House That Time Forgot and Other Stories — Insane pulpitude by Robert F. Young

The House of the Vampire — 1907 poetic thriller by George S. Viereck.

The Illustrious Corpse — Murder hijinx from Tiffany Thayer

The Incredible Adventures of Rowland Hern — Intriguing 1928 impossible crimes by Nicholas Olde.

The Julius Caesar Murder Case — A classic 1935 re-telling of the assassination by Wallace Irwin that's much more fun than the Shakespeare version.

The Koky Comics — A collection of all of the 1978-1981 Sunday and daily comic strips by Richard O'Brien and Mort Gerberg, in two volumes.

The Lady of the Terraces — 1925 missing race adventure by E. Charles Vivian.

The Lord of Terror — 1925 mystery with master-criminal, Fantômas.

The Melamare Mystery — A classic 1929 Arsene Lupin mystery by Maurice Leblanc

The Man Who Was Secrett — Epic SF stories from John Brunner

The Man Without a Planet — Science fiction tales by Richard Wilson

The N. R. De Mexico Novels — Robert Bragg, the real N.R. de Mexico, presents *Marijuana Girl, Madman on a Drum, Private Chauffeur* in one volume.

The Night Remembers — A 1991 Jack Walsh mystery from Ed Gorman.

The One After Snelling — Kickass modern noir from Richard O'Brien.

The Organ Reader — A huge compilation of just about everything published in the 1971-1972 radical bay-area newspaper, *THE ORGAN*. A coffee table book that points out the shallowness of the coffee table mindset.

The Poker Club — Three in one! Ed Gorman's ground-breaking novel, the short story it was based upon, and the screenplay of the film made from it.

The Private Journal & Diary of John H. Surratt — The memoirs of the man who conspired to assassinate President Lincoln.

The Ramble House Mapbacks — Recently revised book by Gavin L. O'Keefe with color pictures of all the Ramble House books with mapbacks.

The Secret Adventures of Sherlock Holmes — Three Sherlockian pastiches by the Brooklyn author/publisher, Gary Lovisi.

Welsh Rarebit Tales — Charming stories from 1902 by Harle Oren Cummins
West Texas War and Other Western Stories — by Gary Lovisi.
What If? Volume 1, 2 and 3 — Richard A. Lupoff introduces three decades worth of SF short stories that should have won a Hugo, but didn't.
When the Batman Thirsts and Other Stories — Weird tales from Frederick C. Davis.
Whip Dodge: Man Hunter — Wesley Tallant's saga of a bounty hunter of the old West.
Win, Place and Die! — The first new mystery by Milt Ozaki in decades. The ultimate novel of 70s Reno.
Writer 1 and 2 — A magnus opus from Richard A. Lupoff summing up his life as writer.
You'll Die Laughing — Bruce Elliott's 1945 novel of murder at a practical joker's English countryside manor.

RAMBLE HOUSE

Fender Tucker, Prop.   Gavin L. O'Keefe, Graphics
www.ramblehouse.com   fender@ramblehouse.com
228-826-1783   10329 Sheephead Drive, Vancleave MS 39565